ANNIE HENRY

Annie Henry

Adventures in the American Revolution

Books 1, 2, 3, and 4

Annie Henry and the Secret Mission
Annie Henry and the Birth of Liberty
Annie Henry and the Mysterious Stranger
Annie Henry and the Redcoats

Susan Olasky

CROSSWAY BOOKS

A DIVISION OF
GOOD NEWS PUBLISHERS
WHEATON, ILLINOIS

Annie Henry: Adventures in the American Revolution

Published by Crossway Books
a division of Good News Publishers
1300 Crescent Street
Wheaton, Illinois 60187

Originally published as separate books: *Annie Henry and the Secret Mission, Annie Henry and the Birth of Liberty, Annie Henry and the Mysterious Stranger, Annie Henry and the Redcoats.*

Cover design: David LaPlaca

Cover illustration: Tom LaPadula

First printing 2003

Printed in the United States of America

ISBN 1-58134-521-6

ML 13 12 11 10 09 08 07 06 05 04 03
15 14 13 12 11 10 9 8 7 6 5 4 3 2 1

Annie Henry and the Secret Mission

For
Marvin

Contents

1

fire!

Annie Henry stood at the second floor window making faces at the men working in the fields below. They couldn't see her, of course, but it gave her satisfaction just the same. Ten minutes earlier she had been outside watching the men from close up. She was full of curiosity about the harvest as she darted back and forth between the mowers with the big scythes and the reapers with their smaller sickles.

Then her almost brother-in-law, John Fontaine, had grown annoyed and ordered her into the house. "Annie, you're in the way," he said. "Go inside and stay where you belong. We've got a harvest to bring in before the rain."

As she remembered his words, her face grew hot. He hadn't even trusted her to go alone to the house but had taken her by the hand and led her there, a quarter of a mile. Annie imagined that she had heard the men laugh as she was led away in disgrace.

Now she stood at the window, a small, ten-year-old, dark-haired girl silhouetted against the glass. Together with her little sister Elizabeth, she gazed out at the flurry of activity below.

It was hard for Annie to stay angry. She knew John Fontaine was right, and from the window she could see a storm coming.

Annie called to her sister who was four years younger. "Elizabeth, look at all those men. Doesn't it look like they are racing the storm?" She showed off the knowledge she had recently obtained. "See the scythe? They use it to cut the wheat. See that other man behind? He bundles the wheat into sheaves."

"Why do they work so fast?" Elizabeth asked.

"Because there's a storm coming," Annie replied. "If we don't get the wheat cut and covered, it will be lost. Look at the clouds over there." She pointed in the distance where a thin line of black clouds lined the horizon.

Elizabeth turned back to her dolls, but Annie continued to watch out the window. On a clear day you could see the mountains near Charlottesville, more than sixty miles away. But not today. As Annie watched, the wind kicked up. In the distance, lightning darted from a cloud.

Her attention turned from the sky back to the men in the field. Other men followed the mowers whose job it was to stack the sheaves into shocks. Eight sheaves stood up on end, and two were laid across the top like a roof so that rain couldn't damage the grain. Soon, shocks of wheat looking like little houses, dotted the field. The men, aware of the advancing storm, worked faster and faster as they struggled to cut and sheave the last field.

Although each man did something different—the mower cut the grain, the gripper bundled it, and a third man tied it—they worked together as one, Annie thought. Each man knew his job and did it quickly. They dropped those sheaves and went on while other men came behind and stacked them. Up and down the field they worked until nothing but the edges were left uncut. Annie knew that poor people could come and glean at the edges of the field and get whatever grain remained.

"They're going to finish, Elizabeth," Annie said with a laugh. "They beat the storm."

The girls looked up at the sky. The clouds were closer, but the rain had not started and the men were finished. She felt a rush of satisfaction. Her father, Patrick Henry, would be glad. As soon as he returned home to his plantation, there would be a celebration.

A flash in the distant sky caught Annie's attention. *More lightning*, she thought, *but it doesn't matter now. The harvest is done. Now all we have to do is thresh the wheat, and that can wait.* She turned her attention to the room in which she stood.

It was a long room that stretched the length of the house. Usually it served as a playroom for the younger Henry children. But on special occasions it would be transformed into a ballroom. That's where the party would be tomorrow when her father returned.

Returning to the window, a look of concern creased her brow. In the distance she thought she saw a fine line of smoke. "Elizabeth, come here," she ordered.

Elizabeth rushed to the window. "Do you see anything out there?" Annie asked as she pointed.

"What do you mean?" Elizabeth responded, peering out the window.

"Do you see smoke?" Annie asked.

Elizabeth shook her head. "I don't see it," she said and went back to her dolls.

But Annie stayed at the window. She wasn't sure she had seen anything. Now it just looked like clouds.

Another bolt of lightning darted down from the

clouds, and she thought she saw another stream of smoke. But when she looked again, what she had thought was smoke had blended so perfectly with the storm clouds that she wasn't sure.

"What if I go down there and tell them there's a fire, and I'm wrong?" she wondered out loud. "John Fontaine would be furious."

Annie waited with indecision. The wind picked up. The branch of a walnut tree scraped the window. She could hear the heavy limbs moan with the wind. A third bolt of lightning lit up the sky, and Annie saw more smoke.

"I know it's fire," she said to Elizabeth. "I've got to warn them. It has been so hot and dry this summer, the stubble in the fields could easily catch on fire."

Elizabeth joined Annie once more at the window. "Wouldn't they smell it?" her little sister asked.

Annie shook her head. "I think it's still too far away."

She tugged at the heavy window but it wouldn't budge. "Help me open this window," Annie said impatiently.

The two small girls struggled with the window but could only move it an inch. Annie knew it was useless to pound on the glass. The men were too far away to hear.

"I'll go down and warn them," Annie told Elizabeth. "Stay here and watch the fields. Surely you see the smoke now."

Elizabeth nodded. There were three distinct trails of black smoke rising to meet the lighter gray storm clouds.

"You have to let us know if the smoke is coming closer," Annie said. "We won't be able to see it from the ground. You'll have to signal." Looking around for something to use as a flag, she finally grabbed the red sash from her dress. "If the fire comes closer to the wheat fields, you must hang this sash out the window. I'll watch for the sign, and I'll be able to tell the men." Annie grabbed her sister by the shoulders and said fiercely, "You have to pay attention, Elizabeth. It's important. Can you do it?"

Elizabeth nodded. Her eyes were wide as she watched the little trails of smoke get bigger and begin to merge as the fire spread. Annie ran down the stairs and out the door. The wind caught up her long skirts and twisted them about her legs, but she didn't stop. She yelled as she ran, but the men were still too far away to hear. Her side ached, but she kept going. Finally, breathless, she reached the harvesters, grabbed the arm of the closest man, and cried, "Fire," while pointing across the fields.

The reaction was immediate. Men jumped up from the ground where they had been drinking water and eating cornbread. Annie watched John Fontaine bark orders. Several men ran to the barn for horses. Minutes later a wagon hooked to a team of oxen appeared loaded with shovels, four large water barrels, and leather buckets. A few men climbed on while others had already started running across the field. John Fontaine grabbed one of the waiting horses and galloped off in the direction of the fire.

No one paid any attention to Annie, who suddenly remembered Elizabeth waiting at the window. Looking over, she saw the red sash hanging out. "The fire is coming this way," she yelled fearfully. "My sister is watching it from the window."

A farmer shouted the news to the men on the hay wagon. In the confusion, no one noticed Annie climb onto the wagon. She could smell the smoke now. Little pieces of ash floated from the sky as the wind gusted. "Oh, Lord," she prayed, "let it rain now. Let it rain."

It was hard traveling across the field because of all the ridges and furrows. Up a ridge the wagon would go, then down a furrow, until Annie felt she would get sick to her stomach. When the wagon finally found a road through the field, travel was easier. But it still took a long time for the wagon to get out to the fire.

The closer the wagon came, the hotter the air grew. Annie found it hard to breathe. Her eyes watered and her throat burned. She could see orange flames blazing up from the dry stubble and wheat shocks. The fire didn't care whether it destroyed the wheat or the chaff. All of it was burning.

Annie shielded her face with the wide sleeve of her dress. The wagon stopped, and the men jumped out, joining the men who were already in the fields. They were beating the flames in a fruitless attempt to put them out. The men grabbed shovels from the wagon and began digging a trench to contain the fire. But the wind was an enemy. Gusts easily carried the burning wheat across the trenches like little torches that sent the dry stubble up in flames.

The men had to retreat before the blazing fire. Several moved the wagon back to get it out of danger. They feared the fire would surround them, leaving them no way of escape.

Others formed a bucket brigade to carry the water from the barrels on the wagon to the fire. One man filled the bucket and passed it down the chain until the man on the end emptied it. Then the empty buckets were passed back. Back and forth went the buckets until the water from the first barrel was all gone.

As they dampened the blaze in one place, it sprang up somewhere else, but the men kept working. Acrid smoke filled the air, making Annie cough until she felt she would faint. A farmer shoved a wet rag at her and told her to tie it across her mouth. Then he handed her a bucket and told her to work.

Annie worked side by side with the men until she was worn out. Then she worked some more. When the rag dried out, she dipped it in the water and tied it back on. Still she labored.

Finally, they had used all the water in all the barrels. They had dug the trenches. There was nothing more to do. And the fire still burned. All around, as far as Annie could see, wheat shocks had burned to ashes. She felt an overwhelming sadness. They had tried desperately to save the harvest, and they hadn't been able to do it.

A bolt of lightning followed immediately by a clap of thunder lit up the field. More lightning meant more fire, but Annie was too tired to care. She walked sadly to the wagon where the men were wearily taking off their gloves. No one spoke a word. Just then she felt something that gave her a spark of hope. At first Annie wasn't sure. Maybe it was just a splash from a water bucket or a piece of ash. But then, as if heaven had opened, the rain began to fall. It fell in a downpour, and the raging fires quickly died out.

A cry went up from the farmers. It sounded unlike any cry Annie had ever heard: a crazy, yelping, howling cry of joy—and Annie found herself yelping along with the men.

John Fontaine did not join the others in their celebration. Annie glanced at him, a lone figure with his head bowed and his knees on the ground, giving thanks to God. Then he roused himself and directed the men. Since the rain had turned the field into mud, John ordered several men to unhitch the oxen and walk them back to the barn.

As he looked around, he noticed Annie for the first time. "How did you get out here?" he demanded. But before she could speak, he went on, "We'll talk later. You ride back with me. Patsy will be worried sick."

John helped Annie onto the horse, then swung up behind her. Before they rode off, he turned to the wet and tired men in the fields. "Thank you," he said to them. "Your hard work helped save the wheat."

Annie's big sister Patsy was waiting on the steps when they rode up. She rushed down the stairs and looked anxiously from John to Annie. "Are you hurt? Annie, what happened to you? What about Father's wheat?" The questions tumbled out so fast that neither John nor Annie had time to answer.

John smiled and took Patsy's hand. "We're all fine. We probably lost a field. I'll know better tomorrow. But thank God for Annie's warning. We were able to slow down the spread of the fire until the rain came."

The three stood under the porch roof for a minute, thinking about the near disaster. Then Patsy said, "You're soaked, Annie. And you're covered with soot. Go inside."

After Annie ran into the house, Patsy turned to John. "What were you thinking, to let a little girl go out to fight a fire?" Patsy's voice broke.

"I'm sorry, Patsy. It was my fault. I didn't see her get on the wagon. But God preserved her."

She nodded. "I know I shouldn't worry so much, John. But I feel so responsible. With Mama ill and Father away, the burden falls on me. Annie takes so many unnecessary risks. Father must do something."

"He will, Patsy. But let your father do it. She needs a mother's gentle touch—and her mother can't give it."

2

Scotchtown

Annie loved every foot of Scotchtown, the plantation house she lived in with her family. Setting on a hill in the fertile farmland of central Virginia, the house was impressive. It was a two-story white clapboard structure with eight large and eight small windows across the front. Large stone stairs led to the front door, which opened onto a long hallway that cut the house in two. Annie sometimes imagined that she could open the doors at both ends of that hallway and ride a pony right through the house.

On either side of that hallway were four rooms, each one heated by a huge corner fireplace. The second story was a single room, sometimes used for large parties, but usually reserved as a nursery for Elizabeth and Edward.

But Scotchtown was more than a house. It was a little village. At the back of the house were separate buildings: her father Patrick Henry's office, the kitchen, bedrooms for her brothers William and John, and one for the children's tutor, Richard Dabney. There was also a dry well—a hole more than twenty feet in the ground that stayed constantly cool. In it was stored milk, butter, and cheese so they would not spoil.

Further away from the house was a dairy, a blacksmith shop, a stable, and many sheds for farm implements. And further still were the small cottages where thirty slaves lived.

Patrick Henry owned 1000 acres, but only 400 were cleared and planted. The rest was woodland and meadow. Scotchtown was a wonderful place for the six Henry children to live. Patsy at seventeen was the oldest. Then came William, fifteen, John, thirteen, Annie, who was ten, Elizabeth, five, and the baby, Edward, who was three.

Annie Henry had explored much of the farm. That's because Patrick Henry thought his children should spend much of their time outside in the woods, running free. Annie agreed with her father. She was a reluctant pupil, and her morning lessons with the tutor were often painful.

But today there were no lessons. Annie whistled with delight as she jumped out of bed. Today Father was coming home. And better still, it was the day for the harvest party—and the farm buzzed with activity.

Patrick Henry had been a busy man in the year of 1774. He had spent weeks in Richmond and Williamsburg on business, sometimes attending meetings of the House of Burgesses—Virginia's legislature where laws were made. Lately, he had been even busier. Tensions had increased between the colonies and the king, and Patrick Henry was a spokesman for many Virginians.

That meant that Annie's father was rarely home. His law practice suffered, and his family missed him. Annie thought she missed him the most.

Standing in front of the mirror, she tried to get her stubborn brown hair to cooperate. It was important that she look just right for her father's return. But her wiry hair had ideas of its own. So she pulled it back in a simple ponytail at the back of her neck and tied it with a ribbon. It would have to do.

Annie wore a dress of white cotton like most girls her age. Its full skirts reached the floor, and its wide ruffled sleeves made good hiding places for books or cookies or pebbles found on her walks. She wore soft leather boots because Patsy insisted. But Annie knew, as did Patsy, that as soon as she ran outside, the boots would come off so that she could run barefoot.

When Annie was satisfied, she went outdoors. The air was heavy after the evening's rain, and it still smelled like wet, burnt wheat. But the rain had washed away the smoke; so she could see a long way. One whole part of the field was charred. The shocks were black; the wheat was ruined.

Her stomach rumbled. She sniffed the air for a hint of bacon or biscuits and was rewarded by inviting smells. Just then, she heard the bell for breakfast. Annie went around the side of the house to a small door. She dashed up the stairs and into the family dining room. Patsy looked up when her sister entered the room. "Gracious, Annie, there's no need to be running in and out of the servants' entrance. You could enter the room like a lady. Come and eat. I don't think I can hold off John and William. They look to be starving."

The two young men, Annie's big brothers, laughed. William shared his father's large nose and deep-set eyes, but John, like Annie, resembled their mother, and like Annie, he was plagued with curly hair and freckles. Neither boy showed any of Patrick Henry's interest in learning. When they could escape the schoolmaster, they went hunting and fishing with friends from neighboring farms. Of course, the boys bragged, their father had been a lazy student also, but Patsy didn't like to hear about that.

Holding her nose, Annie came to the table. "You boys smell like smoke," she said with disgust. "Didn't you bathe?"

"Bathe? Why, we had baths last week. You know it isn't healthful to bathe too often," William said as he pretended to grab the last of the biscuits.

Annie slipped into the seat next to him and plunked the biscuit onto her own plate. "I took a bath, and I suggest you do too. Being next to you is like being in the fire all over again."

"Were you scared, Annie?" John asked.

She nodded. "I didn't know it would be so big and out of control. My arms are stiff from those water buckets. But let's not talk about it. Father is coming home. I'm so excited I don't know if I can eat," she said as she buttered and jellied another piece of bread and put it into her mouth.

"Annie, I don't think there's ever been a moment when you couldn't eat," John laughed. "You're going to become big and fat one of these days."

Patsy laughed. "If I ate like Annie, I'd likely grow as big as a barn. But Annie doesn't sit still long enough. She runs around more than you. I wouldn't be surprised if Annie couldn't outrun you and outfish you, John Patrick."

"And if you got as big as a barn, it doesn't seem likely that cousin John Fontaine would be wanting to marry you, does it?" asked William slyly.

Blushing, Patsy stared at her plate while she chewed

the last bite of sausage. Annie giggled and kicked William under the table.

"Who's going to meet Father?" Annie asked when she had stopped giggling. "I can't decide whether to wait for him or to watch the preparations for the party. I love harvest time."

"Especially this one. Can you imagine if we had lost all the wheat—and Father away?" William asked. "I'm glad we don't have to tell him bad news like that. Now we can celebrate."

Nodding in agreement, Patsy said with some pride, "I'm glad John Fontaine was here to take control. Father left the farm in good hands."

John interrupted, "But it was Annie who deserves the credit. She saw the fire and warned us. If she hadn't, the fire would have spread faster. We would have lost much more."

Annie blushed and smiled gratefully at John. It was nice to be recognized. She thought happily of the fact that Father would surely be told of her role in saving the wheat.

Forcing a smile, Patsy added, "Annie also acted foolishly. She should not have been out riding on a hay wagon in the middle of a fire. She risked her own life and the lives of others."

Annie's eyes welled up. She knew that Patsy was right, but before she could speak John said, "That's silly, Patsy. Annie didn't get in anyone's way. I was there, and I know what I'm talking about. In fact, she emptied buckets and worked like any of the men."

"Hush, John Patrick," Patsy said sharply. "I know where Annie belongs, and it isn't in a hay wagon in the middle of a fire. And I have to say what's right. . . . That's my job even if you don't understand. How would we explain to Father if Annie had been injured? Would you be responsible? No, I would be."

While Patsy spoke, the other children looked around uncomfortably. The playful mood of the group had completely changed.

Excusing himself from the table, William grabbed his rifle from the rack over the fireplace and marched outside. John grabbed his hat and followed. That left only Annie and her older sister. Patsy rose but not before Annie saw the tear slip down her sister's cheek.

Annie looked around the empty room. Minutes before it had been filled with laughter. "I'm sorry, Patsy," she said. "I didn't mean to worry you."

Patsy hugged her tight. "I know you didn't. But you have to learn to think."

Excusing herself, Annie went outside. She walked out back to a small, fenced pen where her chickens pecked at the still wet ground. "You'll have a tasty meal of crickets and grubs after that rain," she said as she scattered dried corn for the hens. Her father had bought her a rooster and three hens a year ago, thinking that raising chickens was a good activity for a young girl. Now she had ten hens that she tended faithfully every morning. She gathered the eggs in her basket and took them to the kitchen where she emptied them into a crockery bowl before returning the basket to the coop.

"I guess I'll go out to the road," she announced. "Perhaps Father will come early. I'm too excited about the party to stay here smelling all that food cooking."

She took off her boots, leaving them on the porch, and set off toward the road. The ground was wet, and Annie's feet were soon muddy. She looked unhappily at the hem of her once white dress.

The road was not paved. It was nothing more than wagon ruts thick with mud after the night's rain. Hitching up her dress, she stepped into the cool mud. It squeezed between her toes. Then she put one muddy foot in a puddle and swirled it until the mud floated off.

Walking a little further, she came to a dry spot under a hickory nut tree where she filled her pockets with green nuts that had fallen during the storm. For the next half hour, Annie amused herself by tossing hickory nuts to the squirrels who chattered noisily in the trees around her. The boldest ones scampered nervously after the nuts. Annie was so busy with the squirrels that she didn't hear the hoofbeats on the pike. But she heard a voice calling her name. She jumped up—and there, about twenty yards down the road, was her father, Patrick Henry.

He galloped to her, reached down, and swung Annie up off her feet in one fluid motion.

"So only little Annie came to watch for me," he said.

She laughed. Her face glowed with pleasure. "I couldn't just sit in the house and wait. I had to come see."

Her father continued to hold her close. "I thought I might find you here," he said with a smile. "I brought a treat back for the child who waited." Pulling a maple sugar candy out of his pocket, he handed it to Annie.

"Here. Let's ride back," he said, putting Annie in front of him on his big black horse and urging the horse toward the house.

"Is the harvest finished?" he asked as he looked about the fields.

"They finished the wheat yesterday, before the rain," Annie said.

"Then I guess we'll have a celebration—or did you celebrate without me?"

"We didn't celebrate. We almost lost everything in a fire. It started by lightning. But John Fontaine and the men fought it—and I think they saved a good deal of the wheat," his daughter explained.

Patrick Henry's face clouded. "That wheat means everything to us since we don't grow tobacco. I'll ride out with John later. But no more bad news," he said. "Tell me about the harvest party."

"You mean we can still celebrate?" Annie asked. "Will you play the violin?"

"Tonight?" he said while yawning. "Oh, I'm much too tired. I must go to bed early tonight, child."

"But you can't," Annie protested. "You have to. . . ." She turned in the saddle to look at him and saw a twinkle in his deep-set eyes.

"Oh, Father. You're just kidding. I knew you'd play the fiddle. You always do."

Patrick Henry laughed.

It was a perfect July night. Stars hung low in the sky. The crickets chirped, and fireflies flashed in the dark. Annie sat on the porch waiting for the guests to arrive. She wore a green silk party dress with tiny white flowers and lace. Patsy had put her hair up with green ribbons, and she wore delicate leather slippers on her feet. Annie felt more like a princess than a little girl from Virginia.

Soon the wagons and carriages arrived, filling up the front lawn. Annie curtsied to the ladies and delivered them to Patsy who waited in the ladies' parlor. The men she led to her father's study.

The men looked like strangers tonight. They had taken off their farming clothes and put on silk knee breeches and hip coats. Their wigs were powdered, and their leather shoes shined.

After receiving the guests, she ran upstairs. The servants were still arranging the tables with food and flowers, but they paid no attention to young Annie. She grabbed a handful of mints from a bowl and inspected the other food. There was cider and punch, ham and beef, pies and cakes, and enough food to feed a small army.

Soon Annie heard footsteps on the stairs, and the guests began entering. The large room quickly filled with Patrick Henry's friends and neighbors, who danced while the children's tutor played the harpsichord. Then Annie's father grabbed his violin and began to play. The dancing switched from the sedate minuet to lively Scottish reels, and Annie joined the dancers.

Finally, her father called for everyone's attention. "It is wonderful to be home," he began, "in the heart of my family. I thank God for them and for my safe travel. But we must also give thanks for the abundant harvest He has given us. And thank you for fighting the fire . . ." Patrick Henry's voice caught, but then he continued, "Thank God none of you were injured, and the grain was saved." He raised his goblet in a toast, catching Annie's eye and winking.

Everyone clapped and the music resumed. Although Annie tried to stay awake until the guests left, she couldn't. She woke up briefly to find herself in bed, her father leaning over her and saying tenderly, "Sleep well, little one, sleep well."

Annie smiled and drifted back to sleep.

3

The Accidental Swim

By October the harvest party was only a memory. Patrick Henry had stayed home for three weeks before leaving again. This time he went to Philadelphia where he would stay two months. He was representing Virginia at the Continental Congress where he and other important men would discuss what they should do about their disagreement with Great Britain.

Annie missed her father desperately. The fall days reminded her of how long he'd been gone. The trees were dropping their leaves. Apples were ripening. The cider presses were running, and the hogs were being butchered.

She wandered out in the pasture watching the men plant wheat seed. They walked up and down the ridges in the field, scattering the seed by the handful. Annie felt at loose ends. Elizabeth was sick with a fever and had to stay in bed. Patsy was busy running the house and didn't have time for Annie. And the boys were out hunting. That left Annie with nothing to do.

Without planning, she found herself by the banks of a

little creek that crossed one of the pastures. It was a favorite place for the boys to fish, but Annie hadn't brought a fishing pole. She walked along the bank until she came to a spot where the roots of a towering willow tree jutted into the water and formed, with leaves and twigs and other debris, a dam. The water was deep, and Annie could see at the bottom a big gray fish that was just out of reach. The fish was playing hide-and-seek with her, swimming out in the open and then darting back under the bank of the creek where the shadows made it hard for her to see.

The day was warm for October, but the water was cold. Annie set one bare foot gingerly on a rock about a foot from shore. She planted her other foot firmly on the creek bank. The fish darted into the shadow. Annie thought for a minute. Maybe she could catch the fish the way the Indians did. Uncle William Christian was always full of Indian stories, and Annie loved to hear them.

She hopped over to the other side of the creek where she found a stick about five feet long and a quarter inch in diameter. She rubbed the end of it back and forth on a rock until a point emerged. Annie kept rubbing until the stick looked sharp. She tested it on her finger and winced as it pricked. Finally satisfied, she thought, *Now I'll get a fish.*

Annie resumed her position of one foot on the rock in the creek and the other firmly on the creek bank. She waited. Then carefully leaning over, she aimed her sharpened stick at the fish. She held that position for a moment before plunging the stick into the water. The fish swam easily out of reach of the makeshift spear.

She tried several more times before giving up, tossing her spear into the stream with disgust. As she began to climb back to shore, her foot slipped on a slimy algae-covered rock. Annie twisted in a vain attempt to keep her balance before tumbling into cold water up to her chest. She tried to stand, but her long skirts were heavy with water.

"Ugh," she groaned dragging herself to the bank. "Now I'm in trouble." Barely had those words left her mouth when she heard the sound of laughter from the other side of the creek. She swung around in time to see a tall, middle-aged woman, dressed in a plain dress with a black calash—a hood-like hat—on her head.

Crawling onto the bank, Annie began to wring water out of her skirts. The woman called out apologetically, "Please forgive me. You looked like you were having such a good time, and then you tumbled . . . and those silly skirts. I am sorry. How rude of me to laugh."

The woman talked as she crossed the creek, walking carefully across on stepping stones until she stood at Annie's side. She held out a woolen cloak. "Please take my coat. You'll catch your death of pneumonia."

Shaking her head, Annie replied, "I couldn't. Look at me." Her cotton dress had a mud streak up the back. Rivulets of water continued to stream from the heavy folds of fabric that clung to her legs and arms. A sudden breeze raised goosebumps on Annie's arms and sent dry leaves scudding across the fields.

"Oh, bother," the woman said. "Of course you'll take it. It can always be cleaned."

Annie hesitated, then gratefully wrapped the cloak around her.

"I'm Mrs. Thacker, a neighbor down the way," the woman said. "We've just bought the farm over there." She pointed out over the fields.

Annie smiled. "I'm Annie Henry. I live up in Scotchtown," she said pointing to the large house behind her.

"I was coming to Scotchtown," Mrs. Thacker said. "Could we walk together?"

The wet girl nodded, and the two set off. They were still about 100 yards from the house when Annie apologized, "I'll have to run ahead. My sister Patsy will spit coals when she sees my dress ruined. It's not the first one this week."

"Surely Patsy has tried spear fishing before," Mrs. Thacker said. "She probably wouldn't begrudge you a little fun."

"Oh, not Patsy. Patsy doesn't know the meaning of fun. Or maybe she's just too old to have fun," Annie said, then caught herself with embarrassment. "Not that old people . . . I mean . . . Oh, you know."

She bit her lip with regret.

Mrs. Thacker laughed. "Even old people like me have fun, Annie. But we also have responsibilities. It takes a while to figure out how to balance the two. Maybe that's what Patsy is figuring out."

"I guess," said Annie grudgingly. "But she'll be angry just the same. I'd rather not give her reason to be unhappy with me. After all, I meant no harm."

"Of course you didn't. You run ahead. I can find my way to the door," Mrs. Thacker said. She waved as Annie ran, dragging the oversized cloak in the dirt. "Oh, well," the woman sighed, "nothing that a little soap and water can't get out."

Annie changed, putting the wet dress in the hamper with the other soiled clothes. She hung Mrs. Thacker's cloak in the wardrobe and then looked for Patsy in the ladies' parlor.

"Where is Mrs. Thacker?" Annie asked.

"She is visiting Mama," Patsy answered.

"Could I visit Mama?" Annie asked wistfully.

Patsy shook her head sadly. "Maybe when Father gets home, Annie." Patsy held a letter in her hand and smiled. "And he is coming home. This letter is dated eight days ago. He could be here anytime." Patsy's face lit up with a smile as Annie realized suddenly how tired her sister looked.

Returning the smile, Annie said, "You look pretty when you're happy, Patsy. I guess you've been working too hard."

Her older sister nodded. "I guess maybe I have. I didn't know getting married was such a big job. There has been my trousseau to prepare, linens to embroider, dresses to have made. Plus all the work of the household. I'm tired. And I've probably been sharp with you."

"You have been," Annie said with a shrug. "But maybe if I was seventeen, I'd be sharp with me too." She laughed, then added, "Doesn't it seem like we're always getting ready for Father to come home? I hope he'll stay this time." She thought for a bit and said, "We just won't be sad while Father's here. Then maybe he won't be eager to leave again."

Patsy shook her head. "Annie, Father doesn't leave because he's eager to get away. Father loves Scotchtown, but business calls him. He can't say no." She thought for a moment. "You're right; we can try to make his stay here pleasant. You must try to be more of a lady. Don't give us reasons to worry about you and fret over you."

Young Annie felt guilty as she thought about the wet dress lying in the hamper and Mrs. Thacker's muddy cloak hanging in the wardrobe. She stared at the floor.

Patsy puttered with their mother's tea chest as she spoke. "My only comfort is that Father will surely see that you need to act more like a lady and less like one of Uncle William's Indians," she said, referring to their uncle who lived in the western wilderness. "He's bound to buy you new dresses soon—and they'll have hoops or bustles. Surely, that will slow you down."

"But I don't want to wear hoops yet," Annie said. "You can't ride a horse in hoops; you can't hike; you can't run; you can't play. That's no fun, Patsy."

Her older sister sighed. "I gave up fun years ago—ever since Mama's been ill. It's about time you helped with some of the burden," she said. "You are too much like Father for your own good. It may be okay for a man to have strong opinions and go on about them. But *you* have to be practical. You've got to learn to sew and tend to matters in a big house. That's the kind of job the good Lord is going to give you. And Father better tell you so—though he probably won't." Patsy looked resigned. "Now get a move on. You go upstairs and play with Elizabeth and Edward."

Only too glad to get away from Patsy, Annie ran up the stairs to the big room—the site of the harvest party. There she found Elizabeth and Edward asleep with their nurse sitting close by.

Annie settled herself in front of a window from which she could see the road that would bring her father home again. She daydreamed, not about fancy dresses, but about the fish that got away.

4

Father's Secret Meeting

Laughter rose from the dining room to the nursery above where Annie had been served dinner with Edward and Elizabeth. Her father had returned yesterday. Today he was entertaining friends and political figures from Hanover County. Although she sat at the top of the stairs straining to hear the conversation below, she heard little more than an occasional burst of laughter.

"Not fair," she said with exasperation. "William, Patsy, and John shouldn't be able to stay with Father while I'm sent off to be with the babies." But Annie knew her father would tolerate no complaints. "Your time will come," he was fond of saying to her.

Annie crept down the stairs and into the family dining room. It was next door to the formal dining room where the guests had been served dinner. But now that dinner was over, her father had taken his guests into the gentlemen's parlor. Patsy had already gone into her room for the night.

She found that the large table was still set as she

entered the formal dining room. Glasses glowed in the firelight; a half-eaten pecan pie sat on the table.

Annie cut a piece and put it on a clean plate. She absentmindedly picked at the pie, savoring the sweet brown custard and the crunchy nut topping. When she finished that piece, she debated about having another. Having decided no, Annie was in a dilemma. She could go to bed as Patsy had done, but she wanted news from Philadelphia, and she knew she wouldn't hear it if she was sleeping. She peeked out into the central hall. Its dark wood floors, worn by the constant traffic, gleamed softly in the soft lantern light. Annie walked carefully toward the gentlemen's parlor, giggling nervously. *I feel like I'm a spy for the king of England,* she thought.

The parlor door was shut tight. Only muffled voices floated through the thick walnut panels. Annie crouched outside the door, her head pressed against it. She could hear John Fontaine's voice and Father's muffled response. But nothing more than that.

Just then, the back door opened. A servant carrying a large stack of books and papers from her father's law office tried to make his way through the heavy door. Annie darted back across the hall into the dining room before the servant could turn around. She watched as he carried the papers to the parlor and knocked. The door opened. Warm light spilled out of the room into the dim hallway. The smell of tobacco drifted out of the room, and a tumble of deep voices broke the silence.

Waiting until the servant left before slipping back into the hall, Annie retraced her steps to the parlor only to find that the servant had not shut the door all the way. It remained cracked about six inches. She settled herself next to the door and sat Indian-fashion with her head leaning on crossed arms and listened.

"Richard and John, I appreciate the work you've done in managing affairs here while I've been away," Henry said. "Have the boys been studying?"

"They aren't as diligent in their studies as they might be," the tutor Richard Dabney replied.

"Nor was I," laughed the elder Henry. "My parents despaired that I'd ever make a success in life. But the law has been good to me. It rewards my gift of gab," he said. "Well, the harvest looks good, the children healthy. . . . I'm satisfied."

"Will you tell us about events in Philadelphia?"

Annie tensed. She didn't recognize the speaker's voice; so she put her head a little closer to the door.

"It was a good convention. The Virginia delegation was divided at first. Richard Henry Lee and I more firm in our aim to stand up to England, others believing that we could still avoid war and compromise with the English governor and the king. But meeting with our brothers from Massachusetts, Pennsylvania, New York, and elsewhere sparked a change of thinking. We are no longer separate colonies dealing with the Crown. We are united as colonies. Our interests are the same."

"What was decided?"

"Sam Adams introduced resolutions that were accepted. All of us, not just the good folks of Massachusetts, are going to resist the Intolerable Acts."

Annie knew that the Intolerable Acts had been forced on the people of Boston as payment for the Boston Tea Party—where men disguised as Indians had thrown all the British tea into the harbor rather than pay a tax on it.

Patrick Henry continued, "The colonies agreed not to pay taxes to the Crown. And we agreed not to import any British goods. Finally, we agreed that Britain has no authority over us except in regulating trade. It was a courageous convention; these are bold steps."

"What do you think? Will Britain drive us to the brink? And if there is war, what will be the result?" John Fontaine asked.

Goosebumps chased up Annie's spine. *War.* Such an awesome word. She listened carefully for her father's reply.

"My frank opinion is that we will have war. England will drive us to the edge—no compromise will take place, fighting will soon begin, and the war will be bloody."

Again John Fontaine spoke, "But do you think that an infant nation such as ours, without guns, ships, or money to get them—do you still think it is possible that we could win against the superior power of Great Britain?"

Paying close attention, Annie heard her father say, "I will be honest with you. I doubt that alone we will be able to win. But what about France? or Spain? or Holland? They are the natural enemies of Great Britain. Do you think they will stand idle? No! They will fight for us. And I am convinced that we shall be victorious, and our independence shall be established, and we shall take our stand among the nations of the earth."

"Hotheads like Sam Adams have brought us to this point." Again the strange voice.

"Sam Adams is a good man. He sees things clearly, and he works from principle. Some things, my friend, are worth fighting for." Patrick Henry sounded like a preacher as he spoke. His voice was soft, but it was hard with conviction.

The strange voice sounded harsher. "This cause is not

one of those things. The Bible is clear that we are to submit to the proper authorities. I've not seen the Crown removed from authority."

"Francis, I'm sorry that you and I are in disagreement here. I should not have spoken so bluntly; nor would I have, if I had known your sentiments. It may be that God is raising up new authorities—the House of Burgessess, the Continental Congress. We aren't criminals. We are law-abiding men seeking to protect and save our liberties in the face of a tyrant."

Annie hadn't heard her father speak like this before. A chair scraped, and she heard the heavy sound of boots crossing the floor. Then Patrick Henry spoke again. "We might still remain friends, Francis. Perhaps we will be in agreement someday."

The response came sharp with anger. "It's not possible to be friends with a traitor. My honor won't permit it. I pray that you pull back, Patrick, while there is yet time. And your duty surely lies elsewhere than on this foolish course you are taking. Give my regards to Patsy and your wife. Good day."

Annie scooted back into the shadows away from the door. From her position she watched as Francis Doyle, a distant cousin and a lawyer, stalked out the front door. The parlor door remained open as he had left it. She crept in front of the door and caught a glimpse of her father, his back turned toward the huge corner fireplace, absent-mindedly stirring the wood with a poker.

John Fontaine interrupted the silence. "I'm surprised at Francis. And I'm worried. Do you think he'll make trouble for you?"

"I don't know. He's always been hotheaded—and certain that he's right. A good man if he's on your side. But no friend if he's not. I'm not sure that our years of friendship and our family connection will mean anything to him if he's convinced I've sold out to the devil, which is what he considers Sam Adams to be."

"Do we need to watch him?"

"What can he do? If he informs Lord Governor Dunmore that I'm plotting treason—well, it won't be news to Dunmore. When I start raising a militia, which I plan to do this month, the news will get to the governor soon enough. Courage! We'll all need it in the days ahead. I don't think we need to worry more about Francis Doyle. Now, I've had a hard week. I'm tired. I think I'll retire."

Annie had crept back to her place near the wall. She felt drowsy and decided to stretch out, her arms pillowing her head. *I'll just close my eyes for a minute,* she thought. The next thing she knew, she was awakened by the sound of footsteps.

"I thought my little Annie would be there," Patrick Henry said with a laugh. "You think you'll miss some excitement if you go to bed?"

Annie blushed while her father reached down and tousled her hair. He lowered his lanky body next to hers. "It's bedtime. The guests have left. Come, child. We'll have time to talk tomorrow."

Annie rubbed her eyes with one hand and held her father's hand tight in her other.

Her father continued speaking: "It's been hard for you, hasn't it? With me away and Patsy in charge. . . . I'm sorry, but sometimes things don't work out as we might hope. . . ." A look of such sadness came over Patrick Henry's face that Annie couldn't speak. She rested her head against his chest while he put his arm around her.

"I went downstairs to visit your mama a while ago.

She looked better, I think. Would you like to go with me to see her tomorrow?"

"Oh, Father. I'd like to see her. Patsy said I couldn't while you were away. . . ." Tears began to stream down Annie's cheek. "She said I'd make Mama worse, but I wouldn't have, would I?"

"No, my sweet, I don't think you would make your mama worse. She's in God's hands now. I'm afraid that only He can make her better—or worse. You mustn't be too hard on Patsy though. She's had a heavy load. She should be thinking about parties and dresses; instead she's been saddled with this house and responsibility. God knows it's a big job, and she's done her best. Without Patsy I don't think I could have gone to Philadelphia. Men count on me . . . and I count on Patsy. You'll have to help her."

A flash of jealousy surged in Annie. Father was talking as though Patsy was doing important work for Virginia . . . what was Annie doing? She straightened up. "I can be a big help too, Father. You'll see. I'll be every bit as much help as Patsy."

Patrick Henry laughed and pulled his daughter up. "I know you'll be a help. But first you need your sleep."

5

Annie's Fall

The next morning Patrick Henry greeted Annie on the back steps. "Hurry, girl. We've got a lot to do today. Get something warm on. We're going to look over the farm."

Annie ran to her room and put on a soft woolen cape that fit snugly around her neck. She wore leather gloves and put on her warm winter boots. She ran out to the stables where her father was already talking to the groom.

"Here she is," he announced as Annie ran up. "Saddle up old Paint for her, Joseph."

Joseph led Paint, a small brown horse, out of his stall. He threw a blanket on the animal's back, then lifted the heavy, well-oiled saddle. Annie stood near Paint's head, patting the smooth neck with her arms, ducking her head when the horse tried to nibble on her hair.

"Okay, up you go," her father said, and he lifted Annie into the saddle. She settled herself in the sidesaddle, her heavy skirts falling on one side of the horse. Patrick Henry mounted his own horse, a big black gelding, and they rode past the kitchen toward the slave quarters and the blacksmith shop.

"Look at that hay, Annie," her father said. "Looks like a good harvest. Scotchtown has done us proud this year." Henry surveyed his farm with pride.

Annie also gazed over the farm. Her glance settled on the cottages where the slaves lived. Even though the buildings were clean and well-maintained, Annie didn't like them. "Why must we have slaves?" she asked her father in a quiet voice. "I wouldn't like to be sold like a sack of flour."

Patrick Henry didn't answer at first. He spurred his horse and galloped ahead, then reined the horse around until he was walking with Annie once again. Only the clip-clopping of the horse hooves broke the silence. Finally, he spoke.

"I cannot justify having slaves," he said slowly. "Slavery is an awful thing. It is against the Bible and destructive of liberty. Every honest thinking man rejects it. . . ."

"Then why do we keep slaves?" Annie demanded. "Shouldn't we free them? Isn't that our duty?"

Patrick Henry shook his head sadly. "I find it hard to believe I am the master of slaves of my own purchase. But, I must confess, I am drawn along by the difficulty of living here without them."

As he spoke, the two came in sight of the stable. "I'm sorry I can't ride longer now, Annie, but I must do some work. We'll visit your mother later." He dismounted and strode to his office without waiting for a response.

Annie stared at her father's back. She was angry. Joseph reached up to help her down, but Annie shook her head. "I'm going to ride a little longer," she said.

Giving the horse a good kick, she turned him back towards the pasture. The horse was eager to run. Annie clutched tightly to the reins and the horse's mane. The wind bit her face. Branches reached out and scratched her, but she ignored them. Her father's words echoed in her head like the clopping of the horse's hooves. Slavery was wrong, Father knew it, and yet he kept them anyway.

Up ahead a tree had fallen over the path. Annie looked at it with determination. "Jump it, Paint," she urged the horse, kicking him sharply with her boot. Paint picked up speed and cleared the trunk, but Annie flew off and landed in a ditch at the side of the path. She lay there, stunned. When she tried to move, a sharp pain ran up her arm. "Oh, Lord," she cried. "Help me."

Paint stood over her, neighing softly. Annie wiggled her toes. Nothing was wrong with them. Then she shifted her legs. They were sore, but there was no sharp pain.

With her good arm, Annie forced herself into a sitting position. She surveyed the situation. She was far from home, alone, with an injured arm. And it would be cold tonight. She had to get back to Scotchtown, but how would she get there?

She needed to tie her arm against her body so that it couldn't move. Annie looked at her skirt. It was already torn from the fall. She grabbed the hem with her good hand and tugged until the skirt began to tear. Soon she had a strip about four feet long. Tucking the end under her injured arm, she wrapped the strip around her back, under her good arm, and over the hurt one as many times as she could. Then she tied the end. Now the injured arm was held snugly against her.

Next, she whistled for Paint who had wandered off to graze. Annie reached up and grabbed the horse's reins, which were trailing in the dirt. She pulled herself up until she was standing, a little shakily, next to the horse.

"Now, Paint," she whispered, "you've got to get me home." Annie knew she couldn't pull herself into the sidesaddle without help. Even when she was healthy, her father or Joseph helped her. By herself, with an injured arm, it would be impossible. But a nearby stump offered hope. She led the horse to it and climbed up. From the stump, the injured girl put one foot in the stirrup. But could she lift herself? She grabbed the saddle horn with her good hand and pulled. Again she prayed, "God help me. Give me strength."

It took several tries, but finally Annie was in the saddle. She leaned over and spoke softly to the horse. "Take me home, Paint."

The horse responded as though he knew something was wrong. He picked his way carefully around the ruts and rocks so that Annie wouldn't be bumped and jarred. Before too long they were back within sight of the house.

Patrick Henry must have seen her approach because he was waiting for Annie at the stables. When he saw that she was hurt, he rushed to her, calling behind to Joseph, "Get the horse and ring the bell." Reaching up, her father gently lifted Annie from the saddle, careful not to touch her injured arm.

"Tell me what happened," he said softly.

Annie couldn't speak at first. But when she saw her father's frightened expression, she took a deep breath and smiled. He carried her into the house and laid her gently on her bed. Patsy hovered anxiously nearby. He sat down by Annie's side.

"You have to tell us what happened, Annie."

Annie sighed. "We were galloping. I asked Paint to jump. He did, but I fell off. I think I've broken my arm."

"Patsy, we must have the doctor. Send John over to Doctor Payne's. He must not delay," their father ordered.

Patsy ran from the room. Her face was drawn with worry.

Reaching for her father's hand with her good hand, Annie said, "I'm sorry, Father. I didn't mean to be trouble. I was angry with you, and I foolishly ran."

"Annie, you aren't trouble. I'm sorry that I have feet of clay. But no one knows it better than I. If it makes you feel better, I think a time will come when we can be rid of slavery. And until that time comes, we must treat those in our care with kindness and gentleness. You will not see one of our slaves mistreated on this farm. That is a promise."

Annie smiled weakly. Her arm ached, and she felt really tired. "Why won't you let me sleep, Father," she said when he continued to talk to her.

"You must not sleep until the doctor comes, little one. I'll amuse you with stories from Philadelphia. But you may not sleep."

Patrick Henry talked on as Annie drifted in and out of sleep. Finally, the doctor arrived. He examined the arm and announced, "A clean break. I'll set it in a splint. It will heal good as new, or nearly so, if you are careful."

Annie smiled and lay back on her pillow. She heard Patsy's gentle voice urging her to drink a sour-tasting potion the doctor said would prevent fever. She drank it and drifted off to sleep while her father sat anxiously at her side.

6

"Rejoice the Soul of Thy Servant"

Even though she felt better, Annie wasn't allowed out of bed for a week. Her father said firmly, "You won't miss anything if you stay in bed, and it's one way I can guarantee that you won't get into trouble."

Annie read a little and sketched until she didn't want to see another pencil. Occasionally her father brought his violin into the room and played. Sometimes the boys brought in cards—but Annie didn't know the games they played. Even Elizabeth tried to entertain her. She brought her dollies and their dishes into Annie's room, and together they played house. Elizabeth smiled a lot. "I like it when you're sick, Annie. Then you play with me," she said.

But finally, on December 1, Patrick Henry announced that his daughter Annie was to get up and dress. More than that, he had a surprise. "You're going to see your mama today, Annie. You asked me last week, before the accident, and I've been waiting until you were strong enough. But I think you must see her now."

Annie dressed awkwardly. Patsy had altered several dresses by opening up the left sleeve to make room for the splint, but it was hard for Annie to pull the dress on. Finally, though, she was dressed and ready to go.

The stairs where he waited for her were outside at the end of the house near the kitchen. The stairs led into the basement which was divided, on this half of the house, into four rooms. Patrick Henry and his daughter walked down the few steps into the basement. The brick floor was cold beneath their feet. Windows near the ceiling let in plenty of light, but the low ceilings forced him to stoop slightly. He peeked into one room where a woman sat knitting.

"Tildy, I want to take Annie in to see Mrs. Henry. How is she today?"

Tildy's eyes swept from her master's face to Annie's. "She's not good, Master Henry. She's not good. But she's as good as she ever is. There's no reason not to let the child see her. Might do her some good, though I don't know about that."

Clutching her father's hand even tighter, Annie could feel the calluses on his palm. At that moment a high pitched moan erupted from the room. Patrick Henry smiled encouragingly. "It will be fine. Come along, Annie." He led her gently into the room and whispered in her ear, "Don't be afraid. It is your mama, even if she doesn't look like it."

Annie took a deep breath and walked toward the rocking chair, turned so its back faced the door. Her father led her by the hand around to the front of the rocker. Sarah Henry was bound by a straight dress. Its heavy cotton strips held her arms at her side so that she was unable to get up from her chair. Her head fell limply to the side, her mouth hung slack, and a bit of spittle dripped from the corner. Frightening moans came from her mother's lips, but

Sarah Henry seemed unaware of them. Annie recoiled from the woman in front of her. She found it hard to believe that this creature was the same mother whose eyes were once warm and alive and whose touch had comforted Annie when she was hurt.

She tried to back away from the chair, but her father's firm grip held her in place. He pushed her toward her mother's chair whispering, "Say something."

Annie obeyed hesitantly. "Hello, Mama," she said softly. "I've missed you so much."

Her mother didn't respond or give any sign that she had heard. Annie didn't know what else to do. She looked to her father for guidance.

"Sarah, dear, I thought it would do you good to see Annie. I know it pains you to be far from your children," Patrick said. "I thought we could visit for a while before going back upstairs."

He tried to talk about the farm and the family. He mentioned his trip to Philadelphia and Patsy's upcoming wedding, but Sarah Henry's expression never changed.

"Let me read you a psalm, Sarah," he said gently as he pulled a little pocket psalter from his vest. "'Bow down thine ear, O Lord, hear me: for I am poor and needy. Preserve my soul; for I am holy: O thou my God, save thy servant that trusteth in thee. Be merciful unto me, O Lord: for I cry unto thee daily. Rejoice the soul of thy servant: for unto thee, O Lord, do I lift up my soul.'"

When Annie heard the words, "Rejoice the soul of thy servant," she could stand it no longer. A huge sob rose up from her chest and racked her shoulders. She began to weep until her throat hurt, and her eyes were swollen.

Minutes went by. She wiped her tears and looked up at her mother. Tears fell from the silent woman's eyes unchecked. Then Annie looked at her father. He held Sarah's hand, and he too was crying.

A bit later, Annie sat at the dining room table across from her father. Light from the candles played across his face, highlighting the wrinkles. *He looks older,* she thought. *Tired.*

"Daddy, what's wrong with Mama? Is she going to get better?" Annie asked.

Patrick looked up at his daughter and shook his head sadly. "Your mama's very sick. She's got a head sickness. She doesn't know who she is; she doesn't know who we are. . . . I don't know if she'll get better."

"But maybe if she came upstairs . . . maybe it's being shut up downstairs that's making her sick," Annie whispered, afraid to criticize her father's decision to keep Sarah Henry in the basement.

The shadow of a smile flitted across Patrick Henry's face. "Honey, the reason your mama stays downstairs with Tildy is so she won't hurt herself or someone else. We don't want to send your mama to the asylum. Here we know she'll be loved and cared for. She is my wife, after all. She is your mama. It's the least we can do."

"But why, Daddy, why is Mama sick?"

"Honey, I don't know why God does what He does. Sometimes His ways are mysterious. But won't the Judge of all the world do what is right?"

Annie was quiet. She didn't know the answer to the question. "I can't believe that it's right that Mama is sick."

Patrick Henry asked, "Annie, do you remember the fire?"

His daughter nodded.

"A great deal of wheat was destroyed. We asked why

God would do that? But I've learned two things from that fire. First, God sometimes has to teach us how much we must depend on Him. Sometimes we think we are in control of our lives, of this marvelous farm, of events. But God wants us to understand that it comes from Him. And second, sometimes these bad things, like the fire, can actually produce something good. John Fontaine tells me that all of the ash in the soil will make that field even more fertile next year. God made a good thing come out of that fire."

Patrick Henry patted her hand. "Come, let's find Patsy."

The next morning, Annie didn't want to get up. She didn't want to see her father, and she didn't want to see Patsy. Rumbling in her stomach, however, reminded her that she was hungry. She reluctantly washed and dressed herself.

When she came into the dining room, everyone else had already eaten. Patsy hovered over Annie. "Are you sure you are well? Should I send for the doctor?" she asked.

"I didn't want to get up," Annie grumbled. "That's all."

"Then you won't eat," Patsy said.

Annie scowled. Then she realized that she had no cause to be angry with Patsy. This trouble was part of God's plan for Patrick Henry's house. "I'm sorry, Patsy. I am hungry. Is it too late for breakfast?"

Patsy set a plate of food before Annie. Then she asked, "Was it awful seeing Mama?"

Annie nodded. "I didn't know it would be so bad. I thought Mama was getting better. I can't bear to think of her down there, all alone except for Tildy."

"Mama's not alone," Patsy said. "When Father is home, he goes down every day. And Mrs. Thacker comes often. She'll be here this morning, I think. Besides, Mama doesn't know who visits and who doesn't."

After finishing her breakfast in silence, Annie went into her bedroom and found Mrs. Thacker's cloak, now cleaned and brushed. She took it with her to a spot under the lilac bush outside Mama's window. Annie sat at the base of it, ignoring the way the dry branches poked at her back. After a while, she saw their new neighbor come around the side of the house and enter the door to the basement as though she had done it many times.

About a half hour later she came out, waved at Tildy, and called out that she'd come again on Friday. Annie waited until Mrs. Thacker was halfway across the front yard and then ran after her. She was breathless when she reached the woman's side.

Mrs. Thacker looked down. "Annie, I didn't see you," she said, and continued walking. "Whatever happened to your arm?"

"I fell off a horse," Annie said. "But I'm fine now." She held out the cloak. "I wanted to return this to you. Thank you."

"You're welcome," Mrs. Thacker replied as she took the cloak.

Annie tried to keep up, but Mrs. Thacker's stride was too long, so Annie trotted and skipped beside her. "How was Mama today?" she asked, biting her lower lip nervously.

"Oh, I didn't see much difference. She was quiet. She listened when I read a psalm. She didn't scream out." Mrs. Thacker spoke matter-of-factly as though Annie was an adult and able to understand.

"Does Mama know you?" Annie asked.

Mrs. Thacker smiled. "I don't think she knows me now. But we used to know each other. We grew up near each other, not far from here. I've known Sarah Shelton for a long time."

"But if she doesn't know you, why do you come?" Annie persisted.

"I guess I come because I love your mama, and I want her to cling to the truth. I believe your mama understands some of what we tell her, at least I pray she does."

They walked together quietly. Mrs. Thacker slowed her pace so that Annie no longer had to trot to keep up.

Finally Annie asked the question that had bothered her all night. "Father says God can turn this sickness into good. Do you believe that?"

Mrs. Thacker paused. She looked at Annie's serious face and understood the struggle the young girl was having. "Let's sit for a minute," she said, lowering herself to the ground. "That's a hard question, isn't it? How can God, if He's good, let such bad things happen?" Mrs. Thacker paused, then asked, "Do you know the story of Joseph?"

Annie blushed. She knew she should know the story and had certainly heard it. She shook her head shyly.

"You don't know the Joseph story? That's one of the most exciting stories in the whole Bible. I can't imagine what your daddy . . . Oh, never mind. Well, it goes like this:

"Joseph was a young man—oh, about Patsy's age, I'd say. He was his daddy's favorite because he had been born when his daddy was getting on in years. One time Joseph's daddy gave Joseph a special coat of many colors. That made Joseph's brothers—he had eleven of them—angry. They believed their daddy loved Joseph best."

"Like Father loves Patsy," Annie interrupted.

"Shhh . . . Just listen to the story," Mrs. Thacker replied.

"One day Joseph had a dream. It was about him and his brothers binding up sheaves of grain in the field. Suddenly, in the dream, the brothers' sheaves of grain gathered around Joseph's grain and bowed down to it. As you can imagine, the brothers didn't like that dream. And then Joseph had another dream where the sun, the moon, and the stars all bowed down to him. Of course, he told his brothers this dream also. They got even angrier. They didn't even like to talk to him."

"But what's this got to do with bad things being good?" asked Annie.

"Be patient, child. You'll see," Mrs. Thacker answered.

"One day Jacob told Joseph to go out to his brothers who were watching the flocks of sheep. Joseph went. His brothers saw him from a distance, and do you know what they decided to do? They decided to kill him.

"But Reuben, the oldest, had second thoughts. He convinced the brothers not to kill Joseph but to throw him into a pit instead. So, that's what they did. But first they took Joseph's beautiful coat.

"You'd think Joseph's brothers would be feeling pretty bad. Maybe they'd change their minds. But these brothers sat down and ate a meal. And while they were eating, some traders came by. The brothers had another idea. They sold Joseph to the traders.

"Then they killed an animal, dipped Joseph's coat into the blood, and took the bloody coat back to Jacob. 'He's dead,' they told Jacob. 'A lion got him.'"

"That's awful," Annie said. "I'd never do that to Patsy."

"No, I don't think you would," Mrs. Thacker laughed. "That was very wicked."

"What happened next?" Annie asked.

"Well, those traders sold Joseph into slavery in Egypt where he eventually became a trusted servant. But the wife of his master accused Joseph of wickedness. It wasn't true, of course, but Joseph was thrown in jail where he stayed a long time.

"A while later Pharaoh, the king of Egypt, had some dreams. He asked everyone to help him figure out what the dreams meant. No one could do it. But one of the men from prison remembered that Joseph knew about dreams. He told Pharaoh about him."

Annie leaned forward to hear the story. Mrs. Thacker's voice gained strength as she told it.

"Joseph was able to tell Pharaoh his dream. He told him there would be seven years of plenty followed by seven years of famine.

"The king asked Joseph what he should do, and Joseph told him to store the grain during the good years so they'd have enough to eat during the bad ones."

"But how is this good?" Annie asked.

"I'm almost there, child. Be patient. Be patient. Well, the Pharaoh did what Joseph said. In fact, he put Joseph in charge. Everything Joseph said came true. When the bad years came, people from all around had to come to Joseph to ask for food because he had stored the grain. And do you know who came? Joseph's brothers. Only they didn't know it was Joseph. They thought he was dead. After a while, Joseph told his brothers who he was."

"I bet he was angry with them. He probably wouldn't sell them any grain," Annie said.

"Oh no . . . he gave them grain. In fact, he didn't take their money. And when he told them who he was, he cried. But you know what Joseph said to them when they said they were sorry. He said—and here's my point, Annie—

'ye thought evil against me; but God meant it unto good.' That means that they meant it for evil, but God meant it for good. You see, if Joseph's brothers hadn't sold him into slavery, Joseph wouldn't have been in Egypt to read the king's dream. The Pharaoh wouldn't have prepared for the famine, and all the people, including Joseph and his brothers, would have starved. That's how God can take bad—even evil things—and bring good out of them."

"But what about Mama?" Annie asked. "How can that be good?"

Mrs. Thacker shook her head sadly. "I don't know. I truly don't know. There is a promise that God works things out for the good of those who love Him. But it isn't always clear to us when we are in the midst of trouble. Your mother loves the Lord. You must make sure you do also."

She stood up and brushed the dry grass off her skirt. "I've got to hurry home, Annie. We'll talk again."

Annie went back to Scotchtown. She felt at loose ends, wondering where her father had gone. She read for a while, but found she couldn't concentrate. Then she went for a walk, but the sights and smells that usually amused her failed to hold her interest. Finally, she found herself outside the kitchen door. A good smell of fried cakes came from inside. Annie followed the smell.

Her brother John was sitting at the heavy plank table with a cup of cider and a plate of cakes in front of him. He looked up when his younger sister entered the room. "Have some fried cakes. They're plenty good," he said, waving a donut in the air.

Annie sat next to him and took the offered donut. A fire blazed in the fireplace. Cast-iron pots hung near the flames with soup cooking for dinner. A chicken roasted on a spit. The good smells of food filled the air.

"Do you know where Father went?" Annie asked her brother.

"Yep."

"Well, aren't you going to tell me?" she asked impatiently.

"I guess if Father wanted you to know, he'd have told you himself," John said.

"You are so impossible. Of course he couldn't tell me. He couldn't find me," Annie said trying to keep her patience.

"Were you lost?" John asked with a mock tone of concern.

Annie slapped the table hard with her good hand.

Her brother laughed. "You better watch out, or you will hurt your good hand. I'll tell you where he's gone. I was only teasing. He's gone to raise an army—or a militia. He took William with him." John sounded angry about that. "Said I wasn't old enough yet."

Annie laughed. "Where'd they meet?"

"Smith's Tavern, of course. They're going to meet there often and practice. I can't believe I can't go. I have to stay around here with women." John shuddered when he thought of the humiliation.

Annie laughed again. "I'm not going to wait."

"Where are you going?" John asked.

"I'm going to Smith's Tavern," Annie answered smugly. "You may be too young to march, but you aren't too young to watch—and neither am I. How will we ever know what's going on if we stay around here? Let's ask Joseph to hook up the wagon. You can drive."

John's mouth opened to protest. Then he grinned. "Let's go. Beat you to the stable."

7

Christmas

Winter was a good time to raise a militia. There was less work for farmers to do once they had harvested their crops and sent their wheat to John Syme's mill where it was ground into flour and packed for sale. Tobacco had been gathered, dried, and prepared for shipping, and the hogs were butchered.

Patrick Henry and his neighbors traveled to Smith's Tavern often. They called it muster day when all the men paraded. They came in their plowing clothes, their muddy boots tapping out the count on the hard-packed field. Children also marched with sticks instead of muskets, while ladies gathered in groups to gossip.

After that first day, Annie rode into Hanover, the nearest village, whenever her father said she could. Her splint had been removed, and although the arm was stiff, she was able to use it a little. The doctor said it would improve with time.

At the square, Annie flitted from group to group. Some days she marched with the boys, tucking her hair into a cap and ignoring their protests. Other times she played hoops and balls with the younger children, and sometimes she stood with the ladies listening to them talk about the price of sugar or who still had tea or good English fabric. None of those products were allowed into the colonies anymore.

Amidst the marching, Christmas, 1774, came to Scotchtown. Its arrival took everyone by surprise. The house had taken on an air of neglect since fall. Patsy Henry was busy with the day-to-day running of the household and plans for her springtime wedding, and Patrick Henry's attention was focused on the militia. Annie figured it must be almost Christmas. The first snow had fallen and melted, leaving nothing behind but clumps of dirty ice.

Still, she didn't think it fitting to have a celebration with her mother so sick. Sometimes she stood outside the window to her mother's room and listened, hoping that her mother might get well and the family might return to normal. But that didn't happen. On good days there was no sound from the window. More often there was more awful moaning and screaming. Then she'd hear Tildy's soft voice soothing and comforting away her mother's tears.

One day their father strode into the family dining room where the children were having supper. He said, "The work is done. It's time to gather some greens and dress up the house for Christmas."

Annie glanced at Patsy. She figured Patsy would say what Annie was thinking: *It's not right to think about Christmas and celebrating, what with Mama being so sick and all.*

But Patsy didn't say it. Instead she smiled at their father as though he were a child to be humored and said, "It's too cold for me. We don't have to decorate this year."

"Nonsense. Christmas comes but once a year, and we are going to mark the day. On Christmas we'll be feasting, and we'll not do it in a house that looks more like it's in mourning than in celebration. Your mother won't be offended." He turned to Annie. "How about you? Won't you come with me?"

Annie didn't want to go—but time alone with her father was rare. She grudgingly nodded but made no move to join him.

"Well, goosey. If you want to go, get a move on. It's going to snow. You can feel it. I want to be back before it does. I'll have Joseph harness the wagon. You dress warmly."

Annie put on her warmest coat and heavy wool stockings under her thick leather boots. She tied a scarf over her head and tucked her hands into Patsy's fur muffler.

She waited on the porch for Joseph to bring the wagon around. An icy wind chilled her even through her heavy coat.

Her father came out of the house in his stained, old buckskin coat and a fur cap. His woolen breeches showed signs of wear.

Annie laughed with delight when she saw him. "You look like Uncle William," she said.

He smiled as he lifted Annie into the wagon and wrapped a heavy fur blanket around her legs. Annie's feet rested on heated bricks. "You know, I didn't always wear fancy clothes," he said. "Folks used to wonder whether I'd show up in court in buckskins."

Annie remembered those days vaguely—before they had bought Scotchtown, before Patrick Henry had become wealthy from his work as a lawyer, before Mama had taken sick. Somehow the sight of the old clothes made Annie sad, wishing for the old days.

A knot settled in her stomach. Her father reached over

and squeezed Annie's thin shoulders, but he said nothing. The horse made its way quickly over the frozen ground until they entered the pine forest.

"Let's see. What do we need? Greens for the windows, surely. That's eight wreaths across the front. We'll need a wagon load of branches to make that many wreaths."

Patrick Henry hopped out. He used a small hatchet to remove limbs from the pines. Annie sat in the wagon feeling the bite of the wind through her coat. She wished she had stayed with Patsy. Her father loaded the limbs into the back of the wagon. He glanced at Annie huddled on the bench. "I think I'll just chop a whole tree down," he said. "We can remove the limbs at home."

He climbed up on the wagon and clucked to the horses. "I want to find one big enough to do the job. Let's go a bit further."

They rode on until they came to a stand of twelve-foot trees. Annie felt a quickening of excitement in spite of herself. "Oh, one of these, please, Father," she pleaded. "They are beautiful."

He smiled. "That's what I thought," he agreed. Taking his ax, he climbed down.

"Stand back," he called to his daughter. "These chips will fly into your eyes."

He raised the heavy ax over his shoulders and swung it with terrific force. The tree shuddered. Over and over again he hit the trunk with the ax, harder and harder. Annie shrank back as she watched her father swing so hard. He was strong, she knew that. But he was also angry, and he was pouring out his anger on that tree. The tree finally fell over with a thud. He wiped the sweat from his forehead with his sleeve. Annie couldn't speak. She watched her father load it onto the back of the wagon.

He then lifted Annie back into her seat. "We'd best be getting home now. Snow's coming," he added looking up at the heavy gray canopy of clouds.

As they rode back to Scotchtown, her father said, "This reminds me of the first winter Sarah and I were married. We had no money and a baby on the way. We were living with Grandma Shelton, who thought we'd done a fool thing to marry so young. No matter. That Christmas your mama and I took the wagon out and cut down a tree. We dragged it back to Grandma Shelton's, pleased that we were going to have enough greens to decorate the whole house.

"But Grandma Shelton wasn't too happy about it. Said she didn't much cotton to all this pagan decorating. She was of the old school—no point in setting up Christmas as any more important than any other day. Just leads to bad habits, she warned us. Well, Sarah and I sat in that wagon with that old pine tree and just laughed. We got a candle and lit it, sang a few carols, drank some cider, and had our own celebration."

Annie had never heard her father talk about the old days. She felt tears burning the back of her eyelids. She squeezed her eyes shut to keep the tears from running down her cheek.

He kissed her gently on her forehead. "Your mama used to be a beautiful woman. That's how I want to remember her." He sighed.

That evening Patrick Henry took out his fiddle. He gathered the children into the parlor and said, "We're going to sing. Annie, find the hymnal." While she found the book, her father played his violin. He said to Patsy, "Come, show this family how to dance." He played, and she danced until everyone was clapping hands and stomping feet. Little Elizabeth ran to her father's knee. "Daddy, Daddy, dance with me," she said.

He stood up, his lanky form towering over his little daughter. "I'd be delighted. Patsy, will you play the harpsichord?"

As Patsy played, Patrick Henry danced with his daughters, first Elizabeth, then Annie. Finally, he fell back into a chair. "Enough. That's enough. I'm an old man and can't dance anymore." He hushed the protests with his hand. Then he looked at the glowing faces surrounding him. "This family has been without laughter too long. We won't go so long again," he said. "I promise. Now let's sing some hymns."

Annie glanced at the family gathered in the parlor—Father sat in his armchair near the fire, baby Edward on one knee, Elizabeth on the other. John Fontaine stood near Patsy at the harpsichord. William and John sat on the floor, their long legs stretched out before them. Mr. Dabney, the tutor, was on the settee. Annie figured she would never forget that night—familiar faces made visible by the lamplight, the sweet smell of apple logs burning in the fireplace, and Father's rich baritone voice singing the words, "Joy to the world, the Lord is come."

Later in her room, snuggled down into the warm comforter, she prayed, "Lord, please make Mama better." Hot tears stung her eyes. She didn't fight them. That night she cried for Mama, Daddy, and for herself.

8

Andrew Thacker

February was marked by an unbroken string of bleak, gray days. The temperature stayed just above freezing, turning whatever snow there was to gray and brown slush.

One cold, drizzly day toward the end of February, Annie had taken refuge upstairs with Elizabeth and Edward. A children's tea party was in progress. She set the table, brought up some biscuits—called scones, and poured tea—actually warm apple cider.

Her younger sister and brother happily sipped the cider and fed small cakes to the gathered dolls and animals. Annie stood near a window watching the rain fall. From a distance, a rider came toward the house. He was covered with an oilcloth to stay dry; so Annie didn't recognize him until he dismounted and uncovered his head as he knocked on the door of Father's office. She recognized the tavern keeper's son.

A moment later, her father opened his office door. The rider held out a letter that he had taken from an oilcloth bag tied to his waist. Annie saw her father take the letter, nod, and then shut the door. The rider put the oilcloth back over his head and strode across the muddy drive to the kitchen.

Not long after, he came out wiping crumbs from his mouth. He gathered his horse from the livery and set off down the road back to Hanover.

She turned from the window back to the children's tea. "I'll have a scone," she said to Elizabeth who had taken over the hostess duties while Annie had been at the window.

"Then you must sit with us, Annie," said Elizabeth. "It's not polite to stand and eat."

Annie pulled a chair up to the table and nibbled at her scone. She looked over at Mary, the nurse who was in the corner knitting. "Mary, will you have anything?" she asked.

"Not me," Mary answered. "I need to finish this sleeve, and I've only a few rows to go. I only wish the light was better."

"Why not sit closer to the window? Surely there's enough daylight to brighten your work," Annie said.

"But the draft is too chilly. I'm cozy where I am. Let me work a little longer though."

Annie walked restlessly back to the window. The rain had let up, but there was still no trace of the sun. "Oh, I wish I could go outside," she said. "I can't stand being cooped up inside any longer. Hasn't this been the longest February, and the dreariest, that you remember? Even the militia isn't drilling. Father hasn't been to Smith's Tavern for weeks."

"We haven't had a nice spell of sun for weeks, you're right. And we're all about to go stir crazy," Mary answered.

As Annie stood at the window, she saw her father stride out of his office, his skull cap pulled down on his head. He walked briskly toward the house, a frown drawing his mouth down at the corners. He entered the back door and called out Patsy's name.

Annie glanced at the children. They were involved in their tea party. Mary was busy. Annie made up her mind to go down and find out what was going on.

Mary looked up at her as she opened the stairway door. "Curiosity killed the cat, little Annie. Spying on other folks won't bring you anything good. If they have something to tell you, they will tell you."

"I'm going anyway," Annie said. She didn't wait for an answer.

It wasn't hard to find her father. His voice carried throughout the house. "What do you mean, you wrote to Cousin Elizabeth Watson? What good could come of it?"

Patsy's response was muffled by her tears. "I only meant to help. I wrote her about John Fontaine . . . and mentioned how poorly Mama's been. I also told her about your activities at the convention. I didn't mean anything by it."

"Well, Elizabeth Watson surely did mean something. She's written a letter." Patrick Henry waved the offending piece of paper. "And she is urging me to send the children to her. She suggests my home is no place for children. I'm too interested in politics, she says, and traitorous politics, she suggests."

Annie fought an urge to rush into the room to defend her father. Instead, she crept closer so that she could hear Patsy's response.

"I never intended for the children to go with her," she said. "But you must think about Annie, Father. The babies

I can handle. They don't know what's going on. But Annie is a wild one. She comes and goes as she pleases. She wanders this farm all day long. I can barely get her to study her lessons. She needs some civilizing, and she won't listen to me."

"Well, she won't go to that family," Annie heard her father say. "If something happens to your mother, we'll talk about other arrangements. But I won't hear of it until then."

Annie barely had time to scramble back to the stairs before her father was out the door, slamming it behind him.

Annie's first impulse was to follow him back to his office. She ran out the back door but halted on the stairs. She didn't want her father to be angry with her for eavesdropping. Nor did she want to go back upstairs and listen to more childish chatter. Instead, she ran down the stairs toward the kitchen, grabbed an oilskin that hung on the porch, and tied it around her. A pair of muddy garden boots also sat on the steps. She pulled them on. They were several sizes too big, but Annie didn't care. She darted around the corner of the kitchen, careful to keep out of sight of the windows.

Soon she was in the orchard. The rain had all but stopped, but the slush-covered ground made running close to impossible, and Annie felt out of breath after going only a short way. The month of staying inside had made her unused to physical exercise.

She continued walking until she was well out of sight of the house and other outbuildings. Then she tried running some more. Her long skirts, now soaked and splattered with mud, twisted around her legs, nearly tripping her once or twice. When she put her foot down, the snow and slush gripped her boots with such strength that Annie felt she would surely lose them. Ignoring the discomfort, she walked and walked until she was far from Scotchtown, far from her father, and far from Patsy's plotting.

Annie stayed outside until her anger passed. She walked along a stream that was close to overflowing its banks. Where normally the water trickled, it now raced with thunderous fury. She sat down well back from the bank, careful to keep the oilskin under her. She threw branches into the water and watched the creek swallow them up and spit them out far downstream. Once in a while, a branch caught in an eddy. Water poured down on it, but the hapless twig could only swirl in circles, unable to break the death grip the eddy had on it. Finally, as though an unseen hand had loosed it, the twig would break free and continue on its course.

That's me, Annie thought. *Caught in an eddy. One thing after another, and I can't get loose.* She stiffened herself, unwilling to cry. She felt her anger burn towards Patsy. But although Annie tried to nurse her anger, she found it hard to hold on to. After an hour she felt tired, wet, and cold—but empty of emotions. *I might as well get home,* she thought. *It's probably lunchtime.*

She hopped up but didn't try running back. She didn't have the energy. Instead, she followed the stream as it meandered toward the house.

As she walked, Annie heard the unexpected sound of music. She climbed a little ridge to get a better look. There was a young man, about John's age, playing a flute. He was a lanky fellow, about as tall as Father, and clad in buckskin. He appeared intent on his music and probably wouldn't have noticed Annie except that her boot slipped on the mud, causing her to fall with a thud.

The young man looked startled. He yelled at Annie, who was still on the ground, "Who are you? What're you doing here?"

"What do you mean, what am I doing here?" Annie answered back. "This property belongs to my father. You are trespassing. I've a mind to report you." Annie's stern tone was marred by a sudden case of the hiccups.

"Your father!" he sputtered. "Not so. My father bought this land from Patrick and Sarah Henry last August. County court just met February 14 to acknowledge the sale. The records are there. Go see for yourself."

Annie bit her lip. She knew her father had been selling off parts of the estate. She remembered last August when some local farmers had been called in to witness the deed. Even Mama had been well enough to sign—that had been right before Father had left for Philadelphia.

"Well, I don't care whose property it is," Annie said. "A gentleman wouldn't talk that way to a lady."

The young man blushed red. A quick grin came to his face. "I'm sorry. You actually scared me. I thought maybe you were a Tory spy—a friend of the king. I shouldn't have spoken so sharply."

Annie's curiosity was quickened. "If I were a Tory spy," she asked, "why would I want to spy on you?"

"Well, 'cause you'd want to know how we patriots are plotting to defend our homes from British tyranny. You'd want to know our plans and see our training exercises. You'd even want names . . . but I'd never tell. If I ever told a spy the names of some of our leaders—why they could be hung in England, that's what they'd be. Who are you, anyway?"

The young man closed his mouth abruptly as he realized what he had been blurting to a stranger.

Annie laughed. "I'm Annie Henry. Patrick Henry is my father."

He blushed again. "Pleased to meet you. You must be a patriot then. Your father is a fine man. He's responsible for Hanover County having raised this militia." The boy paused to think. "Have you heard what's happening in Massachusetts? British troops have poured into Boston. The *Gazette* said fourteen regiments plus Massachusetts Tories have taken over the city. Can you imagine those redcoats trying to take over the Hanover County courthouse? We wouldn't let them."

Annie felt a surge of jealousy. Surely Father knew about Boston. But he never talked about it at home. Not something young ladies needed to worry about, he thought—so his daughter had to hear the news from a neighbor boy. Annie nodded as though she knew what the young man was talking about.

The boy was so taken with his own knowledge that he paid scant attention to the girl's response. "The papers say that Peyton Randolph has called a meeting. Every county is to send two representatives. My pa says your father will be a representative for sure. It's in Richmond next month on March 20."

"Why Richmond?" Annie asked. "Don't the Burgesses usually meet in Williamsburg?"

"This is different. Governor Dunmore has warships in the York River. If the patriots met in Williamsburg, there might be a fight. Maybe the British would break up the meeting or arrest the leaders. Instead, your father and the others are going to St. John's Church in Richmond. You know, that's not so far from here. I'd give anything to go."

Patrick Henry's daughter thought for a moment about the meeting, but then looked curiously at the boy and his flute. "Why are you playing that, and why are you doing it outside on such a miserable day?" she asked.

"I could ask you the same question," the boy answered. "What are you doing outside on a miserable day?"

"Just walking, but at least I'm not fool enough to be playing music," she said.

"I'm practicing. I'm going to play the fife with the Hanover regulars," the boy said proudly. "I'll be marching with your brother William and your father if the British don't hang him first."

Annie gasped. "Hang him? Hang Father? They couldn't do that," she said.

"They will if they catch him in a treasonable act, they surely will. And your father is just the man to say something they might take to be disloyal to the king. . . ." The boy paused for a breath. A look at Annie's pale face made him realize how those words sounded. "I'm sorry. That sounded awful. What I meant to say is that Patrick Henry is the finest speaker in Virginia, maybe in all the colonies. Plus, my pa says your father has a passion for liberty. I just figured that those two things might get him into trouble."

Annie remembered suddenly that she had been gone from home too long. She turned to go and hadn't walked more than 100 feet when she realized she didn't know the boy's name. She turned around and yelled, "What's your name, anyway?"

"Andrew Thacker," he called back.

Annie waved. "Andrew Thacker," she whispered to herself. "He must be Mrs. Thacker's boy." Annie smiled as she ran toward home. Her boots made a sucking sound as they caught in the mud.

She removed the boots and oilskin at the kitchen and left them on the porch; then she carefully made her way across the yard in her bare feet. The wet and grimy hem of her dress rubbed roughly against her ankles.

Trying to sneak into her room so she could change before being seen by Patsy, she walked through the two dining rooms and into her bedroom. As Annie changed, she heard sobs coming from the parlor. She tiptoed to the door, which was slightly ajar. Patsy sat in her mother's favorite chair, head bent, face covered with her hands. She was crying.

Annie felt a sense of dread. Patsy hardly ever cried. She certainly wouldn't be crying over their father's morning anger. No, Annie felt it in her stomach. Something awful had happened.

9

Mama's Gone

Patrick Henry wasn't in the house. Annie ran upstairs. She reached the nursery, breathless, with fear in the pit of her stomach. Annie knew as soon as she saw the nurse cuddling Elizabeth that her fears were right.

"Is it Mama?" she asked.

The old nurse, Mary, nodded. She held out her arms to Annie, inviting her to be comforted, but Annie shook her head. She stumbled back down the stairs. By now the tears streamed down her face. Annie ran out the door around to the side of the house to the stairs that led to her mother's room. The door was open.

One female slave carried out old linens as another carried in mysterious bottles with names like myrtle wax, used to anoint the bodies of the dead.

They ignored Annie as they briskly walked back and forth to do their appointed chores. She crept toward her mama's door. It too was ajar. Shutting her eyes, not wanting to see but feeling that she must, she took a deep breath and forced herself to look. There was Sarah Shelton Henry looking more peaceful in death than she had looked in life—at least in Annie's memory. She had already been bathed. The wretched straight dress that had kept her arms bound was nowhere to be seen. Tildy stood near Sarah's head, rubbing some sort of lotion on her. The old slave looked up at Annie with a kind look.

"Your mama's gone, child. She's in heaven now. No more tears for your mama. Don't cry. Your mama's finally found her peace." Then Tildy bent her kerchief-covered head back down to her task.

Annie stood watching for a little longer. Suddenly, she wanted to see her father. She left the room and dashed outside across the lawn to his office. But once there she felt timid. She couldn't just barge in. Instead, she knocked softly at the door.

"Come in," her father's voice called out. Annie pushed the door open. She saw him slumped in his rocker, staring into the distance. Wearing the skull cap that he sometimes put on his balding head, Patrick Henry looked much older than his thirty-seven years. He looked up when Annie entered and held out his arms to her.

The rest of that week passed in a blur of activity. Patsy wrote letters to out-of-town family telling them the news. She visited with the many friends and neighbors who came to pay their respects. Annie didn't have any particular job to do. She stood politely and curtsied when addressed. She ran errands for Patsy. She stood at Mama's graveside under the lilac tree. During the years of Mama's illness, that lilac tree had been a comfort to her. Even now, although it was still cold and dreary outside, the lilac swelled with the promise of new life.

Annie took to walking. The rain had ceased, and a string of sunny days dried up the mud. She was able to wander far and wide without being missed. Several times she wandered to the stream where she had seen Andrew Thacker, but he wasn't there.

One day she packed a lunch and set off for a walk. The cloak she wore to ward off the cold wind was short and didn't hinder her from running. Annie ran towards the stream until she could run no longer. Her heart felt bursting in her chest, and her throat was raw from the cold air. But she felt good.

She walked until she came to the ridge where she had last seen Andrew. There he was, practicing on his flute. Annie called out, "Hello. How are you, Master Thacker? Mind if I trespass?" She smiled.

He blushed, remembering his words at their last meeting. "Much better weather today," he said.

Annie nodded. She settled herself onto a rock and put the lunch down beside her. "That's true, but a soldier has to march in all kinds of weather. Would you like to share my lunch?"

Andrew grinned. "Ma would tell you not to ask that question. I'm always hungry, and I've never turned down food." He took a seat next to Annie.

Annie took out scones with slices of ham. "I'm sorry, but I brought nothing to drink," she said.

"No matter. The stream is clean. We can drink water," Andrew said as he bit into the biscuit. "I'm sorry about your mother," he said. "I didn't know she was so sick."

She nodded. Annie hadn't cried for days, and she thought she'd like telling Andrew about her mother. "She'd been sick since Edward was born, almost three years. But you know, I always thought she'd get better. I guess I imagined that I'd come home one day, and Mama would be sitting in her parlor working on a piece of embroidery like in the old days. I didn't figure she'd die."

"Sometimes death's a mercy; leastwise that's what Pa says," Andrew said. "I guess sometimes life can be so awful that death is the better thing. Do you think that's true?"

Annie tried to remember what she had heard. "Patsy says that Mama fell asleep in the Lord. She says that Mama will be in heaven—and that I might see her one day. Father said that he'd prayed for the Lord to take Mama. I guess he thought death would be a mercy. But you know, it's awful lonely." Annie thought she might cry. She clenched her teeth and swallowed hard. She did not want Andrew Thacker to see her tears.

As though he could read Annie's mind, Andrew looked down at his food. She quickly wiped a tear from the corner of her eye. Then she said, "I'm probably going to be sent away. Patsy wants to send me to Cousin Elizabeth, but Father says she's a Tory, and he won't have me go. But I heard him talking to Patsy last night. He says I might go to be with Uncle William and Aunt Anne. They're going out west to Fincastle, on the other side of the mountains."

"That's too bad," Andrew said, trying not to gloat. "I get to go to Richmond. Father is going to take a wagon to spring market. We need to buy seed and sell some things. He knows I want to be there, and he said I could go if the chores get done."

Annie swallowed her jealousy and managed to say, "That sounds wonderful, Andrew. I know you're happy."

They finished their lunch in silence, and after a while Annie felt cold. "I'd better get home," she said, "though it is a mighty depressing place to be." She looked hesitantly back in the direction of Scotchtown.

Andrew said quickly, "You come to my house. It's just over the hill. Mama will fix you something hot to drink, and I'll bring you back in the wagon later. How will that be?"

She smiled shyly. "I'd like that. I don't really want to go home quite yet."

The Thacker house was not nearly as grand as Scotchtown. It had only three rooms, not sixteen. It was furnished plainly, in good country style. Mr. Thacker was a farmer—and a good one. He made a comfortable living for his family, but they weren't rich.

Andrew brought Annie into a kitchen that was nearly as big as half the house. At its center was a huge fireplace and a rough-hewed table that could easily seat ten. Mrs. Thacker looked up from her work and greeted Annie with a laugh and a smile.

"Annie Henry. I'd hoped you'd come visit sometime," Mrs. Thacker said warmly, giving Annie a hug.

Andrew looked at his mother and at Annie. "I didn't know you two knew each other."

"We've met once or twice," Mrs. Thacker said. She brushed her flour-covered hands on her apron. "I could fix you some tea; I still have some I've been hoarding, or I could get you some cider. Which will it be?"

"Cider would be fine, Mrs. Thacker," Annie said.

"Spoken like a true patriot. But we wouldn't expect any less from Patrick Henry's daughter," Mrs. Thacker answered.

Annie swelled with pride. She liked being thought of as a good patriot. Mrs. Thacker heated the cider over the fire. She poured herself a cup and one for Annie, shooed

Andrew out of the room, and pulled a chair up alongside the table.

"Cold day to be outside, isn't it?" she began.

Annie nodded, enjoying the way the cider seemed to burn a path from her throat to her stomach.

"Annie, I'm so sorry about your mother. What a sad thing. And your father with such responsibility."

The young girl hesitated for a minute. She felt drawn to Andrew's mother because the woman reminded her of her own mama. Finally, Annie spoke. "Mrs. Thacker, may I ask you something?"

"Of course you may."

"Why do you think Father travels so much? Mama was so sick, and Father was always going to the Burgesses or to a convention. If he had stayed home, don't you think Mama would have gotten better?"

"Oh, Annie. You can't blame your father for this sickness. He did everything he could do for your mother. It would have been easier to send her away to the asylum, but he didn't do that. And as to why he was away so much, I think you need to understand that your father has great skill as a speaker and lawyer. Virginia needs him now. The people respect him."

"But we need him now," Annie protested and began to weep.

Mrs. Thacker drew Annie close and let her cry. She patted her back and smoothed the hair off her forehead. Then she said, "Annie, these may seem like hard words. But I want you to listen. You need to guard yourself that no root of bitterness grows up between you and the Lord, or you and your father."

"What do you mean?" Annie asked.

"I mean anger at the Lord because He's taken your

mother. And anger at your father because he is trying to serve Virginia. God has ordained this moment for your mother to die and a new country to be born. Your father has been called to take part in both events. Think how hard it is for him. Try to help him. Pray for him, but don't be angry with him."

Annie wiped the tears from her face. "I won't be much help to him if he sends me away out west. I don't want to go."

Mrs. Thacker smiled. "I know you'll find a way to help. You are your father's daughter."

Forcing a smile, Annie said, "I guess I'm as stubborn as he is. You're right. I will find a way to help."

Just then Mrs. Thacker glanced out the window. "My, it will be dark before too long. We must get you home before your father is sick with worry." She opened the door and yelled for Andrew. "Andrew, harness up the wagon. You must take Annie home."

When Andrew came around the house with the wagon, Mrs. Thacker gave Annie a kiss. "Take care, dear. I'll be over to see if I can help Patsy." She turned to her son and said, "Andrew, no dawdling. Annie needs to get home, and you've got chores to do."

She stood and waved as the wagon pulled away.

10

Midnight Ride

Annie sat on the front lawn trying to fashion a crown out of a yellow-blossomed forsythia branch. The branch was too stiff to tie, and every time Annie thought she had it, the branch sprang open in her hand. Finally, she gave up. She cut a few more branches off the bush and thought she'd take them to her father. Annie knew he was busy, and Patsy had told her to leave him be. "He has a lot on his mind," her older sister said. "You need to help him by staying out of his way."

But Annie didn't think he'd mind if she brought him some flowers. She walked over to his office carrying the bouquet in her hand. She peeked in his window and saw him hunched over a Bible. She could tell he was busy. His wig was crooked, as if he'd been absentmindedly twirling it. He often did when he concentrated.

She decided the flowers could wait. As she wandered back to the house, a wagon, pulled by the most pathetic horse Annie had ever seen, rolled up the road to Scotchtown. Annie stopped to watch the spectacle. As the wagon drew closer, she saw that it was driven by a woman with two little children clinging to her side. The woman's bonnet was dirty, and her dress was wrinkled as if she had slept in it.

Patrick Henry strode out from his office to meet the wagon. Annie watched him speak to the woman and then help her down. He carried the two children, one in each arm, up to the house. Annie followed this unusual parade.

Her father had seated them in the family dining room. He motioned for a servant to bring food and a pot of cider and sat quietly while they ate. Annie was startled by how quickly they devoured the plates of food set before them. The children ate as if they were starving.

When they had satisfied themselves, they looked up, suddenly aware that the dining room had filled with folks. Patrick Henry, John Fontaine, Annie, Patsy, Elizabeth, and Edward all waited expectantly to hear the strangers speak.

"This is Mrs. Beale of Norfolk, Virginia," Patrick Henry said.

"Thank you," responded Mrs. Beale, "for taking us in like this. We've been on the road for five days—depending on the kindness of strangers. We're headed west, away from this trouble and madness. I have family there. They'll take us in."

"But where's your husband?" Patsy asked.

Mrs. Beale gave Patsy an odd look. "My husband was taken by British soldiers and their Tory friends. He was tarred and feathered because he wrote newspaper stories defending the colonies and begging the king to stop his tyranny."

"Tarred and feathered?" Annie asked.

"He was dipped in hot tar and rolled in feathers," she answered abruptly. "He died shortly after from the burns.

Now my children are half-orphans, and I must depend on the charity of strangers."

The woman sounded bitter, but she did not cry.

The Henry family looked around uncomfortably. They were surrounded with wealth and comfort. Even though they had suffered their own tragedy, they were not homeless. They were not poor.

It was almost more than Annie could bear. "Please let me give your daughters some of my things. I'm nearly ten years old—too old for dolls. Let your girls have them," she begged.

The woman smiled a bitter smile. "They need more than dollies, though I thank you kindly for your generosity. My daughters have been robbed of their future, and you can't give it back to them. I hate this coming war. I hate the king, but I hate the patriots just as much. Why should a good man be taken and his children left fatherless?"

Patrick Henry spoke in a gentle voice. "We grieve with you and hope that you will find comfort in the arms of the Comforter. But Mrs. Beale, you must teach your daughters to be proud of their father. He defended the government of Virginia against the claims of the king and the lords in London who are trying to overthrow our government. I know it's complicated, but your husband's legacy to his children is a proud one. Teach it to them. Teach them to treasure it, not to despise it."

But Mrs. Beale shook her head. Annie understood suddenly what Mrs. Thacker meant by a root of bitterness, and she wanted no part of it.

The Beales stayed for several days at the urging of Patrick Henry. He supplied the girls with new clothes and gave Mrs. Beale some money so that she would not be a burden to her relatives. Annie watched them leave and wondered what would happen to them.

The same day the Beales left, Patrick Henry called Annie and Patsy to his office. They found their father seated at his desk, a letter in his hand. "Sit down," he said. Then a serious look came across his face. "Daughters, you know how sorry I am about your mother. I know you miss her. And now I have to be gone as well. I must go to Richmond again, for the convention."

He paused, then continued, "You saw the Beales. You see that there is trouble in the land. There are spies everywhere. Of course it is worse in Norfolk, but we could easily have trouble here. They'd like nothing better than to arrest me. I have to be vigilant, always watching. I can't let myself be distracted with worry about you."

He stopped speaking for a minute, then continued as though the words were almost too difficult to say. "You know I love you, but, Annie, you'll have to go out west to your Aunt Anne's and Uncle William's. In Fincastle, you'll be safe from spies, and I won't have to worry over you."

Annie protested, "Father, let me stay. Please. I won't be a burden. I'll be a help to you."

He smiled sadly. "I'd like you to help in this cause. I've always known you have a faithful patriot's heart. But you'll be happier at Aunt Anne's."

"I'd be happier with you," Annie insisted. "But I'll do what will help you the most."

A look of relief flooded her father's face. Annie realized that he had expected a fight.

"I'm sorry, Annie," he said. "But this will be best." Then he looked down at his work and said, "I must study a little more now."

Patsy went back to the house. But Annie didn't want to be inside. She ran toward the Thacker house.

The Thackers were all busy doing farm chores to get ready for their trip to Richmond, but Mrs. Thacker sat on the porch with Annie. She listened sympathetically as Annie complained, "I'm going out west. It's all settled. Why must I be so young and a girl? Father isn't sending the boys away."

Mrs. Thacker mused absentmindedly, "You could be a real help to your father—but he knows best, Annie." She looked apologetically at the young girl. "I can't stay and talk. There's too much to do. We have to fill our wagon with harnesses, wool, blankets, and brooms that we made last winter. But I'll be by to see you before you go away."

Annie shrugged. She walked over to where Andrew was carrying baskets of potatoes to the wagon. "When do you leave?" she asked.

"Day after tomorrow, early. Pa says at first light. We have a lot of marketing to do. When does your father leave?"

"Father leaves then also. He says the convention starts the day after. I wish I were going," she said wistfully. "You will have to save up details to tell me."

"I will," Andrew promised.

At home Annie kept out of Patsy's way. At night she slept badly. Her sleep was disturbed by dreams of spies and patriots being tarred and feathered. When she awoke in the morning, she felt uneasy. Surely there was a way she could help her father. Didn't she have an obligation to help? Didn't Mrs. Thacker say she'd be a help? Annie pondered these things without knowing what to do.

The next evening, their father played his violin to the gathered family. From the firelight, she could see that his face was drawn and his eyes tired. He was clearly worried. Then he rose and said, "I've a long day ahead of me tomorrow. I'll say good-bye now because I'll not see you in the morning." He hugged each child, and he whispered to Annie, "Be strong and courageous. I will not be gone long."

Annie couldn't sleep. She lay in bed for hours tossing and turning and listening to Patsy's steady breathing. "Lord," she prayed, "help me to do what's right." Although she knew in her heart she should go west, she couldn't. "Forgive me, Lord," she said. "But I must help my father. I must go to Richmond."

She hopped out of bed and pulled on a warm dress, woolen stockings, and her leather boots. She tiptoed to the door. Patsy didn't move. Annie turned the knob slowly and waited. No sound. Then she pulled the door open and glided soundlessly across the wood floors. Once in the dining room, she stood motionless, listening. Again there were no sounds. The outside door squeaked as she opened it. Annie froze. But the house was quiet. She ran down the stairs into the dark night.

Annie knew there were old coats near the kitchen. She slipped across the yard in the moonlight and found a hunter's jacket hanging there. She pulled it on and filled the pockets with apples from a barrel; then she hitched up her skirts so she could run more easily and started off across the fields.

Annie didn't like the dark. She never had. The tree branches creaked in the wind. Animals made strange sounds, and shadows cast by the moon blanketed the ground in front of her. She shivered, but she was determined to keep going. She knew that she had to reach the Thackers before they set out for Richmond.

Glad that the moon was out and there was some light by

which to find her way, she crossed the familiar fields toward the Thacker house. It took more than an hour for Annie to get there, but finally she spotted the wagon in the yard. She laughed with relief and crept silently toward it. All she had to do now was avoid being seen by the Thackers.

Annie looked around carefully and then climbed into the wagon. She burrowed into the hay and piled some brooms and other things on top of her, hoping that she was covered. Then she fell asleep.

The next morning Annie awoke to the rolling and bumping of wagon wheels. The sun was already out, and she could hear Andrew and his father. Annie wanted to climb out from under the hay and join them, but she knew they would take her back home if she did. She figured if she could stay quiet for five hours, they would be too far from home to return.

The hay tickled her nose, and Annie had to keep from sneezing. She felt her stomach rumble from hunger, and she prayed that the growling, which seemed so loud to her ears, could not be heard by the Thackers. Annie nibbled on biscuits that had grown stale and dry. She savored the juice from her apple, trying to let it satisfy her thirst.

For what seemed like hours, she lay quietly in the back, afraid to move or make any noise at all. She didn't know how much time had gone by when she felt something crawling on her leg. Annie froze. The something slithered under her skirt, tickling her leg.

Quickly and quietly she prayed, but the slithering continued. Finally, she could bear it no longer. She desperately brushed the hay off her face and tried to dig her way out.

Andrew yelled, and Mr. Thacker slowed the horses. "What is the meaning of this?" demanded Thacker.

Annie suddenly felt very foolish.

"There's something under my skirt," Annie cried with a shudder.

"Jump over the side," Andrew said. "Shake your skirt."

Annie did as she was told, and a foot long grass snake fell from her petticoats and crawled away.

Annie recoiled. "Yech, I hate snakes!" she squealed, forgetting for a minute that she was in big trouble. Mr. Thacker's stern face recalled that fact to her. She gulped as he stood quietly, waiting for her to explain herself.

"I just had to go to Richmond," she said finally. "I'm to be sent away to Fincastle next week. This is my only chance to be part of my father's struggle. Please let me stay."

Mr. Thacker was silent. Andrew had turned his back to her, but Annie could tell by the movement of his shoulders that he was laughing. Mr. Thacker was slower to relent.

"You haven't left me much choice. We are only a mile from Richmond. We'll find your father, and he'll have to deal with you. You might as well ride on the seat with us," he said.

Andrew pulled Annie up to the wagon seat. He offered her some water and some fresh food from their basket. "How did you get away?" he asked eagerly.

Annie wasn't sure that Mr. Thacker would approve. She knew that Father didn't like disobedience, and this was surely disobedience. She suddenly realized what a terrible thing she had done. She said, "I slipped away and fell asleep in your wagon; and when I woke up, here we were."

A frowning Mr. Thacker replied, "I'd not like it if my daughter ran away and then tried to pretend she hadn't plotted and schemed. I'd rather she confessed boldly and explained why she did it."

Mr. Thacker urged the horses on. He was quiet the rest of the trip, but Annie thought about what he'd said.

11

"Give Me Liberty, or Give Me Death"

The Thacker wagon was not the only one rolling toward the market town of Richmond. Many farmers were bringing their produce into town. From Richmond it could travel down the James River to Williamsburg, and from Williamsburg goods traveled across the ocean.

Annie waited with anticipation to see the town. Richmond was still small, but it was bigger than Hanover, which consisted only of the courthouse and the tavern. Richmond did not gleam and glisten, as Annie had imagined, but its main streets were brick and cobblestone, not dirt. Some were lined with row houses, little homes that were hooked together on both sides.

The streets were full of wagons and horses. People hurried. Instead of tipping their hats and greeting one another, they seemed eager to get on with their business.

Mr. Thacker drove directly to St. John's Church. It was

a small, white frame building with a square tower. It sat on a hillside, and the tower was visible for a good distance. Not far from the church was a tavern, and Mr. Thacker walked briskly to the tavern after warning the children to stay in the wagon.

As soon as he was out of earshot, Annie turned to Andrew. "Is your father angry? Does he think I'm awful?" she asked.

Andrew laughed. "I think he figures you have spirit. If the patriots have as much courage, we'll be fine." Then Andrew added reluctantly, "But if it was me who did what you did, I'd be in big trouble—even if I did it for a good cause. Pa says children should obey their parents."

Annie groaned. "My father thinks that also," she said. "But maybe he'll not be angry."

They glanced back in the direction that Mr. Thacker had gone and saw him coming back. With him was an obviously angry Patrick Henry. His wig was flopping. His expression was stern. Annie chewed her lip. *Why did I come?*

Patrick Henry reached the wagon first. "What has gotten into you, young lady?" her father demanded. "Patsy is right. You need training. And Aunt Anne will know how to do it. Obviously my methods have not worked. You are as wild as an Indian, with half as much sense."

Her chin quivered, but he seemed not to notice. He continued, "Did it dawn on you that it isn't safe for a young girl to be out at night? Didn't you know there are animals, even wolves, that would find you a tasty morsel? What about thieves or bandits? Even Tories? Annie Henry, didn't you think about Patsy? What must she be thinking?"

Annie gasped. She honestly hadn't given one thought to how Patsy would feel. Annie had only wanted to come to Richmond. She looked up at her father with dismay. "I'm so sorry, Father," she said. "I only wanted to be with you. I wanted to help. I wanted to be a patriot."

Her father's eyes were still hard with anger, and Annie drew back from him. Then he sighed and turned to Mr. Thacker. "I don't know how to thank you. I'll have to deal with her later."

Thacker nodded. "She's not too big to be spanked," he said pointedly.

Patrick Henry agreed and picked Annie up off the wagon seat. "I love you, daughter, but it wasn't right for you to disobey. I can't send you back now; so you'll have to stay. Let's hope you don't get into trouble."

"I'm sorry about Patsy," Annie said.

He nodded. "No matter, we'll send a messenger. Perhaps I should send you back with the messenger," he said. Annie opened her mouth to protest but thought better of it. Her father shook his head. "No, too dangerous. It's hard to know whom to trust anymore. I won't risk it. Now come, and we'll get you situated."

He and Annie walked down the street to a rooming house where Uncle William and Aunt Anne were staying for a week until they returned home to Fincastle. He explained the problem to them while Annie cleaned up. Then he took her out to see Richmond.

There were many men dressed in fancy knee breeches and silks, their hair hidden under powdered wigs. But there were also men dressed in frontier garb who had traveled long distances over muddy roads and through spring rains to get to Richmond for the meeting.

"Who are these folks?" Annie asked her father.

"Men here for the convention," he answered. "The fancy ones are the Tidewater planters. They own the big plantations near the Potomac River. The others come from western Virginia—near where Anne and William live. They've had a hard trip here. Traveling isn't easy in the early spring. But they'll play a role in this convention—you watch."

"How did Mr. Thacker find you so easily?" Annie asked.

"The tavern is where we go to find the news. It hasn't been good, child. There are more stories of patriots being tarred and feathered for what they believe. Two men from Hanover County have been threatened with exile if they don't publicly confess their error in opposing the king."

As Annie listened to the stories, she was glad she had come. She wanted to join Father in the great cause of liberty.

Annie and her father strolled down the sidewalk. Like the Tidewater planters, Patrick Henry was also dressed in silks, knee breeches, and a tie-back wig. Annie thought he looked distinguished. His high cheekbones, large nose, and often-solemn expression made him look more serious than Annie knew him to be. She figured she liked him best when he played the violin. But this meeting was serious, and her father's party face wasn't showing.

They approached a tall, red-headed man walking toward them. He slowed down when he recognized Annie's father. "Hello, Patrick. Who is this with you?"

"Good to see you, Thomas. This is my daughter, Annie. Annie, meet Thomas Jefferson, one of my allies in the cause of liberty."

Annie shyly curtsied, then stood back and listened as her father and Mr. Jefferson discussed tomorrow's meeting. Mr. Jefferson tipped his three-corner hat to her and proceeded down the street.

They continued to walk. Her father pointed out Richard Henry Lee and Edmund Pendleton, but their names meant nothing to Annie. Across the street, near the high churchyard wall, she noted a tall man who had a large crowd around him. "Who is that, Father?" she asked.

"That's George Washington. There's no finer patriot in Virginia. We'll be blessed if he comes on our side, child."

The next day her father left the inn early with her Uncle William. Annie had been sentenced to stay home with Aunt Anne. But to make the sentence sweeter, her father said, "Nothing much will happen the next few days. You stay with Aunt Anne and think about what it means to obey. On the fourth day, you may come to the church."

It was hard to stay in the house for three days, but Annie obeyed. On the fourth morning, the churchyard was filled with spectators who crowded around the windows, which were open to let in the warm spring air. Annie dressed herself hurriedly. "May I go across, Aunt Anne?" she asked.

"Go ahead. But be careful, and watch your manners," Aunt Anne answered. "I don't feel well, but perhaps I'll come over later."

Annie didn't wait. She let out a whoop and dashed out the door and across the street, dodging a passing carriage as she ran. The crowd had grown larger, but she managed to squeeze between people and push her way to a window at the back of the church. Her head came just to the bottom of the window, and she could see in.

She found herself looking into a long, narrow room lined with tall pews. Only the men's heads and shoulders were visible above the wooden boxes. The pews faced toward the window where she stood. The pulpit stood directly in front of the window.

The meeting started slowly. Several men stood up and talked about the good old days and the need to preserve them. But after a while, Patrick Henry rose to speak. He said it was ridiculous to think Virginia could return to the past comforts. Then he offered a resolution—Virginia should set up an army to defend itself.

Immediately the room was in turmoil. Some delegates agreed with him, but others rose to argue against him. They called the resolution rash and reckless. Some said it was rushing into war. Others pleaded for patience. They said in time the trouble would pass, and the good old days would return.

After a time, it seemed certain that the resolution would be defeated. Annie's father rose again. He opened the door to his pew and began pacing as he talked. Annie had never seen her father in the courtroom or the House of Burgesses. She stood enthralled, forgetting her stiff legs and aching back. He spoke softly, shoulders gently slouched, his voice just loud enough to be heard in the church and among those near the windows.

Annie noticed that the men standing near her had drawn close to the window. They no longer talked to each other but were listening attentively as Father spoke. One whispered, "The best speaker this country has," and Annie knew they meant her father.

Patrick Henry spoke like a preacher. He stood slightly bent and said, "War is inevitable—and let it come!"

A gasp went up from the crowd at the windows. But no one called it treason.

By now his voice was louder. He no longer slouched but stood erect so that he looked even taller than his six feet.

"Gentlemen may cry, 'Peace, peace,'—but there is no

peace." Then he added, "The war is actually begun. . . . Our brethren are already in the field! Why stand we here idle? . . . Is life so dear, or peace so sweet, as to be purchased at the price of chains and slavery?"

When he said those words, he crossed his arms in front of him as though they were shackled. He paused, then looked up to heaven and said, "Forbid it, Almighty God!" Then, still standing as though in chains, he looked over at the timid Loyalists and said, "I know not what course others may take," stretching to his full height, he proclaimed, "but as for me, give me liberty, or give me death!" At the word *death* he moved as if plunging a dagger into his breast.

Annie had been so taken up with the speech that when she saw the hand plunging with the dagger, she let out a muffled cry. She stood for a moment in confusion.

The man next to her exclaimed, "When I die, I want to be buried at this spot!"

All around, the people talked. She felt she had to get away to breathe. As she moved from the window, she saw a familiar person also leaving the building. He had an angry look on his face. Annie wondered where she had seen him before. Then she remembered. Francis Doyle! The man who had called Father a traitor. He had vowed to stop her father that night at Scotchtown many months ago.

She felt a quick stab of fear as she saw Francis Doyle hurry away. What if he reported Father's speech to the royal authorities? Could that be treason? Could her father be tarred and feathered or, worse yet, hanged? Annie didn't know what to do; so she followed Mr. Doyle as he briskly walked down the street. She had to trot to keep up with his long strides.

So intent on her task was Annie that she did not pay much attention to where they were going. Before long, though, she realized they were headed for the James River. Annie thought she knew Mr. Doyle's plan. He would take a boat down the James River to Williamsburg where the Royal Governor was.

Annie didn't wait to follow. She ran as fast as she could to the wharf. There she found a busy river with merchant ships and fishing boats lining the dock. She glanced over her shoulder and sighed. Mr. Doyle was still a block away. Annie didn't have a plan, but she knew she had to do something.

A man unloading a load of oysters on the dock turned to her and said in a reassuring Scots accent, "Can I help you, miss?"

She answered, "I'm Annie Henry, Patrick Henry's daughter." She waited for his reaction.

"A fine man, that Henry," the oyster man said with a broad grin. "If you be his daughter, you are much blessed, because they don't come any finer."

She grinned. "I know that. There's a problem that maybe you could help me with. Do you see that gentleman over there?" Annie pointed to Mr. Doyle who had just reached the dock. "He's a Tory. He doesn't approve of my father at all and called him a traitor. And he's just heard my father say that war is inevitable." She repeated the lines still ringing in her head. "My father said, 'Give me liberty, or give me death.'" She waited for a reaction and wasn't disappointed.

"Yes, that's the attitude we must all have," the oyster man said. "No more waiting around for things to get better. They've already gone too far."

Annie interrupted, "I'm afraid Mr. Doyle might be

looking for a boat to Williamsburg. He wants to report my father. Maybe he'll try to stop the convention. Maybe he'll have my father arrested. What can we do?"

The oyster man thought for a minute. Then he smiled broadly. "Don't worry yourself. He'll not find a boat today from this dock. I can guarantee it. We're all patriots here. Wait for me. I'll be back soon."

Annie watched as the oyster man walked from boat to boat, whispering in the ears of the fishermen. She saw them glance toward Francis Doyle and nod, a look of determination on their faces.

Finally, he came to a boat at the end of the dock. Annie noticed with dismay that Mr. Doyle had already climbed aboard and was sitting on a barrel, clearly impatient to be off. The oyster man called to the boat's captain, who came over to listen. Annie saw him nod. He chewed his pipe stem and nodded some more. They shook hands.

Soon the oyster man returned to Annie. "It's taken care of, dear. He'll not get to Williamsburg, leastwise not soon."

Annie pointed at the boat that held Mr. Doyle. "But they're untying the boat, and Mr. Doyle's still on board," she protested.

"Yes, they will sail out of sight of Richmond, but I think they'll have some boat trouble. Probably not get to Williamsburg for a few days. That happens with boats sometimes," he said.

Annie laughed. "Boat trouble. That's funny. Poor Mr. Doyle."

The oyster man laughed also. "Now let me get you back to your father. This isn't the place for a young lady."

Annie nodded gratefully. She realized that she had no idea where she was. She took one last glance at Francis

Doyle on the boat, aptly named *The Patriot,* sailing slowly out into the center of the James River. "Good-bye, Mr. Doyle," she called out quietly.

Up and down the docks the story spread until Annie was surrounded by fishermen eager to meet her and pay their respects to the daughter of Patrick Henry.

The oyster man finally broke away from the crowd. "We must get this lass home," he said to the other boatmen. "Her father will be worried." They took a wagon back to the rooming house. The oyster man touched the brim of his hat and said, "Tell your father that you are a brave little patriot, and that Capt. James Boyd of Edinburgh, Scotland, is proud to have helped."

Annie waved before heading up the walk to the house. Several hours later Patrick Henry bounded up the steps. "Huzzah, Huzzah," he called as he stooped to hug her. "You are the talk of the town, Annie Henry. Everyone has heard the story of how a brave little patriot girl foiled the plans of the wicked Tory. I heard it from the fellow selling apples on the street corner. He didn't even know who I was." Her father's eyes twinkled as he swung her around. "I only wish I had my violin so we could celebrate properly."

"May I stay with you at Scotchtown?" Annie blurted out.

Patrick Henry laughed. "You don't give up, do you?" Then he looked thoughtful. "It will be hard, Annie . . . but what's important is what helps the cause of liberty." He smiled. "You have spirit, Annie Henry, and I love you. Your Aunt Anne's loss is the revolution's gain—and mine. Let's go home."

Author's Note

Annie Henry and the Secret Mission is fiction. However, there was a real Annie Henry who lived in Virginia with her father, Patrick Henry, and her brothers and sisters. Her mother, Sarah Henry, died in early 1775 after a long period of mental illness. Scotchtown and St. John's Church are real places that you can still visit today.

The book is also faithful to the general history of the colonial period. People ate the kinds of food mentioned. They wore the types of clothes described. They performed chores such as fire fighting and harvesting in the manner described in the book.

Patrick Henry played a crucial role in the American Revolution. Whenever possible I have tried to use his own words so that you can get a true idea of what he believed about slavery, war, and liberty. His "give me liberty, or give me death" speech put Virginia firmly on the side of independence. The description of that speech comes from eyewitness accounts.

Many people do not know that Patrick Henry was a strong Christian. He wrote about the Bible: "This book is worth all the books that ever were printed."

Annie Henry and the Birth of Liberty

For my sons:
Pete, David, Daniel, and Ben

Contents

1

A Picnic

Annie Henry looked up at the blue sky. The May air felt warm on her skin as she hurried through her morning chores of gathering the eggs, feeding her chickens, and putting fresh hay in the nesting boxes. Normally, Annie dawdled over those tasks in the hope of delaying her lessons, but today she wanted the morning to fly by because she had planned an outing for the afternoon.

It was not common for girls in 1775 to have regular lessons. Once a girl could read and do arithmetic, she was excused from school. Annie, however, was no ordinary girl. Her father, Patrick Henry, expected all his children to be well educated. As a lawyer, politician, and gentleman farmer, he had enough money to hire a tutor to live on the plantation and teach the Henry children.

Mr. Dabney, the tutor, was a stickler for lessons. Every day at nine o'clock he rapped his willow cane on his desk and called the class to order. The class consisted of Annie, age ten, and her two older brothers, William, fifteen, and John, thirteen. Andrew Thacker, a thirteen-year-old neighbor, came some days if his father could spare him from his chores. The class met in Patrick Henry's library, among bookshelf-lined walls that made it look as though learning was going on. But that wasn't always true.

The boys were hopeless students. They suffered through Greek and Latin, sprawling lazily in their chairs until Mr. Dabney, in frustration, issued a reminder with his willow cane. Then they straightened up and were attentive, at least for a while until the lure of a bird's song or a scent on a soft breeze drew their attention back out the window to the pastures and woods beyond.

Annie liked her lessons, although she didn't like Mr. Dabney, a distant cousin of her father. He could turn an interesting subject like history into a grand bore. Great battles waged by brave soldiers for glorious causes became dried up facts on brittle paper.

Today the boys were supposed to recite a poem in Latin. When it was Andrew's turn, he stood clumsily in front of the class, shifting his weight from leg to leg, never raising his eyes to meet Mr. Dabney's at the back of the room.

Annie stared at her desk, wishing that Andrew could just sit down and be spared the embarrassment, but that was not Mr. Dabney's way. He let the boy suffer for five minutes before excusing him with the words, "Why your father wants to educate you is beyond me. You're the thickest boy I have ever had the privilege of knowing. Sit down."

As Andrew slunk to his seat, he avoided meeting Annie's eyes. William stuck out a long leg, and Andrew tripped over it, nearly falling to the floor. He glared at William, who assumed a look of complete innocence. Mr. Dabney looked up from his ledger book and scolded

Andrew. "Surely it is not too much to ask you to walk quietly to your seat. Please sit down."

When the boy finally reached his seat, it was John's turn to recite. He stood in front of the class and recited the first line of the poem flawlessly. Mr. Dabney smiled, and John flashed a smile in return. Annie relaxed in her seat. For a minute she daydreamed as her brother continued to recite in Latin, but a giggle from William brought her attention back to the classroom. She looked up at John, who was still reciting and over at Mr. Dabney, whose angry face was as red as a British uniform.

"Stop this instant," he bellowed.

Next to her, William hid his face in his hands, barely containing his laughter as John stopped and looked innocently at his tutor. Andrew looked as puzzled as Annie. What had John said?

Mr. Dabney stood in front of the class, his willow rod in hand, looking as though he might explode. "So you think it amusing, young man, to alter the words of a famous poem. And you think it amusing to compare your tutor to a donkey." Even speaking the words caused the timid Mr. Dabney to blush, which set John and William into another round of laughter.

What had come over her brothers? Annie wondered. How could John have insulted the tutor? What would their father say? But that was easy. Patrick Henry wasn't home. The colonies were close to war, and he, as one of Virginia's leaders, was often away.

Just when it seemed as though the tutor had lost control of his small classroom, he glanced at Andrew and Annie. Clenching his jaw, he glared at John, saying pointedly, "If you were attentive like your sister, you would be fine scholars. But instead, you are loafers with heads full of sawdust."

Annie squirmed uncomfortably with the attention, sure that it would bring her brother's disapproval on her head once they were beyond the watchful gaze of the tutor.

Without letting up, the tutor continued his tirade. "You may be excused, Annie. Your brothers will be staying for a while yet. And you, Master Thacker, there is surely no reason to prolong your evident dislike of my classroom. You too may be excused."

The boy didn't hesitate. In two swift strides he was out of the room with Annie close behind. The two tiptoed out of the house so that Patsy, Annie's older sister, would not hear them.

"What will you do now?" Annie asked.

"Don't know," Andrew muttered. "Blasted tutor. Why should I have to learn Latin? Give me one reason a farmer needs to know an old, dead language nobody uses anymore."

As they reached the stable where the boy had tied his horse, Annie asked, "Did you study the poem?"

He shrugged, flashing a smile. "Nope. Didn't study it a minute."

"Then you can't very well be angry that you were embarrassed, can you?"

"That's the kind of thinking that separates boys from girls," Andrew said scornfully as he mounted his horse. "You care about old Mr. Dabney, and I just want to hunt."

Annie waved as her friend rode away. What kind of trouble would he be in when he came home hours earlier than expected? she wondered.

As for Annie, she was pleased with the early dismissal. She walked briskly to the kitchen, a small building behind the main house where several slaves cooked for the family. Earlier in the day, before her lessons, she had asked one of the cooks to fix a picnic basket for her.

She found the basket in the kitchen, full of food. There were fresh current scones—a kind of sweet biscuit—and some slices of ham. It also contained a jar of cold cider and a piece of mince pie. Although Annie had planned to walk, she could barely manage under the weight of the fully packed basket. She lugged it across the yard to the stable where Joseph, the stableman, saddled her small horse. She loaded up the saddlebags with food. Then, with his help, she mounted the horse and rode out of the yard toward the beech woods.

The Henrys owned about 1,000 acres of prime farmland in the middle of Virginia. The land was rolling hills, but on a clear day young Annie could see all the way to the mountains in the west. The largest town was a village about ten miles away called Hanover. It had a courthouse, a tavern, and a small store, but the Henry plantation, Scotchtown, did not need to purchase much from the store. It produced most of its own food and even had a blacksmith who could shoe the horses and make nails.

She had lived there for nearly five years and loved it. Even though her mother had been sick for many of those years and had died just a month earlier, Annie still thought the plantation was a happy place. She particularly liked walking and riding around the familiar grounds. Today she had picked a special place on the bank of the creek for her picnic lunch. It was a hidden place, blocked from view by a grove of trees and shrubs. The young girl tied her horse up to a sturdy branch and pushed through the shrubs until she reached her secret spot. Except for the horse's presence, Annie knew she was invisible to the world.

As she lay back on a blanket and watched the wind-blown clouds drift across the sky, she daydreamed about her recent adventure in Richmond. She had been lying in her special place for a short time when she heard a noise on the other side of the bushes. Raising herself up on one arm, she felt with the other hand for the saddlebags. They were not there! Annie realized she had left them hanging on the horse.

Beyond the bushes, the horse nickered softly. Rising to her feet, Annie listened, sure that someone stood beyond the dense stand of shrubs.

"Who's out there?" she demanded.

When no one answered, the girl felt the first twinge of fear. Her father had said that these were "unsettled times," and that his children had to be careful about strangers. Shaking off the fear, the girl pushed through the bushes. "Nothing to worry about," she assured herself in a voice that was calmer than her feelings.

There was no one around, and the horse was grazing contentedly. Annie was about to go back into the hideaway when she remembered her lunch. That's when she noticed that the saddlebags were missing. "Great," she muttered with a little stamp of her foot. "Just great. Now someone has taken my lunch."

When Annie drew near to the horse to investigate, she saw a crudely written note. "Another way that boys think differently than girls," it said. That's when Annie lost her temper.

"Andrew Thacker," she yelled, "you bring that lunch back now."

She knew she looked ridiculous. Even if Andrew could hear her, and Annie thought he probably was hiding someplace to see her reaction, how would a slightly built ten-year-old girl take back her lunch from a boy who was almost four years older and weighed probably forty pounds more? Impossible.

But Annie didn't always think logically when she was angry, and she was angry now. "Andrew!" she yelled.

The only response was a peal of laughter. Without thinking, the young girl ran towards the sound. She was slowed by long skirts that twisted around her legs. "You'd better not eat my lunch, Andrew Thacker," she shouted as she ran.

When she finally caught up to Andrew in the beech woods, she found him sitting on a log and grinning at her as he stuffed the last of the scones into his mouth. Annie glared at him.

"I hope you enjoy that scone, Andrew Thacker," she said. "I will never, and I mean this, share my food with you again."

She held out her hand and marched forward, expecting Andrew to be sorry and hand over the rest of the lunch. But he just grinned, clambered to his feet, and began running once again. Annie knew that she could not outrun the boy. He was taller and wore breeches. She was slowed down by her long skirts and petticoats that caught on branches and dragged in the dirt. She tried anyway, but the boy's swifter strides soon carried him out of sight. She was following his trail by the sound of crunching leaves and snapping twigs when suddenly there was a thump, followed by silence, followed by a scream.

A few more steps and Annie saw the strangest sight. There was Andrew dancing about, awkwardly hitting himself on the face, arms, and shoulders. The girl began to giggle but stopped laughing when she saw that her friend was no longer running away but running towards her, his hands continuing their wild motions. He drew closer, and Annie saw the problem. A swarm of bees surrounded him.

Without thinking, she turned and ran, ignoring the branches that tugged on her skirts and scratched at her skin. When she reached the clearing, she slowed down to catch her breath. Behind her came Andrew, and Annie yelled, "Run for the creek," as he streaked past. She didn't need to tell him; her terrified friend had already reached the water and plunged in.

Like a turtle stretching for air, the boy lifted his head out of the water, warily surveying the air around him.

"They're gone," Annie yelled. "You can come out."

He rose up and walked shakily to the bank. Annie's first reaction was to laugh. The boy looked ridiculous. His clothes clung to him, and water ran down from his hair into his eyes and mouth. Her laughter turned to fear, though, when she saw how hard he was breathing and watched him lower himself painfully to the ground. She thought he was reacting to the bee stings. She had heard that bees could kill a man. But after a minute's rest, his breathing went back to normal, and she gave a sigh of relief.

It was hard not to stare at the welts forming on the boy's face and arms. His white knee-high stockings were mud splotched, and Annie couldn't tell whether there were stings under them as well. He groaned, and the young girl bit her lip nervously, not sure what she could say that wouldn't make him yell at her.

"Andrew?" she whispered.

He opened one eye and glared at her.

"Are you hurting?" she asked.

"What do you think?"

"Do you want help getting home?"

Andrew groaned louder.

"What's wrong, Andrew?" Annie asked worriedly.

"Pa spared me from some plowing this morning because Ma insisted that I go to school. Now how am I going to explain how I got wet and bee stung at school this morning?"

The tension of the last fifteen minutes dissolved, and Annie hooted with laughter. "What a sight you were," she said, tears streaming down her cheeks. "Serves you right for stealing my lunch."

"How can you laugh when I feel so miserable?" her friend groaned. "Do I look as bad as I feel?"

"Other than a fat lip, a swollen eye, a couple of unsightly red marks, and torn and dirty clothes, you look fine," she answered honestly.

Groaning again, Andrew rose slowly to his feet. "I wish it was just my clothes. But I hurt bad, and there's no way I can hide this from Pa," he said ruefully. "I guess there's no reason to postpone my lickin' any longer."

"Do you want me to take you on my horse?" Annie asked.

"No, thank you. Pa will be mad enough," he answered.

With shoulders hunched he walked slowly in the direction of the Thacker farm. Annie could picture Andrew's father, a stern-faced, hard-working farmer who had only Andrew to help him in the fields, and she didn't like to imagine what Mr. Thacker might say when he saw his son. She watched until she could no longer see the boy. Then she gathered up her saddlebags, got on her horse, and rode back to Scotchtown.

2

Patsy's Wedding

Patsy Henry had been acting strangely for weeks now. Annie would find her seventeen-year-old sister sitting in the ladies' parlor weeping, but when the younger girl would ask what was wrong, her sister would smile weakly and say, "Just happy, I guess, to be marrying John Fontaine."

At supper time Patsy picked at her food. "Where's your appetite, Patsy?" John asked one day, but she only smiled and toyed with her food some more.

Several days after Andrew's adventure with the bees, Annie found her older sister in their bedroom, sitting in the midst of a pile of dresses.

"What are you doing?" Annie asked.

Patsy burst into tears. "I have nothing to wear. Nothing at all. Father doesn't care about it at all. He promised he would come home. The wedding is tomorrow, and where is he?" she sputtered.

"Father will be home. He told you he would," Annie said with more than a touch of annoyance. "And what do you mean, you have no clothes. What are those?" she asked, staring at the dresses.

Turning toward her little sister, Patsy cried, "I can't wear these. Look. Just look. These silks are faded, and the cottons are out of style."

Annie looked more closely at the dresses. Patsy must have owned a dress in every color of the rainbow. They all had full, layered skirts. Some were lace-trimmed, others decked out in beautiful ribbons and bows.

"If Father had been home, I could have ordered new gowns from the dressmaker."

"But Father wouldn't let you buy silk anyway," Annie reminded her.

"He would have made an exception. Father knows how important clothes are. It isn't right for me to take all these old rags into a marriage."

"Fiddlesticks," Annie said. "Father isn't going to break the boycott of British goods so that you can have silk dresses, Patsy. Not especially when you have all these dresses already. And it isn't like you are moving to Williamsburg. You are just marrying cousin John Fontaine. He probably wouldn't care if you wore old flour sacks."

Patsy flushed. "You just don't understand," she said, shaking her head. "Why I even bother to explain it to you, I don't know." With a sharp jerk of her head, the older girl turned back to her dresses, and Annie slipped from the room.

There was confusion throughout the house as servants hustled to clean and prepare Scotchtown for the wedding. The sweet smell of baking cakes and pies drifted through the yard from the kitchen. Inside, the house smelled of lemon-and-oil polish. The table had been set with the best linen and dishes, but all the fancy preparations couldn't cheer up Annie. The house was too lonely when her father was absent.

Grabbing a tart from a tray of pastries, Annie munched on it as she wandered through the house, dropping little crumbs behind her. Glancing out the window, she saw a cloud of dust in the distance. She hoped it would be Father returning from his week in Richmond. She had to wait as the rider came around the bend in the road. As he drew near, she could see that it was, indeed, her father.

He scarcely had dismounted and turned his horse over to Joseph when Annie threw herself into his arms. Staggering back, he said playfully, "My, how you've grown, daughter. Have you eaten all the potatoes?"

Annie laughed, squeezing her father in a tight bear hug. "I knew you'd come back in time," she said.

He disentangled himself as they walked towards the house. "Of course I came back. Was Patsy worried that I wouldn't?"

When Annied nodded, her father smiled. Chuckling, he said, "Let me wash up and get a bite to eat. I've had a long ride. While I'm doing that, you find your sister and brothers. I have some news for you all."

They gathered in the family dining room where Patrick Henry was eating a plate of cold ham and biscuits. He was a tall, slender man, whose long face, deep-set eyes, thin lips, and penetrating stare gave him a serious expression. It was offset, however, by his wig, which was often crooked.

When he finished eating, he wiped his mouth with the linen napkin and cleared his throat. "The *Virginia Gazette* carried a disturbing story today," he began. "There has been fighting in Boston, although the British have not declared war. Nearly three weeks ago the king's troops fired on the militia at Lexington and Concord, and our militiamen returned fire. Altogether, nearly 100 colonists were either killed or wounded. According to the reports, the British tried to take the gunpowder from the storage magazine in Concord, but they were prevented."

"Didn't they already take our gunpowder?" William asked.

"Yes. Governor Dunmore did steal Virginia's gunpowder. And the militia in Virginia let him get away with it. Our leaders said we must be cautious and not risk war. But now we know that the plot to steal our gunpowder was part of a larger plot to steal all the gunpowder in the colonies."

"What will you do?"

"I'm proposing that the Hanover County militia go after the powder. If war breaks out, we will need all of it we can get. Tomorrow the committee will decide what course to take. I expect the men will agree with me that we must go after that gunpowder."

"Tomorrow, Father?" Patsy asked, a stony expression on her face.

"Yes, tomorrow," he answered. "We must not let any more time go by. We've waited too long as it is."

Annie looked at her sister apprehensively. If her father had been more observant, he would have noticed Patsy's clenched hands and tight angry mouth. Now Patsy's voice shook with anger as she spoke. "Do you remember what tomorrow is, Father?" she asked.

He started to answer, but Patsy blurted out, "It's our wedding day. John Fontaine and I have been waiting for months to marry. First mother died. Then you went off on business. Now you go chasing after gunpowder and then back to Philadelphia. You won't be back until August, I imagine. Am I supposed to wait?"

Patrick Henry shook his head apologetically. "I had not forgotten. And I don't want you to wait. But your party will have to be postponed."

"But why?" Patsy challenged. "Isn't there someone else who can go chasing through the countryside after gunpowder?"

"No, Patsy, there isn't," her father said patiently. "I have a responsibility to the militia and to Virginia. I can't ask men to risk their lives and then refuse to go, no matter how good the reason."

"Frankly, Father," Patsy said boldly, spots of color emerging in her cheeks, "I don't care about this matter with England. I want my party." She looked at him defiantly.

"I can understand that," he answered. "But you have not been blessed to be born in a period of tranquility. Sometimes we have to sacrifice our dreams. Going after the gunpowder cannot wait. Your party can."

Annie knew that her sister had been dreaming of a wedding ball. She had talked of little else the past months. Preparations had been made and invitations sent for the dance to be held the day after the wedding. Those plans would all have to change.

Patrick Henry looked at his daughter. "Come, Patsy. You may still marry tomorrow, but we will have to postpone the ball. This is not the end of the world."

"But what is a wedding without a party?" she asked, disappointment written on her face.

"You'll soon see, Patsy. A party is nice, but it pales in importance when compared to many other things."

Grudgingly, the girl gave in. "All right. Tomorrow I'll be married. The ball will have to wait."

The household rose early on Patsy's wedding day. Annie dressed carefully, paying particular attention to her hair, determined to tame its wiry curls. When satisfied, she went looking for Patsy. She found her trying to put on her dress.

"Annie, come help me," the older girl gasped as she wriggled into the tight-fitting bodice of her dress. Annie helped her pull the buttery soft fabric over her head, then finished buttoning the last of the twenty tiny buttons that ran up the back of the gown.

"You're finished," Annie announced proudly, stepping back to view the result. "You look beautiful!"

Patsy examined herself critically in the mirror. "It will have to do," she said. "Do you like the bows?"

"It's perfect. Everything is perfect. But can you breathe?"

"What do you mean, can I breathe?"

"Those bones that hold in your stomach. Don't they hurt?" Annie asked.

"They don't hold in my stomach. They just make the bodice of the dress fit nicely. Of course I can breathe," Patsy laughed.

"Well, I won't wear bones," Annie announced, looking at her own skinny reflection in the mirror.

"I don't think you need to. Not for a while anyway, Annie."

As Patsy pinned her own hair, she told her little sister to run out to their father's office to see if the committee meeting had ended. "It's nearly noon," she added anxiously.

Annie found her father walking back from his office. Dressed in a new blue coat and white silk breeches that reached just below his knee, with his wig on straight, he looked every bit the gentleman farmer. Bowing low to his daughter, he said, "What a lovely lady. May I have the pleasure of your company?"

She curtsied, and he guided her across the yard and into the house. "Patsy sent me to find out if Pastor Sampson is here."

"Yes. He's in my study, and the groom is getting dressed. Tell your sister that we will be ready in fifteen minutes in the ladies' parlor."

After telling Patsy, Annie slipped down to the parlor. It had been decorated with flowers, and a light apple blossom fragrance filled the room. She sat down on a sofa that had been moved against the wall and looked around. In the corner was a massive stone fireplace, and above it hung a portrait of Sarah Henry, Annie's mother. Her mother's eyes gazed out over the room, and Annie wondered what she would have thought about this wedding. It was hard to imagine, because Annie didn't remember when her mother was well. Although she had died in February, she had been sick for years.

The room began to fill with other family members and a few close friends, including Mr. Dabney, the tutor, who played the harpsichord. The groom stood near the fireplace, looking slightly uncomfortable in his stiff Sunday-best clothes. Like Patrick Henry, he seemed most at home in the fields or woods. Despite Patsy's best efforts to dress him up, he'd never make a polished appearance.

Finally, the bride entered the room. All eyes turned to her as she walked toward the fireplace where the pastor stood with John Fontaine. Her dress, despite her complaints, looked beautiful. As the pastor spoke, Annie wondered what Patsy was thinking. Was she scared? She'd certainly acted nervous as a cat all month. Or was she sad that the wedding wasn't fancier? Annie's mind drifted off.

She wondered if the committee had decided to go after the gunpowder.

A rustle next to her brought her attention back to the ceremony. John, seated next to her, was standing up. He leaned down and spoke to her. "You missed the whole thing, daydreaming Annie."

Annie was surprised to see the family standing around, hugging and kissing. Her father caught her eye and winked before leading them to a table loaded with turkey, ham, and various sweets and breads. After eating, Patrick Henry pushed his chair back. "The committee has decided to go for the gunpowder, and we have a great deal to do before we leave tomorrow," he said. "I apologize for having to interrupt such a pleasant and blessed occasion, but I have a job for Annie and John." Turning to the two young people, he said, "You must alert all the farms between here and the village. We'll have other riders going farther out. Do you understand?"

The two children nodded solemnly at their father, but they made no move to leave. Then nodding, he said, "Let's toast the bride and groom, and send these young ones off with a blessing. Pastor, will you do the honors?"

They all bowed their heads as the white-haired pastor stood to pray. "We thank You, Lord, for this couple, recently wed, and ask Your blessings on them and on their children to come. Give them the grace to persevere through hard times, and the ability to take joy in Your works of providence. And bless these young children as they go out today. Keep them from harm, and bring them back safely to their father's house. In Jesus' name, amen."

After they had prayed, Patrick Henry sent Annie to her room to change and John off with orders to look after his sister.

3

Annie's Ride

By the time Annie reached the stable, her brother was already mounted, and Joseph eased the girl up into her saddle. John was quiet as they set off down the road.

"Why so quiet?" she asked finally.

"Just thinking," he answered.

"Thinking about what?" she persisted.

"Thinking that if Father were in his right mind, he would have sent William instead of you."

"That's silly," Annie said, determining that she wouldn't get angry. "William will surely ride with Father tomorrow. Why would Father send him today?"

"That just shows how little you know," John muttered.

"I think you're jealous because William gets to ride with Father, and you have to stay home."

"Don't be foolish," John said. "If Father was thinking straight, he'd have you stay home with Patsy . . . where girls should stay."

Annie ignored her brother. *She who holds her tongue is wise,* she thought to herself. They had ridden about ten minutes, and Scotchtown was well behind them, although its freshly plowed fields stretched out to the right and the left. Already rows of tender, green shoots marched in straight lines in the loose dirt. Early wildflowers bloomed along the road and fences, and their scent gently tickled Annie's nose.

Suddenly eager to be on her way, she said, "I'll see you at the courthouse."

"I'll be there first," John answered. "Don't be stopping to pick flowers or have tea parties," he added as he gave his horse a kick and galloped away.

Annie laughed. The day was too nice, the errand too important, to let John's teasing bother her. She slowed her horse to a trot, not wanting to tire him out too soon. Already she was well out of her brother's sight, surrounded by nothing but rolling farmland and meadow.

The first farm she reached was the Thackers', and she saw Andrew out in the field with a plow and a team of oxen. Annie hadn't seen him since the bee incident several days before. She was glad that he was up and able to work. As she reined in her horse, she caught a glimpse of the boy's face under his tri-cornered hat. With an eye nearly swollen shut and a fat lip, he looked as though he had been kicked in the face by a mule.

"What happened to you?" she asked. "Your father didn't strike you, did he?" Annie couldn't picture Mr. Thacker hitting his son. He was a gentle, although stern, man.

Andrew shook his head. "Of course not. Although I almost wish he had. It's the bees. I must be sensitive to their sting. I'm swollen all over my body. That's why we couldn't come to Patsy's wedding." He rubbed his arm gently, wincing slightly as he touched a sore spot. "And it itches like the dickens. I think I'd rather wrestle a bear than be covered with bee stings."

"Why aren't you inside resting?" Annie asked.

Andrew laughed. "Pa said there's work to be done. He can spare me for school but not to go tease little girls; so I have to suffer the consequences."

Annie was silent. Then she remembered why she had come. "Andrew, I can't stay. I came only to tell your father that the militia is going after the gunpowder tomorrow. They're riding at eight o'clock from the courthouse. Will you tell your father for me?"

Andrew looked enviously at his friend. "I don't suppose he'll let me go," he said. "He'll tell me that I have to learn responsibility at home before I can do such things."

Annie felt sorry for the boy, and she tried to make him feel better. "John's not going either."

"And William?"

"Father's taking William with him," she replied. She saw the envy and disappointment written on Andrew's face. Not knowing what else to say, she mumbled, "I'm sorry," before riding away. After riding a few hundred yards, she turned and saw him attacking the field with a hoe.

For the remainder of the afternoon, Annie visited neighboring farms. In some she was invited into warm kitchens for a rest and a cup of cider. At a few she was met by scowls from farmers who said they were too busy to go chasing after some gunpowder. But that response was rare in Hanover County where the farmers respected Patrick Henry and were eager to serve if he called. Annie didn't spend much time in any place because she did not want to be caught away from the village after dark.

She drew near to Hanover just as the sun began to set, painting the western sky orange and causing the temperature to drop. Annie was glad for the gloves that her father had made her wear. She pulled her cloak, which she had loosened during the heat of the day, up tight under her chin. Weary with riding, she wanted to be off the horse and in front of a cozy fire with John. But when the girl rode into the square, she saw no sign of her brother.

There was a rail and a water trough near the tavern, and Annie walked her horse over to it so he could drink. Once she had tied him to the rail, she stood uncertainly. Was a tavern the place for a young girl to be alone at sundown? She cracked the door and peeked into a nearly empty room.

Hearing the door open, the tavern keeper, Mr. Lewis, looked up and smiled at the small girl framed in his doorway. Nodding in recognition, he said, "Mistress Henry. Hallo. What can I do for you?" As he talked, he walked toward her across the well-worn wood floors.

"I could use a warm drink," she answered. "And have you seen my brother?"

"William?"

"No, not William. John. He's supposed to meet me here." Annie looked longingly at the fire crackling in the large brick fireplace. "Father sent us to alert the militia to be prepared to ride tomorrow morning. They're going after the gunpowder."

The tavern keeper's eyes sparkled. "I'd heard that news already. I'm glad to know it's true." He regarded Annie kindly and asked, "Are you a wee bit hungry, child?"

She smiled gratefully. "I'm starving, but I don't think I should eat in here. Not alone," Annie answered apologetically.

"Of course not. Come back into the kitchen. My own Molly is there. She'll make you a plate and keep you company until John comes. But I don't think you should ride back tonight. It's too dark. Too dangerous. Stay here with us, and I'll send word back to your father. You can see him in the morning."

Annie bit her lip. "Would you wait to send word until John comes?" she asked.

"Of course. We'll wait, and when the lad comes, I'll find a place for both of you and get word to your father. But come ahead. Come see Molly and have a bite."

In the warm kitchen, heating in another large fireplace, a kettle of thick stew hung over the fire, and baking potatoes peeked out from the embers. Molly Lewis, a quiet girl of twelve, sat at a table lit by a lantern, reading a Bible.

"Molly, I've brought you a visitor, Annie Henry. Make her some food, please, and set a place for her brother. He'll be here shortly."

Molly smiled shyly at the visitor. She moved quickly to the fire, and Annie watched as she dipped out the stew and poured it into a pewter bowl. She cut a thick slice of bread, spread it generously with butter, and set the meal in front of Annie.

Molly sat down also. She moved her book to the side, closing it carefully over a ribbon bookmarker.

When Annie glanced up between bites, she caught Molly staring, but the older girl quickly looked away. She was taller than Annie and bigger boned, and she wore her straw-colored hair pulled back without any ribbon or bows. But her clear, gray eyes and pug nose gave her face a friendly look.

"This is delicious," Annie said, wiping her mouth. "I guess I was hungry."

Molly blushed and murmured a thank you, but she

kept her eyes on the table. For several minutes, the two girls sat in an uncomfortable silence, neither one knowing what to say to the other. Finally Annie blurted, "I've been taking messages around the countryside for my father. He leads the militia. They're going to ride tomorrow." She stopped speaking as quickly as she had started, embarrassed to have been bragging, but Molly seemed not to notice.

"And your brother? Has he been helping as well?"

Annie nodded, remembering John suddenly. "Where do you think he could be? He was supposed to meet me here so that we could ride home together. Of course, it's too late now. Your father kindly said we could sleep here. But John should be here by now—unless something happened to him," Annie said, frowning.

Molly stood to clear Annie's plate. "I'm sure he's fine. If he's at all like my brother, he probably stopped to fish or hunt—or maybe play a game of dice. Come sit closer to the fire and don't worry about him."

Annie let the heat from the fire warm her face and hands. Sitting in this bright, friendly kitchen, she found it hard to imagine danger, but Annie knew the night could hide robbers and other threats. She knew her father didn't approve of gaming and didn't think John would play dice, but would he stop to hunt? Annie didn't know.

As she sat before the fire, Annie could feel her eyes grow heavy. She felt a gentle hand on her arm. "Come, Annie. You look tired. There is an extra bed in my room. You can wash there."

Annie nodded and let herself be led to a soft, cozy bed.

4

Molly Lewis

The next morning, Annie felt a hand on her shoulder shaking her and heard a voice saying, "Wake up, Annie. The men are gathering."

She struggled to surface from her dream of horses and fire. She found herself on a small cot in a room not much bigger than a slave's room at home. Sunlight poured through the one window, and Molly, already dressed, was standing next to her with a confused expression on her face.

"Can't I sleep a little longer," Annie said as she stretched her legs. "I swear, every part of me aches today."

Molly shrugged, turned her back to the girl as she made the other bed, and filled the basin with fresh water. After she finished those chores, she turned back to Annie. "I musn't stay any longer. There are too many men needing breakfast downstairs. They say your father should be here soon."

Annie sat up. Of course! She had forgotten that the militia was riding this morning. Hopping out of bed, she washed at the basin and then put on her dress and braided her hair. Glancing out the window, she saw a large crowd of men gathered in front of the courthouse across the street. A few were on horseback, but most stood in dusty boots, their worn coats buttoned tight against the chilly morning air. There wasn't a uniform among them, and Annie thought they looked too scruffy to be an army. Although she searched the crowd, she could not see her father or brother.

Downstairs in the kitchen, Annie found Molly rushing back and forth between the kitchen and the dining room, carrying plates of sausage, ham, and hot griddle cakes to the hungry men who filled the tavern. She looked hot, her face was flushed, and tiny beads of sweat dotted her forehead. Seeing Annie, she said, "Help yourself to breakfast," and then rushed out the door again.

Annie took her food to a corner where she would be out of the way of the bustle. At home the kitchen was in a separate building, and she rarely saw all the activity that went into preparing food for so many people. Here, she was in the middle of it. When the ham ran out, Mr. Lewis sliced another. Molly pulled fresh griddle cakes from the pan over the fire. They worked steadily until the men were fed and began to drift outside to wait for Patrick Henry. Only then did Molly sit and begin to eat her own breakfast.

"I'm sorry to be such a bother," Annie apologized.

But Molly shook her head shyly. "I like having you here. It gets lonely sometimes with no one to talk to."

Annie thought for a moment. At Scotchtown, there was almost always someone to talk to. She didn't think she had ever been lonely, except when missing her father.

After stuffing one last bite of sausage into her mouth, she rose to go. "Did you recognize all the men outside?" she asked.

Molly shook her head. "I don't think they are all from

our county. After you notified folks, they rode out and told others. My pa says that there could be as many as 300 riding from here. And others will likely join as they go."

As Annie got ready to leave, she looked into the dining room at the mess left by the army of recently fed men. The floor was thick with dirt carried in by their farm boots. The tables were sticky with syrup, and soiled plates and mugs still waited to be carried to the kitchen.

In the kitchen, along with piles of dirty dishes, sat Molly, staring sadly at her now cold, half-eaten food.

"I wish I could help," Annie said impulsively, "but I have to find my father."

"Father wouldn't hear of it," Molly answered, dismissing the girl with a wave.

As Annie turned to leave, the older girl called out in a soft voice, "There is something you could do."

Annie turned back to her friend, curious as to what that something could be.

"Promise you will tell me all the news," Molly pleaded. "It will make this easier to bear," she said as she pointed to the mess. Then she clapped a hand over her mouth and turned her eyes away, surprised and embarrassed by her own words.

Annie caught her arm and said, "I promise."

Outside, the young girl set off to find John. He hadn't come in last night according to Mr. Lewis, and Annie was worried about him. But before she could find him, she saw her father astride his black horse, surveying the crowd. Annie waved but he did not see her. She pushed her way through the crowd, trying to keep her skirts up off the dusty ground and keep the men from backing into her. As long as her father stayed on his horse, she had no trouble keeping him in sight.

It wasn't until Annie drew close to her father that she saw that he wasn't alone. Both William and John were at his side. Upon seeing Annie, he dismounted and gave her a hug. "Thank God you are all right."

"Of course I'm all right," Annie said. "You did get the message, didn't you?"

"Yes. Mr. Lewis kindly sent a messenger to us," her father said in a voice that held some anger. Annie glanced quickly at her brothers, but they turned away. When she looked back at her father, he had an expression, dubbed "thundercloud eyes" by the children, that meant trouble for the one at whom it was directed. It was clear that the look was directed toward John.

Patrick Henry broke the silence by pushing John forward, keeping, Annie noted, a tight grip on her brother's arm. He said in a voice that demanded a response, "Tell your sister where you were last night."

John muttered something so softly that Annie couldn't hear, but her father interrupted, "Speak clearly, son. Tell your sister where you were."

Directing his gaze studiously at a point over Annie's shoulder, John said, "Horse rode off," as a blush stole across his cheeks.

"Your horse rode off?" Annie repeated, not understanding.

"Shh," he said through gritted teeth. "I stopped for a short time at Peter Glenn's house. I was nearly finished and almost here. He had a new gun he wanted to show me. We rode out a bit so I could shoot it some. I wanted to try shooting on horseback. But the fool horse was startled, threw me, and then ran off. I had to follow him—he'd gone clear back to Scotchtown—and that's when Father found me."

Annie could feel her father's glare. She wished there

was something she could say to make his anger go away, but she didn't know what.

Just then her father spoke. "I've told John how deeply disappointed I am. I gave him a man's job to do, and he did it like a boy. Plus, he abandoned you because of a fool notion. That could have been dangerous."

"But, Father, Mr. Lewis took good care of me," Annie protested.

"Yes, he did. But John was responsible, not Mr. Lewis."

As her father talked, John stared at the ground, and Annie could tell he was working manfully to keep from crying. Finally, her father loosened his grip on John's arm saying, "Go to the tavern and get provisions for William and me. Some jerky and biscuits, please."

With John gone, Patrick Henry's anger faded. He turned and watched his son crossing the square. "You know this tavern is my old stomping ground. I worked here while studying law," he said, glancing over at the building. "Those were good days," he mused. "We were poor, but we always had food to eat and your mother . . ." His voice broke, and Annie could see him struggle to control his grief. Finally, he said, "Well, enough of that. There's a job at hand." Turning to his daughter, he asked, "Did you have any problem yesterday, Annie?"

"Everywhere I went, the men seemed eager to come. But I didn't know there'd be this many," she replied, pointing to the crowd.

Her father smiled at the men gathering around him. "It's freedom, Annie. We are about to see the birth of liberty. And once we have freedom, men will die to keep it. But let us pray to God that none will have to die today."

As more people saw that Patrick Henry had arrived, the crowd began to push against him, until Annie feared that they would be crushed. Her father mounted his horse, and the nervous animal pranced skittishly until the men moved away a bit. "We are going to recover the powder that Governor Dunmore removed from Williamsburg," he yelled to the crowd. "Some ask, 'Is this necessary?' Just look at what happened in Lexington and Concord. You've heard the news. You know how the British fired upon the colonists. We want only to have our gunpowder for self-defense. We hope and pray for a peaceful outcome. Let us be men of good order."

A lusty cheer went up throughout the crowd before the men fell into line and began to march out of town.

Annie watched them parade by. In their shabby clothes, worn boots, and farmer's hats, they were a ragtag band with an inexperienced lawyer/farmer at their head. Would freedom really depend on an army that looked like this?

Patrick Henry's horse pranced impatiently. Leaning over, he hugged his daughter. "Be good," he said. Then he turned to William, and his voice trembled as he said to his eldest son, "Time to fall in."

Annie hugged her older brother. He looked too young to be going out to fight. She blinked back tears as he joined the marching column.

Her father then turned to his younger son, who said with a breaking voice, "I'm sorry, Father. I failed at my job. Please forgive me."

"I forgive you. We all have failed at one thing or another," his father said. "Learn from this, son, that the world is full of temptations. You must learn to resist them." Then he shook John's hand, saying, "I love you."

To both of them he said, "Don't dawdle on your way back to Scotchtown. Patsy will wonder where you are, and she will worry about you."

As they spoke, the men continued to clomp noisily by, raising dust until Annie's eyes watered. She looked wistfully after them, knowing suddenly that she didn't want to go back to Scotchtown. Not until the men came back. Without thinking, she blurted, "Couldn't I stay here at the tavern, Father? Just until you come home. I wouldn't be a bother. I promise. Maybe I could even help. Please don't make me go home just yet."

Patrick Henry looked at his daughter's serious young face, her eyes pleading to be part of the adventure. He said with equal seriousness, "Mr. Lewis works very hard, Annie. And Molly must work with him. They have no time for play."

Annie nodded solemnly. "I know, Father. But I could be a help. I would learn and work hard. I promise."

"But you're not used to hard work, Annie. What if you tire of it?"

But Annie would not budge. "I promise I will be a help. Please let me."

She could see her father pondering the question. She held her breath, willing him to say yes. When he got off his horse and walked across the square to the tavern, Annie allowed herself a smile. John kept his face fixed stonily on a distant tree. A few minutes later Patrick Henry rejoined them.

"Mr. Lewis has agreed. Apparently he thinks it would be nice for Molly to have a friend for a few days. But I have told him that if you are any bother, he is to send you home."

Then turning to his son, he said, "Now is your chance to prove yourself responsible. You must ride back and let Patsy know that Annie is staying here until I come home."

"How long will you be gone?"

"Could be a week. Maybe longer. If Patsy gets anxious, you remind her that I've promised no shooting unless the

British shoot first." The last of the men had marched down the road toward Williamsburg, leaving silence in their wake. Patrick Henry remounted his horse and waved. "Be good, children. Mind those in authority over you."

"We will, Father," Annie said. "And God be with you."

"Indeed. And God be with you."

After the noise and dust of the militia, Hanover seemed a desolate place. There was an occasional traveler at the tavern, but the daily business was slow. All the local men were gone. Molly said it was unnatural, the way business had dried up, but Annie thought it grand. Although Molly did not have to work constantly doing laundry and dishes and cooking for guests, she still had chores to do. But Mr. Lewis also allowed her to spend time with her guest.

Annie was surprised that Molly wanted to do lessons in the morning. Although the older girl had no tutor, she wanted an education; so each day she worked through her lesson book. Sometimes Annie tried to draw her away, but Molly was firm. "I can't play," she'd say crossly. "I want to learn to read better." Since it was more fun to study with Molly than to play alone, Annie studied also.

On washday, the girls carried baskets of dirty linens down to the river where they scrubbed them on boards until they were clean. Together, they struggled to carry the heavy baskets of damp sheets up the grassy slope to the tavern. At the top of the hill, Annie flopped down in the grass, but Molly set to work hanging her sheets out to dry in the warm spring sun.

"Don't you ever get tired?" Annie complained. "You never just do nothing."

"I guess I don't have time to do nothing," Molly

answered, taking a wooden clothespin from her mouth and putting it on the sheet. "Before my mother died, I had more time. But not now. If I don't help Father, who will?" Molly spoke matter-of-factly, without self-pity.

Annie rose wearily to her feet. Grabbing a sheet, she struggled to hang it on the line, but when she tried to pin it, the other end fell to the ground. Just then Molly looked over and said, "You must keep it up out of the dirt, or we'll have to wash it all over again." Annie could see a smudge of dirt on the sheet, but she hoped Molly wouldn't notice. The older girl meanwhile had finished her basket. She came around to Annie's and said, "Here, I'll help you. We'll get it done quicker that way."

Not all Molly's chores were hard work. She taught Annie to milk the cows, patiently demonstrating where to sit so the cow wouldn't kick and how to gently but firmly squeeze and strip the milk into the bucket. Annie's first attempts were awkward. Sometimes she'd squeeze too gently, and the cow would flick a tail at her. And it was hard to remember to place the bucket just so, in order to keep the cow from kicking it over.

On one particularly warm morning, Annie, with sweat streaming down her cheeks, pushed her stool away from the cow with anger. "This dumb cow has no milk. I've been sitting here for ten minutes, and the bucket is empty. Why don't you have good cows?" she complained.

Molly stood up from her own stool. Her own bucket was filled with warm, foamy milk. Wiping a stray lock of hair out of her eyes, she said, "Look at the udder, Annie. It's full. It's not the cow's fault if the milker is clumsy. Here, let me do it."

Pushing Annie aside, Molly soon had milk streaming into the bucket. Annie sulked in a corner of the barn, muttering to herself that Molly had all the luck. Soon the bucket was full. Molly untied the two cows, slapped their flanks, and sent them back out into the pasture. She turned back to Annie.

"You can pout if you want, but I don't have time. Father said we need butter, and it won't make itself."

"Why can't someone else do this work?" a grouchy Annie asked. "Why must you do it all?"

With a scornful glance, Molly said, "Not all of us own slaves to do our chores. Some of us wouldn't own them even if we could." Embarrassed that she had spoken so bluntly to a daughter of such an important man, the older girl turned back to her work. She knew that Patrick Henry was a lawyer and famous politician while Molly's own father was only a tavern keeper.

Flushed with anger, Annie thought of all the unkind things she could say but caught herself. She knew Molly was right. The only reason Annie did not usually milk cows or churn butter was because someone else did it for her. Determined not to show Molly how much her words had hurt, she said, "I guess I am clumsy. But I can learn as well as you. I'm sorry I gave up on that cow. What was I doing wrong?"

The older girl was eager to be friends again. "Oh, she's a tough old cow. Sometimes you really have to yank hard," Molly said. "I'm sorry I spoke harshly to you."

As the girls walked from the barn, each carrying a full bucket of milk, Annie sighed. "There's truth in what you said. We do have slaves. Father doesn't like slavery, but he can't picture life without them. I guess I'm the same way. But maybe if I learn to work, I'll be better able to."

They had reached the dry well, a small building over a deep hole in the ground—like a well, but without water.

It was cool at the bottom, and things that needed to be kept cold, like milk and butter, were stored there. Molly poured the milk into a metal jug and lowered it to the bottom of the well.

"Come on," she said to Annie. "Let's rinse the milk buckets."

Late that afternoon Annie sat on the porch while Molly finished up something inside. It was cool under the roof of the porch. As she waited for her friend to come out, Annie stretched out contentedly and thought about her father. It had been seven days since the militia had gone out. *Where are they now,* she wondered. When Molly came humming across the grass, Annie turned to her. "Don't you worry about war, Molly?"

The older girl shrugged. "Not too much. My father is too old to fight, and my brother lives out west. I don't see how war will bother me."

"But, Molly, war won't be short," Annie protested. "Father says that with the strength of the British navy and the skill of their troops, we could fight for years. Doesn't that scare you?"

The older girl smiled. "You know much more than I do, Annie. But my father always says not to worry about what tomorrow will bring. Today has enough worries of its own. And I know that one of my worries is getting this butter made before my father takes a paddle to me."

Annie returned the smile. "Show me how to make this butter," she said, "and I'll help."

Molly pulled the metal jug up from the well and skimmed the cream off the top. For the next hour or so the two girls chatted and churned butter, taking turns lifting the paddle up and down until the cream thickened. When the butter was thick but not hard, they emptied it into a large bowl, salted it, and then packed it into molds, which they lowered into the dry well to keep cold.

While the girls worked, clouds gathered in the sky, and now rain threatened. The temperature dropped suddenly, and Annie felt the cold wind bite through the thin cotton of her dress.

Molly straightened up and looked at the sky. "Let's run before we get wet," she shouted through the wind.

The girls ran to the tavern, reaching the porch just as the first heavy drops of rain fell. Soon it was coming down in a drenching flood, bending the branches of the trees to the ground and washing down the hillside in little rivulets. The girls watched from the window. "Won't the militia be uncomfortable?" Annie worried. "I hope we hear news soon."

"We always hear the news at the tavern," Molly answered as she tied an apron around her dress and prepared to make dinner.

Her young visitor leaned back wearily in her chair. "I'm too tired to move," she said. "How can you start another job so soon?"

Molly laughed. "Because I'm hungry as well. And if I don't cook, we don't eat. You had better put on an apron too. There are potatoes to be peeled and onions to be chopped."

"Maybe I'll go back to Scotchtown," Annie said half-seriously as she rose to her feet.

Molly tossed a potato to her. "Tomorrow you can go home if you want—though you'll miss all the news. But tonight there's work to be done."

5

Success!

Loud voices and rowdy laughter broke the morning quiet. Turning over on her cot, Annie cracked her eyes to see if Molly was awake yet. Tangled bedclothes and a hastily tossed nightgown were evidence that the girl had been hurried out of bed.

As she stretched lazily, Annie wondered about the noise from outside the window. In the whole time she had been in Hanover, there had never been more than a few customers at the tavern. All the young men had gone along with the militia. Today, however, it sounded as if an army stood outside. “The militia!” Annie exclaimed, hopping from her bed. “They’ve come back.”

Annie hurriedly dressed and washed, not bothering even to comb her hair. Her eyes danced as she skipped down the stairs and out onto the brick sidewalk. Scanning the crowd, she finally spotted her father engaged in a lively discussion with someone she did not know. She ran across the street and waited, just out of earshot of her father, until the conversation ended. Then she tiptoed up from behind and threw her arms around him. He turned, and when he saw his daughter, he scooped her up in his arms.

"Annie, Annie," he laughed. "How is the little tavern keeper?"

"Just fine, Father. Molly has taught me so much. I've learned to milk, and churn, and properly make the beds, and wash—"

"Sounds like you are set to become a perfect pioneer wife," Patrick Henry said proudly. "Those skills will come in handy someday. And hard work never hurt anyone."

Annie smiled broadly. "What about the gunpowder, Father?" she asked.

"We had success, daughter. We caught up with Governor Dunmore's man in Doncastle. He promised to pay us 330 pounds for the gunpowder, which we can use to buy more gunpowder when we need it, and he sent that money on to Williamsburg. No shots were fired. And we showed the governor that Virginians will stand up for the principle of self-defense."

"Now what happens, Father?"

"I'm already late for the Continental Congress in Philadelphia; so I must leave tomorrow."

"Leaving again? So soon!" Annie wailed. "You're never at home anymore."

"That's all too true, Annie. But I must go. As it is, I will arrive late for the Congress."

As they talked, father and daughter walked hand-in-hand to the tavern where they met Mr. Lewis on the steps. "Thank you for minding my Annie," Patrick Henry said, shaking hands.

"It's been my pleasure. Molly has been happy for the friendship. It's mighty lonely here since my wife passed away. And my daughter works too hard, but your daughter here has lightened the load and brightened the days for us."

"I think it has done Annie good as well. It's not good to grow up without knowing what it is to work hard." Then looking down at his soiled clothes and dusty boots, Patrick Henry said, "There's much I need to do here tonight. I'll require a room and a bath. And these clothes washed. Can you accommodate me?"

With his arm on Patrick Henry's shoulder, Mr. Lewis guided him into the tavern. "We always have room for you here, Patrick. Come, tell us about the gunpowder."

Annie hesitated at the door to the tavern, and her father noticed. "You may come in, child. As long as I'm here."

Annie followed happily behind the two men as they took their seats at a table, and she waited expectantly as Mr. Lewis fetched two glasses of cider before sitting down.

"Well, it wasn't terribly exciting," her father began. "When we marched out a week ago, the roads were dry, and we made swift time for the first two days. Then it began raining. The roads turned to thick mud, and the rivers swelled so much the horses couldn't cross. We had to use the ferry, which could carry only twenty of us at a time. It took us a day just to cross the river, and when we made camp on the other side, we had to sleep in the muck and mire."

"It sounds awful."

"Well, I confess that some wanted to turn back. They had gone with us as a lark. But when it proved to be more difficult than they expected, they lost heart." Then turning to his daughter, he said, "Your brother William, however, proved himself a man. He didn't complain, and he stuck out the journey."

"That William is a good lad," Mr. Lewis agreed.

"By the time we reached Doncastle, we looked most disreputable. Our clothes were stiff with mud, and our guns needed a good oiling. If the redcoats had chosen to fight, I'm not sure we could have overcome them. But Lord Dunmore's man didn't need any persuading. We surrounded the tavern where he was eating and called out to him. When he stood on the doorstep, his jaw dropped, and he quickly looked to see if he could make an escape. When he saw that he was surrounded, he asked me to have a cup of tea with him."

"Tea, Father?"

Patrick Henry looked apologetic. "I know we are boycotting tea, but since he offered, and he was paying . . . and I was surely cold and damp. . . . Well, I accepted. And the tea tasted just fine," he said, laughing. "Anyway, we sat in the tavern with our pot of tea, and before you could say 'boo,' he had agreed to pay the money for the powder."

"Not much courage there," Mr. Lewis said, a broad grin spreading over his face.

"I tell you, friend, the British have no stomach for a fight. We shall be victorious if we go to war." As Patrick Henry spoke, his face glowed with anticipation. "There he sat in all his fine scarlet garments, and we, in our torn and dirty work clothes, stared him in the face—and he backed down. And that's the story of the gunpowder. Once we made sure that the money had been sent to Williamsburg, we set off for home. Again it rained, but we rode our victory home and didn't mind the misery."

Annie looked at her father in his grime-covered clothes. Although he had washed his hands and face, the skin on his arms was gray with dirt. Before she could think, she said, "You aren't going to Philadelphia like that, are you?"

With a laugh, Patrick Henry shook his head. "No. I will wash up here, but I need some clothes from Scotchtown. I think I will ask Mr. Thacker to bring some to me. Andrew is supposed to be meeting him here with a wagon shortly."

Mr. Lewis had gone back to the kitchen. Annie leaned toward her father and whispered, "Father, could I stay here a little longer? It's good to feel useful."

"How will Patsy manage without you?" he asked.

"I have nothing to do but feed my chickens. Elizabeth can do that," Annie said. "Besides, with Patsy just married, she doesn't need me around the house."

Her father nodded. Taking confidence, Annie asked, "Don't you think I could learn a lot by staying here? And didn't you learn a lot before you became a lawyer, when you were a tavern keeper, Father?"

Patrick Henry roared a deep belly laugh. "What I learned as a tavern keeper," he said, pushing his chair out from the table and standing up, "was to appreciate how much news you can hear in a tavern. That couldn't have anything to do with why you want to stay here, could it?"

Annie blushed. Her father always seemed to read her mind.

"Annie, an acorn never falls very far from the oak," he said, pinching her cheek. "There's nothing wrong with wanting news. In fact, even the Bible approves: 'Like cold water to a weary soul is good news from a distant land.'" He looked fondly at his daughter, seeing his own enthusiasms in her eager face. "I don't know. Let me think on the matter. Perhaps an arrangement can be worked out, but I make no promises. Now go and give a hand to Molly."

Annie found Molly in the kitchen, washing and drying the iron pots. The older girl looked up expectantly when her friend came in.

"What news is there?"

Annie returned her excitement with a glum expression. "Success. They were paid for the gunpowder."

"Then why so sad?"

"Father must leave in the morning for Philadelphia. He'll be gone again . . . for months this time," Annie explained. "And I probably will have to go home to Scotchtown." But Annie had no sooner spoken than Mr. Lewis opened the kitchen door and waved for her.

"Your father wants you outside," he whispered.

There on the dusty street her father stood talking to Andrew Thacker, who had just arrived with his wagon. As Annie watched, Mr. Thacker joined them from across the empty square, a piece of paper in his hand.

"Doesn't this just beat all?" he said, waving the parchment in front of him. "The Lord Governor wasted no time."

Patrick Henry raised a questioning eyebrow, and Mr. Thacker for the first time noticed Annie standing next to the wagon.

"Come with me, Patrick," Mr. Thacker urged. "I have something I must show you."

As they walked, the two men carried on a spirited discussion. Annie could see Mr. Thacker talk and her father shake his head. The piece of paper was passed back and forth, and the two men, grim-faced, headed back to the wagon.

"What has happened?" Annie asked.

"Nothing for you to worry about," her father said, making an effort to smile. "But I have decided to let you stay here for another week. I want you to ride home today with the Thackers. Have Patsy pack what I will need in Philadelphia. Then Mr. Thacker will bring you back tonight. Do you understand?"

"But, Father—" Annie began.

"Please don't question me, Annie. Just do what I say. I'll see you later." Then, without another word, he returned to the tavern.

Annie stared after her father while Mr. Thacker loaded the wagon. Then, taking the reins from his son, he motioned the boy into the back with the young girl. They rode along in silence, the wagon bumping over the ruts and rocks that covered the road. Finally, she could stand the silence no longer. "Do you know what is going on?" she whispered.

Andrew shook his head. "I guess we'll find out soon enough," he whispered back.

But Annie doubted that. Andrew might be told what was going on, but she would be kept in the dark. She scowled, and they rode the rest of the way back to Scotchtown in silence.

Their arrival threw the plantation into a flurry of activity. Patsy packed what clothes their father needed for the month or more he would be in Philadelphia. She made sure she packed an extra wig because he would pick at his hair until it looked worse than a bird's nest. All of his things had to fit in several packs that would be carried by a second horse. While she was there, Annie packed a few more clothes for herself. By late afternoon, they were ready and waiting for the Thackers to return.

Annie was surprised when Andrew arrived alone on the wagon. "My pa is coming by horseback," he explained.

As they bumped along the road to Hanover, Andrew said, "I found out what's going on."

"Then tell me," Annie insisted.

"Lord Dunmore has issued a proclamation—an official declaration. That's what Pa had in his hand."

"Well, what did it say?" Annie interrupted.

"If you'd give me a chance, I would tell you."

"I'm sorry. Go ahead."

"The proclamation says your pa is an outlaw. It accuses the militia of trying to stir up rebellion and says Patrick Henry and his followers have caused terror among the king's faithful subjects." Andrew spoke apologetically, sorry to be the one to bring bad news.

Annie's face showed alarm. "A traitor? But they can hang traitors!"

"That's why my pa and other men are riding with your pa to the Potomac River. He won't be alone as long as he is in Virginia."

"But your father—how can he be away from the farm for so long? Isn't this still the planting season?"

Andrew nodded seriously. "He says he is counting on me. If I get the crops in, then we'll eat. If I don't, then the winter will be hard on us."

"But, Andrew, why would he do that?" Annie said with surprise. "You all could starve this winter."

Sitting up tall in the wagon, Andrew showed his anger. "Don't you think that I can do a good job?"

"Oh, Andrew, I didn't mean to insult you. But you have to admit, you aren't always the most dependable person. Remember the bees?"

"Well, my pa thinks I can do it. And I know I can. You just wait," Andrew said, his pride having been wounded. "Besides, Pa says this is one way I can be part of the war. I can't go fight yet, but I can keep the farm going if he has to be away."

The wagon rolled into Hanover, and Annie could see that there were many men standing around. The stable behind the tavern was full of horses, and a neighboring farmer's boy had been put to work tending them.

Annie entered through the kitchen door. There she saw her friend up to her arms in dishes. Molly's face was red, and her hair curled in damp tendrils on her forehead, but she flashed a tired smile when Annie entered the room. "Have you seen my father?" the younger girl asked.

"He's in there, writing letters I think," Molly answered, pointing with her head. Annie hesitated outside the dining room. Mr. Lewis did not allow the girls into the public rooms because it wasn't a proper place for young ladies, but Annie needed to speak to her father.

As she stood there, twisting a lock of hair in her fingers, the tavern keeper walked by and saw her.

"It's fine to go in, child. Your father is the only one there. I haven't opened yet for lunch. Go speak to him if you'd like."

Annie curtsied. She crossed scrubbed wooden floors to the table where her father sat hunched over his paper. She waited silently as he finished writing and set down his quill. He rubbed his eyes and then turned toward Annie tiredly. "It has been a long week."

Annie stood behind him and rubbed his shoulders as he flexed his back. "Does this feel better?" she whispered. He nodded.

"You will be careful, Father, won't you?"

Looking up at her worried face, he smiled. "Yes, child. I will be careful. But I know that my life is in God's hands, not my own. We must not worry."

6

An Unwelcome Visitor

When Patrick Henry left in the morning, trailing his packhorse behind him, he was accompanied by twenty men on horseback. Their long journey to the Potomac River was dangerous and involved crossing many rivers, most without bridges or boats. All along the way they would need to guard against agents of the king, eager to have a hand in arresting the famous patriot.

Only two days had passed when Annie took sick. She complained of a sore throat, and Mr. Lewis sent her to bed. By evening she burned with fever. There was little Molly could do for her. Molly tried to lower the fever with moist towels, but it didn't work. For several days the fever flared, until Mr. Lewis, fearing that Annie might die, sent for Patsy.

That evening John brought Martha, an elderly slave woman who was also a skilled nurse, back to the tavern. She stayed at Annie's bedside, keeping the cool, moist cloths on the sick girl's forehead. It was Martha who forced Annie to take sips of broth and herb tea between her dry, fever-parched lips, and it was Martha who combed her tangled hair and replaced one drenched nightgown with another.

When Annie awoke with a start from a nightmare, Martha comforted her. Annie didn't remember any of this, but Martha told her afterward that she was so sick the family had thought she was going to die. But then the fever broke. Annie awoke again, saw the soft morning light filtered through cotton curtains, and smiled.

Martha, sitting at her bedside, returned her smile. "We've been worried sick about you, child."

"How long have I been ill?" Annie whispered.

"You've been in bed for a week," Martha replied. "At times we thought we had lost you. But you'll be fine now."

Annie caught a glimpse of her arms on the white sheets and shuddered when she saw the rash that covered them. Closing her eyes, she drifted off to sleep. When she awoke again, a tray with hot broth sat on the bedside table, and Martha urged her to eat.

The broth tasted good, and Annie discovered she was very hungry. Soon Martha said she could eat eggs and biscuits, and before long she was devouring ham and cornmeal mush. As the girl regained her strength, the nurse allowed her to leave her bed and sit on the porch with a woolen shawl wrapped tightly about her shoulders. From that vantage point, the child watched the comings and goings of Hanover. Bewigged men in well-cut coats and breeches went in and out of the courthouse. Lawyers probably. Farmers and frontiersman, dressed in homespun and worn boots, came to town to gossip and buy provisions.

One day there was no one but a skinny child whose job it was to tend pigs. The pigs he was minding had escaped from their pen and were rooting and squealing down the dusty road. They darted this way and that, and the boy, with more energy than skill, only managed to excite them further. When he drew near to the tavern, he noticed Annie sitting on the rocking chair, watching him. Sticking out his tongue, he stared back at her until the girl turned away with embarrassment. Then he went back to the chase.

Annie had been recovering for about two weeks when she asked the question that had been pressing on her mind: "Will I return soon to Scotchtown?"

Molly shook her head. "The fever has been bad there. Martha says many of the slaves have been sick, and she returned home to nurse your brother Edward."

Annie's stomach churned. "Is he well?"

"Yes. He's recovering nicely, but your brother-in-law, Mr. Fontaine, and Patsy thought it best if you stayed here until all danger from the fever has passed."

"But I have been such a burden on you," Annie protested, realizing with sadness the truth of her words.

The older girl shook her head. "That's not so. Martha did most of the nursing. And you ate very little."

"But what about my laundry? I know I've gone through piles of nightgowns."

Molly shook her head and would hear no more about it. "You weren't any trouble, Annie. But you could be a help if you would eat and get strong."

It was no longer spring, and the hot summer sun beat down on the hillsides of Hanover County. Annie was now up and about and able to help with the milking and churning, though Mr. Lewis still would not let her help with the heavy chores.

Every day she waited for news from Philadelphia, but little came. Patrick Henry had arrived safely, that much she knew. And the men from Hanover had returned to their farms. There was news also about battles in faraway places.

In Massachusetts, minutemen—men pledged to go and fight on a minute's notice—fought the British at Bunker Hill. In Philadelphia, George Washington was appointed head of the Continental Army. He then traveled with other generals to Massachusetts to bring order to the army there. In Williamsburg, the royal governor, fearful of an uprising by the colonists, slipped out of town by night with his family and escaped to the battleship *Powey*, anchored off the coast of Yorktown. And in Hanover, Annie Henry had her eleventh birthday.

By August Scotchtown was free of fever, and Annie, wanting to see her family again, prepared to go home. Although she hated to leave her friend, who by now was like a sister, Annie couldn't wait to see the familiar house. Mr. Thacker and Andrew brought her back by wagon. It was the first time that Annie had seen the boy since he had driven her to Hanover in the spring.

Already the fields were dotted with shocks of wheat. Before too long it would be threshing season. Annie wondered if Andrew had been able to get his crop planted. She hated to ask in front of his father; so she was glad when Mr. Thacker took over the reins, allowing Andrew to climb back with her.

"You look well," the boy said seriously. "I heard you were awfully sick."

"They've been sick at Scotchtown as well," she said gravely. "But God spared us all. Did you get your crops planted last spring?"

Andrew grinned broadly. "Ma had to help get the last of the seed in, but we finished. Got the whole thing planted before the heavy rains. And the fields look great. Even Pa says so."

"That's wonderful, Andrew," Annie said.

"There's more. Pa gave me a field—covered with trees—and said I could clear it and get it ready for planting. I've been working on that after my other chores are done."

When Annie looked at her friend, she no longer saw a boy. His chest had filled out, and he stood nearly as tall as his father. His face had changed too. All the round curves had become angles, and he had the beginnings of a mustache on his upper lip. But it was his attitude that had changed most. He seemed responsible.

"Have you seen John?" she asked.

"Don't have much time for hunting and fishing," he answered with a touch of regret.

"Don't you come to school?"

"I just haven't had time. Ma helps me with my reading, and I can cipher. I don't need that Latin and stuff."

Finally, the wagon reached the top of a hill, and there in the distance Annie saw Scotchtown. It looked just as she remembered it: A long white house with eight large windows across the front, topped by a brown-shingled barn-shaped roof. The summer gardens were in bloom with asters and coneflowers.

While Andrew unloaded Annie's things, the door was thrown open by Patsy who hurried down the stairs to greet her sister. "We've missed you so much, Annie. Thank God you're home," she said with a weepy voice.

Annie pulled back in surprise. "Look at you. No one even told me you were having a baby."

The older girl blushed and held her fingers to her lips while she glanced at Andrew. He appeared to be busy at his task, but Annie could tell by his red ears that he had heard. It wasn't considered good manners to talk about having babies.

So Annie grabbed her sister's arm and pulled her up the stairs. "Now you can tell me about it," she said. "When is this baby coming?"

"Winter, I think."

"Maybe in time for Christmas," Annie said, full of excitement. "Wouldn't that be great if we could have a baby and Father home for Christmas?"

"Christmas would be a little early for the baby. As for Father . . ." Patsy's silence and her sudden fidgeting with a locket sent a wave of alarm through Annie.

"Father *is* coming home?" Annie demanded.

Patsy shook her head, and tears sprang to Annie's eyes. For a minute she thought something terrible had happened to her father, but Patsy walked over to the little writing desk and picked up a letter. "This just came from him. It says that he has been named commander-in-chief of the regular forces in Virginia. He went straight from Philadelphia to Williamsburg."

Annie was surprised. "But Father isn't a soldier."

Her sister agreed. "I guess he wants to be one, and after bringing back the money for the gunpowder, he proved himself a hero."

"Does that mean he won't be back for a long time?"

"I'm afraid it does. We won't see him this winter, I suppose."

There was silence as the two girls thought about a long winter without their father's presence. For Annie, the news seemed particularly bitter because she had already been away so long, but even this sad news couldn't spoil the young girl's pleasure in being home. She took endless walks across the fields and into the woods, thinking as the smell of dry leaves and wood fires filled her nose that there wasn't any place on earth as nice as her home. Though war might be raging in Massachusetts, and her father might be kept in Williamsburg, at Scotchtown all was well.

That feeling of well-being was shattered one winter night. Something awoke Annie from her sleep. One minute she had been dreaming of her mother, and the next minute she was sitting up in bed awake, uncertain about what had disturbed her. She listened carefully but heard only the sound of raindrops falling softly on the roof. Pulling her comforter up under her chin, Annie snuggled back under the covers. She had just closed her eyes when she heard a distinct noise from outside.

She sat up in the dark and waited. There it was again, a loud pounding on the door. Surely someone would answer the door to see what poor traveler had gotten stranded on such a miserable, rainy night. Her father always made room for visitors. When no one answered, though, she wrapped her blanket tightly about her thin figure and shuffled out into the hallway.

Suddenly she heard a drunken voice yell, "Wake up, you traitors. Get your lazy selves out of them beds. Get out here, Patrick Henry, before I come in and get you."

Annie heard heavy footsteps outside the window. She whispered, "Thank You, God, that the shutters are closed." As the footsteps faded, she tiptoed from the hall to the parlor. There her sister sat, holding a lantern. Patsy held her fingers to her lips, warning Annie to be quiet.

"Who is it, Patsy?" Annie whispered.

"I don't know. Some fool who has had too much to drink. But why does he call Father a traitor?"

Annie knew the answer. She remembered the parchment proclamation from Governor Dunmore. Apparently, no one had told Patsy—probably because of the baby.

"Where is John Fontaine?" Annie asked.

"He had to go to Hanover on business. And the boys are at a friend's house. What should we do?" There were footsteps upstairs and the sound of whimpers. Elizabeth and Edward had awakened and were crying. Annie started to go up but then heard the soft voice of their nurse soothing them back to sleep.

As the sisters stood in the parlor, the pounding began again at the front door. "I tell you, come out," the wild voice demanded. "Patrick Henry is a scoundrel, a coward, a thief, and a traitor. And his family ain't no better. If there is a bounty on Henry's head, I mean to get it."

When Patsy heard the word *bounty*, her face went white. She slumped into a chair, cradling her stomach in her arms. Seeing her sister's fear made Annie angry at the unknown man beyond the door. "I'm going to get the gun," she said.

What she would do with the gun, Annie didn't know. She had never shot it. She hadn't even ever loaded it. But she knew that holding it would make them both feel safer. The girl ran across the wood floors into the family dining room where the gun hung over the fireplace. By pulling a chair over and standing on tiptoes, she was able to reach it. The powder horn and bag of musket balls hung on another hook.

Dragging her blanket behind her, Annie carried the gun back to the parlor. When Patsy saw it, her eyes widened in fear. "You don't know how to shoot it, Annie. You'll kill us both. Put it away."

Her younger sister shook her head. "I've seen the boys do it. It can't be hard. And if he comes in, we have to do something," she argued.

Before the older girl could say any more, Annie drew out a ball from the soft leather bag. Then opening the gunpowder, she tapped a little into the musket's priming pan, as she had seen her brothers do. Her hands shook as she poured the gunpowder, spilling some on the floor. Next she poured a little more powder down the barrel of the musket, wondering as she did so whether it was enough. Finally, she dropped the ball down the barrel. It was at that point that Annie realized she had left the ramrod, a thin pole used to force the ball and powder deep into the barrel of the musket, in the dining room. Laying the musket down, she hurried to get it.

There was silence as Annie got the ramrod, and she wondered if the man had gone. But the silence was short. As she passed through the hallway, the doorknob began to twist. The girl froze, unable to move, but the door held. With a sigh, she went back into the parlor, where she found Patsy still in shock. Ramrod in hand, Annie held the gun tightly between her knees with the barrel up and rammed the pole in. The musket was loaded.

Patsy had watched all this without speaking, but now that Annie had loaded the gun, she began to cry. The younger girl wanted nothing better than to throw down the gun and run into her big sister's arms. But she knew now was the time to fight.

The central hall ran from the front door to the back, and Annie sat down on the floor halfway between the two doors. The hallway was dark; the candles had been blown out hours earlier, and Annie knew she didn't dare relight them. So she sat in the dark on the cold floor, where every sound seemed loud and where the frigid air cut through her thin nightgown, chilling her to the bone.

When her back grew stiff sitting one way, she shifted her position. All the while, she prayed, "Dear Lord, keep us safe," holding the heavy musket, ready to fire. Finally, she could stand the waiting no longer. She crept to a window, loosened a shutter, and peeked out. The night was still dark, but the rain had passed, and by the moonlight Annie saw two figures come towards the house at a run. Then she heard a yell, saw a flash of light, and heard the explosion of one musket followed by another.

From the parlor, Patsy screamed, and Annie aimed the musket at the backdoor. There was more pounding; only this time the voice that went with it was familiar. William! With relief, Annie ran to the door and swung open the latch.

William, water dripping down his hat and coat, brushed past his sister into the hall. "Are you both all right?" he demanded.

Annie's voice shook. "Yes."

"Where's Patsy?"

"She's in the parlor," the girl answered.

William ran to the parlor and found his older sister sobbing on the settee. "It's all right, Patsy," he murmured. "It's over. No one will harm you now. Try to get some sleep," he commanded gently, pulling the blanket over her and turning again to his little sister. "I have to go help John. You stay here with her; do you understand?"

Annie nodded solemnly. The boys were gone about thirty minutes, and then John returned, ashen-faced. As he removed his wet coat and boots, he tried to keep his face hidden from Annie, but she saw his shaking hands and red-rimmed eyes.

"Where did the man go?" Annie whispered.

William, who had come in behind John, answered, "He won't bother you anymore. Tell us what happened."

Annie recounted the night's terrors as her brothers listened. William's face was grim, and he glanced several times at John who stared at the floor. Once Annie thought her younger brother was going to speak. He lifted his head, but only a sob came forth.

"What's happened?" Annie demanded when she could stand it no longer.

"We saw him from the distance, but when we shouted, he turned and fired his musket. John fired back and hit the man. He's dead," William added.

For John, the effort to hold back his tears was too much. Rasping sobs shook his body, and he said over and over again, "I never meant to kill him."

William patted his brother's arm. "You did what was right, John. Father would be proud of you."

"But I killed a man," the boy sobbed.

"You were defending your family," William answered.

"Why couldn't Pa be here?" the weeping boy asked.

William said softly, "Come, brother. It's been a long night. And tomorrow will be a long day. Let's see if we can get some sleep."

7

An Early Arrival

John Fontaine arrived home two days later and found Scotchtown in confusion. The slaves had been put on alert for other trespassers, and John and William kept the house under close guard. William had even ordered a cast-iron bell to be hung near the porch so that his sisters could ring it in an emergency.

Patsy had taken to bed amidst worries that she might lose the baby. When Annie tried to cheer her up by talking about planning a party to celebrate the birth, her older sister shook her head. "There are more important things than parties," she said, echoing her father's words without realizing it.

The responsibility of protecting the household seemed to help John recover from that night, but Annie didn't have anything to take her mind off those nightmarish memories. She found herself afraid to go outside alone and jumpy if she had to cross from the house to the kitchen or her father's office. She hated the hours she spent alone because that's when she imagined what might have happened if her brothers had not come home.

Under John Fontaine's calm guidance, Scotchtown returned to order. One day, not long after his return, Annie found Patsy lying in her dimly lit room. Annie settled herself into a chair near the bed, feeling better just being with someone else. That's when she saw Patsy's face tighten in pain and beads of perspiration dot her lip. After a few seconds, the pain seemed to pass, and her sister opened her eyes.

"Patsy," Annie asked, "whatever is the matter? Is it the baby?"

Smiling wanly, Patsy replied, "They've been coming like this for hours. You've got to find my John. Is he home yet?"

"He's home, but I can't leave you like this."

As the older girl lay there, her hand clutched the blanket, and her jaw tightened as she held her breath through the pain and then relaxed. Opening her eyes, she whispered, "Please, Annie. Hurry."

Annie dashed from the room onto the porch. Desperately scanning the yard for her brother-in-law, Annie saw no one. Then she remembered the bell. She rang it furiously until one of the cooks appeared at the kitchen door.

"What's wrong, Miss Annie," she asked.

"The baby is coming," Annie answered. "We must find Mr. Fontaine and Martha, and I can't leave here." Annie heard her voice crack over the words.

"We'll find them. Don't you worry, Miss Annie. Go on and stay with Miss Patsy."

Annie hurried back to the darkened room where she found Patsy dozing fitfully. She prayed as she sat by the bed, knowing there was nothing else she could do. "Please God, let the baby be born well, and keep Patsy safe," she whispered.

The half hour before John Fontaine came seemed like an eternity to Annie. Every move that Patsy made, every groan, brought fears of immediate birth and possible death. But finally he arrived, and Annie sighed with relief. "You're here."

He stood awkwardly at the door, his hat in his hand, his farm boots still muddy from the field. "Is she all right?" he whispered worriedly.

"I think she's sleeping," Annie said softly. "Sometimes she groans, but otherwise she's quiet."

"Do you think she can hear me?" he asked.

"Come, sit by the bed and talk to her," Annie urged. "I'll go and wait for Martha. Will she be here soon?"

"I don't know." John Fontaine sat gingerly on the side of the bed. He held his wife's hand and smoothed her damp hair back from her forehead.

There was nothing for Annie to do but wait. Finally she saw Martha making her way slowly across the yard to the house, weighed down by the heavy satchel that she carried in one hand. The girl ran to meet her.

"Will Patsy be all right?" she cried. "Isn't it awfully early for the baby to come?"

Wrapping one bony arm around Annie's shoulders, Martha said, "You let Martha do the worrying. I ain't lost a baby yet, and I don't intend to start now."

Annie looked at Martha's well-worn, wrinkled face, which spoke of many years' experience. The girl relaxed. Martha was in charge, not Annie. All would be well.

They had reached the house, and Martha released Annie. "Take my satchel inside and then fetch me some some water and rags." When Annie hesitated, Martha shooed her away. "Go on, child. Hurry. It will be hours before this baby comes, but we want to be ready."

Annie had been gone only a short time, but when she returned to Patsy's room, it looked different. Patsy was propped up by pillows in her bed. Sunlight flooded in through opened shutters, and a cozy fire blazed in the fireplace. John Fontaine had been sent outside to wait.

Martha busied herself in one corner. When she saw Annie watching, she put her to work bathing her sister's face with a cool cloth. Throughout the day, Patsy labored. The pains came more frequently and with greater strength, but still the baby was not born. Annie began to worry. Would the baby never come?

She whispered that question to Martha during one of the periods between pains, but the nurse just smiled. "Things are going fine, child. Now go see if you can't make Miss Patsy more comfortable."

Shamefaced, Annie returned to her sister's side. She mopped Patsy's forehead with a damp cloth and rubbed her lower back as Martha had shown her. Just then Annie's stomach grumbled. She remembered that she hadn't eaten since breakfast, more than eight hours before. Timidly, she looked at Martha and mouthed the words, "I'm hungry."

The old woman nodded. "Go get some food. We don't want you to faint from hunger."

"I'll bring back something for you," Annie offered.

She found her brother-in-law pacing in the hallway and reassured him. "She's fine, Martha says." Outside in the yard, her brothers were pitching horseshoes. They looked up when Annie came out. "Just getting food," she said. "Nothing's happened yet."

In fact, nothing happened until early evening. Annie did her best to make her sister feel comfortable, but still Patsy cried out with pain. Finally, there was a shout, and the nurse said, "Here it comes!" The next thing Annie knew there was a baby lying in Martha's arms. The old woman wiped his face with a damp cloth, thumped his bottom, and out came a forlorn little cry. Then she lay the little boy on his mother's stomach.

He was the tiniest little thing that Annie had ever seen. His skin looked too big, and it hung in wrinkles around his ankles. With his feet tucked under him, he looked no bigger than a hand. The minutes after the birth were full of confusion. Patsy laughed and cried as Martha washed her face and dressed her in a fresh nightgown. She looked delightedly at the little boy who now lay in her arms, wrapped in blankets. "Just look at him," she whispered. "Isn't he beautiful?"

Martha gave Annie a poke. "Don't just stand there, Miss Annie. Go tell Mr. Fontaine that he has a beautiful son," she ordered.

John Fontaine stood right outside the door. "I heard the cry," he said. "Are they both well?"

"It's a boy, and they are both just fine." Annie grinned. "He's little as a peanut and red as a beet, but Patsy says he's beautiful, so I guess he must be."

John slumped down in a chair, exhausted. "Thank You, God," he prayed.

"Aren't you going to come see?" Annie asked.

"May I come now?"

"Martha said to get you, and whatever Martha says, goes," the girl said with a smile. "Come on. Patsy is waiting for you."

Annie felt out of place in the happy birthing room. Being on the outside felt funny, as if she had just taken part in a miraculous event and then been shoved to the side.

"I'm being silly," she told herself later that night when the feeling came over her again. She had been lying in bed for hours, too tired to sleep. Every time she shut her eyes, her mind would start working, and then she'd be wide awake again. One minute she was reliving the night with the drunken man, the next she was feeling sorry for herself because Patsy was now the center of attention. As much as she tried to squelch the feelings, they kept popping up.

With relief Annie saw the first rays of the sun. Morning: Now she wouldn't have to pretend to sleep anymore. She crawled from her bed and splashed her face with water from the wash basin.

Her brothers already were seated at the breakfast table. John speared a slice of ham as Annie came into the room. "'Morning," he said. "Cornbread's hot."

Annie took a seat at the long trestle table and looked without interest at the food. "I'm not very hungry," she said.

He smiled. "That leaves all the more for me." He stabbed another piece of ham. Annie grabbed a piece of cornbread and nibbled on it. She grew aware of William staring at her.

"Why are you staring at me?" she demanded.

"Just thinking."

"What does that mean? Thinking about what?"

"About teaching you to shoot a gun," he said.

Annie looked with surprise at her brother. It was unusual for a girl, at least one who lived on a plantation, to know how to shoot. Afraid to show any eagerness, she asked, "Why?"

"Simple," William replied. "We can't always be close to home. When spring comes, John Fontaine, John, and I will be off in the fields. Patsy will be busy with the baby, and we can't leave you unprotected in the house."

"But there are always people around," Annie stated.

"That's true. But Lord Dunmore has encouraged the slaves to revolt—to leave their masters and to join with the British. Our people seem loyal, but we can't be certain they will stay if trouble comes."

"Does Patsy know?" Annie asked.

"How could she know? She's just had a baby. We aren't going to trouble her about something like this."

That made sense to Annie. John had kept quiet during the discussion, and so Annie turned to him. "What do you think?"

He shrugged. "Shooting isn't everything, but sometimes it's necessary. Better that you know how, I guess, than to be defenseless. But Pa won't like it."

William looked impatiently at his brother. "Pa doesn't have to know. Besides, he's in Williamsburg, and we are here. We have to do what we think is right."

Biting her lip, Annie looked at her big brother. "Will you tell Father what happened?"

He returned her glance, then turned away. "John Fontaine doesn't think it wise. What can Father do? We will write and tell him about the baby, but that's all."

Annie could see the sense of it, but an uneasiness settled over her. There was sure a lot going on at Scotchtown that Patrick Henry didn't know about, but there wasn't much she could do about it. Eager to change the subject, she asked, "When do we start?"

"Today. Let's go to the woods, and we'll teach you to load this old gun," William said.

"But I know how," Annie reminded him. "Remember, I loaded it when the drunken man was here."

The brothers looked at each other skeptically. Then John spoke. "We think the gun was already loaded. When we get to the woods, you can show us how you think it works."

John grabbed the musket, and the three set off down the road to the woods.

8

The Lesson

They followed the path that meandered through fields, past slave cottages, finally passing through a tall beech woods. Upon reaching the woods, Annie stopped for a minute, letting her eyes adjust to the shadows. Turning toward her brothers, she held her hand out for the gun. "May I load it now?" she asked.

William and John stood and watched, prepared to tease their sister if she loaded it wrong. She sat down on a log, laying the gun over her knees.

"You don't sit down to load a musket," John laughed, but Annie ignored him. She made sure that the gun would not slide, then opened the powder horn, and gently tapped its edge against the priming pan. When that was done, she sprinkled more powder into the barrel. Then, standing up, Annie leaned the musket against her leg while she bent to get the ramrod. She looked at her brothers, who were watching carefully. With a flourish, Annie pushed a musket ball and some paper down into the barrel with the rod.

When she had finished, she fixed a challenging stare on her brothers. "Well?" she asked. "Did I do it right?"

John looked surprised, but William smiled broadly. "That's great, Annie. Looked like a girl doing it, but at least you got the job done." Then pointing at a tree, he said, "Go ahead, Annie, shoot at that tree over there."

Annie raised the musket to shoulder level, trying to hold the long gun steady. After sighting down the barrel, she pulled the trigger, and the musket came to life, knocking Annie down on her backside. John and William hid their smiles behind their hands. "That's good," John said.

"Make sure you plant your feet," William added, wiping his eyes.

Annie picked herself up, brushing the dry leaves off her skirts. She rubbed her shoulder and asked, "Did I hit the tree?"

The boys grinned. "We forgot to look," William replied.

John ran over to the tree. He searched the scarred trunk of the old beech, but could find no evidence of the musket ball.

Annie shrugged with disappointment, and William patted her awkwardly on the shoulder. "That's fine, Annie. It was your first shot. By the end of the day, you'll be shooting like a drilled militiaman." Then he scratched his chin. "I have an idea. Sometimes people learn to do something best on their own without teachers hanging over their shoulders. John and I want to make you a challenge."

John looked at his brother curiously. William continued, "No sense in wasting ammunition by shooting at trees. Maybe you should have to get us dinner. A couple of squirrels or doves, maybe an opposum or a raccoon. What do you say? You get us dinner, and John and I will admit that you're a good shot. Do you accept the challenge?"

Annie knew that William was laughing at her. But she took the challenge anyway. "It's a deal," she said. "I'll be back at dinnertime—and I'll have something for dinner, or . . ." She paused. "Or . . . or I guess you'll go hungry tonight," she finished lamely.

"No. If you don't bring back dinner, John and I will think of a punishment. Come on, John, let's leave Annie to her hunting."

Annie watched her brothers walk out of the beech woods. So much for shooting lessons. Now she was left with the problem of what to do. "Load the gun, you ninny," she scolded herself. After she had reloaded the gun, she felt more confident.

The woods were quiet except for the occasional squirrel's chatter or bird's song. It made her nervous to be alone in the woods for such a long time. What if there were bandits or outlaws? What if there was another angry loyalist? She thought she heard a musket shot, then another. Each time she felt more nervous. Suddenly, the hours before dinner seemed endless, and Annie wished she was back in sight of the house. Without thinking, she began to run, eager to put the shadows of the beech forest behind her.

A noise! Were those footsteps?

She swung around but saw nothing. Then, grabbing her skirt, she ran again. Behind her she heard the crackling of pine needles. Darting behind a tree, she turned to face her pursuer, but the woods were quiet. Annie could hear only her own rasping breath and the sound of her heart pounding in her ears.

It was not more than twenty-five paces to the clearing. Grabbing the hem of her skirt in her hand, she ran for the the light, not once turning to see who was behind her. Branches reached out, scratching her arms, and a log rose up to trip her. She stumbled but did not fall. When she reached the field, the sun welcomed her, and she stood under its warm rays until her legs stopped trembling, and she could catch her breath. It was then that Annie realized she still clutched the musket in one hand and her long skirt in the other.

She stared at the gun for a minute, then slowly brought it up to her shoulder. It felt too heavy, and her arm trembled under its weight so that Annie could not aim it. Nonetheless, she stood facing the woods, ready, she thought, to shoot her pursuer. She stood there for a minutes until she heard a voice behind her.

"What are you doing?"

Annie turned with a start. "Don't scare a girl like that," she yelled at a puzzled-looking Andrew Thacker. "I could have shot you."

The girl still held the gun to her shoulders, but now it was pointed shakily at Andrew, who held his hands up in front of his face as if to ward off a musket ball.

"Well, put it down, Annie. Don't you know guns are dangerous? Who gave you that musket anyway?"

Annie, breathing heavily, let the musket down to the ground. "I'm sorry," she said. "I didn't mean to point it at you, but there was someone in the woods."

Andrew looked as though he wasn't sure whether or not to believe her. He had heard the story about the intruder at Scotchtown as had just about everyone in the county, and now he figured Annie was imagining things. "You were just spooked, more than likely," he said. "I don't see anyone there."

Annie turned back toward the woods. "But I know

someone was there," she insisted. "When I ran, he ran. When I stopped, he stopped. I heard it with my own ears." She knew she sounded shrill, and she could tell from Andrew's expression that he felt sorry for her. That only made her angry. "Don't be feeling sorry for me," she demanded.

"I've got to get back to work," Andrew said, pointing at the field behind him. "Will you be all right now?"

Still clutching the musket to her side, Annie nodded. Her eyes took in the field where Andrew had been working. It was pitted where stumps had been, and their remains littered the field. The oxen were chained to a stump where Andrew had left a long metal bar sticking up out of the ground. Still nervous, but not wanting to admit it, Annie tried to prolong the conversation. "What're you doing in the field?" she asked.

"Remember the plot of land Pa gave me?" Andrew asked with a grin. "Well, this is it. I guess it's part of the land we bought from you last year. Anyway, Pa said I should clear it, and maybe next year it'll be ready to plant."

"Next year. Isn't that a long time?" Annie asked, amazed that it could take so long to get a field ready for planting.

Andrew grinned. "Feels like forever, but I can only work on it after I do my other chores. This field looked like those woods before I cleared it. Now I've got to remove all the stumps. Ain't easy," he said shaking his head. "I have to get back to work. Pa still keeps a pretty close eye on me."

"Go ahead. I'm sure whoever it was is long gone by now. I've got to get back to the house anyway," Annie said, all thoughts of bringing back dinner gone from her head.

She walked along the edge of the woods, feeling safe because she knew Andrew could still see her. As she turned back to watch him, she heard a noise coming from the woods on the right. Before she could scream or raise the musket, her brother John stumbled out in front of her.

"What do you think you're doing, John Henry?" the girl demanded. "Was it you who was chasing me? Was it? 'Cause I don't think it was a bit funny."

Her brother looked at her sheepishly. "I didn't mean to scare you," he said. "I changed my mind about leaving you alone, but when I came back, you seemed so skittish I thought I'd play a trick."

Though his words sounded apologetic, Annie could see the beginnings of a grin forming on his face. She was not going to let him off the hook. "You know I almost shot Andrew. I could have killed him, just because you scared me," Annie scolded.

"Well, you didn't," John replied.

"But I could have."

Annie began walking briskly toward home, and her brother hurried to keep up with her. "Don't you think I should get some credit?" he asked. "Didn't I come back?"

Annie turned on her brother, her face crimson with anger. "You scared me half to death, John Henry. That's what you did." Then she began to cry, which only made her angrier. She knew she looked ridiculous standing out in the middle of a wheat field with musket in hand, arms scratched and dress torn, glaring at her brother, who looked close to tears himself. She tried to nurse her anger just a little longer, but suddenly the situation seemed so silly that Annie began to giggle. What started as a small giggle grew into a roar, until she was bent double with laughter. John stared at her with a worried look.

Annie saw it and swallowed a new wave of laughter long enough to say, "I'm fine. Really. Everything just seemed so silly all of a sudden."

John gave her a questioning smile. "So you aren't angry anymore?"

Annie shook her head as she wiped tears from her eyes. Then she began to giggle again. "What am I going to do about dinner?"

Looking at Annie, the musket, and the empty game bag, John laughed. "I can help you there. Come on. Let me show you how to shoot that gun." The two walked in companionable silence, John pointing out the squirrels and Annie refusing to shoot them. When they were about 100 feet from a wheat shock, John turned to Annie and said, "Shooting isn't that hard. And you don't really have to be able to hunt in order to protect yourself. It would be better if you could hit a target like that wheat. Go ahead, shoot and see if you can hit it."

During the next hour, Annie practiced shooting and loading the musket until her shoulder was so sore she could barely lift her arm. She rubbed it and winced as her fingers touched her tender skin. Peeking under her sleeve, she saw an ugly bruise beginning to form.

Looking up at his sister, John noticed her pained expression. "I should have warned you about the gun's kick," he said. "That's why we wear a jacket or a vest when we're shooting." The sun was getting lower, and the wheat shocks began to cast long shadows in the field. "Time to get back," he said. "William will be waiting for you."

"But what about you? Aren't you coming back?" Annie asked.

"Not with you. William will think I'm weak if he knows I helped you. You'd better go back alone."

"A lot of help you've been," Annie grumbled. "I still don't have anything for supper."

John grinned. Reaching around his back, he pulled out his own game bag. In it were two squirrels. "I shot them before I came back to you," he said. "Thought you might need them."

Annie pulled back from the limp bodies that John held in his hands. "Poor things," she sighed.

"Oh, Annie," John reasoned, "God gave us these squirrels to eat, just like he gave us pigs. I don't see you giving up your ham and bacon."

"Well, you put them in my bag. I don't want to touch them." Annie held out the bag to John. Once the squirrels were in the bag, the two set off. John walked with his sister until they were in sight of the house; then he ran around the back way.

Annie went straight to the barn. There she found William as she expected. She handed him the game bag without a word, turned, and marched out of the barn. John, who entered the barn just as she was leaving, winked as she passed by.

William must have seen the wink because Annie heard raised voices, and the next thing she knew, William was chasing John out of the barn. When he saw her, he turned and began to chase her toward the house. Annie ran quickly, but her long skirts got in the way. Besides, William was much bigger and stronger. He caught up to her on the steps leading to the backdoor and pulled her down until he had pinned her to the ground. Annie gasped for breath as William rubbed dried grass in her hair.

"Stop, stop," Annie shrieked. "Let me catch my breath."

Just then the door opened, and they heard a deep voice. "Since when do near-grown boys knock young girls down to the ground?"

William climbed to his feet looking shamefaced. "Mr. Dabney," he blustered, "we were just playing."

Scrambling to her feet and brushing off her skirt, Annie felt her face burning with embarrassment, but the tutor was not looking at her.

"I think, Master William," Dabney said with a touch of sarcasm, "you would be better served if you concentrated on your schoolwork. I know it is late—nearly dinnertime, I believe. But I'd like to see you in the schoolroom. Now." Then he turned and walked away, fully expecting William to follow.

William scowled before following the tutor to the classroom. John raised his eyebrows in an imitation of the tutor and said to Annie in his best adult voice, "And you, my dear, would be best served by concentrating on dinner. I expect to see you in the dining room. Now."

With laughter, they went in to eat.

9

On to Williamsburg

The baby, Benjamin, grew fat over the remainder of the winter. No longer did his skin seem too big for him. He lost his baby fuzz, and the hair that replaced it was thick and curly. He had big brown eyes and a smile so broad it caused his cheeks to dimple and his eyes to squint. When Patsy was tired, Annie watched him. He couldn't yet crawl or sit, but he laughed when Annie acted silly, and she loved him.

But Benjamin was winter's high point. Otherwise, it was a lonely time. Patsy was devoted to her husband and her baby. She no longer sat around thinking about clothes and scolding Annie. Now she lived and breathed baby Benjamin and John Fontaine. John and William found endless ways to keep busy outside, and they made it clear that girls were not welcome.

Patrick Henry stayed in Williamsburg all winter. He hadn't come home for Christmas, and, because of the baby being born, the holiday had slipped by without anyone taking any note of it, leaving Annie feeling sad and neglected. If only Father could come home.

That didn't seem likely. The letters from him were few and far between. One reason was the weather. It was harder for post riders to move the mail during cold and rainy weather. To Annie it seemed as though her father had forgotten them, and though she knew he hadn't been told about the night with the drunken man, she still felt like he should have known about it somehow. If he really loved her, wouldn't he know when she was in trouble?

In late January, the weather broke. The temperature warmed to the sixties, and the air had the soft feel of spring. Stepping outside into the warm weather was like an invitation to play. Annie went to the stable and had Joseph saddle her horse.

As she rode away from home, Annie felt her spirits lift. For the first time since the drunken man had come and since the baby had been born, she felt free and unafraid. She rode farther and farther from the plantation, crossing the familiar pastures and fields, now brown and dead. A few scrawny cows grazed there. An occasional deer, looking for food, crossed her path.

Annie wasn't certain when the idea formed in her head. But she had been riding for little over an hour when she made up her mind. If Father would not come home, she would ride to Williamsburg to see him. The day was clear, the temperature mild, and her horse was full of energy. Nothing stood in her way.

As if the horse could sense her excitement, he picked up the pace until Annie was flying over the fields. She let him run for ten minutes before reining him in to a trot. "Don't want to get tired, boy," she said. "We've got a long way ahead of us."

By noon, Annie's stomach began to growl, and she realized that she had neither food nor money. She felt a twinge of alarm, but it passed quickly. After all, she was Patrick Henry's daughter. It should be no problem getting a meal at any house she passed. Virginians were known for their hospitality. Annie could remember any number of travelers who had been fed and given shelter at Scotchtown.

Her stomach growled again; so Annie began to look for a house. Finally, on a small rise, she saw a cabin about the size of the Thackers'. Annie walked the horse up to the front porch. She tied him to a post and knocked at the door. It was answered by a young woman, maybe Patsy's age, holding a baby in her arms. A blond-haired toddler peeked out from behind her skirts. The woman looked surprised.

"Hello," Annie greeted her. "I was wondering if you might be able to give me a bite to eat."

Although Annie had heard many travelers make that request, she had never done it before. Somehow it seemed embarrassing. It was like begging. She blushed and looked away.

The woman smiled and opened the door wider. Behind her was a single room with a table at one end and a bed and cradle at the other. Dried herbs hung from the beams, and a loft held barrels, probably filled with apples and potatoes. The table was set, and the smell of fresh-baked bread filled the room.

"My name is Abigail Byrd," the woman said. "My husband, Nathaniel, will come shortly for lunch." She paused, and Annie realized with embarrassment that she was expected to introduce herself.

"Um, I'm Annie Henry," she said. "I'm on my way to Williamsburg."

"Williamsburg! Why, that's a far piece. And you're all

alone?" Abigail exclaimed. She set the baby down on the bed and beckoned the girl over to the table. Then, picking the little boy up and carrying him over, she set him on the bench and placed a plate of dried apple slices and hot corn bread before him.

Annie watched while she performed these tasks. Abigail's mousy hair was pulled back into a simple coil at her neck. Her face was freckled as though she spent too much time outside without a bonnet, and her hands were rough from work. But she had a nice smile and clear gray eyes. She reminded Annie of Mrs. Thacker, except Abigail was younger.

Having settled the boy, Mrs. Byrd turned her attention to her guest. "I don't mean to be nosy," she said, motioning the girl to sit at the table, "but what is a young girl doing going to Williamsburg?"

"I'm going to see my father," Annie answered.

"And he's in Williamsburg?"

"Yes."

"Does he know you're coming?"

Annie avoided Abigail's eyes. "Not really."

"Hmm," Abigail said. "Let me guess. Your father is Patrick Henry. He's been very busy, and he doesn't know you're coming."

"That's right," Annie admitted. "But he'd be happy to see me. He's been away for so long. I know he misses us."

"Of course he does," Abigail said. "But won't your folks at home worry about you?"

Annie felt a twinge of guilt. They would worry about her. She knew they would. Why hadn't she thought about that earlier? She chewed her lip. Just then the door opened. A stocky, bearded man came into the room. Abigail rose to meet him. He handed her his coat, which she hung on a hook next to Annie's. She whispered something to him, and Annie saw him glance in her direction. He was big, much bigger than Father, and seemed to fill the room. His hair had been blown by the wind, and it stood in unruly tufts on his head.

After he had removed his boots, he strode over to the table where he towered over the young girl. Holding out his hand, he said, "I'm Nathaniel Byrd. Welcome." Then he sat down.

Abigail set the bread, dried apples, and ham slices before them. They prayed and began to eat. The man, obviously hungry, ate and ate. When he had finished, he leaned on both elbows and stared at his young guest. She blushed and looked away. "Why don't you tell us about yourself?" he invited.

Annie took a deep breath and began. They were such good listeners that she found herself telling them about the past year, about her mother's death, her father's absences, the drunken man, Patsy's baby, and the lonely winter. While she spoke, Abigail moved to a rocking chair where she nursed the baby and put him to sleep in the cradle. She cleaned up the little boy and laid him on the big bed before slipping back to the table.

Finally, Annie finished speaking. "That's quite a tale, Miss Henry," Nathaniel Byrd said. "I know, as a father, that I wouldn't want a child of mine to go to Williamsburg on her own. It's dangerous."

Annie started to speak, but Nathaniel held up his hand. "I ain't got the authority to stop you, but at least spend the night here. I know it's only midday, but there's rain coming, and the creeks can get riled. It wouldn't be safe to go on tonight. This way, you'll have a dry place to stay and can leave at first light."

Without waiting for a response, Nathaniel rose to his feet. He nodded at Annie, kissed his wife, and pulled on his coat. "It was a pleasure to meet you, Miss Henry. But I have to get back to my work," he said. "Stay as long as you like with us."

"Thank you," Annie said.

When he had gone, Abigail cleared the dirty dishes. "Let me just run out to get some water from the well," she said. "You rest for a minute."

The couple was visible outside the window. Mrs. Byrd lowered the bucket into the well and pulled it up again, dumping the water into a kettle that she had carried out with her. Nathaniel joined her and they talked, glancing at the house. Then Annie saw Abigail nod and Nathaniel walk away. In the west, a line of gray clouds appeared, and the wind began to pick up. A dead leaf, pushed by the wind, skipped across the dry ground.

When Abigail returned to the house, she set the kettle over the fire. "Nathaniel took your horse around to the barn and gave him some oats. The rain is coming up fast. You will stay, won't you?"

Annie sighed. "I guess I'd better. Do you know how much farther to Richmond?"

Abigail picked up some sewing from her basket and began to work, glancing up at Annie from time to time as she sewed. "It's several hours in the best of weather. With this rain, it could be longer. The roads will be muddy and the rivers swollen. One river has no bridge or boat. You'll have to cross on horseback."

"Then it must not be deep," Annie said.

"That's true," Abigail admitted, "except when there's

rain. Then the river swells terribly. Takes hours to drop. That's why Nathaniel wanted you to wait." She turned her face back to her sewing.

Annie felt jumpy. Sitting still was hard to do. She wanted to go, but she knew that wouldn't be wise. She walked over to the window. The sky was dark in the west, but the storm still looked miles away. Should she try to get to Richmond before the storm? Annie didn't know. She came back and sat down in front of Abigail.

"From Richmond, I just follow the river to Williamsburg, right?"

"That's true, but if the water's high, you won't be able to follow the river very closely. There'll be flooding."

"Well, then, I could take a boat," Annie said, remembering all the boats she had seen docked in Richmond.

Biting her thread as she peered at Annie, Abigail nodded. "Yes, there are boats. But have you ever considered the kind of man who is likely to be on a boat? They are often rough and mean. They spend their time on the sea, without people about. They aren't to be trusted."

"But last year a very nice captain helped me in Richmond," Annie protested.

"Oh, I'm not saying there aren't nice and decent boatmen. But they are rare. And what if you get on board with one who isn't so nice?"

Annie chewed her lip, as she often did when she was nervous. If what Abigail said was true, then she shouldn't go on to Williamsburg. But she had come so far. How could she turn back now?

Abigail must have seen her indecision because she said, "I'm not trying to discourage you from seeing your father. But you've bitten off a big mouthful, and we'd hate for you to get hurt."

"I know you mean well," Annie said. "But now I don't know what to do. I feel like if I don't see Father, I will explode. I just have to go. I really can't wait." She ran out to the barn.

Abigail came after her. She wanted to stop Annie, but seeing the determination in her young face, she said, "At least take some food and a coat. If it rains, you'll be cold. And come back if you have difficulty."

Annie nodded. Now that her mind was made up, she wanted to leave. While Annie saddled her horse, Abigail fixed a bag with food and water and brought out the coat.

"I wish you would stay," Abigail said. "Won't you?"

The woman looked so worried that Annie hugged her tight. "I'll be fine, really," she said as she mounted the horse.

It was a cold wind that nipped at the girl's cheeks as she rode. Glancing over her shoulder, she saw the Byrd farm grow smaller and smaller and the lone figure of Abigail Byrd fade from view. Annie felt tears come to her eyes, and her throat burned. She let the horse run, not caring that the wind was raw against her tear-streaked cheeks.

Annie came to a river. She reined in the horse and surveyed her options. The river was too wide to cross at this point; so she explored the bank in both directions. Finally, she found a place where the river narrowed to about twenty feet. She edged the horse down the sandy bank. He put one hoof into the water and stopped. She urged him forward into the swirling water with gentle pressure from her knees. Immediately, her skirts were wet, and the icy coldness of the water took her breath away. Still she urged the horse on. Reluctantly, he stepped forward until he reached the middle of the river where the water came to his shoulders. Then he stopped.

Despite Annie's urging, the horse would not go forward. He moved nervously in the water until Annie, frustrated and cold, kicked him hard. The horse reared back, tumbling his rider into the water. Although the creek did not appear swift, there was a rapid current under the surface, and Annie could feel herself being pulled along. Her skirts and leather boots, heavy with water, weighed her down. The numbing cold of the water made her sleepy. *If I could just close my eyes a minute,* she thought.

Then she felt the strong body of the horse next to her. Rousing herself, Annie reached out an arm and grabbed the rein. She struggled to keep her head above water as the horse pulled her back toward the bank. At last, feeling the solid ground under her, she scrambled up the bank and flopped on the ground.

For a long time she lay there, too exhausted and scared to move. Finally, though, she roused herself enough to look around her and then fell back in frustration. The horse had taken her back to the near bank of the river. She still had to cross it if she wanted to go to Williamsburg. She began to cry.

Red-eyed, she wiped the last tears away. Using the wet skirt of her dress, she blew her nose. Then she mounted the horse and turned back toward the Byrds. The wind blew fiercely in her face. It pressed Annie's sodden dress against her like an icy skin. She kept her head down, letting the horse pick his way back. Soon she felt the first pinpricks of rain. Each icy drop felt like a needle jab. Reining in the horse, Annie pulled on the oilcloth coat that Mrs. Byrd had lent her. It kept the rain off her dress but couldn't do anything to make her dry and warm. On they traveled until in the distance she saw a light.

As if sensing warmth, shelter, and oats, the horse picked up his pace, galloping the last fifty yards through the mud. Annie prayed that he wouldn't twist a leg or fall. The Byrds must have been expecting her. As soon as she arrived, the door opened, and Nathaniel carried her into the cabin.

While he took care of the horse, Mrs. Byrd removed Annie's wet clothes, wrapped a warm towel around her, and put a cup of herb tea before her. "You silly girl," she said in a voice that was comforting, not scolding. "We were worried sick about you."

Too tired to speak, Annie took the tea and drank it gratefully. Then Mrs. Byrd dressed her in a nightgown that had been hanging by the fire. Its toasty folds of fabric warmed the girl's skin as she lay down on the bed to sleep.

10

Father Returns

When Annie awoke, she found herself in a strange bed in a strange house. She looked around and saw the plain, well-scrubbed trestle table and benches, the empty crib, and the herbs hanging from the ceiling. Yesterday's memories came flooding back.

Outside, the sky was a deep blue, but moisture on the window meant it was cold. Annie quickly slipped into her dress, which she found hanging near the fire. Its fabric felt stiff, but it was warm and dry, and that's what mattered.

She found Abigail in the yard and the two children bundled under a bear rug in the wagon with only their faces exposed to the sun. The woman turned when she heard Annie, and a broad smile spread across her face.

"Good morning, Annie. How are you feeling today?"

"Much better, thank you," Annie said, glancing over the bright landscape, her eyes taking in the startling blue sky and the iced-over wagon ruts and hoofprints. Abigail's cheeks were rosy, and her eyes glowed with good health.

"I'm sorry about yesterday," the young girl said. "I didn't mean to worry you."

"We know that," Abigail reassured her. "Sometimes we all let our hearts rule our heads, but I should have done more to stop you."

Kicking at a skim of ice with her toe, Annie sighed. "Do you think life will always be like this until England gives us our freedom?"

"I don't know. But the wisest thing is to remember what St. Paul said, 'I know both how to be abased, and I know how to abound; everywhere and in all things I am instructed both to be full and to be hungry, both to abound and to suffer need.'"

"What do you mean?" Annie asked.

"I mean that we can't wait for circumstances to be perfect in order to be happy. You've been born to a family that is blessed in many ways, but your father is gone a great deal of the time. You can't say, 'I'll be happy when Father comes home,' because you don't know if he'll ever be home all the time. You need to be content right now."

Annie turned her back so that the older woman wouldn't see her wipe away the tears that trickled down her cheek. "I just want Father to be home. I want a family like yours," Annie said.

Abigail hugged her. "And if you had our troubles, you'd want something else," she said softly. "You'll have to learn that you can't find happiness by getting something. It comes only when you trust God to supply what you need. Now come along to the barn with me. Nathaniel's there with a visitor you'll want to see."

Annie followed at Abigail's side, hoping the large man would not be angry with her. It took her eyes a minute to adjust to the dim light of the barn. When they did, she saw Nathaniel cutting a piece of wood with a saw. Another man sat on a bale of hay nearby. As she drew closer, her heart stopped. The man looked up, saw Annie, and rose to his feet, but before he could stand, she had thrown herself on him.

"Father," she cried, "you did come home!"

Nathaniel and Abigail left the two Henrys alone in the barn. Patrick Henry said in a soft voice, "You worried the whole family, child. What were you thinking?"

"I just wanted to see you," the girl whispered. "It had been so long, and you hadn't come home. And everyone is so busy . . ." She let her voice trail off.

Pulling her close, he said, "I'm sorry, Annie. I have been away too long. Too long for me and too long for you."

"But how did you get here?"

"Nathaniel rode over to Scotchtown to tell everyone where you were. I had just come home. If only you had been a bit more patient, child."

"I'm so sorry," Annie said, hiding her face behind her hands.

"It was foolish, yes," Patrick Henry said. "But good came out of it," he added, his eyes twinkling.

"How?"

"I was beginning to think I was not needed at home."

"Oh, Father, that's not true," Annie protested.

"I know that now, but I had been thinking it. Is Scotchtown being tended to?"

Annie nodded.

"Are you eating meals regularly?"

Again Annie nodded.

"Doing your schoolwork? Getting new clothes? Going to church?"

Annie looked embarrassed.

"Well, then, you see, I figured I wasn't needed," her father said with a regretful sigh. "But now I know better. Come, Annie. We need to say good-bye to these good people and go home."

As they rode back to Scotchtown, Annie listened to army stories. Patrick Henry described the tents set up in rows behind the College of William and Mary and the men—farmers mostly—learning to drill for the first time. But the worst of it was the boredom. For months the army did nothing but drill as they received battle reports from Massachusetts. "Army life is one thing for General Washington," her father said. "It's quite another thing for those of us here in Virginia. And for your poor, old father, military life was nothing but training. I never met the enemy, never engaged the British, and now I've been relieved of my command."

When he said that, Annie's eyes flashed. "What happened?"

"The Continental Congress reorganized the armies. There are no more independent Virginia regiments. Maybe it's not my calling to be a general."

Annie pondered this news. "Does that mean you'll be home more?" she asked finally.

"Yes, unless God has some other purpose for me."

"Won't you miss being a leader?" Annie wondered.

"I love Scotchtown," he answered. "My heart is never so happy as when I'm home under my own fig tree, tending my own land and in the company of my own family."

They rode together in silence. Then Patrick Henry said, "You know, Annie, war is inevitable. The king will not swallow his pride and let us go easily. And it is too late for us to change our minds. We have grown used to making our laws, worshiping our God, leading our lives without interference from the king. He wants to make us a little London, but our ancestors risked their lives to escape that corruption and build a better country here. They came for liberty. Do you understand?"

There was an urgency in Patrick Henry's speech, a passion that Annie recognized, which both excited and frightened her.

"The thought of war scares me, Father," she admitted. "Last year it seemed like an adventure, but now it seems too close."

"Annie," he said, "I wish we didn't have to make these choices. But we know now that keeping our liberty is hard work. It takes diligence and sacrifice. The Henrys have had our share of sacrifice, and God may call us to sacrifice even more."

Finally, Scotchtown came into view. They walked their horses around the house and tied them to a post. Together they walked to Sarah Henry's grave.

"You remind me so much of your mother," Patrick Henry said. Annie nodded, her eyes filling with tears, and he drew her close. "I miss her. And yesterday, when I wondered what had happened to you, the thought that you were in danger was almost more than I could bear. But I have learned that God is able to comfort us in our trouble. Have you learned that, Annie?"

Annie shrugged. She had worked so hard to be strong and brave. She had done so many foolish things. Now she was just confused.

Annie looked up and saw her father watching her, a sad expression on his face. She longed to comfort him, but the words stuck in her throat. Instead, she fixed her eyes on a cluster of boulders near the grave.

She could feel the weight of her father's arm on her shoulder. She heard the gentle tone of his voice. "The only thing that has enabled me to get through this year is the knowledge that God, the creator and sustainer of all things, knows me and cares for me. What a comfort to know that although He knows my sin, my pride, and my anger, He is still my friend and my redeemer."

There was a struggle inside Annie. Part of her wanted to throw herself on her father's shoulder and weep until there were no more tears. But at the same time, Annie wanted to pull away. She wanted to say, "I'm fine. Do we have to talk about this?"

For minutes they sat on the bench, neither one speaking. Then her father told her stories about her mother, most of which Annie had never heard. As he talked, Annie's own memory brought up images, long buried, of Sarah Henry before she was ill. Annie fought to hold back the tears, but that only made her throat ache, and the tears came anyway. She cried on her father's shoulder until she couldn't cry anymore.

When the tears stopped, Annie rubbed her eyes. Her father said, "You can't deal with problems by pretending they aren't there, Annie. Take them to God, because He is your only comfort in life and death."

Annie felt tired; so when her father said he had to go to work, she just nodded and watched him walk back toward the house. Then she prayed.

That night Annie understood for the first time the story of the Prodigal Son. Instead of scolding, she received hugs. That evening after a feast when the remains of a half-carved roast and a small ham sat on the table, Patrick Henry looked around at his family.

"I heard an interesting tale as I rode home this trip," he began. "It was about a family hiding a terrible secret. Something about an intruder and a death."

As Patrick Henry spoke, he looked deliberately from one to another. Annie squirmed uncomfortably under her father's stare, but she didn't speak.

At the other end of the table, John Fontaine cleared his throat. Annie saw Patsy squeeze his hand and nod encouragingly.

"Father," he said, "you have heard correctly. We did have trouble a while back, but it seemed at the time the best part of wisdom to keep the knowledge from you. I thought that the news would distract you from your other duties, but I was wrong. Please forgive me."

"Thank you," he answered. "There is no duty more precious to me than the duty to care for my family. If by my absence I've conveyed something else, then please forgive me." Then, breaking the somber mood, he pulled out his fiddle. "Let not our hearts be troubled. This is a joyous night. We are all together, and tomorrow we'll have all the time in the world to talk."

11

The Birth of Liberty

It was May, a year after the gunpowder incident. Annie was nearly twelve. Early one morning she walked down to the barn to go riding. There she found John in a panic. Joseph, the slave who tended the horses, had taken the wagon into town. Marie, the gentle saddle horse that had belonged to Mrs. Henry, had been in labor all night and was about to give birth. She lay heavily on her side, her belly bulging with foal. Tiredly, she picked up her sweat-soaked head and strained before dropping it once again to the straw-covered ground.

"What's wrong?" Annie asked. Even her hushed voice seemed too loud.

"The foal is in a breech position," John explained. "Feet first, and the cord is wrapped. They'll both die if the foal doesn't turn." John crouched by the horse's head, sponging her off with a warm wet rag. "Come on, girl," he whispered to the horse. "Come on, girl."

With every contraction, the foal was thrust more firmly into its deadly position. All that was visible were the tips of the foal's hooves struggling without success to be free.

Annie felt herself cheering on the mother. "You can do it," she whispered. But the horse had no strength. The mare groaned, a shudder wracking her body before she fell still. John knelt over the animal, listened for a heartbeat, then rose wearily to his feet. "I'm afraid she's gone. She just plumb gave up."

Annie started to cry. "Isn't there a way to save the baby?"

John was suddenly energetic again. "We could try." After a moment's hesitation, he looked at Annie, saying sharply, "Get a knife, a sharp one."

Annie quickly came back with the knife. Then she watched, unable to look away, as John sliced open the mare's belly and removed the still-breathing foal.

John moved swiftly to remove the bloody mucous from the foal's nose and mouth. He looked up, a bleak expression on his face. "He's not breathing."

But Annie didn't want to give up. "Keep rubbing," she urged him, grabbing a rag and rubbing the back and legs of the colt. Tears streamed from her eyes until she could not see, and yet the two continued to labor over the colt. Then Annie felt a shudder. She wiped her eyes and saw the colt's chest heave, his head shake, and then he came to life, struggling to stand on his spindly legs.

"Yes!" Annie cheered softly.

John rose wearily to his feet, wiped his bloody hands with a rag, and grinned at Annie. "We did it," he exulted. "We really did it."

Together they watched the colt take his first tentative steps. He looked like brown velvet with white boots and a white blaze marking on his head.

"If only Father could see you now," Annie said proudly to her brother.

John blushed. Then he looked at the dead mare. "Let's cover her up," he said. They found an old cloth in the barn and placed it over the mare. They then turned their attention to the colt.

"How will we feed him?" she asked.

"We'll have to bottle-feed him," John replied. "Unless we can find a mare who will adopt him." His face brightened. "I think the Thackers just lost a foal. Maybe their mare would do. I'll go ask Andrew after we fix up a bottle."

"How will we make a bottle?" his sister asked.

"You get a bottle from the kitchen. A tall narrow one," he added. "I'll see if I can find a piece of leather to make a nipple."

Annie brought back the bottle, which they filled with fresh milk. They then took the piece of leather, tied it to the bottle, and poked a hole in the end. Annie held the makeshift bottle up to the foal. Clumsily the colt nudged the bottle, unable to grasp the nipple in his mouth. As he butted the bottle with frustration, it wiggled back and forth, always just out of reach. Annie wanted to give up, until she remembered what she had learned about milking cows: You can't blame the cow if the milker is clumsy.

Her brother frowned. "Annie, you must hold the bottle still. Put it between your body and your arm. Like this," he said while demonstrating. "Then it won't move on the colt."

Annie tried again, wedging the bottle against her body with her elbow, the nipple jutting forward. Gently, John nudged the colt forward, guiding his head until the colt, smelling the milk, grabbed the bottle in his mouth. Annie felt a tug, but she held on tight. The colt played with the leather nipple for a minute until he got the hang of it; then he drank thirstily.

"He's drinking." Annie smiled. "He's really drinking."

"That's fine." John nodded. "You're doing real fine, Annie. Do you think you can do this several times today until I get back from Andrew's with the mare. That means you must stay right here with the colt," he said, fixing a serious glance on her.

Without hesitation, Annie nodded. "I can do it," she promised.

"Let's move the colt," he said, nodding towards the dead mare. "We'll put her at the other end of the barn."

Annie led the way, using the milk bottle to encourage the still wobbly colt forward.

When the colt had finished the bottle, John took it from his sister. "You must wash the bottle before using it again, or else the sour milk will make the colt sick."

Annie nodded solemnly. When he had gone, she settled herself on the hay near the colt. "You'll need a name," Annie said to him. "It could be something like Brownie or Butterscotch. But those names are so ordinary. You need something special." For the moment, though, Annie couldn't think of anything.

It was past noon when Andrew finally came with the mare. Annie had nursed the colt three times and was tired, but she had not left. Andrew spoke softly to his horse, rubbing her chestnut mane with his one hand while he tightly held the reins in the other. He urged the mare over to the colt, and Annie gave the foal a push toward the mare.

For a minute the two horses sniffed each other curiously. Then the foal smelled the mare's milk and began nuzzling until he grabbed onto a teat and began to nurse noisily and hungrily. Annie grinned, and Andrew, seeing that the mare had adopted the colt, let go of the reins.

"They'll be fine together," he said as they walked from

the barn. Annie nodded. For a minute they were both silent. Then the boy let out a whoop.

"What's that for?" Annie asked, staring at her friend. "You look like the cat who swallowed the canary."

The boy had a pleased expression on his face and a look of pent-up excitement. He didn't answer but kept looking at Annie as if to say, "I know something you don't know."

"Come on, Andrew," the girl urged, "tell me. What's going on?"

"Race you to the house," he challenged. "If you win, I tell you. If you don't, you'll have to hear the news some other way."

Annie took off running as soon as she heard the word *race*. She could hear Andrew's heavy step right behind her, but she kept running, swinging her arm to the right to keep Andrew from passing.

She reached the back stairs of the house half a step ahead of him and sat down with a plop. "Now tell me."

He sat next to her, breathing heavily and laughing. "You cheated. Tried to trip me with those big skirts of yours."

Between breaths, Annie gasped, "I have to run with them. All you have to do is run around them. Now tell me."

"The reason I was so late getting the mare over was that Pa had me go into Hanover to pick up something at the tavern."

"And that's the news?"

"No, silly. The news is what I heard when I was there."

"So what was it?"

"You are kind of impatient, Annie. Don't you know that patience is a virtue."

Annie glared at Andrew, then burst into laughter. "Okay. You tell me when you're good and ready. I have all the patience in the world."

"That's better. Well, the news is . . ." Andrew's soft voice rose to proclaim loudly, "VIRGINIA HAS DECLARED HER INDEPENDENCE FROM ENGLAND!"

Annie's eyes grew wide. "Are you serious? Is this true?"

"Yes, it's true. And there's more."

"What?"

"Your pa is the new governor—governor of the independent colony of Virginia."

Annie gave Andrew a hard stare. "My father? Governor?"

"Yep," her friend answered with a grin. "Patrick Henry, governor of Virginia. And in a few weeks the Continental Congress will do the same. You'll see. They'll write a Declaration of Independence, and then we'll be free."

Looking about at the home she loved, its white walls standing in gleaming contrast to the green fields all around, Annie shook her head. "We won't be free," she said slowly. "But our fight for freedom will have begun."

Annie had mixed feelings. Patrick Henry would be distracted from his family once again, but the job had to be done. Patsy now had a baby, Andrew had made a field, John had birthed a foal, and she was growing up too.

Then shaking off the serious thoughts, she smiled. "I now know the name for the colt. Father said we would see the birth of liberty, and I guess we just did. Liberty. That will be his name."

Annie Henry and the Mysterious Stranger

For
The Hahns: Paul and Fran
Thank you for your faithfulness.

Contents

1

An Accident

From her seat in the family carriage, twelve-year-old Annie Henry watched the countryside roll by. The pitted road was in spots little more than two worn wagon tracks through the sun-baked fields. On either side were thick stands of corn, wheat, and tobacco. Houses were few and far between and sat back far from the road.

Mile after boring mile the coach lurched along on its way from Scotchtown, the Henrys' home, to Williamsburg, the capital of Virginia. It was early September of 1776, and Patrick Henry, the newly elected governor of Virginia, was returning to the capital after a summer of serious illness. The doctors, uncertain of the diagnosis, had used all the tools available to them. First believing the problem was sick blood, they attached leeches to his skin to suck the "sick blood" out. When he did not get better, they gave him doses of awful medicine. Finally, they threw up their hands and did nothing. At that point, he began recovering.

Now her father was strong enough to travel, but as he lay across from Annie in the coach, she could see the toll his illness had taken. He was thin and pale and even now, after all these weeks, a violent cough sometimes shook his thin body, causing his forehead to bead with sweat. Then Annie would dip her handerchief in the jug of water she carried and mop his forehead.

For Annie, this was only her second trip away from Scotchtown, and it was the first time she had ever lived outside rural Hanover County. She left behind an older sister, Patsy, and Patsy's family, as well as three brothers and a younger sister. Thinking about them brought quick tears to her eyes. *It will be lonely in Williamsburg,* she thought.

For the week before leaving, ever since Patsy had decided Annie must go to take care of their father, Annie had felt queasy in her stomach. She knew she wasn't sick, but her stomach felt topsy-turvy, and she had to force herself to eat. Sometimes she woke up at night and could not get back to sleep. It did not help when her older sister tried to comfort her with advice not to worry about tomorrow—today had enough worries of its own.

Now here she was, alone except for a sick father and Phillip, the driver, journeying through this unknown territory. Phillip had assured Patsy that they would stop at an inn to sleep, but Annie still felt uneasy.

She stuck her head outside the carriage window. Still no sign of Richmond, their next stop, and the pink horizon behind them warned that sunset was near. Suddenly the carriage jerked forward as the horses galloped crazily from side to side.

"Whoa," the driver shouted.

Annie clutched the leather edge of her seat. Across from her, Patrick Henry's head bumped the wood-paneled wall of the carriage, jerking him awake.

"Runaway horses," Annie whispered.

"Pray, Annie," he whispered, closing his eyes.

For several desperate minutes the horses ran out of control while the driver struggled to halt them. Then, just as suddenly, the carriage stopped, shuddering violently before tilting dangerously to one side.

Inside the coach, the wicker picnic basket slid across the floor. Annie screamed as her father rolled off his seat, hitting his head sharply on the floor. She scrambled to his side, holding her breath as the coach rocked. He appeared dazed but was able to lift himself back onto his seat.

"Are you all right, Father?" she whispered.

He nodded his head, but then closed his eyes and seemed to drift off to sleep. Annie sat there anxiously. Should she stay near him or climb out of the carriage and look after Phillip? She sat still for a moment, thinking through her options, but the deepening shadows told her the sun was setting rapidly, and soon they would be in darkness. At least Annie could light the carriage lanterns before that happened.

Because the carriage was partly on its side, one door was pinned shut by the ground. Slowly she inched her way across the seat until she could reach the handle of the other door. She turned it and pushed the door open. Then, putting her hands on both sides of the opening, she pulled herself through. From her perch on the edge, she leapt to the ground, holding her breath as the carriage rocked and then settled back into its unsafe position.

"Phillip?" she called.

There was no answer, and Annie feared the worst. She circled the carriage and saw, lying against a tree, the shaken but conscious driver. He was rubbing his forehead where she could see a black-and-blue lump already forming.

"What happened?" she asked.

"I don't know. Those crazy horses . . . I don't know what spooked them. It almost sounded like a gunshot, but it couldn't have been. Not way out here. Anyway, they've gone and broke the wheel clear in two. Let's see about the axle."

Bending down, he looked under the carriage. Then standing up, he brushed the dirt off his hands. "Axle looks fine," he announced. "That's luck for you."

"Or God's providence," the girl whispered. "Can you fix the wheel?"

"There's a spare on the back," he said. "But I'll need help to raise the carriage. You aren't big enough, and your father isn't strong enough. We may have to wait until daylight, then I can ride for help."

At those words, Annie let the tears flow that she had been trying desperately to hold back. The driver reached out awkwardly to pat her arm. "Don't cry, Miss Annie," he pleaded. "We'll be safe here. Why, we must not be more than an hour from Richmond. There won't be no trouble, and you can sleep comfortably in the carriage. Please don't cry."

Phillip's words shamed the girl into silence. But she trembled when she thought of spending the night out in the dark countryside.

"What about Father?" she asked.

"Was he injured?" Phillip asked, a worried expression on his face.

She bit her lip uncertainly. "He banged his head hard and then drifted off to sleep."

"Sleep is the best thing," Phillip nodded in reply, relieved that his poor driving hadn't injured the governor.

"Couldn't we light the lanterns?" she pleaded as she looked around at the deepening shadows.

"Sure. That's a good idea. Then I'll unharness one of the horses and ride back to those woods and gather some wood. We'll need it for a fire."

"But," Annie protested, "you wouldn't leave me here alone. Why do we need a fire? It's warm out."

"You ask too many questions," Phillip said, annoyed at her chatter. "Let me go to work. Without a fire, who knows what kind of animals we'll have creeping about."

Annie bit back her reply. She wouldn't let him see how frightened she was. "At least leave me the musket," she requested.

After he finished lighting the candle inside one of the carriage lamps, he lowered the glass. The flame flickered, then glowed. Its soft light brightened the area around the carriage, putting Annie a bit at ease. She watched as he unhitched the horse, saddled it, and tied the other lamp to its saddle. "I won't be long," he said.

She carried the musket over to a tree about twenty feet from the road. Its low-hanging branches made it perfect for climbing, and she tied her long skirts out of the way and scampered up. By now it was pitch dark, except near the carriage where the lantern softly glowed. Annie felt fairly safe in her hiding place. She kept her eyes on the road Phillip had taken, wishing he would return.

She must have dozed because the sudden sound of horse hooves jerked her to attention. *Can it be Phillip already?* she wondered. Peering through the gloom, her eyes picked out a heavyset figure on a dark horse. *It can't be Phillip,* she thought. *He's not nearly that big.*

She drew the musket a bit closer to her. "I never loaded it," she groaned. Had Phillip done so? She watched as the rider got off his horse some distance from the carriage. He walked silently toward the disabled carriage, looking about him secretively. *He means no good,* Annie thought, pulling back against the trunk of the tree.

"Please, don't let Father wake up," she begged. "Let him be quiet."

In the light of the lantern Annie thought she saw a glint of silver. Was it a knife? She held her breath, uncertain what to do. In the dim light she knew she had little chance of hitting the man even if the musket were loaded. It would be better to wait until she knew her father was in danger before even trying to shoot. So she held still.

Closer the man crept toward the carriage until he came to a stop before a dark shape on the ground. Then, as the girl watched, he held out a long dagger and bent down toward the shape. She leaned forward in her branch trying to see better what he was doing. There was a tearing sound as the man struggled with the dark object. *The trunk,* Annie thought. It had come off the carriage during the accident. She could see now that he had forced open the lid and was rummaging about, throwing clothes this way and that as he searched for anything of value. Several times he paused, looked around and listened intently before continuing his work. When he had finished at the trunk, he rose and began to walk over to the carriage where Patrick Henry slept.

Annie's finger tightened on the trigger. The heavy weapon trembled in her sweaty hand, and she prayed that she wouldn't have to use it. When the man reached the carriage, he started for the door. Abruptly, though, he turned and pulled the lantern from its hook. Using the light, he returned to the trunk and continued his search. She watched him pocket several small items. Money probably, and maybe her father's silver buttons. When he finished, he once again crept toward the carriage, carrying the lantern in his hand.

The wind blew, and a broken branch fell from Annie's tree. The sound it made as it rustled through the limbs and crashed to the ground startled the girl. The highwayman paused and stared directly at her hiding place. She froze, certain he could see her. As he stared, he held the lantern a little higher so that Annie, for the first time, caught a good glimpse of his face. He was a heavy man with a fleshy face and thick neck. His small, deep-set eyes were almost swallowed up by his puffy eyelids.

For a minute the two were frozen in a silence. The stillness was broken by the sound of Phillip's horse. Louder and louder came the hoofbeats as the horse drew nearer. Silently—and quickly for such a big man—the highwayman rose and ran to his horse. He seemed to melt into the darkness, disappearing without a trace, with only the sound of his retreating animal.

"Who goes there?" Phillip shouted when he heard the other rider. He rode into the circle of light and seemed to hesitate. Should he follow the highwayman?

When Annie saw that it was Phillip, she shimmied down the trunk of the tree, ignoring the pain as the rough trunk scraped her legs. "Phillip," she screamed as she ran toward him. By this time he had dismounted his horse and was examining the mess before him. There lay the ransacked trunk with the broken lock. Shattered lantern glass glittered on the ground.

"What happened here?" Phillip asked, his face white. "Your father . . . ?"

"It was a highwayman," Annie whispered in a trembling voice. "I hid in a tree."

"Let's check on the governor."

Together they walked to the carriage, and Phillip lifted the slender girl until she could peek through the door. Her father still slept, his chest gently rising and falling.

"Now tell me about this man," Phillip asked, looking about nervously. "Was it one or a gang?"

"Just one," Annie said. "He tethered his horse a ways from the carriage and walked over. Then he broke open the lock and took some things from Father's trunk."

"Did he have a gun?"

"Not in his hand," she answered. "Only a dagger. What do you think he would have done if you hadn't come back?" she asked.

"Only God knows," he replied nervously. "But I wish we could go on tonight. I wouldn't have expected highwaymen to be operating so close to Richmond. Have we lost all respect for the law?"

"At least let us make a fire," the frightened girl begged. "I have had enough surprises tonight. I don't want to meet a bear."

Immediately Phillip set to work building a fire, and soon the flame burned brightly, sending little sparks drifting up into the sky. Although the night was hot, Annie shivered. Even the hot fire couldn't seem to warm her.

Looking up from his work, Phillip shouted at the girl. "Get back from there. All we need is for your long skirts to catch fire."

She drew back and looked at the driver apologetically. She knew he felt extra concern because she was there.

"I want you to get back in the carriage," he said after

he had picked up the scattered contents of the trunk. "Your father will feel better knowing that you are safe inside."

With his help, she climbed back into the carriage. Her father roused himself momentarily. "Why haven't we fixed the wheel?" he mumbled.

"It's too heavy for Phillip to manage alone," she answered. "We'll sleep here tonight, and he'll get help in the morning. Richmond isn't far." Annie spoke soothingly, knowing that her father was still dazed from the accident. "Sleep now, and in the morning we'll be able to continue our journey to Williamsburg."

Although her father soon slept, Annie could not. She tossed and turned on the uncomfortably tilted seat. Sometimes she felt herself drifting off, but then the howl of a wolf or the hooting of an owl startled her awake. Once she peered out of the carriage and saw Phillip on guard, puffing his pipe and holding the musket on his lap.

It was the sound of birds singing that Annie heard first. She opened her eyes sleepily and looked about the cramped carriage. Her father was sitting up on his seat. Although he looked gray and weak, she was glad to see him awake. Before she could speak, though, she heard the sound of horses. Holding her breath, the girl put her finger to her mouth in a warning to her father to be quiet.

"Hello," a voice called out. "Do you need help there?"

It was a friendly greeting, and Annie relaxed, but her father shook his head. Even highwaymen could pretend to be friendly. Why didn't Phillip answer?

She heard the scuff of a boot on the dry ground and then a hearty laugh. "Startled you, didn't I," the stranger said. "I saw the smoke from your fire and thought I might get some food. I didn't expect to be put to work this early, but I'm glad to help."

From Phillip came a groggy response, and Annie guessed that he had been found sleeping.

"I'm Spencer Roane," the stranger said.

Annie saw her father smile.

"It's okay, daughter," he assured her. "Mr. Roane is a law student in Williamsburg. We'll be safe now."

2

The Governor's Palace

With Mr. Roane's help Phillip was able to fix the wheel, and soon the carriage was on its way. When the law student realized who was inside, he became excited. Riding his horse alongside the coach, he leaned down to talk to the governor.

"We are so glad that you are well," he said. "There has been worry that you might not come back. Many, including Mr. Jefferson and Mr. Madison, feared that without your leadership, the factions would not hold together."

Annie listened to them with one ear. She was glad to see her father sitting up and taking an interest in the world about him. Talking politics with this young man seemed to energize him. The two men ignored her; so she turned her attention to the countryside. From the window, she caught glimpses of the river—probably the James—and saw the tips of white sails against the blue autumn sky. War seemed far off in this peaceful setting. But then she remembered the highwayman and realized that it wasn't. She listened to Mr. Roane's news.

"I've been riding from Philadelphia," he said. "The news from New York is not good. General Washington has been fighting valiantly against General Howe on Long Island. But Howe's massive numbers forced Washington to retreat to Manhattan. They believe further attacks by the British are coming."

"How are his troops holding out?" Henry asked.

"There are many deserters—boys who joined the militia for adventure but were not prepared to fight," Mr. Roane replied. "Others have already fulfilled their terms and are ready to leave. If we don't send Washington more soldiers and food and the clothing to supply them, we will surely lose this war."

The words were grim, and the mood turned somber as the carriage rolled into the outskirts of Williamsburg. Once into the safety of the town, Mr. Roane said goodbye and spurred his horse on, eager to get to the Raleigh Tavern to spread the news.

By now they had entered the town, rolling past the red-brick buildings of William and Mary College, past the Bruton Parish Church. The carriage slowed and turned. Patrick Henry said, "Look out your window."

Annie looked. In front of her was a long tree-lined green. Looming at the end of it was a large two-story brick mansion behind a tall brick wall. "That's our home, Annie," her weary father said.

Annie gazed at the mansion in silence wondering, *Will Williamsburg ever be home?*

When Annie awoke the next morning, she was in a bed in a strange but beautiful room. She looked about at the green-flowered paper-covered walls and at the three tall windows that lined one side. From her canopy hung green and purple flowered curtains that matched the coverlet on her bed.

A wardrobe filled one wall, and a small table with two chairs sat in a corner. Annie climbed down from the tall bed, using the step stool that stood next to it. She opened the wardrobe and saw that all her dresses had been hung neatly. On the washstand was a pitcher of water. She stuck her finger in; it was hot. Pouring a bit into the washbowl, Annie washed the road dust off her face and neck. She brushed her hair and tied a ribbon in it.

After dressing, Annie opened the drapes and saw that the windows all overlooked the green. From her perch she could see the comings and goings of all the people who had business at the governor's palace.

Eager to explore the rest of the house, Annie opened her door and slipped out into the hallway. Her father's room was across the hall, but Annie didn't want to bother him yet. Instead, she ran outside where she found the kitchen and scullery. There slaves were already busy washing dishes. There was a bathhouse and a smokehouse, and a livery where two men were already working on the damaged carriage. Smoke billowed from the chimney of the blacksmith's shop. Behind the walls of the Palace, a small village existed. Almost everything the governor needed was produced on his own land.

Slaves watched the young girl curiously as she ran from place to place. Children giggled and pointed at her. There was so much to explore that Annie wished her brothers were there to enjoy it with her. She knew Edward would like playing hide-and-seek in the wine cellar. From behind the kitchen, she caught a glimpse of the canal and knew that William and John would be fishing this minute if they were here.

A grumbling in her stomach led Annie back indoors. She found that a table had been set for her in the dining room, and she ate breakfast alone, something she had never done at Scotchtown. Even though she didn't have to fight her hungry brothers for the last biscuit, Annie found her food strangely tasteless. "I'd rather have less and be with my family," she said to herself, "than to have all these riches and be alone."

"I won't go!" Annie insisted. "I didn't come to Williamsburg to go to school."

From the bed where Patrick Henry lay came a deep chuckle.

"But, Father, I've seen those city girls at church. They are sillier than our cows back home, and to think of having to spend every day at school with them . . ."

Annie sat down on one of the chairs that had been left behind when the last royal governor, Lord Dunmore, had escaped out the backdoor of the Palace, fearing for his life. Dunmore had the misfortune to be the king's representative in 1776, just at the time that American colonists were ready to throw out British rule.

Annie's father sighed. "Maybe I should have left you home," he muttered.

"But, Father," the girl protested, "you know you were too weak to come back to Williamsburg alone. Patsy and the doctor wouldn't have stood for it. But they warned me how stubborn you could be."

Another chuckle came from the area of the canopied bed on which the sick governor lay.

A week had gone by since the Henrys' arrival in Williamsburg. From the first, Patrick Henry had talked about sending his daughter to school. But Annie had protested. Now, however, thinking her father's mood had softened, the girl leaned forward to state what she thought was her best argument against going. "I can't very well take care of you if I'm at school all day, can I?" Leaning back in the chair, she crossed her arms and waited for her father to give in.

But when the governor spoke, it was only to say, "Well, lass, the matter's already settled. I've paid Mistress Hallan your first month's tuition. You start on Monday." Before Annie could protest, her father yawned. "Not now, Annie," he said. "I have to rest. Please close the door behind you."

Annie stared at her father, not really believing that the argument was over just like that. Without a word, she rose from the chair and left the room, banging the door closed behind her. She stood for a minute just on the other side of the door, debating whether it was worth trying one more time to get her father to change his mind. She stood in a large open room at the top of the stairs where royal governors had entertained visitors. It was a gloomy place with dark walls that matched Annie's mood.

The floor smelled faintly of lye soap, and wet patches near the walls gave evidence that it had just been scrubbed. The girl walked across the room to the door of her own bedroom, scuffing the soft leather soles of her shoes against the floor's planks.

Coming to Williamsburg to nurse an ill father had been one thing; going to school with city-bred ladies was another. She stormed into her bedroom and threw open her wardrobe doors. The sight did nothing to cheer her up. There hung the little frocks she had worn for years at Scotchtown. But now she saw them with Williamsburg eyes, and she knew they were out of style. If she were to wear them to school, she would be marked as a baby and a country girl. Proud as she was, Annie didn't think she could bear the ridicule.

Tears of frustration welled in her eyes. From the Henrys' high-backed church pew, Annie had seen the young ladies in their hoop skirts and satin dresses. They seemed silly, and Annie didn't want anything to do with them. And most especially, she didn't want to go to school with them.

She rubbed away the tears savagely. "You're twelve years old," she said to herself. "Too old to cry."

Just then, outside the door, Annie heard footsteps. Smoothing her hair, she turned to face the door, trying to rub away every trace of tears. There was a knock and then Mr. Goodacre, the butler, said, "Mr. Thomas Jefferson is here to see Governor Henry. Is your father well enough for visitors?"

Annie opened the door. "My father was just taking a nap," she said. "Perhaps it would be best if you told people that Father would only receive callers in the morning. He seems much stronger then."

With a nod and a bow, Mr. Goodacre turned and went back downstairs. Annie slid quietly across the floor and leaned over the bannister to get a glimpse of the famous visitor. In the reception room downstairs, the tall and handsome Mr. Jefferson talked earnestly to Mr. Goodacre. As Annie leaned over to hear what they said, her foot caught the hem of her dress, and she stumbled. Catching herself, the girl looked down just in time to meet Thomas Jefferson's gaze. He winked before turning to leave.

With cheeks blazing, Annie rushed back to her room.

It was bad enough to be clumsy and almost fall down the stairs. But to do it when a man like Thomas Jefferson was watching. And for him to know that she had been eavesdropping. Annie shuddered and burrowed her head under her pillow.

3

Mistress Hallan's School

Monday dawned bright and cold. Annie had wanted an earthquake or a tornado—anything to keep school from meeting. But she was disappointed. Now she was on her way to the dreaded destination. Under the yellow canopy formed by the towering catalpa trees that lined the Palace green, Annie shuffled her way to Mistress Hallan's. Her boots kicked up the dried leaves that had gathered in the gutter along the side of the road, and her thoughts turned toward school. Even thinking about entering the strange classroom set Annie's stomach churning. She thought for one panicked moment that she was going to be sick right there on the green. But the queasiness passed, and the girl plodded on, her boots clip-clopping along the cobblestone road.

When she reached the corner of Duke of Gloucester Street, Annie looked wistfully back at the Palace. No familiar face stood at the gate watching and waving. With a sigh she crossed the busy street, careful to step around the piles of horse manure. Mistress Hallan's little house was on Queen Street, just around the corner from Duke of Gloucester, no more than three minutes away, but Annie managed to walk so slowly that she didn't arrive for fifteen minutes and was late.

She knocked hesitantly and then waited. Eventually the door was opened by a maid, who silently ushered the nervous girl into the parlor.

In a minute, a stern-looking woman entered and looked pointedly at the mantel clock. "Ten-fifteen," she said. "My school is run on time, even for the governor's daughter."

Annie blushed and whispered an apology. The sour-faced teacher nodded and led her charge into the school room. Five pairs of eyes looked up as Annie entered. She knew right away that she was all wrong for this school. She looked like a country cousin amidst all the city finery. Though she had thought it wouldn't bother her, she found that it did. She was suddenly self-concious of the cut of her dress and the style of her hair.

For a minute she wished she could disappear, but then she heard a soft voice in her head telling her to stand up straight and be proud. She was the governor's daughter. So Annie did. She smiled stiffly, the way she had practiced in her bedroom whenever she imagined herself a queen, until each one of the girls was forced to smile back.

Mistress Hallan interrupted this silent ritual. "Let me introduce the other young ladies. Letitia Gray," she said, pointing to a pretty girl with her hair piled six inches higher than her forehead. "The governor's daughter, Annie Henry."

The girl nodded and Annie winced, fearing the mass of hair would fall into her face. "Next to Letitia is her cousin Diana North," the teacher added, as a white-capped young lady in a satin sack dress looked up. "Diana is related to a cousin of the king. Isn't that so, Diana?" The girl nodded, barely able to restrain the pride that showed on her face. "And this is Grace Jones," the teacher went on. "Grace's father is a very prominent attorney in Williamsburg," she added with an anxious smile at the tall girl, who nodded at Annie.

After the first three girls were introduced, Annie noted a change in the teacher's attitude. "This is Virginia Galt," she said as she pointed at a pale girl with mousy hair tucked into a white cap. "Her father has the apothecary shop. And this is Kate Marsh." Kate kept her eyes on the table, and Annie thought she heard snickers before the teacher shushed them away. "Hush, girls. Your parents don't expect you to go about snickering."

The other girls settled back to work, and Annie removed her own ink and quill from her satchel. As she readied her paper, she observed the others secretly. All the girls except Kate and Virginia were dressed in fine gowns with hoops, and lace on the sleeves. All the girls wore white caps, except for Letititia, who wore pearls tucked into her tower of hair.

As Annie observed the girls out of the corner of her eye, she found that Diana was watching her. Embarrassed, Annie brought her attention back to her work. She carefully dipped her quill in her ink well and began writing out one of the *Poor Richard* sayings by Ben Franklin: "A stitch in time saves nine."

Over and over each girl formed the words until Mistress Hallan was satisfied that their letters were perfect. Annie had no patience for this kind of careful work. She worked hurriedly, smearing her still wet letters with the side of her hand so that she would have to start again. Sometimes she loaded too much ink on her pen and created an unsightly blob on her paper. The other girls worked quietly and neatly, and Annie could feel her face get hot as she struggled vainly to get one page done without error.

"I guess country girls have no reason to learn to write," she heard Letty whisper to Diana.

Then Diana smiled sweetly at Annie and said out loud, "Don't worry. By the time Mistress Hallan is finished with you, you'll be able to write a beautiful letter. My father already lets me write all his correspondence. But then, the governor probably doesn't need any help from his daughter."

Annie was thinking of a reply when Mistress Hallan interrupted and announced it was time for tea. The girls moved to the dining room where a pot of herbal tea sat on a sideboard along with a tray of small sandwiches and sweet cakes, which a maid served to each young lady. Even during tea, the lessons continued.

"Ladies, when inviting someone of your own station to supper, it is polite to say, 'Sir, you shall oblige me very much if you will do me the honor to take my poor dinner with me.'"

Kate asked shyly, "But why don't we say it plainly, ma'am?"

Diana and Letty, who had been whispering together, looked with exasperation at Kate. "Because we're not plain, Kate," Letty said primly, while Diana giggled behind her hand.

Annie bit her tongue. She wasn't going to get into fights today, but she determined to become friends with Kate, even if it cost her the company of these fine young ladies. Mistress Hallan turned to Kate. "These are rules for polite company. You may never need to use them." Kate blushed a deep red, and the other girls tittered, but the tutor seemed unaware that she had insulted one of her students.

For the next several minutes the girls ate the meal spread before them, conciously keeping one hand in their laps and saying the many polite phrases Mistress Hallan had taught them. When the teacher left the room for a moment, Letitia stood up, glancing around to make sure she would not be overheard by the mistress.

"Young ladies," she trilled in a poor imitation of the teacher, "bite not thy bread, but break it, but not with slovenly fingers." She pretended to stuff food into her mouth.

"Shh. Sit down, Letty, before the old biddy comes back," Diana hissed. But the girl wasn't ready to give up her stage.

"Spit not, cough not, nor blow thy nose at thy table if it may be avoided," she said, daintily wiping her nose with her handkerchief as the other girls roared with laughter.

Grace took up where Letty left off. "Stuff not thy mouth so as to fill thy cheeks," she said, puffing out her cheeks like a little chipmunk. "Be content with smaller mouthfuls." With those words she turned and stared meaningfully at Annie who had just put a small cake in her mouth. All the girls giggled, while Annie tried to swallow the offending sweet. Just then footsteps on the wood floor sent Grace back to her chair.

The girls were choking back laughter when Mistress Hallan returned. Kate, whose back was to the teacher, didn't see her enter the room. She caught the teacher's wrath.

"Kate, it is low to carry on like that at table," the

teacher said with a prim scowl. Poor Kate blushed scarlet again, and Annie squirmed.

With relief, Annie left school at the end of the day. The minute they had been excused, Virginia and Kate hurried out the door. Annie hurried after them but was interrupted by a voice behind her.

"Why are you rushing so?" Grace called.

"I'm just glad to be done, and I do want to see Father," Annie answered.

"Don't rush off. We usually go buy a sweet and gossip for a bit. Will you come?"

Annie could see Letty and Diana standing a few yards away. She felt torn. She knew she should get home to see her father, but she wanted desperately to go. "I guess I had better not," she said regretfully. "Father has been sick, and I should get home to him."

"Oh, come," Grace urged. "Your father has servants who can look after his health."

It took only a little urging for Annie to change her mind. "I'll come," she said. "But I must not stay long."

The girls giggled as they walked along Duke of Gloucester Street. "Why don't Kate and Virginia come?" Annie asked.

"They are lucky to get out of work at all even for school," Grace said with a laugh. "You should see that Old Mrs. Wythe. She keeps a tight reign on Kate. That's why that girl is such a goose. She's afraid her own shadow might jump out and bite her."

"My father says that old Mr. Galt is as tightfisted a man as he ever knew," Letty added. "It's a wonder he lets Virginia go to school. He's certainly not going to let her have a pence to go for a sweet."

Annie was about to tell how she had worked at a tavern the previous summer when Grace spoke again. "Work is so boring to think about. I'm grateful for servants. My mother says that my job is to catch a good husband."

That set all the girls to giggling, and soon they were talking about dresses and dances. It wasn't until the church bell chimed that Annie realized an hour had passed. By then a fall breeze had begun to whip up the leaves along the gutter and send them scudding across the street. Regretfully, Annie looked at the darkening sky. "I really must be going," she said.

"Come again tomorrow," they called out after her.

"I will," she agreed, as she quickened her pace toward home.

4

An Emergency

For several weeks, Annie went back and forth to school. She fell into the rhythms of Mistress Hallan's classroom and learned what was expected of her. And she also learned the rules of Williamsburg society. It was clear that Grace was the leader at Mistress Hallan's. The other girls tried to dress like her. They put on bored faces when Grace was bored. And when Grace suggested a prank, all the girls went along.

Because Annie was the governor's daughter, Grace didn't tease her as much as she teased Kate or Virginia, but Diana and Letty never failed to make snide remarks about her clothes. One day Annie arrived at school just as Kate was setting up her desk. Kate put her small jar of ink on the table and placed her quill carefully alongside her one piece of paper. Annie knew that Kate did not have much extra paper because it was so expensive. Her work was done painstakingly so that every line was used and none wasted.

Once her table was in order, Kate went into the parlor to wait for the other girls. In the meantime, Annie set up her own table, laying out her ink and quill pen. As she worked, Grace rushed through the back door, her long cape flapping behind her. Setting her satchel on the floor, she removed from it two jars of ink. One she placed at her own seat, but the other she put at Kate's. Then she removed Kate's own jar.

Annie gave her a puzzled look but said nothing. *Maybe Grace is giving Kate some better ink,* she thought. Everyone knew that Kate made her own ink with water, ink powder, and vinegar to make it go further. Putting the matter out of her head, Annie followed Grace into the parlor where they had morning prayer and Bible reading.

Several times Annie saw Grace exchange secretive glances with Diana and Letty. When Bible reading had ended, the girls went into the classroom, filing through the doorway one at a time because their hoop skirts filled it completely. Annie dipped her own pen in the ink and began writing, carefully blotting the wet ink so that it would not get on her hand and white cuff.

The other girls seemed strangely quiet, and when Annie looked up, she saw them waiting as Kate dipped her pen into her ink. She turned to see what was so interesting. Kate seemed unaware of the attention. Carefully, she pressed her quill to the paper. With horror, Annie watched as a stain, which looked like blood, spread from the sharpened point of her quill. Kate screamed and threw down her quill, splattering the blood-red ink all over the table. Grace's shoulders twitched, and the other girls struggled to hold back giggles. Then Kate burst into tears.

The noise brought Mistress Hallan, who had been in the parlor, rushing into the room. "What's going on here?" she demanded as she saw Kate crying before her ruined work and the other girls sitting in innocent silence.

"There's blood in my ink," Kate sobbed.

"Oh, nonsense," Mistress Hallan said after gingerly picking up the spoiled paper and sniffing the red stain. "It's nothing but berry juice. Can't you even make a decent pot of ink?"

"But my ink is black," Kate said with an injured look. "This isn't my ink."

"And just whose is it?" Mistress Hallan challenged. "You've made a mess not only of your own paper but of my table as well." The teacher began scrubbing the red liquid off her table, muttering in a voice loud enough for them all to hear. "This is what comes from trying to be generous."

As the mess was cleaned, Kate sat sobbing in her chair. The other girls looked at her awkwardly until Diana snapped, "Hush, girl. Do you want Mistress Hallan to send you home? Then what would Mrs. Wythe say?" The threat of being sent home was enough to silence the girl.

Amidst the confusion, Annie watched Grace who never let on that she knew about the ink bottles. She helped wipe up the mess, patted Kate sympathetically, and made herself useful, until Annie began to doubt what she had seen. Over and over again she played back the scene, trying to make sense of it. Meanwhile, her own work suffered because she couldn't concentrate. Mistress Hallan would have thrown up her arms in complete exasperation if Annie hadn't been the daughter of the governor.

With relief, Annie gathered up her belongings at the end of the day and rushed to be the first one out the door and up the street. Even though she heard her name being called, she didn't stop but walked as briskly as she could towards home. When she entered through the gate, she finally relaxed. At least at the Palace she could count on people behaving normally. Because she didn't want to see anyone, especially not the butler who seemed to stand sentry near the front door, Annie crept around the side of the house until she heard voices and laughter. There, under an enormous magnolia tree, sat Patrick Henry, his head covered with a silk turban, looking a bit like a scrawny buzzard. But what caught Annie's attention was the fact that her father wasn't alone.

At his side sat a young woman who, at that moment, bent forward and whispered something to him. He threw his head back and laughed so heartily that Annie feared he might have a fit. She had never seen her father behave that way. But then as the girl watched from behind the tree, the strange woman reached out her hand and touched his arm. And he kissed her hand. It was so unexpected that Annie almost cried aloud, but she caught herself just in time.

Dropping her satchel on the lawn and kicking off her shoes and stockings, the girl ran past the kitchen to where the garden still flourished despite the changing weather. Rows of potatoes and sweet potatoes, cabbages and brussel sprouts, herbs and other late crops grew on the terraced hillside. Annie skipped down the slope until she came to the pathway that meandered around the banks of a canal.

The trees still wore their fall colors. They rose up in orange and yellow splendor, and their reflections were caught in the calm waters of the canal. Several swans swam toward Annie, expecting to be fed, but she hadn't brought any crumbs with her. Shuffling her feet through the dry leaves, she walked along the bank, stopping now and then to pick up a pebble and try to skip it across the water's glassy surface.

Before too long she was out of sight of the Palace and deep in the woods and gardens that bordered the canal. As long as Annie stayed on this side of the canal, it wasn't possible to get lost. The gardens—and even the woods here—were tame compared to the countryside around Scotchtown. This was the governor's land—and Annie knew it would be a very bold trespasser or poacher who would dare to come on the governor's property.

Just like at home, Annie found the woods to be a comfort. She let herself be soothed by the sound of the wind and the chattering of the squirrels. She followed one path after another, until she was quite confused about where she was. There was a wide path that led from the canal to the side of a hill. There Annie found the icehouse buried in the hillside. The path had been made by servants dragging heavy blocks of ice from the canal in winter to the small building. From the top of the hill, Annie looked down onto a maze sculpted out of boxwood plants, and beyond that she could see the formal gardens nearer the Palace.

Surrounded by the great beauty of the gardens, Annie felt all alone. She had yet to make a real friend in Williamsburg. In fact, the longer she stayed, the less she understood. And now her father, the one person she had thought she could count on, was acting odd. It was too much for the girl to bear. Suddenly, she wanted nothing more than to go riding.

Running back to the house, Annie rushed upstairs and put on a pair of sturdy boots. The sun was low in the sky; so she wrapped a cape around herself and went down to the stable. The governor had many horses to choose from, but Annie asked the groom to saddle a gentle one. She didn't want to be bucked off.

He put her saddle on a small bay mare and helped the young girl mount. "I'd keep off the streets, Miss Annie," he said. "You aren't used to all the traffic."

Annie nodded as she walked the horse to the gate. They picked their way over the cobblestone road at a leisurely pace. Annie didn't want to run until she reached an open field. Once there, she gave the mare its head. For the first time in a long time, Annie felt the rush of the wind against her cheek. She bent low over the horse's neck, letting the animal's warmth warm her skin. Finally, she pulled up on the reins until the horse stopped. She let him graze for a minute while she looked around.

Across the field, Annie saw the college. The tents she had seen when they had driven into town still stood forlornly against the darkening sky. Annie urged the horse on toward them, curious to see what the army looked like up close. As they drew near, she could see young men squatting near their fires, looking tired and dirty. There were no uniforms to be seen, and the men looked too scraggly to be of much use to General Washington or anyone else.

"Hello, ma'am," a young soldier said, lifting his tricorner hat as Annie rode by. She smiled and waved at all the boys who looked so much like her brothers. Some played cards, and a few were tossing a dagger into the ground. A bit away from the crowd, a group of boys about her age were marching. Their leader bellowed at a fellow who lagged behind his companions, "Monroe, James Monroe." Annie watched with amusement as the slowpoke ran to keep up.

She made her way around the outskirts of the camp where she was overtaken by a young man on a horse.

"This may not be the safest place for you to be riding," he said.

"I wasn't meaning any harm," Annie answered apologetically, looking up at him. He looked familiar.

"Of course not. But an army camp is not the place for a young lady, especially one alone. May I help you back to your home?" he asked.

"No, I'm fine," Annie answered, puzzling over where she'd seen him before. "The Governor's Palace is not far, and I have plenty of light. But thank you."

"So you are the governor's daughter?" he said.

"I'm Annie Henry," she answered.

"I'm James Madison," he said, tipping his tricorner hat. "Your father and I have often been allies.

Annie smiled in recognition. Under Mr. Madison's watchful glance she urged her horse back to the Palace grounds. By the time she reached the stable, the sun was setting, and a sharp north wind had begun to blow.

That night seemed long to Annie. She had barely spoken to her father at dinner because he seemed to be thinking about something else. She had tossed and turned all night, finding it hard to sleep. In the early morning she drifted off and then slept too long. When she woke up, she saw that it was late, and she would be tardy unless she hurried. There was no time to say good-bye to her father. Snatching up her satchel, she ran out the gate and up the Palace green to Duke of Gloucester Street. In the churchyard, a deacon talked to a man dressed in black as several slaves labored to dig a grave in the hard soil.

When she arrived at the teacher's house, Annie found the school mistress all aflutter. She looked nothing like the efficient woman of the day before. Today her cotton cap sat crookedly and from under it sprang several unruly clumps of hair.

Kate stood forlornly in a corner, and Annie felt a twinge of guilt as she remembered Grace's cruel practical joke. Because she felt guilty, she didn't go talk to her. Instead, she stood in another corner waiting for the other girls to arrive. It wasn't long before Letty and Diana swept into the room.

"Whatever is the matter?" Diana asked as she looked at her teacher.

"Is it the gout?" Letty asked, not knowing what gout was, but knowing that it made her father terrible to be around.

"Probably dispepsia," Diana whispered.

For some reason, that set the two girls into a fit of giggles, but Mistress Hallan didn't seem to notice.

Letty joined Annie in the corner, but Diana took Mistress Hallan by the arm and urged her to take a seat. "I wish Grace was here," she said. "She'd know what to do."

"Mother always has a cup of tea when she swoons," Letty said. "Why not get some tea?"

Diana looked around for the maid and said sharply, "Please bring a cup of herb tea to your mistress. She is not feeling well."

By the time the maid brought the steaming cup, Grace had arrived. She immediately took things in hand. "What troubles your mistress?" she asked the maid.

"Mistress got a letter this morning and has been acting flighty ever since," the maid answered.

Grace knelt by the teacher's chair. "What has happened to disturb you so?"

"I'm worried," the woman said, barely holding back

the tears. "I've had a letter saying that my mother and sister have come down with the pox. They refused vaccination last year, and now they are both at death's door. I must go to them. Duty requires it. But I don't like to leave my responsibilities here," she whispered, barely able to restrain the tears.

Grace nodded her head. "Of course you must go home," she said. "We don't need to have school until you get back."

The other girls looked at each other, all thinking the same thing: vacation.

Immediately, Diana chimed in, "You must go to your family in their time of need. Wouldn't you agree, Letty?"

Letty had joined Diana at the teacher's side, and the two girls both nodded their heads vigorously. Letty added, "We'll miss you terribly, of course, but there is no other solution. Of course you must go." Then, turning to Annie, she said with a bright smile, "Wouldn't you agree?"

Annie was glad that school would be canceled, but the feeling was followed quickly by shame. How could she rejoice in Mistress Hallan's sadness?

With the six girls twittering about, it seemed certain that someone would faint. But Grace took control of the situation. "Since there's no school today or in the coming weeks, there's no reason for you all to stay here. Letty and Diana, why don't you leave."

Annie could see that the girls were torn. The fun of playing sympathetic listeners had quickly worn off, but the two girls hated to miss anything. Grace understood their hesitation. "Did you see the new hats at the milliner's?" she asked. "There were several pretty ones in the window this morning." She smiled blandly at the girls, who immediately began to put on their cloaks and hoods.

When Letty and Diana had gone, Grace turned to

Virginia. "Go to your father and find out what medicines Mistress Hallan should take with her. Tell him to charge it to my father's account and bring those things with you." When Virginia looked uncertain, Grace gave her a gentle push. "Tell him to send everything that would be helpful."

Now it was just Kate, Annie, and Grace. Mistress Hallan seemed willing to let the girls take charge. Grace looked at Kate. "Have you ever packed a trunk?"

Kate nodded. "I help my mama do it for Mrs. Wythe all the time."

"Then go and pack a trunk for Mistress Hallan. Her girl is not very helpful, but if you take her with you, she can show you where to find things." Kate didn't hesitate. Within seconds she had taken the servant girl in hand and begun the job of packing.

Now Grace looked at Annie, who felt ashamed that there was nothing practical she could do to help. But Grace had other ideas. "Can you run?" she asked.

With embarrassment, Annie said yes. She knew young ladies didn't run.

"Good," Grace answered, obviously pleased. "Would you be willing to run to my house and get a carriage. Mistress Hallan's family lives about fifteen miles from here, and there's no reason for her to rent a coach. My family can spare one. I sent my carriage back home, but if you wouldn't mind going after it, I could finish up here and we would be ready by the time you came back."

Annie hesitated only a minute, but it was long enough for Grace to blush. "I would go myself, you understand, but with these silly hoops, I'm helpless. I just saw that you were more sensibly dressed."

A grin flashed across Annie's face. "Of course I can run," she said, immediately wanting to be out the door. It seemed even more fun because there was something slightly improper about it that appealed to Annie's sense of mischief. "Who would ever connect the governor's daughter to a girl running down the street?" she laughed. "Shouldn't you write me a note?"

"Of course," Grace answered, as she took a sheaf of paper from Mistress Hallan's desk and dipped a quill into the inkstand. She scrawled a note, blotted it carefully, put it in an envelope, and sealed it with a drop of wax. "Just hand this to the doorman. He will know what to do."

Annie had opened the door and was down the stairs before she realized she did not know where Grace lived.

"When you get past the capitol, turn to your right. You will see the Hall in the distance past York Street. If you have trouble, just ask at the gunsmith's. He will help you."

Once out the door, Annie began to run. Instead of going down busy Duke of Gloucester Street, she cut through the gated backyards until she reached Francis Street. She ran past the little houses that lined the street and past the dying vegetable gardens. Several cows grazed in a common area, and the sheep seemed to graze anywhere there was grass. When she developed a stitch in her side, she slowed down to a walk, ignoring the curious glances of the townsfolk who were going about their business. Finally, on the right, she saw the gunsmith. She knocked timidly at the door of the house that was connected to his shop. A white-haired woman answered and pointed the way to the Hall.

Annie walked up the long tree-lined driveway to Grace's house, aware that her cheeks were red and her hair had tumbled out of its cap. She paused near a tree, taking a minute to wipe her face on a petticoat and to smooth her hair. Footsteps on the oystershell drive gave her a start, and she looked up to see a tall, thin man about Patsy's age gazing at her with curious gray eyes. "Good morning," he said in a deep voice. "May I give you some assistance?"

Straightening up, Annie curtsied, feeling the heat rise in her cheeks. "Excuse me," she stuttered. "I'm Annie Henry. Grace sent me to get a carriage for Mistress Hallan who must go home because of the pox." The words tumbled out so fast that they were hardly understandable to the man.

With a small bow, he introduced himself. "I am Spencer Roane, a cousin of the fair Grace, and confused about your errand. But I'm sure that the ever-organized Grace has sent along a message explaining it." He looked expectantly at Annie, who only then remembered the letter she carried in her hand. She held it out to him, and he tore the seal and read it quickly.

"Let us go back to the carriage house and see what is suitable for this trip." He held his arm out to her, and Annie placed her fingers on his elbow as she had seen fashionable ladies do. She almost stumbled over her feet as she sought to keep up with his long stride.

Between Mr. Roane and the groom, a decision was soon made about which carriage and horses to send. Then Grace's cousin, as though realizing he'd had a dreadful lapse in manners, said, "I'm so sorry. I should have offered you some refreshment. Would cider do?"

Annie nodded, unable to utter even the most simple phrases. Never had she felt so tongue-tied as in the presence of this gentleman. He stared at her intently. "Didn't I meet you with your father coming into Williamsburg?" he asked.

All of a sudden Annie recalled the young man who had fixed their wheel and escorted them from Richmond. She blushed as she realized how messy she looked. "I didn't recognize you," she said apologetically.

"Nor I you," he added with a laugh. They stood there awkwardly for a minute before he, sensing her discomfort, abruptly excused himself and walked toward the house.

Soon the carriage was ready, and the driver helped Annie inside. She laid back against the soft leather seat and thought that this carriage, with its polished wood and gold trim, was not the carriage of an everyday lawyer. Certainly Patrick Henry had never owned anything like this.

At Mistress Hallan's they found the schoolteacher out front with her trunk, waiting on the brick sidewalk, Grace at her side. As the driver helped the teacher into the carriage, Annie stood next to her classmate. The teacher waved at the girls as the two black horses, responding to the urging of the driver, set off down the street.

5

Williamsburg

The sun was out; the air was crisp and clean-smelling. And best of all, there was a whole day ahead with no school. "What do we do now?" Annie asked with anticipation as she watched the carriage disappear down the street.

Grace grabbed her hand. "Come with me, and I will show you Williamsburg."

Hand in hand, the girls walked toward the main street, which was filled with carriages and wagons.

"I've never seen so many wagons here," Annie said.

"Market Days are coming next week," Grace answered. "These folks are setting up early to get the best spots."

Indeed, the streets were full of people and wagons. Small boys ran in and out between the carts, causing more than one driver to raise his whip as though to strike the grinning children.

Next to the courthouse there were many bewigged gentlemen. "Court is in session," Grace whispered. "They'll be holding trials for all the thieves and scoundrels." As the girls passed the courthouse, Annie saw a man with his arms and head in the stocks. She turned away in embarrassment as a small boy threw a hickory nut that hit the man on the head.

"What's he done?" Annie whispered.

"Probably public drunkeness," Grace answered.

"Look," Grace said, pointing to a poster that had been hung on a wall. "There will be horse racing and a play called *The Tragedy of Othello*."

"Does your family allow you to go?" Annie asked, feeling every bit the country girl she was.

"Of course. Everybody goes. The town will be so full, there won't be a room in a tavern that's not taken. Papa says that men even share a bed because it's so crowded. Relatives come to visit us from all over. Why, I remember two fairs ago we had twenty-five extra people staying at our house, and they stayed for weeks even though the fair lasts only three days."

"I met one of your relatives," Annie remarked shyly.

"And who might that have been?" Grace asked.

"He said his name was Mr. Roane." Annie couldn't figure out why the tall stranger had made her so tongue-tied.

"Oh, Cousin Spencer. He's awful handsome, don't you think?" Grace glanced at Annie mischievously. "They say he's one of Virginia's most eligible bachelors."

By this time Annie knew she was blushing terribly. To change the subject, she pointed to another broadside. "Look at this," she said, and then began reading the notice:

THURSDAY NEXT, THERE IS TO BE A TRYAL OF SKILL, WITH BACK SWORDS, PERFORMED ON THE PUBLICK STAGE BY TWO GLADIATORS, ONE

AN ENGLISHMAN. THEY BOTH DESIRE SHARP SWORDS, A CLEAR STAGE, AND NO FAVOUR.

"What does that mean?" she asked her friend.

"Oh, it will be sword fighting. Very dramatic, I should think. And there will be crowds of people about the stage, and the men will be wagering."

"But might someone get hurt?"

"I don't think so. I rather think it's a show and the men just pretend to go at each other with swords and daggers. But I'm only guessing. Mother says the outdoor sports aren't for children or ladies. She won't let me go to the cockfights or the bearbaiting either; I've heard they are awfully bloody; so I don't really want to see them anyway."

They'd been so busy talking that Annie hadn't realized they had come upon the Raleigh Tavern. A crowd had gathered in front of the white clapboard building, and Annie and Grace paused to see what was happening. From a small platform, a man held up a clock. Around him, men dressed in wigs stood alongside laborers who wore their own hair pulled back and tied behind their necks, raising their hands and nodding their heads in a kind of silent ritual. Only the man with the clock spoke, and he did so in a singsong voice.

"An auction!" Grace cried. "I do love auctions. Watch how they raise their bids."

Annie watched, and soon she began to understand the meaning of the jerky hand motions. Between items, there was much teasing and joking back and forth, and the crowd of men did not seem to be taking the bidding all that seriously

"Look," said Grace, "isn't this pitiful? Parson Field's

widow is selling all her things so that she can go out West. I wouldn't go West even if you paid me. Can you imagine living in those horrid conditions? With wild Indians about." As Grace spoke, she rifled through the boxes, tsk-tsking at the odd assortment of goods being sold. "Who would buy some of these things?" she asked.

Annie shrugged, ready to move on. The auctioneer had just sold a table and lamp, and was moving toward the box of knicknacks. He looked up at the girls, an annoyed expression on his face. "This is hardly the place for you," he said. "Why don't you go on about your business and let me get back to mine?"

Two little red circles flamed in Grace's cheeks. "I'll have you know that you are speaking to the governor's daughter," she said haughtily, pointing at Annie. The man had come so close that the girls could smell the tobacco on his breath and see the grease stains on his shirt front. He stared at them boldly. Then he took a soiled handerchief from his pocket and wiped his nose, all the time keeping his smallish eyes on her.

The man frightened Annie. If it had been her choice, she would have run away, but Grace grabbed her arm and held it so tight that she couldn't move.

"I don't think you want to be rude to the governor's daughter, do you?" Grace persisted. "After all, he could shut down your little auction business if he wanted to."

The man looked furious. The veins in his neck pulsed with anger. For a minute, Annie thought he was going to curse at Grace. But then he seemed to think better of it. He trained his piggy eyes on Annie, who flinched under his gaze. A small smile stole across his face.

"I didn't mean to be rude to our nobility," he said smoothly. "Let me make it up to you," he continued, holding out to her a little box. When she hesitated, he pushed it on her. "Now you take this as a present from me, and we'll be friends, won't we?"

Annie began to protest, but Grace pinched her arm so hard it brought tears to her eyes. She felt her fingers close over the box. Immediately Grace began tugging at the girl's arm, pulling her away from the auction scene. When they reached a clearing, Annie turned on her friend.

"How could you do that?" she demanded. "My father will be furious."

"Oh fiddlesticks," Grace answered. "That's how things work here. People are glad to do favors for you, and you should let them do it. All the other governors did that. The people expect it. Open the box, anyway. What did he give you?"

Annie shoved the box at her friend. "You take it if it means so much to you," she said. But Grace would have none of it.

"I didn't figure you to be such a prude," Grace said with disgust. "I should have come with Diana and Letitia, though they are frightfully boring."

Annie didn't like to be thought of as a prude. Besides, she was curious. What had the man given her? She lifted the hinged top of the small wooden box, and nestled there was a beautiful tortoiseshell hair comb.

"It's beautiful," Grace said with surprise. "I thought he'd given you some awful glass beads, but this is a lovely comb. Take off your cap and put it on," she demanded.

It wasn't the first time that day that Annie had felt a little like a marionnette puppet being jerked around by her demanding friend. Nonetheless, she pulled off her cotton cap and slipped the comb into her thick brown curls. Annie knew from Grace's admiring expression that the comb looked good on her, but she asked the question anyway, "How does it look?"

"It looks wonderful," Grace said. "It will look even nicer when you get some proper clothes."

Annie didn't let Grace's insult bother her. She felt a growing sense of pleasure. It could be fun being the governor's daughter. Her father had told her she would enjoy it. Maybe this is what he meant.

For the next hour the girls amused themselves by strolling up and down the sidewalks in front of the shops, giggling behind their fans when they saw any of the young men staring. Annie found that she enjoyed the stares, and she wondered why she had fussed so about getting older. Maybe Patsy had been right all the time. It was only after a while, though, that Annie remembered to ask Grace a question that had bothered her all morning.

"Why did you change Kate's ink?"

"It gets so dull at Mistress Hallan's. I thought it would be something different. But I never thought Kate would be so upset. She's usually so . . . quiet."

"It seems so unfair that Mistress Hallan blames her for everything. Why didn't you confess?"

Grace gave Annie a quizzical look. "If you had played a prank, would you confess if it might bring shame to your father? Would you really want to disgrace him and make his job harder?"

Thinking of it that way, Annie was no longer certain. She shrugged.

"Well, that's how I felt. Kate doesn't have a reputation. She's a servant. But my father is an important attorney. You heard Mistress Hallan. I can't be the one to dishonor him."

"But why not be nice?" Annie couldn't help but ask.

"Now you're acting like a prude again. Don't you ever want to do something fun if it doesn't hurt anyone?"

Grace's voice rose, and Annie saw several people turn to look at them. She didn't want to fight. Besides, Grace was fun. She was bold, and it was certainly good to have a friend in Williamsburg, especially one with so much style; so she changed the subject.

"I'm hungry. Is there someplace we could eat?"

"We can eat in the dining room at the Raleigh but not in the tavern," Grace answered.

The girls headed across the street, dodging the carriages. They took their seats near a table where sat two men dressed in striped silk breeches and long velvet coats. On their heads the men wore stacked and curled wigs in an outrageous style.

Annie couldn't help but stare. But Grace merely giggled. "Aren't they handsome?" she whispered. "Father says there are many macaronis in London, for the people are much more stylish there."

As the girls ate, the dandies rose from their chairs and made elaborate bows toward the two young ladies, which made Annie blush and caused even Grace to giggle.

"I think it would be excellent to live in London," Grace said later. "Just imagine the fine life we would have."

"But I thought you were a patriot," Annie said with surprise.

"Oh, we all are patriots," Grace said dryly. "The patriots are winning, and Father says it is best to be on the winning side. But I think the British soldiers look very handsome in their red coats."

Annie wasn't sure whether her friend was serious or not, so she laughed. They finished their bowls of sorbet and then left the Raleigh. They admired hats in the milliner's window. Annie saw in the silversmith shop a belt buckle that she felt sure her father would like. In the barber shop they saw a man with a long cone over his nose and mouth. Behind him, the barber (who doubled as the surgeon) sprinkled powder over the man's wig until the air was full of fine white dust. With the help of the tube, the man was able to breathe until the dust settled. Finally, he stood up, removed the cloth that had protected his shoulders from the dust, and glanced admiringly in a mirror at his newly powdered wig. Annie gasped when he turned around. It was her father.

She turned her head abruptly, not wanting to meet him on the street. "I need to go home now," she said to Grace. "I don't want to worry my father."

"He won't be missing you yet, will he?" she asked.

"I don't know. But I want to get home."

"All right. But at least walk me to Mistress Hallan's. That's where my carriage is coming to pick me up."

By the time they reached the market square behind the courthouse, there were twice as many wagons as before. And already the smell of roasting meats and the call of cheery vendors had begun filling the air.

Annie gazed wistfully at several country boys in their worn breeches, wrestling in a clearing. Though dust-covered and shabby, the boys brought back to Annie memories of her brothers. Despite her best efforts, her eyes began watering, but she was determined not to let her friend see her cry.

"Just a bit of homesickness," she said when she saw that Grace had seen her wipe away a tear. "I guess I miss the boys."

"You have brothers?" Grace asked.

"Oh, yes," Annie said, but for some reason she was reluctant to tell Grace about them.

"How could those country boys remind you of your brothers?" Grace asked.

Annie shrugged and said, "You know, boys . . ."

Annie was glad when they reached Mistress Hallan's and saw Grace's carriage, which had come back to take her home. She waved and said, "Thank you for the tour of Williamsburg."

"It was fun," Grace replied. "And rewarding for you."

At those words, Annie's hands flew to her head where she could feel the comb under her cap. She couldn't keep the grin off her face.

"Perhaps we can go to the fair together," Grace said.

"I'd like that," Annie replied with a wave as Grace's carriage rolled down the road.

6

Miss Dandridge

By the time Annie arrived at the Palace, her father was already there. He greeted her enthusiastically and said, "I feel stronger today than I have in a long time. Come, sit with me outside. Soon it will be winter and too cold."

When they had taken seats out in a sunny spot on the lawn, Patrick Henry asked about Annie's day. Glad for his undivided attention, she told him about Mistress Hallan and then about her tour of Williamsburg.

But Annie didn't mention the auction, sensing that her father wouldn't approve. She nervously fiddled with the comb, which she could feel under her cap, and she was glad that she didn't have to explain to him how she had gotten it.

Annie wasn't used to hiding secrets, and having one made her eager to go inside. She rose to go back to the house, but her father held her arm. "There is something I want to tell you," he said, turning his face away from her.

His expression was not one that Annie had seen before. He looked younger, in a way, and a secret smile played about the corners of his mouth. When he caught Annie staring at him, a slow blush colored his cheeks.

"We'll be having a guest for dinner," he said abruptly. "You should dress for the occasion."

"But I don't have any dresses," Annie said. "I only have the clothes I brought with me from home."

"And what is wrong with those clothes?" her father asked.

"There isn't anything wrong with them," his daughter said shyly. "But none of the girls at school dress like this . . . except for the girl who works for Mrs. Wythe."

Her father was quiet for a minute. Clearly, this was news to him. "Well, it isn't fitting for my daughter to be improperly dressed," he said. "But what do we do about it?"

Annie shrugged. She didn't know anything about dressmakers. That had been Patsy's job.

Patrick Henry smiled suddenly. "Miss Dandridge—she's the guest who is coming to dinner. She'll know what to do about it. We'll leave your clothes in her hands."

With a frown, Annie considered her father's words. She didn't want to depend on the lady she had seen with her father. On the other hand, the woman would know about clothes. Feeling confused, the girl excused herself and ran inside.

Later, when Annie entered the dining room, she saw a flower-decorated table laden with food. But Annie's eyes did not linger on the table because behind it stood a pretty young woman, whose hair was piled high and dressed with pearls. She was laughing playfully with Annie's father, who stood next to her, until both of them became aware of the young girl's presence.

Abruptly, they broke off their conversation, and

Patrick Henry introduced the woman. "Miss Dandridge, I would like you to meet my daughter, Annie. Annie, Miss Dandridge."

Annie could feel their eyes upon her as she curtsied. She was glad when it was time to sit down and eat. Despite the best efforts of her father and his friend, dinner was an uncomfortable affair filled with awkward pauses. Every time Miss Dandridge tried to engage her in conversation, Annie couldn't think of the simplest thing to talk about.

Finally, Patrick Henry cleared his throat. Annie held her breath, fearing that he was making some kind of announcement. But instead he said in a loud voice, "Dorothea, we must do something about Annie's clothes. She tells me she is not dressed properly for Williamsburg, and I have been negligent. Well, I want to remedy the situation, but neither I nor Annie know anything about it. Will you take pity on this poor child and see that she is outfitted correctly?"

While this little speech was going on, Annie thought that she would die. Especially when her father made her stand and turn so that Miss Dandridge could see the problems with her current dress. How could he be so clumsy? She refused to smile or even look at her father's friend.

Finally, when she thought the humiliation would never end, she heard Miss Dandridge say in a sweet voice, "Why don't we have a little music. Patrick, won't you play for us?"

He excused himself and went to the fortepiano, which sat in the corner. As soon as he left the table, Miss Dandridge reached out a hand to sullen Annie. "Your father meant no harm, child. He didn't mean to embarrass you, nor did I. If you are willing, though, I would love to help you pick out some fabrics for some new clothes. I have a marvelous dressmaker, and it would be my pleasure."

It was hard to be angry at Miss Dandridge. After all, it wasn't this woman's fault. With a shy smile, Annie agreed.

"Good. I'll come for you tomorrow morning," the woman said. "Now let's go over to the piano and sing."

The next morning Miss Dandridge and Annie rode in a carriage to the dressmaker's house, which was behind a milliner's. Miss Dandridge sent the carriage away with orders to come back in an hour. As Annie hung back, looking admiringly at some of the feathered hats in the milliner's window, Miss Dandridge knocked on the dressmaker's door.

Once inside, they were in a room full of fabric. Some was silk, obviously imported years before, and now being sold for very high prices. But there were also pretty cottons, damasks, and satins, some from America, but mostly from France. Miss Dandridge looked around and began pulling out bolts of fabric. "Do you like this? Do you like that?" she asked, and Annie, who felt too timid to answer, merely shrugged.

The dressmaker smiled at the confusion, and when there were eight bolts on the table, she said, "I think that's plenty to choose from."

"So it is," Miss Dandridge said, satisfied that she had done her job. "Now this little girl would like several dresses, three I think, suitable for school. And one dress for parties."

"Four dresses," Annie gasped. "What will Father say?"

"Your father will be glad," Miss Dandridge answered.

"Have you ever worn hoops?" the dressmaker asked.

Annie shook her head.

"Well, then, we must start you with a pair of pocket hoops. She pulled a contraption off a shelf. "This is a pocket hoop farthingale," she said as she buckled the leather strap around Annie's waist. From the leather belt hung four metal braces, and from the braces were three half-circle hoops on each side. The top hoop was smallest, the next a little bigger, and the bottom hoop was the largest. These hoops were strung together, and if a woman needed to fit through a small door, the hoops on one side could collapse.

Annie surveyed herself with the hoops and sighed. "Will I be able to run?" she asked.

"I'm sorry," the dressmaker said. "Once you are in hoops, your running days are over."

Before Annie could change her mind, Miss Dandridge said, "Look at the bright side of things. You'll soon be old enough for courting and marriage, and you won't even want to run."

Annie rolled her eyes, but she was too polite to argue with the older woman. Next, the dressmaker removed a petticoat from a shelf. "You will need new petticoats to go over these hoops," she said. The petticoat was heavier than anything Annie had ever worn. It was made of two layers of fabric quilted together, with wool batting in between.

Miss Dandridge laughed when she saw the effect that the petticoat and the hoops made. The slender child had grown a foot wider on either side, as the hoops held the skirt out at the hips. But since the hoops didn't extend in the front or the back, Annie looked perfectly flat.

"I look like a loaf of bread that has been run over by a wagon," she said. "Flat from front to back, and bulging at the sides."

The dressmaker tsked and continued her measuring and pinning until at last she announced that she was finished. "Now choose your fabrics," she said through a mouthful of pins.

Annie looked at the pretty cottons that sat before her and finally settled on three, with the help of Miss Dandridge. Choosing fabric for a party dress was more difficult, but she finally decided on a dark green satin.

"Could you have one of these made up right away?" Miss Dandridge asked. "I know Miss Henry would like to have a new dress for market days."

The dressmaker nodded. "I will begin it today. It's not too fancy. I can have it done early next week, before the fair begins."

Miss Dandridge nodded with satisfaction. "Send it by the governor's house just as soon as it is ready, please."

Annie was quiet on the ride back to the Palace.

"That wasn't so hard, was it?" the older woman said.

"The dresses will be lovely," Annie admitted. "But will I like wearing them?"

"You really don't have much choice, my dear. The fate of all young girls is to become young women. That is the way God planned it. The hard part is becoming a young woman of good character—a godly young woman. That doesn't happen naturally."

"Did you ever wonder why people act so funny?" Annie asked.

"What do you mean?"

The girl shook her head. She wasn't sure what she meant, but she surely felt confused.

The carriage stopped at the governor's house, and Annie stepped down. She smiled shyly at her father's friend. "Thank you for helping me," she said.

"I loved doing it," the older woman replied. "I hope you'll let me be a friend."

7

The Fair

Time seemed to crawl as Annie looked forward to market days. Finally the first day arrived, and the poor girl woke with a throbbing headache. She cracked her eyes opened and winced as the sun poured through her bedroom window. With a groan, she pulled the covers up over her head and tried to go back to sleep. But the headache, which had been a mild irritation as she slept, now strengthened, and Annie worried for a minute that she was sick again as she had been about a year earlier with the fever.

She heard a knock and the door opened. Then came the sound of the maid's soft footsteps across the floor. Still Annie didn't budge. It wasn't until the maid said, "I've brought you some hot tea and a letter from home" that she threw back the coverlet and sat up abruptly in her bed. The maid saw her wince. "Are you ill, Miss Annie? Should I get your father?"

"No. I just have a terrible headache, and the light from the window is awfully bright," she said, trying to keep the whining out of her voice.

The maid pulled the drapes closed, and Annie felt better almost at once. Taking a quick sip of the hot herb tea, she turned the letter over in her hand, but she didn't open it. Instead, she waited impatiently for the maid to pick up some clothes off the floor and smooth the covers because she did not want to open the letter while anyone was there. It was hers, and she wanted to read it alone.

Finally, when the girl thought she could bear it no longer, the maid left. She quickly slipped the blade of the letter opener under the sealing wax and broke the seal. The letter smelled of lavender and brought back memories of sachets made from the dried blossoms that grew in the herb garden at home. It was funny the things she remembered.

> Dear Sister,
>
> We have been poorly at Scotchtown. Such a season of illness I do not remember, but God has spared our lives though many are still weak from the effects of this bout of flu.
>
> The rain continues, day after day, and I feared the crops might be lost in the fields, but husband John has managed to bring them in, and I think we will do well.

Annie looked up from the letter and thought about the hard work of bringing in the wheat. It had been only two years since she had helped save the crop from fire.

> Your brothers chomp at the bit to be off with General Washington's army, but John Fontaine has reminded them how the army in the north depends on food from our Virginia farms. We have been divided into sections, each with the duty to send a portion of our bounty to the army. John Fontaine has worked hard to gather meat as well as corn and wheat to send up

> north. We have tried to cut back on our own needs so that we have more to send.

As Annie sat on her canopied bed, she felt a twinge of guilt. Never had she lived so easily as during these weeks at the Governor's Palace, and yet the family at Scotchtown was sacrificing for the army. She turned back to the letter.

> Baby grows, and with all the sickness about, he has worn me out. I worried about his taking ill, and now I find I have little energy to manage. And nurse has had her hands full with Elizabeth and Edward. But I must not complain.
>
> The Thackers are well and ask about you. In fact, Andrew and his father are going to market in Williamsburg. Perhaps you will see them. We miss you. Though I was often exasperated by your behavior, I find that our home would be happier if I could hear your laughter and the sound of running feet. Keep Father from getting sick, and remember how much we love you.
>
> Your loving sister,
>
> Patsy

Annie laid the letter aside and brushed away the tears that wet her cheeks. For a fleeting moment she wanted nothing more than to rush back to Scotchtown and see the familiar faces. But then she thought of her father, still weak from his own illness, trying to do the hard work of a governor. "I'm needed more here," she said aloud.

There was another knock on the door, and once again the maid entered. This time she carried a tray loaded with food and a bottle of some sort of medicine "guaranteed to take away the headache," she promised.

Annie forced herself to eat some of the hominy. Under the maid's watchful eye, she swallowed a spoonful of the bitter remedy, washing the foul taste down with another sip of tea.

"There is a card for you, miss," the maid said hesitantly.

Annie reached for the engraved card that was on her tray. Printed on heavy ivory paper was Grace's name. On the back, in her friend's neat handwriting, was a note.

> Come to the fair with me today. Could you meet me at the church yard at noon? Send a response with my driver.

Annie considered. Did she feel well enough to go? Carefully, she turned her head from side to side. Her headache seemed to be going away—it no longer hurt when she moved her head. Rising from her bed, she walked over to her desk where she kept her pen and ink. In a careful hand, she wrote that she would be pleased to go and signed her name. After blotting the paper, she handed the letter to her maid with instructions to take it down to the waiting driver.

There was no need to hurry; so Annie rested a little longer. But when the clock chimed eleven o'clock, she rose from her bed. The water in the pitcher on her washstand was already cold. She splashed it quickly on her hands and face. Then she looked in the wardrobe. Only yesterday a package had arrived with one of her new dresses, the hoops, and petticoats. Annie had carried the clumsy bundle upstairs without anyone seeing it. *Now,* she thought, *I will wear my new dress.*

When the maid returned, Annie asked her to help. Together they strapped on the hoops. Then Annie pulled on the heavy petticoat. Finally, with the maid's help, she struggled into the tight gown the dressmaker had sewn. It had narrow sleeves with a band of lace at the bottom. There was lace around the collar. The skirt was gathered so that the pretty petticoat showed underneath. She moved this way and that in front of the mirror, admiring the way the hoops made her skirts stick out on the sides. The whole costume weighed at least fifteen pounds. "I look all grown up," she said to herself.

Although Miss Dandridge had given Annie a pair of tiny leather shoes, they didn't look as though they could stand up to walking; so Annie put on a pair of sturdy boots. No one would see them under the dress, she thought.

By the time she left the Palace, it was close to noon. She tried to hurry, but she had to squeeze through sidewalks full of people. There were fancy people and tradespeople in plain dress, farmers, and macaronis. The market itself was on the green near the courthouse, but the Palace green was also crowded with carriages and horses. From a distance, she could hear faint music coming from some sort of high-pitched instrument. It was nearly drowned out by a multitude of voices. Twice the girl was nearly run over by a runaway horse that galloped back and forth across the street.

Annie could hardly take everything in. There was a juggler on one side and a man with two monkeys on his shoulder on the other. Up ahead she saw a roped-off area where two boys wrestled while the crowd cheered them on. Just when she wondered if she should return home, she saw Grace alight from a carriage. Ignoring the crowds around her, Annie pushed forward to meet her friend. In her haste and because she was not accustomed to her hoops, she bowled over a small child without realizing it. His cries caught her attention, and she stopped and picked him up, ignoring the teasing of an older boy who said, "Watch where you're going, miss."

Grace was tapping her foot impatiently while she waited for Annie. When she saw her friend, she grabbed Annie's arm. "You look marvelous! That's a lovely dress. Now come. We don't want to miss a thing."

"Where do we start?" Annie asked.

"Let's go see the sword fighting," Grace answered, a mischievous smile on her face.

"But I thought ladies didn't do that," Annie answered a bit uncomfortably.

"Oh, pshaw," Grace answered. "That was a rule set by the royal governor. But we don't have a royal governor anymore. We can make our own rules."

Annie thought about that. It seemed to make some sense; so she followed behind her friend.

They walked across the green, away from the street. The farther they went, the fewer girls and ladies Annie saw. Up ahead a small stage had been erected, and upon it two men dressed only in breeches and loose, white shirts held their swords aloft. A signal was given, and the men began their dance, lunging at one another with their swords as the crowd around them cheered. Spectators were betting on the outcome of the fight, and men in the corners had their hands full of money.

It was dramatic, and Annie found herself moving closer to the stage as she watched it. She blushed when she heard the cursing going on, and several times she thought someone said something crude to her as she walked past. But the girl was so enthralled by the fight that she lost track of time and place.

Finally, the fight was finished when one of the swordsmen managed to pin the other against the rope at the side of the stage. Annie felt a tug at her arm. She turned to go but found that it wasn't Grace who was tugging at her. It was a foul-smelling man carrying a large jug of ale. His fat, red face was uncomfortably close to Annie's.

"Ah, the governor's daughter," he sneered. "You want to come and have a friendly drink with me?"

Annie recognized the drunken man as the auctioneer. She tried to pull away, but he had his dirty hands on her dress, and she was afraid it would tear. She looked around desperately for Grace but couldn't see her anywhere.

"Let go," she hissed at the man, but he held her arm more tightly with his dirt-covered hand.

"I thought we were going to be friends," he whispered, his breath hot against her cheek.

Annie was about ready to scream when she felt a hand on her other arm. "I've been looking for you, young lady," said a tall man on her left. "Cousin Grace asked me to find you, and so I have."

Annie had never felt so relieved in her life. It was Spencer Roane, Grace's cousin, who stood protectively next to her. He looked at the red-faced man and said firmly, "I'll take my little friend with me."

Annie thought for a minute there would be a fight, but the man let go, muttering insults all the time.

Her cheeks burned as she heard the things the auctioneer said about her and realized that Mr. Roane had heard them too. Annie could feel the hot tears stream down her cheeks. She tried desperately to wipe them away. Blindly, she followed her rescuer, who held her tightly by the hand as they pushed their way through the crowd. Eventually they stopped, and Annie felt his arm on her shoulders. "You girls were foolish to go there," he said. Annie looked up and saw that Grace was standing, white-faced, next to her. Her normally confident manner had disappeared. She nodded wordlessly as Spencer Roane continued scolding them. Annie felt her headache begin pounding again.

Spencer sighed. "You girls look as though you could use some refreshment. Come, I'll buy you a cider."

They followed meekly behind as he led them to an outdoor stall where fresh cider and doughnuts were being served. Even after Mr. Roane left, with a strict warning that they should stay near the street, Annie and Grace said little.

"I didn't mean to lose you in the crowd," Grace said sheepishly. "I'm so sorry. I'm glad Spencer came by at the right time."

"Me too," Annie whispered.

"Do you want to go home?"

Annie thought about it. She had been scared, but there was no reason to be afraid any longer. As long as they stayed near the street and among the vendors, there would be no danger. And her headache seemed better after the cider and doughnut. Annie shook her head: "But let's not get into any more trouble," she stated.

Grace grinned. "Let's not."

The rest of the afternoon was full of many strange sights. Vendors of all sorts sold produce and goods they had brought from all over Virginia and the world. Men and women roasted chestnuts over fires, and small pigs turned on spits over others. In the middle of the green, the girls heard laughing and saw many children racing to see. They found themselves witnessing a soaped pig contest. There, a pig whose tail had been soaped was let loose, and children of all ages chased him around a clearing, trying to grab on to his slippery tail.

The crowd cheered as a mud-covered boy dove at the frightened pig and brought him down. Annie watched for a minute as boy and beast wallowed together in the mire. She only turned away when Grace pulled her in another direction. Then she heard a voice behind her yell, "Annie . . . Annie Henry."

Turning around she came face to face with the mud-covered boy from the pig contest. She stared at him for a minute until she spied, through the mud, the smile of her friend from back home, Andrew Thacker.

With a whoop, she ran forward, ready to throw her arms around the muddy boy until he said with a laugh, "You'll be an awful sight if you become as muddy as me."

She paused. "Andrew Thacker!" she exclaimed. "I can't believe I'm seeing you."

"Well, I can't believe I'm seeing you," he said, staring at her fancy dress.

Annie blushed as she remembered the scrapes they had been in together. There was an awkward moment and then Annie remembered Grace, who stood behind her waiting to be introduced. "Oh," she said with embarrassment. "Grace, let me introduce Andrew Thacker, a friend from home . . . and, Andrew, this is my friend Grace Glendon-Jones."

Andrew removed his cap and bowed, saying, to Annie's astonishment, "Pleased to meet you, miss."

Grace nodded, amusement written on her face. Annie glanced from one friend to the other and grew increasingly uncomfortable, but Andrew rescued the situation. "I have to go now," he said, bowing again. "It was nice to see you, Annie."

Annie watched as he turned and ran through the crowd, wanting to yell out after him but catching herself.

"Interesting friends you have," Grace said slyly. "Not a typical Williamsburg fellow."

Annie began to protest, but that made Grace grin more. Shrugging, Annie wondered why she should defend Andrew anyway. He had looked ridiculous covered with mud.

She felt her headache returning and was glad when it was time to go home. After gratefully closing her bedroom door, she pulled the drapes on the crowds down below. She removed her dress, which she let slide to the floor, took off the heavy petticoats and hoops, and slid under the covers of her bed.

A knock on the door several hours later woke her. The maid whispered into the darkened room, "Miss Annie, your father is asking to see you. Will you go to him?"

Rubbing the sleep from her eyes, Annie stared for a minute without understanding. Her body felt heavy, and her legs and arms ached. When she tried to talk, her tongue felt thick, and her mouth was dry. The maid slipped a cool hand against her forehead. "You're hot. I knew you shouldn't go off to the fair today. I'm going to get you something to make you feel better."

As she pulled the door shut behind her, Annie smiled at the memory of the fair until she remembered Andrew. "What's wrong with me?" she moaned with embarrassment, pulling the coverlet up over her head. "How could I have been so rude to my friend?" Her headache pounded behind her eyes, and her nose was so stuffed up that she could hardly breathe. Annie felt more and more sorry for herself.

In the midst of her despair, there came a firm rap at her door. The knob turned and Annie heard the door open, but she kept her back toward it, not wanting the maid to see her cry.

"I've brought you something to make you feel better," a gentle voice said. Annie turned to see Miss Dandridge sitting on the side of the bed. When the older woman saw the girl's tear-streaked face, she asked, "What's wrong, my dear? Would it make you feel better to talk about it?"

Annie shook her head.

"Never mind. We don't need to talk now." Miss Dandridge smiled as she wiped Annie's forehead with a cool cloth. "Just shut your eyes, and we'll see if we can't get that headache to go away." Soon Annie felt herself drift off to sleep.

8

The Race

It was morning again before Annie awoke. Her headache was gone, but the maid would not let her out of bed. "Orders of your father and Miss Dandridge," she said.

Several minutes later, Patrick Henry peeked in the door and looked relieved to see Annie sitting up in bed and eating a bit of breakfast.

"You worried me, daughter," he said, pulling a chair alongside the bed and sitting down in it. "But I can see that Dorothea was correct. She said you were overtired, but she did not think you were ill. She'd like to visit you again if you would enjoy it, and she gave very firm orders that you are not to leave your bed."

As her father spoke, he smiled, clearly enjoying sharing this responsibility with Miss Dandridge. He looked happy. No longer was his skin pale and sickly looking, and his deep-set eyes looked less brooding than Annie had seen for a long time. She tried to think how to describe the change. Crisper? No, that sounded too much like a piece of toast. Happier? Well, he was clearly that, but the word didn't capture all she was seeing. Brighter? Certainly his eyes and smile were brighter, but there was something more. Then she had it. Jaunty! Her father looked absolutely jaunty. There was a spring to his step and a liveliness to all his movements that Annie hadn't seen before. She grinned, and her father, who had been chattering about something, grinned back.

"You seem happy this morning," he observed.

"And you also, Father. I haven't seen you looking so jaunty," she said, trying out the new word, "since I was a little girl."

"'Jaunty,' you say? 'Jaunty?'" Patrick Henry roared with laughter, then spoke seriously: "I am happy. And I'm pleased that you noticed. I have news for you."

Annie held her breath and felt her smile fade.

"Miss Dandridge and I plan to marry," her father said, not noticing her change in mood. "Isn't that good news?"

"When?" Annie squeaked.

"Early spring," he informed her. "We want the family to come, and travel is too uncertain in the winter. So as soon as the roads are dry, we will wed."

"Isn't this very sudden, Father?" Annie asked, trying to hide her disappointment. It didn't matter that Miss Dandridge was kind. The girl didn't want to lose her father to another woman.

"I wasn't intending to mention it quite yet," he said, looking at his daughter fondly. "But she told me yes last evening, and I do hate to keep secrets." He looked so pleased with himself that Annie didn't have the heart to show her true feelings.

"It sounds wonderful," she said. Then, slipping back down under the covers, she said, "I'm feeling very tired. Maybe I'll take a little nap."

Her father hopped to his feet. "You rest, daughter. I

must keep some appointments." After brushing her cheek with a kiss, he paused at the door. "Andrew and Mr. Thacker will be coming to dinner tonight. I hope you are well enough to join us."

Annie looked surprised. "Will Miss Dandridge be there?" she asked.

"Of course. I'd like her to meet our friends from home."

There was a pause, and Annie fidgeted with the bed-covers. As her father turned to leave, she forced herself to speak. "Won't you be embarrassed?"

"By Miss Dandridge?" Patrick Henry asked. "Not at all; she has lovely manners."

With exasperation, Annie glared at her father. "Not by Miss Dandridge. By the Thackers. They don't seem like Williamsburg people," Annie said, repeating Grace's words.

Patrick Henry shrugged as though Annie had told a joke. "I guess if the Thackers aren't fit for Williamsburg, I'm not fit either. We're Hanover County boys, pure and simple. Now you have a quiet day," he ordered as he left the room.

Annie fell back on her pillows, thinking about her father's words. It was a lot easier for men, she thought. As long as you could shoot a gun and tell a good story, you could belong. But for girls, it was harder. Annie didn't think her father understood at all. Shaking off the gloomy thoughts, she turned her attention to the sounds she could hear from the window.

It was the second day of the fair, and the crowds were as noisy today as they had been yesterday. It was impossible to ignore them. Annie didn't want to have a quiet day, especially upon the orders of Miss Dandridge. She felt fine. She threw on one of her old dresses and went barefoot across the hall to her father's room. There a large window opened out onto a balcony that overlooked the Palace green. From her perch, she could see the wheelwright working on a carriage and the grooms walking some of the governor's horses.

A crowd was gathering along an oval course where a group of men and boys were removing their waistcoats and tricornered hats, which they laid in a pile on the ground. Annie watched the men break into groups of five. With much laughing and shoving, one group of five lined up at the starting line and waited. A gun went off, and the men burst into motion. The girl watched them race around the course, their ponytails streaming behind them, arms chugging as they stretched toward the finish line. "That looks like such fun," she said wistfully.

When the first group of runners had finished, another lined up at the start and waited its turn to run. She could feel her own heart beating as she longed to be outside running with the others. "Why shouldn't I go?" she asked herself.

Once the idea entered her mind, Annie bustled about her father's room to see if there were any boys' clothes that would fit her. She put on one of the baggy, unbleached cotton tunics that tradesmen wore, and although it was large, it didn't much matter. But breeches would be another problem. Her father's would all be too big. She searched the wardrobe and found nothing. Then she caught sight of the trunk they had brought with them from Scotchtown. It was almost empty, but in the bottom was an old pair of breeches that had belonged to William. It had been packed by mistake in all of the confusion surrounding their departure. Annie pulled them on, fumbling with the buttons. She secured a pair of her father's stockings with garters, slipped her feet into a pair of her own buckle shoes, and admired herself in the mirror.

In all her concern about clothes, Annie had forgotten her hair. "How will I hide it?" she wailed, running over to the window to assure herself that the races were still going on. It looked as though the runners had taken a break while children ran after a flock of sheep that had wandered onto the track.

"I can't wear a hat," she said because she had noticed that all the other runners had removed theirs.

On one table were Patrick Henry's wigs. One had been freshly curled and powdered, but another was in need of grooming. It was dirty, and its ponytail looked straggly. "Father must have worn this in a rainstorm," she muttered, looking at the limp item. "How will it look on me?"

The wig was too large for Annie, but once she tucked her long hair up underneath, it fit fairly tight. She shook her head back and forth and was glad to see that the wig stayed on. Cracking the door, she peeked out and, seeing no one, tiptoed over to the stairwell. Mr. Goodacre was nowhere around. "Now if only I can get downstairs without being seen," she whispered. "It's as good a time as any."

Taking a deep breath, the girl glided silently across the floor and stepped lightly down the stairs. At the bottom, she looked furtively around. Then she dashed for the door. Once outside, Annie slowed down. She hoped she looked like any other young boy walking about.

By now the sheep had been herded away and the races were about to resume. Annie watched several more from the sidelines before gathering her courage to go forward. When the last group lined up, she knew it was now or never. She joined them, taking the outermost lane. When the gun sounded, Annie leapt forward, but the men were much faster than she. Although she ran her hardest, she could only overtake one of them. The race ended with Annie a long way out. But the girl glowed with excitement. It had been fun to run even if she hadn't won.

Bending over to catch her breath, Annie almost fainted. There, not more than ten feet away, was Spencer Roane. She ducked her head but not before she saw him glancing at her curiously. Keeping her head down, she hurried away, making sure that Mr. Roane did not follow her. After she had slipped into a crowd, Annie turned her attention back to the races. The winners would now compete against each other. Annie picked out Spencer Roane as one of the runners, but there was another who looked familiar. It was Andrew Thacker. Annie would have known his slightly bowlegged walk anywhere. The boy looked nervous. He stood slightly off from the group and glanced every now and then up at the Governor's Palace.

When the gun sounded, Annie jumped. Silently she urged her old friend forward. "Go, Andrew," she whispered and groaned as her friend slipped going around the first curve. But he got up and continued running, gradually overtaking several of the other runners. "Faster, faster," she said a little louder as he rounded the second turn. Soon the runners were close to where Annie stood, and the girl shouted, "Come on, come on," ignoring the strange looks that others gave her. *They are all yelling,* she thought. *Why are they paying attention to me?*

Rounding the last curve, there was only one man ahead of Andrew. It was Spencer Roane, Grace's cousin. "Go, Andrew. You can do it," Annie yelled as loudly as she could. It was only when she heard a whispered comment about girls in boys' clothing that Annie realized she had given herself away with her screaming.

Ducking her face, she pushed into the crowd that was milling about, letting it push and pull her until she was near to the governor's gate. Quickly she slipped through the gate and walked briskly until she was once again in the safety of the Palace. She held her breath, hoping no one would see her as she ran up the back stairs to her room.

She had left her clothes in a jumble on her father's floor. Hurriedly, she pulled off the boys' clothes and pulled on her nightdress, wadding up the breeches and tossing them in the trunk. By this time, her hands were shaking as she realized what she had done and how close she had come to being discovered. As she looked up, she caught a glimpse of herself in the mirror and burst out laughing. For there she was in a simple white gown with a man's white ponytailed wig on her head. She pulled it off and jammed it on the wig stand. *There,* she thought. *Now I look like a frazzled little girl.* Taking another deep breath, she opened her father's door and almost ran into Mr. Goodacre, the butler, who stood in the hallway.

"Miss Annie," he said with surprise, "were you looking for something in your father's room?"

"Just watching from the window," the girl answered with wide-eyed innocence as she hurried into her own room.

Safely there, Annie found that she was exhausted. She slipped back into bed, where she was soon asleep.

Later that afternoon there was a surprise with Annie's tea. The maid brought up the tray, and hidden among the plates of food was a small box. "A gentleman brought it to you, miss," said the maid with a slight smile.

Annie tried to look indifferent, but she couldn't hide

the smile that played around her mouth or lit her eyes. "Are you sure it's for me?" she asked.

"Yes, miss. He said it was for you especially and made me promise to give it to you with your tea."

The maid took her time plumping up pillows and straightening the room, giving a glance every so often at Annie, who was determined not to open the box until the maid had gone. Finally, the woman left the room, and Annie took the top off the box. Nestled on a piece of cotton wool was a pair of silver shoe buckles, the prize from the race, and a note. "If pluck and daring were enough to win races, these would be yours," the note read. It was signed with the initials "S.R."

Annie's face burned with embarrassment. Spencer Roane had recognized her. Now Grace would know about her foolish idea to run—and so would her father if Mr. Roane talked about it. The girl held her head in her arms and groaned. "When will I ever learn to think before I act?" she moaned.

At seven o'clock, Annie entered the dining room. She had taken special care in dressing and wore her new dress. The maid had helped curl her hair, which she wore piled on top of her head. The girl was determined to be a lady beyond reproach that evening.

Since her father had invited a large group, tables had been set in the supper room at the back of the house. Someone played the fortepiano while the guests stood in groups talking. As she entered the room, Annie could feel people watching her, and she suspected they were laughing at her. Holding her head high, she walked over to the fortepiano and saw that it was her father who played.

"Daughter," he said, "we have been waiting for you.

Come, let us sit down to dinner." He held his arm out to her and led her to a place at one of the tables. Soon all the guests were seated. As the food was served, Annie had time to examine the guests. Next to her father sat Miss Dandridge, and on her other side was Mr. Thacker. It was with surprise that Annie watched the woman talk and laugh with Andrew's father.

Andrew looked less comfortable in his dress-up clothes, and several times Annie caught the boy scowling at her from his place across the table. She didn't know most of the other guests. They were all well-dressed, and she suspected that most were members of the new legislature. The conversation swirled around her as people talked about war and taxes. News had reached Virginia about a British victory in New York. General Washington had lost more than 1,400 troops and had been forced to retreat from Manhattan.

Annie listened with one ear as she thought about her brothers back at Scotchtown. William would soon be eighteen and off to war. *Those lost troops could include him next time,* she thought. Even Andrew was getting older and would soon be able to enlist without his father's permission. She could tell by the way he listened to the war talk that he would join General Washington as soon as he was old enough.

When dinner was over, the guests moved into the ballroom to dance. Annie stayed in her chair, not wanting to join the festive group in the other room. Andrew startled her when he said, "Would you go for a walk with me?"

Looking up at her old friend, she shrugged. "Let me get a coat, and I'll meet you out back."

9

The Maze

Annie had changed from her thin leather slippers to a pair of buckle shoes and put on a long, hooded cape. In each hand she carried a lantern, which she brought from the house. Not wanting to go through the ballroom carrying the lanterns and wearing the coat, she left through the side door and circled around the house until she found Andrew shivering in the garden.

"Here," she said, holding out a lantern to him. "It's very dark in the yard."

"Where do you go to get away from this?" the boy asked, waving at the house.

Shrugging, Annie said, "Don't you like the Palace?"

He screwed his nose up. "It's so, so. . . showy," he said finally. "It may have suited the royal governors, but it's hardly fitting for the elected governor of the people of Virginia."

Annie frowned. Andrew had a way of making her angry. "Well, I guess maybe even an elected governor deserves a nice house," she proclaimed.

"Oh, you think so," he sneered. "And all these servants and slaves?"

"Why not?" she asked, though she had often thought there were too many servants for such a small household.

"Because we are at war," Andrew said, marching ahead through the yard. "Some people are sacrificing for our freedom. I guess I thought the Henrys would be among them. Besides, Thomas Jefferson's Declaration of Independence said that all men are created equal. How can you keep all these slaves?"

Annie's anger incrreased. She did not want to argue slavery with Andrew Thacker. "You aren't the only one who has ever sacrificed," she said, quickening her step to keep up with him. "And for your information, Williamsburg suits me. There are real ladies and gentlemen here," she said pointedly. She didn't have to add the next phrase, "unlike in Hanover," because Andrew understood exactly what she was saying. He scowled, and she quickened her pace, trying to put some space between them.

"I just don't understand how you could have become so stupid in such a short time," Andrew said to the girl's back. "I always thought you had more sense."

Annie turned and glared at her friend. "Well, that good sense tells me I should go back inside," she said. "Did you ask me to go for a walk so that you could scold me?" Turning again, the girl walked away in a huff.

"Truce," the boy called out apologetically. When Annie turned, he smiled and said in his friendliest voice, "I won't talk anymore about how snobbish and silly the people are in this town." Annie narrowed her eyes and was about to continue the argument when she had an idea.

"Let's go in the maze," she suggested. "I've never been in it at night. Do you dare?"

The boy nodded, and together the two ran through

the garden until they reached the boxwood shrubs that formed the maze.

"The goal is to get to the middle," Annie explained. "You go one way; I'll go the other, and we'll see who gets there first."

Before the girl had stopped talking, Andrew set off down his path. The boxwood was thin in places, not nearly as lush as it would be in summer. In the daylight, she could see through the shrubs in spots, but because it was so dark and she had only a lantern, she had to feel her way along. She held the lantern out before her, letting the candle light the path. She ran her other hand along the edge of the hedge, feeling for an opening on the side. Up and around the dark path she walked, occasionally seeing the flicker of light from Andrew's lantern or hearing his muttered words as he tripped over a rock or twig.

"How are you coming?" Annie called out nervously.

"I'm almost there," came the confident reply.

That's not true, the girl thought, but quickened her pace just the same. She had walked so far without coming to the center clearing that she began to fear that she was lost. *This is silly,* she thought. *I can't get lost in a maze in my own yard.*

"Andrew?" she called out. When he didn't answer, she called again, a little louder. Again there was silence.

Suddenly the girl was afraid. Surrounded by thick darkness, she was overcome by the feeling that she was trapped.

"Andrew Thacker, answer me this minute," she yelled, hating the sound of fear she could hear in her own voice. From behind her she heard a deep chuckle, and the girl whirled around. There, standing perfectly still, was Andrew. He had ducked into a path, and Annie had just walked by him without realizing he was there. When she saw his grinning face, she became furious. "How could you do that to me?" she screamed.

Andrew looked surprised. "I didn't mean to scare you that much," he said apologetically.

She was not in the mood to hear an apology. "I hate you, Andrew Thacker," she cried. "You are mean and a big bully, and I hate you." Then she burst into tears.

Andrew looked around him uncomfortably. He had a temper of his own and thought about leaving the angry girl in the maze to teach her a lesson. That was too cruel, he decided. *If there is ever a time to turn the other cheek, now is it,* he thought. Out loud he said, "I'm leaving the maze. If you want me to help you find your way out, come with me."

"And let you get me lost?" she sneered. "I'll get myself out."

"Suit yourself," the boy said. "I trailed a string behind me. Learned it from one of those old stories that Mr. Dabney was so crazy about. Remember the minotaur?"

Annie didn't answer; so he turned and began walking away.

Seeing that he wasn't going to beg her forgiveness, Annie struggled for less than a second about whether to follow him. She hurried to catch up, careful to leave a gap between them. On they walked, saying nothing, until Annie tripped. Her lantern fell to the ground, and the candle snuffed out. Suddenly, it was very dark.

"Andrew," she called, "I've lost my light and twisted my ankle," she cried.

While she waited for the boy to return, she heard rapid breathing from the hedge at her right. Startled, she twisted around to see who was there. "Who's in there?" she demanded with as much authority as she could muster. "I will bring the governor's soldiers to get you," she added when there was still no movement from the bushes. Annie heard Andrew's footsteps and saw the light from his lantern.

He held his hand out to her and pulled her to her feet. She winced as she put weight on the twisted ankle. "Who are you talking to?" he asked.

Annie nodded toward the bushes and whispered, "Someone is in there."

The boy looked at her skeptically. "How do you know that?" he asked.

"Listen. You'll hear breathing."

They were quiet, and for a minute there was no sound. Then both of them heard a ragged breath. Andrew said sternly, "Come out from there, now."

The bushes shook, and by the lamplight they watched as first one bare brown foot, then another, appeared. The legs were followed in short order by the rest of a young, rag-covered body, topped by a tiny tear-streaked face. The child cowered before Andrew and Annie, keeping her face turned toward the ground.

With her hands on her hips, Annie said, "Get up," as she looked with disgust on the dirty, dark-skinned girl standing before her shivering. Her nubby hair was braided in tight corn rows, and her bare brown legs were gray with dust. Annie's harsh response set the small child shivering.

In a gentle voice Andrew said, "Let's go someplace where we can talk. This child is nearly frozen."

Annie scowled but let herself be led by Andrew, who carried the trembling child. Clumsily they made their way out of the maze. When they had reached the clearing, Andrew paused. Where can we go where we won't be disturbed?" he asked.

"I suppose they're through in the kitchen," Annie muttered. "There'll be a fire there; so it will be warm."

The three stumbled through the gardens to the kitchen, which was dark. Hot embers still glowed in the fireplace. Andrew set the girl down on the stone floor and lit several lanterns while motioning Annie to close the door.

The little girl sobbed where Andrew had set her. Annie, who suddenly felt very tired, snapped, "Stop blubbering. It can't be that bad. What reason do you have to carry on so?"

Her harsh words only made the stranger cry louder. Andrew looked impatiently at Annie. "That's enough." Then turning his attention to the little girl, he asked softly, "What's your name?"

At first she didn't answer, and Annie was about to say perhaps she was deaf when the girl turned to Andrew and whispered, "Deborah."

"How did you come to be in the maze?" Andrew continued, never raising his voice. He had lowered himself to the floor near the little girl and spoke so quietly that Annie, who was standing up, could barely hear.

"I was hiding," she whispered.

"Speak up," Annie said. "What is it? Have you run away? Your master must be looking for you."

"Annie!"

She ignored Andrew and turned back to the little girl. "You'll have to go back, you know. You might as well tell us who your master is, or the guards will force it out of you."

With a desperate voice the child cried out, "Oh, missy, please don't get the guard. Have mercy."

Andrew's voice dripped with disgust. "Annie, go back to the Palace. I'll take care of this."

She turned to argue, but Andrew shook his head. "You've said enough tonight. Now go home."

Like a wounded dog, Annie turned her back on her friend and slipped out the door. Blinded by the tears that streamed down her face and burning with anger and indignation, she ran to the Palace and slipped in the side door. She could hear voices and music coming from the ballroom, but she turned away from the cheerful sounds and ran up the stairs where she took refuge in her room.

Throwing herself on her bed, she cried and cried. "I hate you, Andrew Thacker," she said, pounding her pillow. Then she remembered her own ugly behavior and turned her fury on herself. "What has come over me?" she wept. "Why have I become so ugly? Oh, God, help me. I'm so confused."

10

An Errand of Mercy

Annie's twisted ankle swelled horribly, and for several days she had to stay in her room. The doctor said there was no help for it but rest and tight bandages. From her window, she watched as the remaining merchants and farmers took apart their booths and loaded up their wagons. An army of young boys flocked over the green, looking for any treasures that might have been left behind.

Once they had gone, the green looked desolate. The catalpa trees had shed their last leaves, which lay in sodden clumps along the road. A heavy night rain had washed mud from the fields onto the streets where it sat inches deep along the gutter. It was hard to imagine that Williamsburg could ever look clean again. "It's like my own soul," the girl said to herself. "I've become ugly like this field, and I don't even know how it happened. Is there any hope for me?"

Just then a wagon rattled down the street toward the Palace. Two men sat on the seat. As it drew nearer, Annie recognized the Thackers. She watched as Mr. Thacker climbed down and entered into a heated discussion with her father, who had been waiting on the steps. Both men stepped aside as a small, blanket-wrapped bundle was loaded on the wagon. She tried to see what was in it but couldn't tell. Finally, the two men shook hands before Mr. Thacker climbed back up and drove off.

As it rolled away, Annie glimpsed two dark brown eyes peering out from under the blanket at the back of the wagon. "They've taken that child," she said in amazement.

It was not until later that day, though, that Annie was able to ask her father about what she had seen. He seemed somber and thoughtful when he came to her room for a visit. But he didn't look surprised when Annie asked, "Where are the Thackers taking that girl?"

Her father didn't speak right away. He studied her face before answering in a sad voice. "I didn't want to believe the story Andrew told me the other night. . . ."

Though her eyes welled with tears, Annie struggled to hold them back. Lifting her chin, she said in a shaking voice, "I wasn't the one who was rude, Father. It was Andrew. He ordered me back to the house as if I was a child." The injustice of it still burned.

"Yes. Andrew apologized for his rudeness. But I am less concerned with that than I am with your attitude. I have never known you to be cruel."

"Cruel?" she demanded. "I only wanted to let that child know that she couldn't take advantage of the governor."

"Oh, Annie," her father said sadly, rubbing his eyes with the back of his hand. "Did you listen to her story? Did you even stop scolding long enough to listen?"

It was hard for Annie to lie there under her father's disapproving eye. She stared at the blanket rather than meet his gaze, and she felt her heart harden. *He doesn't understand,* she thought. *He is always standing up for other people—and not listening to me. He should know that I'm only worried about his reputation. After all, Virginia counts on him.* When the girl finally looked up, her sulking eyes met her father's sad ones. He shook his head.

"I'm going to tell you her story," he said. "I want you to hear it from me, and then I want you to think about it." Patrick Henry lowered himself into a chair across from her bed. Then he began speaking, his voice so soft that Annie had to strain to hear him.

"Andrew came to me the other night after settling Deborah—did you know that was her name?—in the kitchen. I found her trembling with cold. Her right cheek was swollen and crusted over with dried blood in a wound that was obviously infected. She had been branded."

Annie interrupted her father. "A brand? Who would brand her?"

"Her master—a man named Mr. Penny from Roanoke."

"I bet she ran away," Annie said. "See, I knew it."

Her father shook his head, closing his eyes as though he was almost too tired to continue. Then his soft voice began again. "Her mother ran away and took Deborah with her. They were caught and given back to the master who branded them—but the mother became sick and died on the trip back to Roanoke. Then, as they were crossing a flooding river, the wagon tipped, and the girl was swept overboard. She grabbed a board that came loose from the wagon. It carried her downstream until she ran into the riverbank. Since then she has been wandering, without food or warm clothing, praying she wouldn't be caught and sent back to the man who put a brand on her face."

Annie shivered even though her bedroom was warmed by a blazing fire. Her father slumped back in his chair and stared past Annie, deep in thought. Annie felt terrible, but her pride and anger wouldn't let her admit it. Finally, her father rose to leave. As he reached the door, he said, "Miss Dandridge has been asking me to let you go with her for several days. I thought it was too cold. But I think the change will do you good. As soon as your leg is better, you will go with her."

For several days Annie puzzled over her father's statement. Where was she going? Why with Miss Dandridge? But he refused to answer any questions. Finally, all the swelling had gone, and Annie was able to walk without pain. That's when he told her, "Today Miss Dandridge will come for you about noon. See that the maid has packed your clothes."

"Yes, Father," Annie said as he pulled the door shut behind him.

After giving the maid instructions about her clothes, Annie felt at loose ends. She decided to go for a walk. The weather had turned cold, but there was no sign of snow. She put on a cape, tucked her hands into a fur muff, and then set off down the street, not caring where she went. The wind blew fiercely, biting her cheeks and bringing tears to her eyes. Stopping in front of the print shop to catch her breath, Annie saw a young boy inking type with a leather-covered ball that he dipped into a pan of gooey black ink made of lampblack and varnish. Then he reached up on tiptoes and pulled a long lever, called a devil's tail, which lowered the heavy plate onto the paper. After checking the printing, the boy hung the wet sheet of paper on a drying line.

He glanced up as he worked and caught sight of Annie peering through the window. Screwing his mouth into an awful grimace while crossing his eyes, he stared so intently at her that she blushed and hurried on her way.

The wind had picked up. It howled between the houses, banging a loose shutter on one of them. The streets were nearly empty with only a few brave souls venturing forth. Annie huddled on the sidewalk, pulling her hood more tightly about her face and burying her cold cheeks in the warm fur of her muff. For a minute, she stood uncertainly on the sidewalk, before turning around and heading back to the Palace. She reached the gate at the same time as a carriage pulled by two gray horses. Miss Dandridge leaned out the window and smiled. "Getting a head start on the cold?"

Barely managing to smile, Annie nodded. "I must get my case and say good-bye to Father. Then I will be out."

Mr. Goodacre carried out a small valise with Annie's clothes. Meanwhile, Annie found her father in the study, still sitting in his chair, brooding. "I'm going, Father," she said, trying to be cheerful.

He looked up, a startled expression on his face. Rising to his feet, he said, "I hope it will be a good trip for you, Annie." He put his arm around her shoulder and walked her out to the carriage.

"Take good care of her, Dorothea," he said with a smile at Miss Dandridge.

"One day she'll be my daughter, Mr. Henry. I'll treat her as one today."

The girl climbed up into the carriage where Miss Dandridge quickly tucked a heavy fur around her and placed hot bricks at her feet. Even before she was settled, the carriage began moving. By the time Annie looked out the window, her father was almost out of sight. She felt queasy in the stomach and almost shouted for the carriage to stop. Why was she being sent away? And where was she going?

If Miss Dandridge sensed her confusion, she gave no sign of it. Every time Annie looked at the older woman sitting across from her, she had her eyes closed and her head bowed. How could she sleep, the girl wondered. Annie poked her head out the window and watched each farmhouse pass by. The wind stung, but she didn't care.

Then she became aware that the older woman was watching her. "Where are we going, anyway?" she asked sullenly.

"I have friends in the country who need help. Your father was kind enough to lend you to me."

"What kind of help?" Annie asked, curious about this woman's friends.

"You'll meet them, and God will show you how best to help," Miss Dandridge answered calmly. "It's a long ride. You don't want to freeze."

Annie scowled but pulled back from the window. It wouldn't help if she started out on the wrong foot with this woman her father seemed intent on marrying.

The rest of the trip was quiet. Miss Dandridge was content to doze as Annie stared out the window watching the trees go by. The carriage made good time despite the muddy ground because the road they traveled was well used and maintained. But at a certain point, the carriage turned, leaving firm ground and heading out onto a bumpy, rutted road that was little better than a path. They made their way, lurching and swaying, along the path until up ahead Annie caught sight of a small dwelling—little more than a log shack. A mangy-looking dog ran out to greet them with ferocious barks, which brought a small boy from the house. He stood on the ramshackle porch, arms drawn close to his shivering body.

As the carriage pulled to a stop, the driver dismounted and helped Miss Dandridge, followed by Annie, out of the coach. It was close to dusk, and the wind, which had died down, picked up again. It carried a putrid smell, which Annie thought came from a poorly located outhouse. Wrinkling her nose in disgust, the girl turned to Miss Dandridge and was about to comment, but the older woman shook her head and walked briskly toward the ramshackle house, paying no attention to the smell.

With a scowl, the girl lifted her skirts, trying to keep the hem from dragging in the dirt. She quickened her pace to keep up with Miss Dandridge, not wanting to be left outside with the dirty-looking boy who stared at her. He stood in the middle of the doorway, forcing Annie to walk around him, trying to keep her skirts from rubbing up against him. She felt his dark eyes staring at her back as she entered the dimly lit house.

A miserly fire smoldered in the fireplace, giving off little heat. Every time a gust of wind blew outside, the fire flared, fed by the wind that leaked through large gaps between the logs in the walls. Miss Dandridge, ignoring the dirt and cold, put down the satchel she had carried in. She hugged the grimy little boy who had followed them into the house. Annie couldn't help but look to see if the boy's dirty face had left a stain on the older woman's pretty dress.

"Here, Thomas, I've brought you some lovely apple butter and some biscuits to put it on. Why don't you go wash your hands, and then you can eat," she urged gently as the boy plunged his dirty little hands into the basket of food.

"Yes, ma'am," he said, racing out the door to the well, but not before giving Annie a warning look. She moved away from the basket, thinking to herself, *I don't need his biscuits. He doesn't have to worry about me.*

Miss Dandridge went into the bedroom and pulled the room's only chair over to the bed. On it was a woman with a weatherbeaten face. Her arms and neck were covered with scabs. *The boy's mother,* Annie thought.

Miss Dandridge took from her satchel a new shawl, which she wrapped around the other woman's shoulders. "Hello, Mary. How are you this day? Are you eating the food I brought you before? And are you taking your medicine?"

Mary nodded feebly. "The doctor bled me last week," she said in a faint whisper. "Said it would make me better."

Annie shivered thinking of the slimy leeches used by doctors to *bleed* patients. But Miss Dandridge didn't even wince. "I heard that your sister left for Bermuda. We were surprised that she would go."

"Once Mama died, Sissy said there weren't no reason for her to stay. She stayed only long enough to make sure I wouldn't die. She's gone to be with family."

"I guess she feared that if she waited any longer, she wouldn't be able to sail this year. Try not to be bitter. She was fearful of the war."

"I'm not bitter, Miss Dandridge. But it's awful lonesome knowing that there's only me and my boy left here in Virginia."

"You just eat and rest and get your strength back so

that you can take care of your boy. You want him to grow up and be a fine man, don't you?"

The sick woman nodded feebly.

"Good. Then I'm going to warm some broth for you, and you are going to eat it." Miss Dandridge softened the words with the gentle voice in which they were said.

"Oh, I almost forgot. I brought a helper with me. This is Annie Henry. She was in your sister's class for a while."

Annie had started to smile, but when she heard those words, the smile left her face. Could this really be Mistress Hallan's sister, the one with the pox? Her eyes questioned Miss Dandridge.

"Yes. This is Mary Hallan, sister to your teacher. Sadly, their mother died. But Mary is recovering nicely, and we are here to help for a few days."

Annie looked around the dirty house again. How could Mistress Hallan, so prim and so impressed with position, be related to this person? Annie's face must have reflected her thoughts because the next thing she knew, Miss Dandridge had pulled her to the side. "I won't have you putting on airs or being rude to my friends," the woman said quietly. "If you cannot help, then you may go outside to the carriage."

Annie blushed red and nodded. The little cabin was quiet except for the sound of the wind through the cracks. The fire flickered, which seemed to rouse Miss Dandridge from her thoughts. She rose and left the small bedroom. Annie followed her and heard her ask the driver to look for some wood for the fire. That would be a job, Annie thought. There weren't any trees around at all. What a stupid place to build a house.

Just then she heard a little voice behind her. The boy, Thomas, held a biscuit in his hand.

"I saved this for you," he said. "I wasn't going to give it to you because I wanted all the biscuits for myself. Then I saw your face, and you looked so angry that I knew I should give you one."

Annie stared at the boy. His lips were smeared with apple butter, and his face was unwashed. He held the biscuit in a hand that, although it had been washed, still was dirty. He smiled shyly at first, until he saw Annie's answering smile. Then a big grin spread across his face.

"Why do you think I'm angry?" she asked finally.

"'Cause you look like Aunty, who had a sour face every day she was here," the boy answered bluntly.

"Well, I'm nothing like your aunty," Annie answered, insulted by the comparison.

"Do you want the biscuit?" the boy asked again, looking at it wistfully.

"No. You can have the biscuit," Annie answered. The boy didn't eat it but continued to look at her expectantly.

"Thank you," she finally said. With that, the boy ate.

11

Annie Comes Back

While Thomas finished the biscuit, Annie looked around the small room. It certainly needed cleaning. Thomas followed her as she peeked out one of the windows.

"Where does your mama keep a pail?" she asked him.

"On the porch," he said. "Want me to get it?"

"Fill it with water, and we'll clean up this mess," she answered brusquely. As she waited for the little boy to return with the bucket, she looked around. Where could she start? Why had Miss Dandridge brought her to this place? Surely she could have brought a servant. She felt a tug on her skirt and found Thomas standing there with the pail.

"Put it down," she snapped. The little boy's chin quivered, and Annie fought to keep from saying something awful.

"I guess we'll need a broom," she said. "Do you have one?"

"It's on the porch, too. I'll get it," he said, racing out the door and letting it swing shut with a bang.

Annie pushed up her sleeves. She sighed as she looked at her nice new dress with its hoops and lace. It wasn't intended for housework. If Miss Dandridge had told her she was going to be a scullery maid, she could have dressed in her old clothes. For a minute, the girl rebelled. Why should she clean someone else's dirty house? It wasn't her job, and no one could expect the governor's daughter to do it.

The bucket was heavy as Annie lugged it across the plank floor to the corner. There was some lye soap in a cupboard, and Annie scraped some into the water, stirring it with a wooden spoon. She found a clean rag, dunked it into the water, and scrubbed the rough, plank table. It was made of logs that had been smoothed on one side. Bearing down with all her weight, the girl scrubbed and scrubbed until the wood shone. She didn't even hear the boy come back with the broom.

The girl's hands were red from the lye, but she didn't notice. "Thomas, do you know how to sweep?" she asked.

"Yes, miss," he said.

"Then you sweep the dirt out of this house. I'm not doing all the work myself."

The little boy handled the broom awkwardly, but he managed to rid the floor of most of its dirt. "Now I'm going to scrub," she said. But the girl found that it wasn't easy getting on her hands and knees in the clumsy hoop skirt. Putting her hands on her hips, she sighed with frustration. "Turn your back, Thomas," she ordered.

The boy turned.

She reached under her skirt and undid the buckles that held on her hoops. Slipping them out from under her, the girl felt suddenly free. But she found that her skirt hem dragged on the floor. It was much too long without the hoops to hold it up. "I'm going to have to tie up my hem," she muttered, pulling up the skirt as she spoke. She tied it in several places, letting her petticoat show beneath. Then, plopping down on her hands and knees, she scrubbed.

By the time the floor was finished, Annie's hands were raw. Her back and knees ached, and her skirt was dirty. But the floor had a well-scrubbed look, and the cabin no longer looked so dingy. She stood up and stretched, feeling satisfaction at a job well done.

Thomas, who was standing near the doorway, smiled broadly when he saw how nice the room looked. "It's just like Mama's well again. She used to keep the house neat," he bragged. "But Aunty wouldn't clean. Said she had a maid at home to do it. And Grandma couldn't, so it just got dirtier and dirtier—I didn't know how to fix it."

Annie nodded, feeling a spark of tenderness toward this grubby little child. "How old are you, Thomas?"

"I'm seven," he said proudly. "Old enough to be the man around here, Mama says."

"You're a real help to your mama. I know you are," Annie said. "Come on, there's just one more thing that we need to clean before we're done."

"What is it?" the boy asked, looking around the room.

"It's you, silly," she answered. "Where's your wash tub? I'm going to heat some water, and you're going to have a bath."

"A bath," the boy moaned. "I don't need no bath. Mama don't make me take one."

"But your mama is sick, and I'm in charge. And I say you need a bath," the girl said laughing. "Go fetch the water and hang it over the fire. I'll get the tub."

Annie found an iron tub on the porch. It was too cold for Thomas to bathe outside; so she dragged it into the house. Over his protests, she filled it with water that had heated over the fireplace. Only after she agreed to hang a privacy blanket would Thomas undress and climb into the hot water. She waited on her side of the blanket. When it was too quiet in the tub, Annie threatened to come around and make sure the boy was really in the water and using soap. "You scrub behind your ears," she said. "And wash your hair."

While the boy was bathing, Miss Dandridge came out of the bedroom. "Look at this place, Annie. You've done wonders. Where did you learn to clean like this?"

"Last summer when I stayed with a friend at her father's tavern," Annie said, smiling despite her earlier anger.

"Where is Thomas now?" Miss Dandridge asked.

Annie pointed to the blanket behind which splashing sounds could be heard. "He's bathing," she said. "But what do I do with his clothes?"

"I brought some nice winter breeches and a wool shirt for the boy," Miss Dandridge said. "They are in my satchel. Would you get them?"

Annie tiptoed into the bedroom, careful not to wake Mary. She reached into the satchel and dragged out the bundle of clothes. As she pulled, out fell a piece of paper. The girl bent over to get it when she saw her name written in her father's hand. Looking guiltily over her shoulder to make sure Miss Dandridge wasn't watching, Annie began to read. It was apparently the page of a letter written from Patrick Henry to Miss Dandridge. "I worry about Annie," it read. "She doesn't seem like the same sweet child who came with me from Scotchtown. Last summer she begged to be allowed to stay at the tavern in Hanover—eager to work, she said. Now she has adopted the Williamsburg sneer at everything simple. I fear that the homely virtues of faithfulness, diligence, perseverance, and kindness seem old-fashioned to her."

After reading the letter, Annie sank back on the floor, letting it drop back into the satchel. Was it true? she wondered. Had she changed so much? Looking about guiltily, Annie hopped to her feet, certain that Miss Dandridge would be coming after her in a minute. She picked up the bundle of clothes and hurried back where she found Miss Dandridge drying the little boy off.

"I don't want her to see me," he screamed.

Annie tossed the clothes to a grinning Miss Dandridge and turned her back on them.

After a few minutes, Miss Dandridge called to her, "I'm not a cook," she laughed, "so I had cook prepare us a picnic supper. In fact, there's enough food here for several days. Are you hungry?"

"I'm hungry," Thomas shouted. "I'm starving. I could eat all that food."

Annie scowled. "I'm not hungry," she said.

"Well, come sit with us anyway," Miss Dandridge urged. "Maybe seeing us eat will give you an appetite." She ignored Annie's downcast face. The little boy began eating as soon as the food was set before him. But Miss Dandridge reached out a hand to him. "We have not prayed." Then she looked at Annie and said, "Would you ask the Lord's blessing?"

Bowing her head, Annie started praying. She found that even the simple words of thanks stuck in her throat. It had been a long time since she had prayed. Finally, she managed to croak out a few words, feeling embarrassed as she did so.

They ate and drank, and even Annie found the food too tempting to ignore. Though Miss Dandridge made pleasant conversation, Annie was distracted. She thought about her father marrying a new wife, and about her mother who had been sick and died. Why would God heal Mary and not her mother? she wondered. Her attention was brought back to the present when Thomas asked, "Is my mama going to live?"

Miss Dandridge smiled. "Such ideas you have, Thomas. Of course she's going to live."

But Annie spoke out loud some of the things she had been thinking. "Sometimes mamas don't live," she said. "My mama died."

Miss Dandridge froze in her seat. Thomas's little face crumpled into tears until the older woman said bluntly, "Your mama will not die, Thomas. She's getting better. In fact, I have a surprise for you. We're going to take the two of you back to Williamsburg. We'll take our warm carriage, bundle you both up, and bring you to our home where your mama can get strong."

Annie threw her napkin down. "You're not God," she screamed as she rose from the table. "You don't know what will happen."

Miss Dandridge spoke calmly, but there was a no-nonsense look in her eye. "Sit down, Annie," she ordered. While the girl sat down, Miss Dandridge regarded Thomas, whose face showed confusion.

"Thomas, Annie is right that I'm not God. I don't know all His plans. But I do know your mother is getting better. Her fever is gone, and her strength is increasing. With care, she will be fine." The boy looked trustingly at the older woman, who turned to face Annie.

"Annie, I want you to think for a minute before you speak. Thomas needs you to tell him the truth. When your mama died, what did you learn about God?"

The question brought back a rush of memories, good and bad. Several times she began to speak, but each time Miss Dandridge said, "Have you thought it out carefully, Annie?"

Finally, the girl smiled a weak smile. She looked at Thomas and said, "I know that God, who made the heavens and the earth, does only what is right," she answered.

That answer seemed to satisfy the boy, but it didn't satisfy Annie. She worked quietly while they washed the dishes and packed away the food. Miss Dandridge tucked the little boy into his bed, and Annie was left alone in the room. For the first time she wondered where she and Miss Dandridge were going to sleep.

The older woman tiptoed out of the bedroom. "I guess we should go to bed also," she said.

"But where?" Annie asked.

"There's a barn out back. It has plenty of hay. I asked our driver to lay the blankets in the loft."

"Where will he sleep?" Annie asked.

"In the carriage, I gather."

"Won't it be cold?"

"He has blankets," she said. "Let us take a lantern and see what arrangements he's made for us."

They walked by lantern light to the barn, which was filled with sweet-smelling hay. There was a ladder up to the loft, and Miss Dandridge regarded it with amusement. "How will I climb this in my hoops?" she mused aloud.

Annie laughed. "Take them off," she said. "I did."

With a feminine shrug, Miss Dandridge removed the awkward and bulky hoops and climbed the stairs to the loft. Annie, not wanting to be left alone, clambered up behind her. They found two beds made of furs and blankets on hay. The girl snuggled down in one of them, pulling the warm blankets up close to her chin and breathing deeply of the barn smells. Next to her, Miss Dandridge settled down and then blew out the lantern. Suddenly the barn was plunged into darkness.

They lay there quietly for a few minutes until Miss Dandridge asked, "What else did you want to tell Thomas?"

The girl didn't answer right away. She listened to the older woman's gentle breathing and the sounds of the wind outside the barn. "I guess I wanted to tell him that things can get pretty confusing. But then I thought he was probably already confused, and I didn't want to make it worse," she said.

"What do you find confusing?"

Annie thought. "I find the rules confusing," she said. "Like why do people act one way at Scotchtown and another way in Williamsburg. And I find God confusing. Why is He so far away?"

Now it was Miss Dandridge's turn to be quiet. Annie thought she had fallen asleep, but then she heard the soft voice. "I think God seems far away when we know that we've done something to displease Him," she said. "Some people live their whole lives like that. They never humble themselves and confess their sins. They pretend that they are perfect, even though they know deep down that they sin. We all get angry and act selfishly. We all want what doesn't belong to us."

Annie shivered and pulled the cover up tighter. Then Miss Dandridge continued, "I believe what the Bible says—that if we confess our sins, Christ is faithful and just and will forgive us our sins and cleanse us from all unrighteousness."

"Even me?" Annie whispered into the dark.

She felt Miss Dandridge's hand reach across and take hers. "Even you, my dear," the older woman said. "And as for manners in Williamsburg: Too many confuse money and style with good manners. Some people even think their fine clothes make them Christians. Others believe that since we have no king, we are free from all rules. They have confused liberty with license to do whatever they wish. They couldn't be more wrong. God has given us liberty so that we might do good. And we will not hold onto our liberty long if we lose our virtue. This is one of your father's greatest worries. But enough. You need your sleep, and I need mine. Good night, dear."

Annie turned her back to Miss Dandridge and thought about the woman's words. She felt herself at a turning point. She could be self-righteous, pretending that she was perfect, or she could humble herself and admit her faults. One was the way of pride, the other the way of forgiveness. *I'm not so bad,* she thought. But then she remembered a hundred cruel things she had done. Every time she tried shaking off the feeling and sleeping, she couldn't.

Finally, as the first rays of sun poked their way through the rafters, Annie knelt beside her blanket, confessed her sin, and begged God for forgiveness. Then she fell into a deep and dreamless slumber.

Annie slept until noon. When she awoke, the bed next to her was empty. She lay there for a minute, enjoying the cold air on her face and the cozy warmth under the blanket. She knew she'd have to throw off the covers soon and make a dash for the house. Just then something pinged on her blanket. A second later, she felt something hit her toe. "What's that?" she said, bolting upright.

A giggle from down below gave her a clue. She found

a little chestnut—a buckeye—near her arm and another by her foot. "I'll get you," she chuckled, pocketing both nuts. Then crawling to the edge of the loft, she peered over. No sooner had her head appeared than she was beaned with another buckeye.

"I got you," the boy chortled, falling on his knees. "I got you good that time."

Annie let fly with one of the chestnuts she had stashed in her pocket.

"Ouch," the boy yelled, rubbing his leg where Annie had hit it.

From above, the girl grinned. "Truce?" she asked.

"All right, truce," the boy agreed, still rubbing his thigh.

Annie climbed down from the loft, straightening her wrinkled dress as she went.

"I thought you'd never wake up," Thomas said. "I only threw the buckeyes to get your attention."

"Is Miss Dandridge in the house?" Annie asked.

"Yep, she's helping Mama get dressed. We're going to Williamsburg today," the boy said eagerly.

"Today?" Annie asked. "I had best get ready. I look a mess."

"You sure do," Thomas agreed readily. "You look like you slept in those clothes."

"Well, that may be because I did," Annie replied. "Now shoo. Let me get ready."

The boy ran off with the skinny dog that Annie had seen earlier. She followed behind, shivering as she crossed the yard in her dress. In the cabin, she found a fire blazing. "Oh, it's nice in here," she said as she stood in front of the fireplace.

"Good sleep?" Miss Dandridge inquired.

"Hardly," Annie replied, remembering the fitful night. she had. "It was so odd," she continued. "After we talked, I felt so wound up. My stomach was churning, and I worried over every bad thing I could ever remember doing. I felt as if I would go crazy, and when I tried to calm down or count sheep, I became even more stirred up. Finally, there seemed to be no choice. I pleaded with God to forgive me and to give me a fresh start. And I felt a peace come over me as if He had answered. The rest of the night I slept like a baby," she said with a laugh, "that is, until Thomas woke me up."

Miss Dandridge had been listening carefully, a slow smile coming over her face. Then she bent and hugged Annie, whispering a prayer of thanksgiving to herself.

While they talked, Thomas ran back and forth from the porch. "May I take this?" he asked, holding up an old hoe.

"Let's leave that," Miss Dandridge said with a grimace.

The little boy carried the rusted tool out to the porch, but then he returned with a cracked pottery pitcher. "This is Mama's favorite," he said, holding the blue pitcher up. "We must take it with us."

Annie looked up from the satchel she was packing. "Oh, Thomas," she blurted without thinking, "that old thing is better left in a junk pile."

Tears welled up in the little boy's eyes as he appealed to Miss Dandridge. "My daddy gave this to Mama," he said. "It's her favorite."

Annie looked humbled. "I'm sorry, Thomas," she said. "I didn't mean to hurt your feelings."

Meanwhile, Miss Dandridge looked around the room where the piles of things that they planned to take were growing. "There's just not room in my carriage for all your belongings," she told Thomas. "Let's leave some things here so that when you come back, your home will be ready for you. We'll only take what you'll need for the winter in Williamsburg."

"I guess that will be all right," the boy said. He looked around as though he were thinking of something. "I'm hungry."

"There are some apples and some cheese in the basket," Miss Dandridge offered. "I'm going to get your mama up, and then we'll be ready to go." Then, looking up, she noticed that Annie was still dressed in her same crumpled dress. "Annie, you need to change before we set out. I'll not have your father think that I neglected you."

Annie smiled. "Only made me work like a slave and sleep in a barn," she said, giving her a sly grin.

Miss Dandridge laughed. "Some people don't respond well to luxury," she said. "They need to remember who they are before God."

Annie removed her soiled dress and put on a fresh one. She moved quickly, before the little boy could do anything to embarrass her. By the time she was finished, the carriage was loaded with Mary inside on a makeshift bed. Thomas was happy to ride above with the driver; so Annie and Miss Dandridge squeezed together on the other seat.

By the time they reached Williamsburg, Annie's back and legs were sore from the bumpy trip. She was tired and glad to reach the Governor's Palace. When the carriage stopped and the driver helped her out, Annie saw Thomas's wide-eyed wonder at the size of the house.

"Do you really live in that place?" the boy asked.

"Yes," she said. "And you can come visit me here."

"Really?" he asked. "You'd let me come inside?"

"Of course," the girl promised. "My friends can visit me anytime they want. And you're my friend." She reached up and shook the boy's hand, handing him the last of the buckeyes as she did so. "I'll be praying for your mama," she said.

"Me too," he answered.

Annie heard the door open behind her and saw her father's slender figure come down the stairs and stand by her side. She slipped her arm around his waist and said softly, "I'm back, Father. Annie from Scotchtown is back."

12

A Christmas Ball

Annie found an invitation waiting for her when she entered the house. There was to be a Christmas ball at Grace's home, and Annie and her father were invited.

"A Christmas ball?" she exclaimed when she read the neatly engraved invitation. She hadn't realized the fall had passed so quickly.

Annie ran to her closet to examine the green satin party dress that Miss Dandridge (would she ever call her Mother?) had helped her pick out. It was a beautiful gown, and Annie felt full of excitement as she thought about wearing it.

The week plodded along. But finally Friday came, and Annie was able to dress for the ball. With the maid's help, she curled her hair, making sure that the hot curling iron didn't burn it. Then, reaching into a box that she kept in her wardrobe, Annie found the tortoiseshell comb that the auctioneer had given her. She had not worn it since that day.

She slipped into the dress, not even minding the feel of the hoops because the effect was so beautiful. When she twirled, her skirts billowed out around her. "Now I can use my dancing lessons," she said as she remembered the sometimes painful sessions that she had been forced to endure.

Annie and her father pulled into the driveway at the Hall, announcing their presence with the sound of carriage bells and the twinkling of lights. They were not alone. Ahead of them were twenty carriages, each unloading its load of happy partygoers.

Annie waited impatiently for their turn with her face pressed against the carriage window. The house glowed like a lantern with the light of thousands of candles. Faint sounds of music drifted to her waiting carriage. Next to her, Patrick Henry, elegant in his satin waistcoat and breeches, tapped his foot in time to the music. "Will you dance with me?" he asked.

"I'll write you into my program," she answered playfully.

By that time their carriage had reached the veranda, and a uniformed servant opened the door and helped Annie out. She waited for her father, who guided her up the stairs and into the house. She felt overwhelmed by the press of people who crowded around, eager to shake Patrick Henry's hand. He nodded and smiled at them as he guided his daughter into the ballroom where the music played. "Let us have good music and dancing," he said to his friends. "There will be time for talk later."

Just then, Annie caught sight of Grace. "Come with me," Grace whispered in her friend's ear. "We're having our supper in another room. Then we can join the adults for dancing."

Hand in hand, the girls skipped out of the ballroom. In a large drawing room, Annie found her friends from school, as well as many young people whom she had never met. Grace drew her into a circle of friends, and for the next few minutes, they admired each other's dresses and hair. Even Kate was there. Annie made her way next to her and said, "You look so pretty tonight."

Kate smiled shyly. "Mrs. Wythe gave me the dress. I hope it's all right?" she said, a little self-consciously.

"It looks wonderful to me."

At that moment, Grace interrupted, carrying two cups of punch. "I thought you might be thirsty," she said. "There's plenty to eat as well." She pointed at a table laden with food.

Kate drank down her punch quickly and then giggled. "I think I'm nervous," she confided to Annie.

"I am too," Annie said. "I've never been to a ball like this either. I guess we can be nervous together."

The two girls walked toward the buffet and began filling their plates. They had just taken seats when Grace came again. "Here," she said. "I didn't think you could carry a plate and a cup; so I brought you some more punch."

Annie, who hadn't finished her first cup, gave Grace a funny look. But Kate accepted the fresh cup gratefully. "Thank you," she said.

The two girls settled down to eat. Kate nodded her head and tapped her toes in time with the music.

"Do you like to dance?" Annie asked.

"I never have," Kate answered. "I'm probably all left feet. But I love music, and Mrs. Wythe has been letting me play her harpsichord."

"Do you think someone will ask you to dance?" Annie asked, wondering if she would be asked by anyone other than her father.

Kate shrugged and took a last sip of her punch. "It makes me nervous just to think about it," she admitted.

The two girls watched the scene around them. There was some mild flirting going on between several older girls and boys. Annie watched the way the girls hid behind their fans, giggling. "If that's what it takes to get a husband," she whispered to Kate, "I guess I'm doomed to be an old maid."

"What are you two whispering about?" Grace asked as she reappeared with two more glasses of punch. "Don't the two of you know that you're supposed to mingle, not sit alone and whisper?"

The two girls blushed guiltily. "We didn't mean to be rude," Kate apologized. "We're just finishing eating."

"Here's some punch then," Grace said. "After you finish it, you must promise me to mix with the other guests. I don't want my party to be a failure."

Kate accepted the scolding, but Annie shook her head. "I don't know why Grace is acting like such a busybody," she said. "We aren't the only ones sitting in chairs." She felt like grumbling some more but caught herself. *That's not kind,* she thought.

When Kate had finished her third cup of punch, she stood up. "I'm to mingle," she said just a trifle loudly. "Wish me success." As she stood, she swayed slightly.

Annie looked at her friend curiously. "Are you feeling all right?"

"Wonderful. Just wonderful," her friend replied. She turned abruptly and plowed into a waiter who carried a platter of cold meat pies. "Excuse me," she said as the tray tumbled to the floor, scattering food everywhere.

When Kate saw the mess, she sank to her knees and began crawling around, trying to pick up the meat pies.

"I'll get them, miss," the waiter said. "You go on."

But Kate moaned. "My fault, my fault."

Annie looked around, wondering what to do. She saw Grace standing in a corner, a smug look on her face. Meanwhile, a small crowd had gathered around them. Annie heard the titters and the talk. "Girl's drunk. That's what I heard. Probably brought a flask to the party. Wait until Mrs. Wythe hears."

Without waiting to hear any more, Annie reached down and grabbed Kate by the waist. "We need to get some air," she said quietly. "Come with me."

Kate rose to her feet unsteadily, but with Annie's arm around her, they walked to the door.

Just then Grace called out to Annie, "Where are you going?"

"For some air," Annie answered. "My friend needs some air."

"Your friends are inside, Annie," Grace said. "Let the servants help her."

"No. Kate's my friend, and she needs me," Annie answered. Next to her, Kate giggled.

"Oh, Kate," Annie whispered. "Be quiet. Someone will hear you, and you will really be in trouble."

"But why?" Kate asked. "I'm only having fun at the party."

"But why'd you have to go and get drunk?" Annie asked. "Mrs. Wythe will never forgive you."

"Drunk!" the girl said in a loud voice that Annie was sure would bring someone to investigate.

"Hush. Yes, drunk. Did you bring a flask?"

By this time, Annie's harsh words had begun penetrating Kate's drunken mind. She shook her head as though to clear it and sank down onto the floor.

Annie tightened her grip. "You can't just sit down here," she hissed. "Let's go out in the yard."

"But it's dark," Kate wailed.

"Of course it's dark," Annie said. "That's why we're going there. You don't want to be seen like this, do you?"

Kate shook her head miserably. "I don't feel that well."

"You'll feel better when we get outdoors."

Annie pushed and pulled the other girl along the dark hallway until they reached a door leading to the backyard. Pushing it open, the girls tumbled out into the cold, black night.

"It's too cold," Kate moaned. "Oh, Annie, it's cold."

"Look, Kate," Annie said in her best matter-of-fact voice, "I'm cold also. Maybe if we go to the . . . Let's see, the kitchen will be too busy, as will the scullery. I know—the smokehouse. The walls are thick, and we'll be out of the wind."

Since the yard was strange, Annie wasn't sure where the smokehouse would be, but she figured it should be near, but not too near, the kitchen. Keeping in the shadows, they walked until they could see the lights of the kitchen. Finally, the two girls stumbled into the smokehouse. The room was dirty with ash, and the odor of smoked bacon and ham was overwhelming.

"I may be sick," Kate whined as she seated herself on the brick floor.

But Annie wasn't paying any attention. "I just can't figure out how this happened," she puzzled. "What did you have to drink tonight?"

"Just the punch that Grace brought to me," Kate sniffled.

"Grace Jones," Annie said with disgust. "That's cruel." She suddenly remembered Grace's smug look when Kate had bumped into the waiter. "She must have mixed something in the punch."

"But didn't you drink the punch?" Kate asked.

Annie shook her head. "I didn't like the taste of it," she confessed.

"And I drank three glasses," Kate moaned. "No, four. I drank one of yours as well."

From outside the smokehouse, they heard the sudden sound of footsteps, and then the heavy door creaked open. Before either girl had a chance to be afraid, a voice said, "So that's where you ran off to."

Kate screamed, but Annie stared white-faced at the coarse, whiskered man who now stood about two feet from her. He peered at her from beady eyes. Out of the corner of his mouth he spat a stream of brown liquid that splashed on Kate's white dress, sending the girl into a new round of wailing. Annie knew she had seen him before.

"Who are you?" Annie asked.

"I think you know me," he growled. "I know who you are."

The man drew closer, and Annie screamed as she recognized the auctioneer. He clapped a rough hand over her mouth and snarled, "Shut up. I'll see your father, the fancy governor, pay a pretty penny for your return."

Keeping his hand pressed tightly over her mouth, the man lifted her as though she were nothing more than a sack of feathers. Then, as the lantern light glowed softly on Annie's hair, the man saw the tortoiseshell comb. "It's a beautiful thing, isn't it?" he said as he yanked it out of her hair and stuffed it in his pocket.

Ignoring Kate, who lay moaning on the floor, the man pushed through the door and stumbled with Annie into the darkness. She struggled against him, but he easily subdued her with his massive arm. He squeezed harder until she thought he might squeeze the breath out of her. Still, she struggled. "There's no point in all that wiggling," the man said. "Ain't no one going to hear you. My horse is just behind those trees there. We'll be gone, and there won't be no hope for you unless your pa wants to pay a ransom. Like that nice comb. I got that from your pa. I bet you didn't know that."

Annie stopped wiggling, wanting him to continue his story. As she relaxed, so did he. "Yep. Course, I didn't know it were your pa. I saw a broken-down carriage and ransacked a trunk. Didn't know 'til later that your pa were in it—could have held him for ransom if I had. But now I got the daughter, and my guess is the governor will pay quite a bit to get you back."

While he talked, the man slowed his pace, stopping often to catch his breath. He cursed softly. Though she was light, she made an awkward bundle because her hoop skirts kept getting in the way. He loosened his arm as one of the wire hoops bit into his flesh, and Annie took that opportunity to free her arm from his grasp. Now, instead of both arms being tightly held against his body, one of her arms hung free. The man didn't notice.

"We're almost there," he muttered to himself. Carefully, Annie reached into the man's pocket and felt for the comb he had stuffed there. Grasping it tightly in her hand, she drew it out. Then, with the courage that comes from desperation, she jammed the comb into the man's ear until he screamed in pain. He opened his arms and dropped the girl, who ran clumsily away. When she had put about twenty yards between them, she screamed as loudly as she could.

From down the hill Annie heard voices, and she screamed louder. Behind her she heard heavy footsteps, so she kept running, blinded by the tears that flooded her eyes.

"Whoa," a voice said, as two strong arms grabbed her. Annie swung her fist until it connected with the face of the man who held her. "Ouch," he said. "Here, perhaps you'd better take her. After all, she's your daughter."

Hearing those words, Annie stopped her kicking and screaming. "Father!" she cried.

"What happened to you, Annie?" he asked as he folded her into an embrace.

"Oh, Father. That disgusting man. He's the one who robbed the coach. And he's the one who tried to grab me at the fair. And he's the one at the auction—"

"What auction? What fair? What man? This is all confusing. Let's go back to the house and hear this story."

"But, Father, he's getting away," Annie cried. In the distance, they could hear the scrambling of feet. "He said he has a horse there."

By now they were close to the stable. "Round up some men, and we'll go after him," a young man told a groom. He rubbed his bruised jaw ruefully. Annie looked at him, and the young man smiled. "You certainly know how to find excitement, Annie Henry," he said. "But perhaps your father needs to teach you that the quiet life has its virtues as well."

"Did I hurt you?" she asked.

"I would never admit that you did," he answered, climbing on his horse.

When the posse had ridden off, Annie turned to her father, who held her arm tightly. He said, "That Spencer Roane is a fine young man. I'd be proud to have him for a son." And for some reason Annie blushed.

Later, after they had rescued poor Kate from the smokehouse, a group gathered at the governor's mansion to discuss the night's events. Kate and Annie were a mess. Their dresses were soot-covered, and Annie's was torn from her run through the trees. Their hair was bedraggled, and Kate complained of a splitting headache.

Word came that the outlaw had been caught and now sat in the public jail. Mrs. Wythe came to collect Kate. Instead of being angry, she winked at Annie and said, "It's that Grace Jones, not my good Kate, who should be punished."

Miss Dandridge sipped a cup of warm herb tea. "I can't get over the lawlessness of some men," she said for the fifth time.

Taking her hand in his, Patrick Henry said, "We shouldn't be surprised. Sin lurks in all our hearts. But I pray that God would restrain evil and change us for the better. If we are not a virtuous people, we won't long be a free people."

Then, looking at his daughter, he said, "I hope you've learned your lesson about using my position to gain favors."

She nodded, hiding a yawn. "I didn't know it was your comb, Father."

"But that isn't the point. I bought that comb for Miss Dandridge, it is true. By accepting it from the auctioneer, you brought into question my integrity. You made it seem as though the man had to pay a bribe to get into my good favor."

"I'm sorry, Father," Annie answered.

"Then I'll say no more."

13

A Wedding

One day in early January, Annie and Miss Dandridge sat sewing in the parlor. A huge fire roared in the fireplace; outside, several inches of new snow blanketed the ground.

"I remember when Patsy was preparing for her wedding," Annie said, thinking back two years.

"I wish I had met your sister," Miss Dandridge said. "We live too far from your family, I think."

"But they'll come here for the wedding, won't they?" Annie asked.

Miss Dandridge set down her sewing on the settee. She stared dreamily at the fire. When she didn't answer, Annie looked up from her own stitching. "They'll be at the wedding?" she repeated with a touch of anxiety.

Miss Dandridge shook her head as though chasing away cobwebs. "I'm sorry, dear," she said. "I wasn't paying attention. Of course they'll be at the wedding." But then her face took on a sad look.

"What's troubling you?"

"You may think I'm silly," the older woman said sheepishly.

"I won't think that of you," Annie answered with a smile.

"Do you think your father would mind being married at Scotchtown?"

"Scotchtown?" Annie asked. "But why? You have the beautiful mansion here, and all your friends are here. Why would you want to go to Scotchtown?" As she talked, Annie paced back and forth in front of the fireplace, her skirts making a noisy swishing sound as she passed.

"Annie, sit down," Miss Dandridge said, a bit impatiently. "Your pacing is making me nervous."

Annie blushed and sat down. Miss Dandridge had never snapped at her like that. For several minutes both were silent. Then Miss Dandridge said apologetically, "I'm sorry. I am all a flutter over this wedding."

Again the room was quiet. Only the ticking of the clock broke the silence before the older woman spoke. "I'd like nothing more than to be married at Scotchtown," she said. "That home has been such a big part of your family's life. . . . I guess I'd feel more a part of the family if our wedding took place there."

Annie thought about that for a minute. "And you wouldn't mind not being married in the Governor's Palace?" she asked.

"Not at all," Miss Dandridge replied. "Your father has only one more year as governor, and then we'll leave Williamsburg for good. This is not our home."

"But what about all the people you know here?"

"Annie, most of these people are not friends. They are political friends or allies. They like your father because he is the governor. But in Hanover, he has true friends. Some were his friends when to most of the world he was a failure."

"What does Father say?"

Now it was Miss Dandridge's turn to blush. "I haven't asked him. I'm afraid maybe he has his heart set on being married here, and I'm willing to do whatever will make him happy."

"That's silly," Annie declared. "I bet Father doesn't care. Why don't you just tell him what you told me."

"I will," Miss Dandridge promised. "But would you do me a favor first? Will you find out your father's thinking on this subject?"

"Do you mean right now?" Annie asked.

"Well, it doesn't have to be this instant," Miss Dandridge said. "But . . ."

By this time Annie was on her feet and at the parlor door. "Why don't you send for tea," she suggested. "I won't be but a minute."

She took the stairs two at a time despite her skirts. Outside her father's door, she paused to catch her breath. Then she knocked.

"Come in," he called.

She found him sitting at his writing desk, a stack of letters before him. "I find this writing to be tedious," he complained. "I wish you would make progress in your penmanship so that you could do some of this for me."

Annie looked shamefaced. Despite her best efforts and the patient instruction of Miss Dandridge, her handwriting was still plagued by ink splotches. Annie sat on the edge of her father's tall canopy bed. He turned in his chair until he was facing her.

"Well, daughter?" he asked.

"I wanted to know where you are getting married," Annie blurted.

"That's Miss Dandridge's decision," he answered, turning back to his letters.

"Wait," Annie said. "You don't care where the wedding takes place?"

"I've assumed it would be here at the Palace or maybe at the Bruton Parish Church. But why not ask Dorothea?"

"Why not Scotchtown?" Annie asked, looking intently at her father.

Her question took him by surprise. He rubbed his jaw as though thinking about it for the first time. "I couldn't ask Dorothea to get married in the country," he said finally.

"But is that what you'd want?" Annie persisted.

"It would certainly make things easier," he said. "There would be no need for the whole family to come to Williamsburg, and we could just stay for the summer. We must not remain in this dank town during the wet summer months." Then he shook his head. "No. I couldn't ask her to make that sacrifice."

Annie hopped down from the bed. She placed a kiss on her father's cheek before saying "thank you" and skipping out. Her father stared at her retreating figure, a puzzled look on his face.

Back downstairs, Annie drank the cup of tea that Miss Dandridge held out to her. Despite the older woman's eager expression, she kept silent, enjoying her chance to tease. Miss Dandridge was too well-bred to beg, so the two drank their tea in silence until Annie tired of the game.

"Father says it's up to you," she said finally.

Hearing those words, Miss Dandridge's expectant smile faded. "That means he'd prefer the Governor's Palace, doesn't it?"

"He said . . ." Annie tried to hide her smile but failed. "He said it would be more convenient at Scotchtown, but he couldn't ask you to make that sacrifice."

Suddenly Miss Dandridge laughed. "That's wonderful," she said. "I choose to be married at Scotchtown. Now to tell your father and write to Patsy." She paused for a minute. Worry furrowed her brow. "Will Patsy think it too much trouble?" she asked.

"You don't know Patsy," Annie said with a grin. "She loves a good party—and you'll give her great pleasure preparing for it."

"Good," Miss Dandridge answered. "Then I must write to her and ask."

In May, 1777, Annie returned triumphantly to Scotchtown with her father and Miss Dandridge. The house was filled, not only with the Henry family, but with the many guests who had come from all around for the wedding.

The house was noisy and filled with laughter. Annie's brothers and sisters demanded to hear all the news from Williamsburg, and there was much bragging and teasing. Several days after arriving, Annie wandered outside near her mother's lilac tree, which was laden with sweet-smelling blooms. She sat on the bench near the tree, glad to be alone, if only for a few minutes.

"You'd like Miss Dandridge," she whispered out loud, as though talking to her mother. "She's kind and good, and she loves Father very much. She even likes me," Annie said shyly. She hugged herself with happiness. Annie looked awkwardly around her to make sure no one was listening. "I love you, Mama," she whispered. "I feel so happy because I love Miss Dandridge also."

Later that week the little Anglican church was filled with guests as Patrick Henry and Dorothea Dandridge became man and wife. It was through tears that Annie watched the ceremony. Her brother John poked her. "Why are you so sad?"

"I didn't know I'd ever be this happy again," she said. "Isn't it grand?"

"It will be," her brother agreed, "if she doesn't try to put me in silk breeches." His words were softened by the wide grin he couldn't seem to get off his face.

"She has her ways," Annie laughed. "You won't even know what hit you."

At the ball that followed, Annie danced and danced. She even danced with Andrew Thacker. There were a few awkward moments when Annie apologized for her behavior in Williamsburg. But those soon passed, and the two friends joined the other young people in a fast Virginia reel. Andrew moved with more energy than grace, and by the end of the dance Annie felt she had been through a whirlwind. She let Andrew lead her rather shakily to a chair where she gratefully sipped a cup of punch. Andrew withdrew to join his friends, and Annie sat tapping her toe as she watched the brightly dressed dancers moving gracefully across the floor.

Just then her father joined her. "Are you too tired for one more dance?" he asked.

"Too tired for one with Andrew," she answered with a smile.

"I don't have his energy or dancing talent," her father said. "Would you join me?"

Annie followed her father to the dance floor. For several minutes, they joined the circle of dancers without speaking. Then her father looked at his second daughter. "Are you happy to be home?" he asked.

"I never was happier," she answered.

"Any regrets about your year in Williamsburg?"

"Not regrets really," she said slowly. "But I wish I hadn't been so foolish."

"Places like Williamsburg bring out the fool in a person," he said. "But . . . they can also make you wise."

"I think I'm learning that," Annie whispered.

Annie Henry and the Redcoats

For
Mom and Dad

Contents

1

A Dangerous Journey

"I sure wish that baby would stop crying," Elizabeth complained. "Why doesn't Dolly feed her?" She tucked a few stray pieces of hair back under her blue gingham sunbonnet and scowled at the howls coming from the wagon behind.

Next to her on the seat at the front of the big Conestoga wagon, her older sister Annie smiled. "At least we know the baby has good, strong lungs. She's been crying for the past hour and doesn't seem at all tired of it."

"But I'm tired of it," twelve-year-old Elizabeth grumbled under her breath.

Annie pulled her sister's bonnet down over her eyes, letting her own laughter drown out the younger girl's complaints. "I'll make you switch wagons if all you do is complain," she warned. "Perhaps you should go sit with the cooking pots. They won't mind your grumbling."

Next to them on the seat, Joseph, one of Patrick Henry's many slaves, yawned. They had already been on the trail for two days, and he was used to listening to the girls' mild bickering. He wiped a handkerchief across his sweaty brow and pulled his tricornered hat lower over his eyes. The afternoon sun was bright.

"I don't know why we couldn't travel in a more comfortable coach," Elizabeth complained as she vainly fanned herself. "It's hotter'n blazes. I can hardly breathe."

"We couldn't bring a nice city coach out on this trail," Annie answered. "Just look at the ruts and rocks. Why, we'd never get to Leatherwood. Already it's going to take nearly seven days."

Elizabeth groaned. "Why couldn't Father have stayed in Richmond? Aunt Anne said he could make a fortune as a lawyer, and if Dolly keeps having babies, he'll need a fortune. I don't know why we have to go out to the frontier."

Annie closed her eyes and let the sun warm her face. Her own bonnet hung down her back despite her sister's constant reminders that the sun would bring out unsightly freckles. At nearly sixteen, Annie was still small. Although not beautiful, she had lively gray eyes and a quick smile that was attractive. She wore her wiry dark hair in a plain style, away from her face, because she wouldn't spend hours every day having her hair styled as many women did.

Letting the rhythm of the wagon lull her into near sleep, she thought about the changes in store for her family. It wasn't easy to leave the luxury of the Governor's Palace for a house on the frontier. But that's what her father, the famous patriot Patrick Henry, had wanted.

He had always loved the land. From the time he had bought Scotchtown in Hanover County, he had dreamed about going farther west where the land was good and neighbors were far away. Politics and duty had kept him in the city. But now, having finished two terms as governor, he had sold Scotchtown and bought 16,000 acres in Henry County, Virginia, right on the frontier. She smiled as she thought about living in a county named after her own father.

It wouldn't be an easy life. After all, it was 1779, and the Revolutionary War still raged. For two years the British had been stirring up the Indians all along the frontier and encouraging them to raid the white settlements. Things were worse on the other side of the mountains, especially in Kentucky, but her father said that all settlers had to be constantly alert.

Annie's thoughts were interrupted by a yelp and the sound of hooves against the sun-baked ground. Sitting up, she caught sight of her nine-year-old brother Edward charging toward the wagon on his pony.

"Whoa, Master Edward," Joseph shouted as he steadied his own team of skittish horses. "Slow down before you cause an accident."

The sweating boy brought his horse under control. "You can't get the horse all lathered up like that on a hot day like today," Annie scolded. "I don't know when we'll find water." She stopped scolding, though, when she saw the frightened look on his face.

"Something scare you?" Elizabeth teased. "Maybe Indians," she added. "You've been telling us you've seen Indians all day."

The boy blushed. "It wasn't Indians," he said. "It was a rattler, fatter than my fist. Lying smack in the middle of the trail. I thought at first it was dead, and so I pulled up close. Then I heard the rattling. The snake raised its head and looked at me. Lightning didn't wait to see what would happen next. He just bolted out of there. Nearly knocked me from the saddle." The boy gulped for air as the words tumbled out of his mouth.

"A rattlesnake?" Annie looked skeptical. "I've never seen one. Are you sure it wasn't just an old grass snake?"

"Do you think I can't tell the difference?" the boy said scornfully. "I'll tell Father. Maybe he'll let me shoot it."

Without waiting to hear more from his sisters, Edward rode off in search of his father. Just finding him would be a job. There were ten wagons carrying household furnishings for Patrick Henry, his second wife, Dolly, and their new baby, also named Dolly. In addition, the caravan included Annie, Elizabeth, Edward, and their older sister Patsy, all of them Patrick Henry's children from his first marriage. Patsy traveled with her husband, John Fontaine, and their three small children. The Henry household also included many slaves. Livestock brought up the rear of the caravan. There were cows, oxen, horses, and even pigs.

From her place in the first wagon, Elizabeth shuddered. "I don't like snakes," she said.

"Don't be silly," Annie admonished her. "A snake would have to have wings to get up on this old wagon."

For the next few minutes the girls were silent as the wagon bumped its way along the rocky trail. Next to them, Joseph pulled up on the reins. Annie saw that the trail led down to a creek about fifteen feet across and then resumed on the other side. Behind them the other wagons creaked to a stop.

Joseph hopped down from his seat and helped the girls down. Annie stretched. She felt stiff from riding all day, and the tight corset that she wore under her dress bit into her side. "I'd give anything to be ten again," she whispered to Elizabeth.

But the younger girl shook her head scornfully. "Not

me. I love looking all grown up," she said, smoothing out her own hooped skirt.

Next to her sister, Annie felt rumpled and hot. Her dress hung limply at her side while Elizabeth's looked cool and crisp. Though four years separated them, she sometimes felt Elizabeth was the older one.

While the horses and cattle were watered, the girls wandered back to the second wagon where Dolly, their stepmother, had finally managed to coax the baby to sleep. Annie thought back to when she had first met Dolly; she had known the woman then as Miss Dandridge. Then she was Dorothea, and now Dolly.

Dolly smiled wanly at the girls, and Annie felt a twinge of worry for her new mother. "You must be awfully tired," she said, offering her a drink from a jug of cider. "Father shouldn't have made you travel when the baby is still so young."

Dolly laughed. "Do you think I would let your father move to Leatherwood without me? I'm tired, but otherwise I'm perfectly well, and I'm strong as an ox. You just have to stop worrying about me," she said, with a smile that told Annie she was grateful for the concern.

"Well, I don't know why you couldn't convince Father to stay in Richmond," Elizabeth said, still not happy with the idea of being a frontier girl.

"I could no more keep your father in Richmond than you could keep Annie looking properly dressed," Dolly answered. "They both just go their own way."

"Annie looks wonderful," a new voice rang out.

The three turned to see Patrick Henry walking toward them with a spring in his step. He was a tall man but stoop-shouldered, and his balding head was hidden under a tie-back wig. He wore leather breeches and a stained leather vest that Annie knew was at least twenty years old.

"I think we'll camp here for the night," he said, looking around him. Annie's eyes followed his, and she could see that it was a good spot. The ground was level, with plenty of grass and water and a good view of the trail behind them. It would be hard for a stranger to sneak up on them.

"Are we almost there?" Elizabeth whined.

"Now, Elizabeth, you know I said the trip would take seven days if all went well. And we've been on the trail for only two. By my reckoning, that means five more days."

Elizabeth scowled. "Couldn't I have stayed with Aunt Anne?" she said.

The others exchanged glances, but Patrick Henry looked annoyed. "You're becoming tiresome, Elizabeth. I don't want to hear any more complaints."

Just then Annie remembered that she hadn't seen Edward for a while. "Did Edward ever find you?" she asked. "He saw a snake and wanted permission to shoot it."

Her father frowned. "I never saw him," he said. "How far back was that?"

Annie and Elizabeth looked at each other. The younger girl shrugged. "I wasn't paying much attention," she said.

Annie bit her lip. "He came riding hard out of a gully on the right. Maybe a mile back, but maybe not that far. Do you want me to go look for him?"

Patrick Henry shook his head. "He'll turn up. If he doesn't after a bit, I'll look for him." He bent over and kissed his wife. "There's plenty of work to do here."

For the next half hour everyone was busy pulling the

wagons into a circle, unhitching the teams of horses, gathering wood for the fire, and spreading out blankets for beds. Soon an aromatic stew bubbled in a big iron pot over the fire, and Annie felt her stomach grumble. Still, Edward hadn't returned; so Patrick Henry set out to look for him.

By looking at the sun, which hovered over the tree line to the west, Annie could tell it wasn't long until nightfall. She worried about her father and Edward. Finally Annie grew impatient with the wait and began to search among the wagons for her little brother. From one wagon to the next she looked, but there was no sign of him. Someone thought he had seen him get a musket, but no one could remember when that was. Annie wasn't worried that her brother had the gun. At nine he was a good shot and had hunted often with his father. But that was at Scotchtown where everything was familiar. Here there were unfamiliar hills and gorges. A boy could easily get lost. Worse still, he could have been captured by Indians. The thought made Annie shiver and raised her determination to find him.

She retraced the trail that the wagons had traveled, hoping to catch sight of her father, until she had gone a mile or so. With the deepening shadows, it was hard to guess where the snake had been; so Annie looked for evidence of her brother. Finally her sharp eyes saw where branches had been broken. She turned off the trail, thinking that this must have been the spot where Edward had come charging out of the gully.

"Edward," she called, while searching the brush for more clues. Her eye caught a glimpse of something white hanging from a tree branch. Scrambling off the path, her feet slipping on the loose gravel and her long dress catching on the branches as she brushed by them, she reached and grabbed hold of a piece of cloth. It was a piece of white muslin like the shirt that Edward had been wearing.

Annie knew her brother had been this way, but was it recently or earlier in the afternoon? Should she go forward or back to the wagons? Glancing up at the darkening sky, she knew that it would be night very soon. If she didn't find Edward, she would be alone with only wild animals to keep her company. That thought almost sent her scurrying up the path to the wagons.

"I can't leave him out here alone," she told herself. "I know Father is looking, but he didn't even know where to start. I don't want them to worry about me, but what can I do?" So she plunged on down the slope where she had found the piece of muslin. The dense brush caught at her skirt and scratched her arms. "Edward!" she called again out loud.

By now evidence of Edward was everywhere. Even Annie could see hoofprints in the wet soil near the creek at the bottom of the hill. How he had ever brought the horse into such deep brush, Annie couldn't tell.

All this time she had put fear out of her mind. She had to find her brother. But as the shadows deepened, Annie grew less confident, and tears welled up in her eyes.

In the dimming light, Annie strained to see in front of her. "Edward, Edward," she yelled. When she paused to listen, she heard the first sounds of the night. There was the hooting of an owl. Fireflies flickered, but her tears blurred their light. Had she been wrong to go after Edward? It certainly seemed so now.

Wiping her eyes on the back of her hand, she pushed forward through the trees. Desperately she called out her brother's name and paused to listen. Was that a whimper? Again she called, this time more loudly.

At first it sounded like the cry of an injured animal, but as Annie listened, she heard her own name being called in response. Try as she might though, she couldn't see her brother.

"I can't see you," she yelled. "It's too dark. Yell louder."

The boy let go an awful cry that startled Annie with its closeness. She stumbled in the direction of the noise, fighting back tears of relief as she drew closer. Finally she saw him propped against a tree, his leg twisted awkwardly behind him. With a sob, she threw herself on her brother, letting her tears spill onto his head. That was enough to stop his noisy crying. He pulled away, wiping his hand across his shaggy hair. "Stop crying on me," he grumbled.

"All right," Annie agreed, wiping her eyes, but she didn't take her arm away from her brother's shoulder, nor did he try to move it.

"Whatever happened to you?" she asked when he had dried his own tears.

Sniffling noisily, Edward said, "I went back to shoot that snake. Thought I had killed him, but when I rode Lightning up to take a look, the snake struck him on the shank. The horse reared back and threw me. I must have rolled down that hill. And then I tried to crawl to a safe place, but my leg is twisted. It hurts awful bad. I don't know where the horse went." His lip trembled as he thought about the wounded animal.

"Poor Edward," Annie sympathized, patting him on the back, not wanting to think about the horse's fate.

The boy seemed to be watching the shadows. "You aren't alone, are you, Annie?"

She smiled ruefully. "I'm afraid I am. Father was out

looking for you, but he didn't come back, and I couldn't bear to think of you out here alone, and so I tried to find you myself. Problem is, night came too soon. I guess we'll have to spend it here together."

"No," Edward screamed. "I can't be out here alone. Have you heard all the sounds?"

Annie hadn't been paying attention, but suddenly in the silence, she heard a distant howl.

"That's wolves," Edward whispered. "There could be panthers, foxes, bears. We can't stay here alone."

"Well, we can't go back," she said matter-of-factly, though the thought of the wild beasts terrified her. "And there isn't any use in crying. That won't protect us. We're going to have to build a fire. A big one. Only problem is, I don't know how."

Edward sat up straighter. "I have a flint. I can build a fire, but I can't get the wood. Not with this leg."

"Well, that's easy," Annie said. "I'll gather some wood. First, though, I'll have to move you." By pulling the boy up and letting him lean against her, they were able to shuffle off into the clearing. Being careful to keep her brother in sight, she filled her long skirt with twigs, which she carried back and forth to the site of the fire. Although there was no way of cutting larger pieces of wood, she found plenty of short pieces, which she dragged over.

Meanwhile Edward stacked the wood, placing twigs and dry leaves at the bottom. When he was satisfied, he pulled his flint out of his pocket and scraped it against a rock. It was hard work, but finally a spark flashed in the dark, setting fire to the dry leaves and twigs. Soon the small pile of wood began burning. Annie gathered another skirt-load, venturing a little farther this time since now she had the fire by which to see. Sparks spun their way into the night sky. Annie wondered if anyone could see them.

By the time she had gathered enough dry wood, Edward had slipped off into sleep. Annie huddled near him, musket at her side, and listened to the strange sounds that came from the dark forest. She knew her family would be worrying about them, but she also knew that it would be foolish for anyone to go out at night to find them. *In the morning,* she reassured herself. *We'll be safe in the morning.* As the fire crackled, she drifted off to sleep.

2

Leatherwood

"Wake up," Annie urged her brother. Around her, the trees were shrouded by mist. Above them, the first hint of morning light brightened the sky.

"Do you hear that?" she whispered in his ear.

Edward wiped the sleep from his eyes. "I hear you," he grumbled. "Let me sleep a little longer."

By now Annie was impatient to get back to her parents. She shook her brother until he sat up. "Listen," she demanded. "Don't you hear that noise?"

For a minute, the two sat in the shadows, straining to hear. "There it is again," Annie said. "It sounded like twigs cracking."

"Probably a bear," he muttered.

"It isn't a bear. I think it's people," she said, brushing the dirt from her skirt. She began throwing dirt on the embers of the fire until it was extinguished.

"If you don't get up," she said to her brother, who remained seated on the ground, "I'll leave you here."

"How am I supposed to walk?" he asked her. "Remember, my leg is sprained."

Annie felt like strangling Edward. It was bad enough

that he had gotten lost and hurt, but now he was acting like a whiny baby. "If you get up, I'll help you up the hill," she managed to say, biting back the harsher words she felt like saying.

"I remember when you broke your wrist," Edward said. "No one treated you mean. Why can't you be kind?"

"I'm trying," Annie said.

Annie took a deep breath but said nothing. She was thinking how miserable and ungrateful he was when she heard their names being called. "Annie . . . Edward . . ."

"We're down in this gully," Annie screamed, hoping her voice could be heard.

She heard a shout and then another, then her father's voice. "I'm coming down to get you," he yelled.

Annie and her brother waited as Patrick Henry scrambled down the steep slope. Finally he stood before them, relief etched on his face.

"Thank God we found you!" he exclaimed. "I searched until dark last night, and when I found Annie missing as well, I didn't know what to do. I couldn't leave Dolly and the baby. I couldn't sleep, thinking about you out here by yourselves." Then glaring at his son, he said, "Don't ever ride off alone like that. You could have caused great sadness."

Edward hung his head while Patrick Henry turned his attention to his daughter. "And you are old enough to know better." Annie frowned. She knew her father was right, though she didn't like hearing it.

He helped Edward up the steep, wooded slope. There they met the rest of the search party that had left camp at dawn. Edward rode in front of his father while Annie rode behind John Fontaine. When they reached the camp, a cheer went up among all the people.

Later, when Annie was alone with Elizabeth, she

learned that Dolly had been awake all night praying for their safe return.

After Edward's adventure, the trip was uneventful. For five more days the train of wagons bumped and lurched its way along roads that got progressively worse until they were little more than worn ruts in the grass. They forded creeks and rivers and were glad for the large wheels of the Conestoga wagons that kept the wagon beds dry.

Annie and Elizabeth walked alongside the wagon when the bumping became more than they could bear. When their feet grew sore, they were forced to ride along some more.

What a sight they were! Annie marveled at the size of her father's household. And she wondered at his desire to move so far out on the frontier. It seemed ridiculous to carry a fortepiano out into the wilderness, but that's what the Henrys were doing.

On the seventh day, the wagons climbed steadily up the hilly terrain. In the far distance, Annie could see a line of blue-gray mountains—the Blue Ridge, her father told her. The Henrys wouldn't be going past them but would settle in the foothills. This wild land thrilled Patrick Henry. Ever since the mountains had come into view, he had been excited. When they traveled through woods so dense that the sun never reached the forest floor, he pointed out various trees and animals.

More than once, Annie and Elizabeth were startled by a flock of wild turkeys that thundered up before the oncoming wagons. Edward, confined to his wagon because of his leg, grumbled that he wasn't able to get a shot off at the inviting targets.

"How much longer?" Elizabeth asked for the hundredth time that day.

"Not more than a couple of hours," her father answered. "Isn't it beautiful?" Just then they heard the roar of a river and, looking over to the right, saw the swirling waters of Leatherwood Creek. "We need only to follow the creek, and we'll be home," he said.

"Will it look like Scotchtown?" Elizabeth asked. "I don't want to share a room with anyone. Will I have my own?"

Patrick Henry sighed and looked at Annie, who had remained silent. "I trust, daughter, that you will be content with whatever provision God has made for you."

Elizabeth blushed. "Couldn't God provide a nice big house like the Governor's Palace?" she whispered to Annie after her father had moved on.

"Shh," her sister cautioned her. "If you set your heart on a big house, you will surely be disappointed. Think of this as an adventure. Then you won't mind so much."

"That's easy for you to say," Elizabeth responded, her hand on her hip. "You had your chance to mix with society in Williamsburg. Now Father wants to bury us out here in the middle of nowhere. I swear I'll die."

Annie giggled at her sister's words and her long face. "You might die at the hands of Indians or maybe even from a fever," she said dryly. "But I don't think you'll die for lack of luxury."

Before Elizabeth could respond, their father came riding back at a gallop. "It's just ahead," he announced, hardly able to keep the grin from his face. "Take the wagons on about a mile," he told the driver, "and you'll see the house."

On down the line of wagons he went, giving the good news to his family that the long journey was finally at an end. Annie leaned forward with anticipation. Finally they would see the place where they would make their home for the next several years.

The horses strained to pull the wagons up the last hill, and there at the top, Annie saw Leatherwood for the first time. She looked quickly at her sister, whose shocked expression told the whole story.

"Let's get down and go look it over," Annie urged. Elizabeth bit her quivering lip, trying hard not to cry. But tears, great big tears, slipped silently down her cheek.

"It's not so bad," Annie tried to reassure her. But Elizabeth would not be cheered; so the older girl hopped down from the wagon and went around to find Dolly. She found her stepmother near her wagon, holding little Dolly in one arm, with her other arm around her husband.

"Do you like it?" Annie heard him asking eagerly.

"It's good land," her stepmother answered. "Look at the timber. I've never seen anything like it. And we'll never want for game or fish. One can raise a family out here. I must admit that I'm glad to be far from war. You've already sent two sons to fight. Is it selfish to want the rest of us to be safe?"

Without answering, he turned to his daughter whom he had just noticed. "Come, Annie. What do you think?"

She didn't want to hurt his feelings, but her face gave her away.

"I know the house is small," he said. "It isn't much more than a cabin really. But we can add on to it and make it comfortable. There's plenty of good work to do, and we brought enough hands to do it."

Annie nodded doubtfully, but her father was so excited that he didn't seem to notice her lack of enthusiasm. He rode off to give instructions, leaving Annie and Dolly watching in bemused silence.

Finally Dolly said, "How is Elizabeth taking it?"

Annie smiled. "Not well, I'm afraid. Her heart is broken. She had hoped for a fine house like Monticello."

"Elizabeth has much to learn about the value of things. I think Leatherwood will be the place to learn it," Dolly said. "Now let's go see how bad it is."

Together they strolled toward the house, calling to Elizabeth to join them.

"It's sturdy," Annie said finally, after the shock of seeing the tiny two-room house had passed. "Father was right to say it's sound. There aren't any holes in the roof, and the brick is tight."

"But it's so small," Elizabeth protested. "Where will we all sleep?"

"There's the loft," Dolly answered. "You and Annie will sleep up there. Father and I and the baby will take one of the rooms, and we'll put the table in the other."

"No," Elizabeth wailed. "What about parties? And won't we ever have visitors?"

Dolly was firm. "Elizabeth, you need to be content with what your father has provided for us. We can add on to it, but for now, the house is tight and secure. I know we'll be crowded, but we'll also be together. Your father has given Patsy and John Fontaine 2,000 acres down the creek. They'll build their house over there. There are barns to build, quarters for the slaves, a place for Edward. . . . We have too much to do to waste time worrying about parties."

While Elizabeth sniffled back her tears, Annie went through the house and out the backdoor. "There is a kitchen," she announced. "Looks as though there's a smokehouse also." She remembered the lessons she had learned in Williamsburg—character, not position, counts. "It's not so bad."

Outside, there was all the commotion of a small village. Some slaves were unhitching the six mules from each wagon and leading them to a fenced pasture that Annie hadn't noticed before. Others were beginning to unload the family's furniture, carrying beds and tables and chairs into the two-room house.

Patrick Henry, striding out from the house, interrupted the work by calling to his foreman, "Nathan, moving this furniture can wait. I want two portholes built on each side of this house, big enough for a rifle to shoot through. Do you understand?"

The foreman nodded. He turned and spoke to several of the slaves nearest to him, who in turn nodded and went in search of tools.

Dolly, overhearing her husband's command, looked at him with surprise. "Portholes?" she asked. "Rifles? In our living room?"

"Now don't you worry, Dolly," he answered her soothingly. "It's only a precaution. You know there are Tory sympathizers and their Indian friends out here on the frontier. I'd be less than a good husband if I didn't try to protect you from them."

His wife nodded her head, but there was a look of sadness on her face, and Annie saw her hug her sleeping baby tightly to herself. Fearing that Elizabeth would throw another fit if she watched the slaves cut gunholes in the walls of the little house, Annie guided her sister away from the crowd. She found her older sister Patsy playing a guessing game with her son Ben.

"Where will you live, Patsy?" Annie asked curiously. "Will you stay at the house with us?"

Her sister shook her head. "Father offered, but I want to be with John Fontaine," she answered softly. "I think they'll have a lean-to built by tomorrow, and then they'll set to work on a sturdy cabin. It won't be fancy, mind you, but it will be snug. I'll have the fortepiano, and so I'll be content. Ever since John was injured in the army, I've wanted to be as far from war as I could get."

Glancing about, they both laughed. "It would be hard to get much farther away," Annie agreed.

Looking around at the dense woods that crept up one hill after another, Annie said, "There's no shortage of timber. But it seems as though there isn't much land cleared for farming. How will Father ever make a go of it here?"

"I'd wager that he'll sell some wood," Patsy answered. "John Fontaine told me that they'll girdle some of the trees this fall."

"What's that mean?" asked Elizabeth, who had been daydreaming nearby.

"He says the men will cut all the bark away in a ring on each tree. Then next spring when the sap rises, it won't be able to, and eventually the trees will die. They'll harvest them, and we'll have plenty of lumber to build houses here."

"Just think of the exciting stories you'll have to tell," Annie coaxed her little sister. "Someday you'll be at a stuffy dinner party, where the only subject of conversation is how many rows of ruffles should decorate a lady's gown. You'll be able to spin a story of daring exploits in the wilderness. You'll shock them," she said with a grin on her face, enjoying the picture she was painting.

Elizabeth giggled in spite of herself.

Then Annie added with a broad smile, "Don't you know that Father's enemies would enjoy hearing about our present situation? They'd love to think that Father is suffering in the wilderness. So we just have to prove them wrong. We'll show them what the Henrys are made of."

3

Squatters

Fall of 1779 came to Leatherwood in a burst of color. Trees cast off their green clothes and put on yellow, orange, and outrageous shades of red until the nearby hills looked as if a huge patchwork quilt had been thrown over them. In the far distance, the mountains of the Blue Ridge seemed to stretch to the ends of the earth.

Annie felt surrounded by beauty more awesome than any she had imagined, and for the first time, she began appreciating what her father saw in the frontier.

They were isolated. For days at a time, they saw no one outside the immediate family. They were hungry for news. So whenever travelers passed by, the Henrys urged them to stay and visit.

In November, a late-leaving group of settlers passed by on their way to Kentucky, bringing bad news of the war. The British had sent 3,000 troops by ship from New York to Savannah, hoping to capture the Georgia city. The British easily defeated the 800 Americans who defended it. Now the redcoats had an army in the South that promised to do much damage.

Annie despaired. Could it be that after more than four years of war the British would win? She did not worry for the Henrys' own personal safety. Savannah was a long way off, and their house was well-protected with the portholes, but she grieved for her country.

Though the colonies suffered, Leatherwood prospered. When she looked outside the house, Annie could see progress. The air was full of the rich smell of smoking hams. They wouldn't run short of meat that winter. Although they had arrived too late to plant crops, the ground was ready for spring planting. The Henrys had brought enough corn to see them through the winter.

The men kept busy building houses and clearing land while the women tried to make their rude dwellings into homes. It fell to Annie to teach Elizabeth and Edward. Neither liked studying, and more than once the older girl threw up her hands in frustration.

After one particularly hard day of teaching, Annie came upon her father, slumped over his desk, a letter in his hand. He didn't hear her at first, but when she saw him like that, she called out his name in a worried voice. Rousing himself, Patrick Henry tried to sit up and pretend that nothing was wrong, but his daughter saw the sweat on his forehead and the pallor underneath his tanned skin.

"Are you feeling sick?" she asked anxiously.

"I'm tired, and I think the fever may be coming on again," he said. "The air is so good here that I'm trusting not to be laid low by it, but all of the bustle of moving and building has sapped my strength and left me ripe for another bout."

"Then you must take to bed!" Annie urged him. She knew the fever, caused by malaria that he had caught in the swampy city of Williamsburg, was often bad and had kept him in his bed for weeks at a time. "Maybe if you rest now, you can avoid the worst of it."

He gave her a weak smile. "There's wisdom in what you say, daughter," he admitted. "But there is still much to be done before winter."

"It can be done without you," she said to him. "I'm sure Dolly would agree. Where is she?"

"She's gone to see Patsy for a bit. She'll be home soon," he replied.

"Then you must go to bed now, and I'll have Martha come and tend to you."

Patrick Henry protested, but one look at his daughter's determined expression settled the question. When he rose to stand, she saw his legs sway, and he would have tumbled to the floor if she hadn't rushed to his side. He leaned heavily on her as they shuffled to the bed in the other room. No sooner had she settled him than his teeth began chattering, and a drenching sweat broke out upon his brow.

With damp cloths Annie tried to bring down the fever. She paced nervously back and forth, listening anxiously for the sound of Dolly's return. Her father turned fitfully on his bed, groaning pitifully. Once he sat upright, looked at his pacing daughter, and said grouchily, "You're giving me a headache. Can't you be calm?"

She bit her lip and forced herself to sit in the chair near the bed. Though she could make her body stay still, she couldn't keep her toes from tapping or her fingers from nearly rubbing the skin from her thumb. Just then Dolly came into the little house.

Annie heard the door open and was out of her chair in an instant. Grabbing her stepmother's arm with relief, she said, "Father is ill with the fever. I've put him to bed, but I didn't know what else to do."

Dolly hurried into the sickroom and saw that her husband had fallen asleep. Calmly, she straightened his bedcovers, rinsed the cloth and placed it back on his forehead, and closed several of the shutters so the light in the room sank into dim shadows. Then turning to Annie, she said, "You did everything necessary. All we need now is some of Martha's good potion. Would you go to her and have her bring some up to the house?"

Annie nodded and fetched Martha, the slave woman who was gifted in medicine. She knew how to use herbs to heal almost any disease. Then Annie hung about the house, feeling that there was more she should do for her father. Finally Dolly came to the door. "Why don't you take out one of the horses and go explore for a while? Your father should be fine. Hasn't God healed him each time? Doesn't Martha know how to treat him?"

Annie hesitated, unable to put away her worry.

"Come," said Dolly reassuringly. "Pray with me and then go. We'll leave your father in the hands of his Father and Martha."

They prayed, but Annie still wouldn't go until Dolly said, "You aren't helping your father one bit by wearing a hole in the porch. Go!"

Reluctantly Annie walked toward the stable, casting worried looks over her shoulder. But when she reached the barn, her spirits lifted. She hadn't been riding for a long time. Dolly was right. She already felt better.

Joseph saddled her horse and led him out of the gated paddock. "Now don't you go too far," he scolded her. "No telling what kind of thing is prowling around out there."

But Annie, glancing up at the cloudless blue sky and

feeling the crisp air on her cheeks, paid little heed to the warning of the groom who seldom ventured out much beyond his stable.

She walked the horse slowly down the lane that led to the house and then turned him into one of the cleared fields. They trotted across, carefully avoiding stumps and rocks that littered the way. Once they were out of sight of the house, Annie felt her breath quicken. She loved exploring. She always had, and age had done nothing to dampen her enjoyment. In that way she was like her father, who never seemed able to settle in one place.

She had been riding for nearly an hour when she saw smoke wisping up over the next hollow. Cautiously, she urged the horse forward, hoping to see what was causing it. *It could be travelers,* she reasoned. *But why would they be so far from the main trail? Could be Tories.* They were the colonists who sided with the king. *But why would they be on Henry land?* It didn't make sense.

She stopped near a clump of trees and decided to go the rest of the way on foot. Sliding down from her saddle, she loosely tethered the horse to a tree branch. She crept forward, carefully avoiding sticks and leaves that would alert anyone to her presence. When she reached the top of the hillock, she cautiously peered over the crest and saw below a little shanty village made up of three makeshift houses clustered closely together. A little farther off was a fire with a huge kettle hanging over it.

Annie crouched behind a large outcropping of rock so that she was not visible from below. While she watched, three scruffy-looking children, no older than Edward, came tumbling out of one of the lean-tos. Behind them was a bearded man dressed in buckskins, a musket in his hand.

He bellowed at the children to keep quiet and then yelled back into the dark shanty.

Out peered a bonnetless woman, who looked ancient to Annie. Her face was deeply lined. She had gaps in her mouth where her teeth should have been. A long pipe hung between her lips. She scowled at the loud-mouthed man before bustling toward the kettle. Grabbing a long iron ladle, she began stirring whatever was in the pot, shooting sullen looks at the man. Meanwhile he continued swearing at her until Annie's ears rang with ugly words she had never heard before.

Annie scooted back down the hill, eager to get away from the unpleasant scene. She mounted her horse and was ready to ride away when she thought again of the children. Could she just leave them there?

What else could she do? she asked herself. Those were surely their parents. Those children belonged with those adults. But maybe she could help them some way. The horse danced impatiently under her, eager to run in the crisp autumn air. Annie chewed her lip. What should she do?

Finally she made up her mind to tell John Fontaine. He would know who they were and what to do.

John was not at the Fontaines' little cabin. Patsy sat on a rocking chair on the front porch, a baby in her lap, and the two little ones playing contentedly in the dirt nearby. Laundry hung from the line behind the house.

"Where are you going in such a hurry?" Patsy called out to her.

"I need to find John," Annie answered.

"I haven't seen him since breakfast," Patsy said. "He took a wagon and some shovels and went out that way. Said he was going to be putting up fences."

John wasn't more than half a mile away. She heard hammering before she found him supervising a crew that was fencing in a pasture for the cattle that the Henrys had brought with them from Scotchtown. When he heard Annie yelling and saw her galloping toward him, her dress flapping in the wind behind her, he threw down the piece of timber he was holding and ran toward her.

"Is it one of the children?" he asked, his face full of worry.

"Everyone is fine," Annie assured him, realizing how her sudden appearance must have scared him. "But I saw something that worried me." Annie sketched out the scene to her brother-in-law as quickly as she could.

After asking several questions, he frowned. "Squatters," he said.

"What?" Annie asked.

"They are squatters, I imagine. Folks told us there were some rough ones in these parts, but we hadn't seen them yet. They don't want to do honest work. Sounds like they are making whisky, probably to sell to the Indians."

"Is it serious?"

"Could be. Maybe they'll just leave if I tell them to. But that isn't likely. I think I'll go see Judge Lesker and have him supply a small posse to help me get them off the land. We don't want any trouble with them."

"What can I do?" Annie asked.

"You'll have to take me over to their camp," he answered. "Then I'll ride to the judge and see what he suggests. You get Patsy and take her up to your house. I don't want her alone until we know they're gone for good."

"How do we know they're the only ones?"

"I expect they aren't. That's one reason I want Judge

Lesker and some help. Usually these squatters will set up different camps. If one is found, they all move on to another."

John barked out instructions to the crew and then mounted his horse, and they were on their way. Annie didn't have any trouble finding the camp again.

"Get Patsy and take her up to your father's," John commanded. "It probably isn't necessary, but I'll feel better knowing she isn't alone. I'm going to get the judge. No telling when I'll be back."

At Patsy's, Annie helped her sister pack up some clothes and ready the babies. Together they hitched up a wagon, tied Annie's tired horse to the back, and drove over to the larger house. For once she was glad for her father's foresight in putting in the portholes.

Only when she came in view of the house did she remember her father's relapse. In all the confusion, she had put it out of her mind. Turning to her older sister, she said, "Father is in bed again. He looks bad, but we caught it early this time, and Dolly says not to worry. I wanted to tell you, though, so you wouldn't be taken by surprise."

The color drained from Patsy's face as she listened calmly to her younger sister. Her eyes stared into the distance. Only her trembling lip revealed her worry.

All of Annie's own fears returned. Yet she knew that her worrying wasn't going to help her father. "I believe God will preserve him a little longer," Annie whispered, as her sister buried her face in her nursing baby's hair. "You will have to trust Him for that."

There was confusion when the sisters reached home. Now instead of six, there were ten people in the house, one of whom was very sick.

Edward whined because he was left at home with the

girls. Elizabeth cried because she didn't like living in the wilderness. Though Dolly tried to bring order to the confusion, Annie could see she was on the verge of tears herself.

"Elizabeth," Annie ordered, "you take care of the baby and let Dolly go back to Father." When Elizabeth began to protest, Annie interrupted, "I'm going to take Benjamin and go for a walk with Edward."

"But you can't leave," Patsy objected.

"We won't go out of sight of the house," Annie promised. "The boys will climb the walls if we stay."

Outside, the sky had darkened. Thick thunderheads billowed above, and the leaves of the nearby trees flashed silver in the wind.

"Doesn't it smell like rain?" Annie asked, trying to distract the boys while hoping to catch a glimpse of John Fontaine.

"If it rains, they'll come home, won't they?" Edward asked.

"I think they'll probably stay until the job is done," Annie answered.

Benjamin squealed as the first raindrop plopped on his face. "Rain, rain," he chanted. The drops fell one by one at first, but then the sky opened, and the torrent poured down.

"Run to the house," Annie shouted, scooping up Benjamin in her arms.

They pushed through the door, laughing and letting the water drip off their clothes onto the floor. Patsy looked up. "Don't tell me it's raining," she moaned, putting down her sewing and hurrying to the window to look out. "Look at it come down. Surely they'll come home and not stay out in the rain."

But John did not come home that night or the next day,

even though the rain continued. To the ten anxious souls crowded into the small house, the rain seemed to go on forever. At the first sign of a break in the weather, Annie announced that she was going to the stable.

"Is it safe?" Dolly asked.

"Of course it is," Annie replied. "We haven't seen or heard a sound for days. I can't stay inside any longer."

"Then go if you must," Dolly said in a weary voice. "But take the musket with you. John left it loaded."

Annie carried the heavy gun outside with her. The air was crisp and frosty, but bundled up in her cloak, she was warm. Crossing through the muddy yard, she was glad for the galoshes on her feet.

Once she reached the stable, she didn't want to stay there. She asked Joseph to saddle her horse, feeling confident because of the musket. Off she rode, letting the horse determine the direction in which they went. She had intended to stay near the house, but gradually they rode farther afield until the smoke from the chimney was no longer visible.

Now curiosity took over. Annie led the horse on the path toward the squatters' camp, sure that John had chased them away by now. She rode the horse boldly up the hillock, not bothering to hide her presence. When she reached the top, it was just as she had thought. No fire burned, and there was no sign of anyone.

She led the horse down the rocky trail toward the camp, keeping her hand on the musket. Once at the bottom, she tethered the horse and explored. The little dirt-floored shacks were empty of everything except a few pieces of chipped pottery. Annie didn't know if they had ever held furniture, but whatever had been there was now gone.

She was glad to leave the pathetic little camp. Riding

on, she heard the sound of horses and the creaking of wagon wheels. A bit farther on, she saw a bedraggled band of squatters walking slowly down the trail, two men pulling a cart loaded with household items behind them.

Watching the procession, muskets at their sides, were John Fontaine and a band of ten mounted men. He turned when he heard the sound of Annie's horse coming from behind him. When he saw her, his face darkened with anger. He broke off from the watching group and rode toward her, a grim expression on his face.

Annie tried to smile and explain, but he interrupted. "Didn't I tell you to stay inside?" he barked.

"Yes, but—"

"I don't want to hear any 'yes, buts,'" he said bluntly. "You don't know what kind of danger you might have walked into."

"Oh, but, John, you don't know how hard it was to wait. Inside with all those people, and the rain," she said, hoping he would soften.

"Annie," he said sternly, "it hasn't been easy being outside in the rain either. But we had a duty, and we did it. You also had a duty, which you chose not to do. You cannot be driven by how you feel. You must learn to do what's right, even when it costs you comfort or tries your patience."

The straggling pack of squatters had passed from sight with the mounted men behind them. John watched until the horsemen too were out of sight. Then sighing, he said to his sister-in-law, "Come, let's go home."

Annie sighed. She didn't like being scolded by John. It made her feel like a little child once again. As they rode along in silence, she thought about his criticism. Maybe he was right. Maybe she had acted on a whim, doing what she felt like. She would need to think about it more. She glanced sideways at her brother-in-law. His wet coat hung heavily, and water dripped from his tricorner hat. He slouched in his saddle, his eyes closed as if he were asleep.

For several minutes longer they rode along without speaking. It was John who broke the silence. “Aren’t you curious about what happened?” he asked.

“Of course I am, but I thought you were too weary to tell me.”

“We found five camps. That’s what took so long. They were hidden in hollows that were near impossible to find. There were a few women and children, poor things, but mostly it was ragged men. I wouldn’t be surprised if some weren’t deserters from General Washington’s army.”

“Deserters?” Annie asked.

“Men who couldn’t take the long winters in the North without any food or proper boots. General Washington’s army lives on air, don’t you know?”

That brought a small smile to his quiet face.

“Was there fighting?” Annie asked.

“None worth speaking about,” he said. “Several of the men were so drunk they couldn’t even put their trousers on straight. None of them could shoot a gun, not in the condition they were in.”

“Where will they go?”

“I don’t know. Judge Lesker told them that if they were found in Henry County, they’d be arrested as deserters, and that seemed to scare them. He’s escorting them to the North Carolina border. I don’t think they’ll come back, not to these parts anyway.”

By now they had reached the house. “You go on in,” Annie said. “I’ve got some thinking to do.”

4

A Wild Ride

When winter came to Leatherwood, the snow made travel extremely difficult. Mail already took weeks to reach them, and the snow only made it slower. In January, 1780, Dolly gave birth to another daughter. They named her Sarah Butler, which Annie liked because her mother's name had been Sarah. Now the house was more crowded than ever.

In February, Patrick Henry received notice that he had been elected to the Virginia legislature by his neighbors in Henry County. The notice came to him so late that the session had already started. When he received it, he and Annie were sitting in the barn where he was oiling his saddle.

"It's seven days ride in the best of weather," he told Annie, glancing up from the letter he had just received. "I can't make it in less than ten in these conditions. Besides, Dolly would hate to have me go so soon after the baby's birth."

"Won't they miss you though?" Annie asked. She

pulled her long cloak more tightly around her neck, feeling the sharp wind as it blew through the drafty barn.

"They may miss me, though Governor Jefferson might welcome my absence. In any case, the letter is so late in arriving that I couldn't get there in time. I'll write a letter saying I can't attend this session. Perhaps in May I'll go."

Annie groaned inwardly. The whole family had thought that moving to Leatherwood would bring an end to Patrick Henry's frequent absences from home. But it seemed as though his neighbors thought too highly of him to keep him out of the legislature.

"How will you tell Dolly?" Annie asked him gently, knowing that her stepmother wouldn't like being left with two small babies on the frontier.

Her father rubbed his jaw and gave his silk cap an absentminded tug. "Dolly knew when she married me that I had a duty to Virginia," he said. "She won't be happy, but she'll accept it as my calling from God."

"I almost wish that I were going," Annie confessed. "I'm feeling a bit crowded in this little house with all these people. I need some kind of work to do, I think, because I fritter away my time in so many fruitless tasks."

Patrick Henry studied his daughter's serious face. "I thought you were teaching Edward and Elizabeth," he reminded her. "That's important work."

"Indeed it is," Annie answered. "But they are such poor students. Elizabeth would rather daydream about missed parties in Richmond, and I can't force her to study. She just looks at me and shrugs. And Edward. He's even worse. His Latin is poor, and my Greek is worse. Between the two of us, we scrape through the lessons. But, Father, surely you see that I'm not equipped like Mr. Dabney to teach."

He smiled. "Edward doesn't take much to learning,

that I know," he answered kindly. "And Elizabeth is so pretty, she probably won't have to know more than she does right now. Some young man will want to marry her, not for her book learning and conversation, but for her good temper and pleasant company. Do the best you can, my dear. Neither I nor God would ask anything else."

Annie sighed. She knew her father's words were true. She knew enough to teach her sister and brother all that they might need to know. Edward would probably be a frontiersman all his days. The reading and ciphering he already could do put him ahead of many of the men of that type. And he was right about Elizabeth also. She was pretty and self-confident, and when she wasn't complaining, she did have a sweet, gentle spirit. Then why did his words make Annie so sad?

She rose from the hay where she had been sitting. "I must go and do something," she said in response to his worried look. "Every part of me wants to scream for being cooped up so long. I wish I could just go run like I did when I was a child. I almost regret getting older. I'm trying," she confessed, "but I don't seem suited for those womanly tasks."

Her father reached out and patted her shoulder. "You'll find your calling, and God will equip you for it," he encouraged her "Go inside and see if you can't relieve Dolly of some of her burdens. You'll see. Helping her will take your mind off your own troubles."

Annie pulled her cloak more tightly around her shoulders and headed out into the bitter winter cold. The wind, whipping through the opening between the house and the barn, caught Annie in the face, making her gasp for breath. Underfoot the frozen ground crunched as she crossed the yard. She was trying so hard to keep her skirts off the ground that she didn't spot a patch of ice. When her foot slipped out beneath her, she swung her arms wildly, trying to maintain her balance, and landing on her seat on the ice. Her cloak flew open, and the bitter wind found its way inside her woolen dress. As she stood up, Edward appeared from behind the house.

"Ha ha," he laughed, pointing at Annie. "I saw that."

"Oh, be quiet," she muttered as she stumbled up the stairs.

The wind followed her into the little house, until she slammed the door on it. Inside, Elizabeth and Dolly stitched and talked in front of the fireplace while the children either slept or played nearby.

"Come in and get warm," Dolly urged, looking up at her wild-haired stepdaughter standing near the door. "You must be freezing."

"What I'd like to do," Annie blurted out, "is go visit Patsy. She's probably feeling housebound, and if I took a wagon I could be there in a half hour or so."

"But it's too cold," Dolly objected. "You'll get sick."

"I'll put on extra clothes," Annie promised. "And we can heat some bricks to put by my feet. There's a heavy bearskin rug . . . Why, I'll be toastier on the wagon than you are here by the fire."

Dolly sighed. "I know you're feeling housebound, dear," she said sympathetically. "You may go, but you bundle up tightly."

At that moment, Annie loved her stepmother more than ever, and tears welled up in her eyes. She always seemed to understand what her stepdaughter was feeling even when Annie couldn't put it into words. She smiled gratefully at the older woman, who blew her a kiss across the room.

Edward barged in the door behind her. "Can I come

too?" he begged. Annie groaned inwardly, but she didn't need to worry. Dolly shook her head.

"Shut the door and take off your wet clothes, young man. We'll let your sister go off on her own for a little bit."

By the time Annie was settled on the wagon, the wind had died down, but the air was still frigid, and her cheeks burned with the cold. Under the bearskin, however, she was toasty warm. She urged the horses along the frozen trail, up and down the small hills, until the Henry house was out of sight behind her.

There was a high point between the two houses. When Annie reached it, she stopped the wagon and listened. Out on the frontier it was quiet. Except for the creaking of a branch in the wind, there was no sound at all. No sound of slaves working in the fields. No sound of hammering or sawing. No sound of horses. No laughing or talking or running or crying. It was completely silent, and Annie imagined for a minute that she was the only person alive.

She shivered at the thought. Is that what she wanted—to be alone? Rousing herself from her daydream, she clucked to the horses, urging them on toward Patsy's. Annie was about halfway there when she came to a long stretch of road that went through dense forest. They had cleared a trail only wide enough for a wagon to pass. On a bright sunny day when the leaves were in full leaf, the leaves were so dense that little light reached the forest floor. Even on a winter day when the trees were bare, the path was plunged in shadows.

She urged on the horses. Suddenly, and without warning, they stopped. Though Annie slapped the reins and clucked until her mouth was dry, the two horses would not budge. "Now what's wrong?" she muttered into the frosty air as the horses nervously pawed the ground. She stood up on the board seat and looked around.

As she stood there, trying to see what had set the horses off, one of them reared up and threw himself against his harness. The wagon lurched forward, and Annie was thrown to the ground.

She landed with a thud on the bearskin that had slipped off her lap when she stood. "Fool horses," she muttered as she rubbed her hip where she had hit the ground. About fifty feet ahead, the horses stopped. They pawed the ground and acted so skittish that she feared they might run away.

Gathering up the bearskin, she crept forward, not wanting to scare them off. It was then that she saw what had frightened them—two wolves lurking behind the trees about twenty yards from the wagon. Their bony bodies looked half-starved, but that only made them appear more dangerous. Annie quickened her pace. Had they seen her?

The closer she crept to the wagon, the closer she drew to the wolves. They were walking in a circle, keeping Annie and the wagon in the center. The girl scanned the trees, but she did not see any others. Didn't they always travel in packs? By now the two horses were going crazy, scraping the ground, rearing and tossing their heads.

When Annie was about five yards away, she began to run. At the same moment the wolves rushed forward. She threw herself on the back of the wagon, her legs tangling in the long skirt of her dress just as the horses took off running. Clinging to the flat bed of the careening wagon, Annie inched forward until she had reached the seat.

The two snarling and growling wolves snapped at the wooden wheels as the horses gathered speed. They were joined by five more that Annie hadn't seen before. The pack raced along, seeming to keep pace with the horses. Clinging desperately to her seat, she looked at the reins hanging just out of reach. If she couldn't grab them, the horses would run the out-of-control wagon into a tree.

Annie clutched the seat as the wagon veered off the track and almost hit a tree. "If I don't grab the reins, we'll surely crash, and then I'll die," she moaned, closing her eyes as if that would keep her from harm. "Lord, help me," she prayed.

The words had barely left her lips when she opened her eyes and looked at the reins again. She inched forward on the seat, turning slightly so her right arm was closer to the reins while she continued clutching with her left. "Now!" she said to herself as she reached and caught the leather straps in her hand. The smooth leather cut into her hand as the horses strained against the reins, but Annie ignored the pain and wrapped the straps around her palm so she couldn't let go. She tried to calm the horses without slowing them, but it was a hopeless task with the wolves snapping at their heels.

There was a thump. Annie looked behind her and saw the crumpled body of a wolf that had somehow been crushed by the wagon. The other wolves slowed and circled back. She turned away, not wanting to see them tear into its warm flesh.

On they ran through the last of the forest trail, going much faster than was safe on that wild stretch of road. Finally they reached the open trail again, then up a rise, and Patsy's cabin came into view. Aromatic smoke drifted from the cabin's stone chimney. The horses, sensing safety, finally heeded Annie's direction and allowed themselves to be brought under control.

Annie drove the wagon around to the barn, ignoring

the cold. When she stumbled across the threshold of the snug little cabin, Patsy could see immediately that something had happened. She put down the baby and poured a cup of hot herb tea, which she urged on her sister.

Annie couldn't keep her teeth from chattering. Everytime she tried to talk, the words got lost in sobs. Finally Patsy shushed her. "Just drink the tea and warm yourself," her sister urged. "There will be time for words later."

5

A Great Wind

Spring brought more bad news to the colonists. The victory at Savannah gave London's generals confidence to try an attack against Charleston, South Carolina. In February, 10,000 British soldiers attacked Charleston. About 5,000 Americans were waiting for them, but only half were professional soldiers. The rest were militiamen who had come from their farms to defend Charleston and all of South Carolina. Reports from the continuing battle were vague, but the British seemed to have the upper hand. The Henrys at Leatherwood, like patriots everywhere, prayed for good news.

Annie was becoming impatient. Even watching spring come to Leatherwood couldn't cheer her. Everywhere there were signs of new life. Leaf buds swelled on the trees, and tender grass sprang up from barren ground.

It was too soon, of course, to put away winter clothes and blankets. In March there could still be a month of cold weather ahead. One day while she was walking, Annie noticed that not all of Leatherwood's trees had come to life. Some stood naked against the blue sky, not a bud on their barren branches.

"Father, why do some of the trees look as though they are dying?" she asked one night at supper. "There's a large grove of hardwoods without a leaf."

"Don't you remember? Those are the trees that we girdled last autumn," he told her. "We cut a ring through the bark so the sap can't run. They're dying, and it will make it easier for us to cut them down next year."

"You'll wait a whole year?" she asked.

"It takes a long time to kill a tree," he replied. "But without any leaves, the sun will finally reach the ground and warm the soil so we can plant corn around them."

Edward pondered. "Won't it be hard to plow with all the trees in the way?"

"We won't harvest as much, but we'll get a crop. Next year, when the trees are completely dead, we'll clear them out."

"But what about all the other trees?" Edward asked, since only one grove had been girdled.

"You'll have to wait and see," his father replied.

Several days later, Annie woke to the sounds of branches scraping against the roof. The wind moaned as it chased through the cracks under the doors. Though it was still dark outside, she heard her father's voice and saw light through the door of the loft.

Elizabeth muttered in a voice thick with sleep, but Annie ignored her, knowing that her sister would drift off if left alone. The older girl shivered in the cold loft. She darted from the warmth of her bed and found her dress and woolen stockings, which she put on as quickly as she could before scurrying down the ladder.

Someone had already put fresh logs on the fire, and voices from her parents' room let her know that both Dolly and her father were awake. Annie poured herself a cup of herb tea, grabbed a biscuit, and had breakfast in front of the fire while she waited for them to come out. Something was going on, and Annie wanted to know what it was. Maybe they had heard from her brothers at the war.

Soon her father opened the door. When he saw his daughter sitting in front of the fire, a smile split his face. "I'm not surprised to see you up," he remarked.

"I heard voices, and since it's still dark outside, I thought I would see what's going on," she explained.

"I could tell you to go back to bed," her father said smiling. Just then Dolly walked out of the room carrying baby Sarah in her arms. She looked sleepy, and Annie saw that her stepmother hadn't bothered to dress. She had pulled a warm dressing gown over her nightgown, and her hair was still mussed from sleep.

"Did he wake you as well?" Dolly asked with a wan smile. "I told him to whisper, but you know your father."

Annie smiled. "You look like you didn't get much sleep. Was the baby fussy?" she asked sympathetically.

"I don't know what it is," Dolly admitted with a worried frown. "She fussed most of the night, and just when she had fallen to sleep and I had dozed off, your father heard the wind."

"But, Father," Annie said, "what's so special about the wind?"

"We're clearing acres today," he said with a gleeful look.

He poured himself a glass of cider and munched on several biscuits left over from the night before. "I promised John Fontaine that I would be over at first light if there promised to be a good wind today. I must be hurrying," he added, peeking out the window.

A look of confusion crossed Annie's face. "I don't understand," she said.

"If you want to come with me," he told her, "then you will see why I'm so excited by the wind. If you'd rather stay here, I'll tell you about it later."

It took Annie about five seconds to decide that she'd rather be outside with her father than in the little house with a fretful baby, a tired mother, her cranky sister, and a toddler who would need minding.

Annie rose to find her cloak and muff.

"Wear thick boots," her father instructed. "And make sure you're plenty warm. We'll be gone all day."

With all her layers of clothes, Annie felt as she imagined a bear would feel in his winter fur. She waddled out to the waiting wagon where Edward, similarly bundled, bounced eagerly on a bale of hay. "Isn't this grand?" he said excitedly, tying a red knit scarf tightly around his neck.

Annie smiled at her brother. Looking in the back of the wagon, she found many axes. Her father strode forth from the house, dressed like a woodsman, anticipation on his face.

They set off slowly for the Fontaine cabin, the wagon slogging through the muddy trail. At the far edge of the woods that separated the two houses, Patrick Henry stopped the wagon. Before long John arrived with a wagonload of slaves. Annie watched her father and John talking, their conversation punctuated by gestures as they pointed at various trees.

Annie huddled under a bearskin. The crew of men walked toward a stand of trees to her right. Soon the forest echoed with the sound of metal against wood as the men cut triangle-shaped notches into the trees. Wood chips flew until the air was thick with dust.

For several hours the men worked, sweat pouring down their faces despite the cold. Annie's ears rang with the noise, and she started wishing she hadn't come. Then suddenly the noise stopped. The sweating men drifted out toward the trail, sawdust stuck to their wet clothes and skin.

They quenched their thirst with dippers of water from the barrel and mopped their foreheads with the back of their sleeves. She watched them and didn't notice that one man had stayed in the woods. The sound of his ax rang out, startling her. When she turned, she saw a powerfully built man standing at the base of a tree that towered above all the others. He looked small against the trunk of the huge tree, and his ax seemed a tiny tool to take on the mighty trunk.

The wind roared, forcing Annie to pull the bearskin more tightly around herself. "Boom," went the sound of the ax against wood. On the lumberman labored, each stroke of the ax seeming as strong and steady as the first blow he had landed. Finally he had cut a notch about halfway through the trunk. He looked up at the tree, which swayed in the wind, and took one more swing before running out of the forest faster than Annie had ever seen a man run.

She was more puzzled than before. They had cut notches out of nearly one hundred trees, as near as she could tell. But not one had come down. How were they supposed to clear a field like this?

Just then her father strode around the wagon. "Are you ready, daughter?" he asked, a broad grin stretching across his face.

"Ready for what?" she replied. "I must not understand tree clearing because it seems to me you haven't cleared a one."

"Patience," he answered with a sly grin. "Before this day is done, this whole stand will be clear. Remember, things often don't seem as they are."

Her father walked away from the wagon, clearly enjoying his mystery. Annie smiled and let him have his fun. The trees moaned in the wind, and overhead a flock of blackbirds squawked noisily.

It was hard to wait, especially when she didn't know what she was waiting for. The men huddled around, telling each other stories and laughing as they ate cornbread and drank cider, not at all minding the rest from their work.

Out of the corner of her eye, Annie caught a glimpse of red darting behind a tree. When she turned to get a better look, it was gone. Thinking it was a cardinal, she stared into the woods, hoping to see it again.

The next time she saw it, she realized it was too big to be a bird. Suddenly Annie remembered Edward. Hadn't he been wearing a red scarf? She tried to remember. Climbing down from the wagon, she ran a few feet into the woods. "Edward," she called out.

There was no answer; so Annie ran in a little farther and called his name a little louder. Then she saw the flash of red again. "Edward!" she screamed.

"Help me," he called to her.

Annie felt her heart beat faster. Now what trouble was he in? She found him squatting on the ground. "What are you doing?" she asked.

"I found this perfect skeleton," he answered. "If I try to pick it up, it will break apart."

"Oh, Edward," Annie said a little crossly, "what do we need with a dirty, old possum skeleton anyway?"

"Come on," he whined. "It will be part of my collection. I can draw it and study it. Please?"

"Well, what do you want me to do?" she asked.

"Put it in your skirts," he said, as though that were the most obvious thing in the world.

Annie looked with a mixture of fondness and exasperation at her little brother. "All right," she answered. "But I'm not touching it. If you want the dirty, old thing, you pick it up yourself."

The boy carefully lifted the small bundle of bones and set it on Annie's skirt, where she cradled it in the folds. "Now, we better leave these woods," she said. "The men are waiting for something."

The two walked slowly toward the trail, Annie being careful not to jiggle the bones that her brother had gone to such lengths to get. Just then there was an enormous gust of wind, followed closely by the loud cracking of wood. The girl looked up and saw above her the huge tree trembling and shaking. Its enormous trunk swayed violently as the wind blew against it. There were more sounds of wood cracking, and Annie understood instantly the danger that she and Edward were in.

"Run!" she screamed at her brother, dropping her skirts and running as fast as she could.

He bent over as if to grab the skeleton that she had just dropped, but Annie screamed again, "Don't bother with it. Just run!" Even as she spoke, the tree swayed further as its trunk, where it had been notched, began to give way.

Annie and her brother stumbled out of the woods just as the tree was torn from its stump and crashed into the tree next to it. That tree, which had also been notched, trembled and shook. Unable to stand up to the weight of the huge tree that leaned upon it, that tree also snapped, falling on the tree next to it. One after another the trees fell, the ground shaking as their heavy trunks crashed to the forest floor. When Patrick Henry saw his children dash out only a moment before the first tree fell, he ran to them.

By the time he reached them, they were at the wagon, where Annie hugged the frightened boy while she fought off tears.

She didn't know whether to laugh or cry. Laugh, because she was saved. Cry, because she had come too close to death.

Patrick Henry faced them with stunned silence. When he could finally speak, he said to Annie sharply, "What were you doing in there?"

Her eyes welled with tears, but before she could answer, Edward said, "She saved my life, Father. Don't be angry."

From behind them came the din of splitting wood as more trees thudded to the forest floor. But the drama of the trees seemed like nothing compared to the drama of life and death in which they had almost been a part.

Clutching his children tightly to himself, Patrick Henry bowed his head and prayed.

By the end of the day, not a single tree stood in what had been a dense stand of forest. The ground was littered with their heavy trunks, which lay in piles where they had fallen. It would take days for the men to drag them away, and still more days for the stumps to be burned and hauled away. Finally the field would be ready for planting.

There would be time in the future to think of those tasks. Patrick Henry looked out over his land with a contented sigh. "This is good land," he told his children. "We serve a most gracious God. How blessed we are!"

6

A Horrible Discovery

In May, 1780, the news from the war was worse. The American soldiers in Charleston had surrendered, and the British were in a position to control all of South Carolina. From there they could threaten North Carolina and even Virginia. "Why is this happening?" Annie cried. "I thought we were going to win the war. I never expected that we would lose."

"Patience, Annie," Dolly answered. "Doesn't your father always say that there is much that goes on beyond our sight—and even beyond our understanding. Surely you have learned to trust the Lord."

"Feebly, I guess," came Annie's reply. "It's always easier to trust when things are going well."

"Ah, yes," Dolly said smiling. "But faith is believing in things not seen, in things yet hoped for."

Annie thought about Dolly's words the next morning as she lay in bed listening to the blue jays yammering outside. Pulling her pillow over her ears, she tried to block out the noise, but it only grew worse as the gray squirrels added their chatter to the confusion.

The girl threw off her pillow, which hit Elizabeth on the ear.

"Annie," her younger sister complained, "why did you throw your pillow at me?"

"Just listen to those birds," Annie grouched. "How can you sleep so soundly?"

Elizabeth rolled over in the bed the girls shared. "You're just out of sorts because Father has gone to the assembly," Elizabeth said. "Now go back to sleep and stop bothering me. I'm tired."

Annie glared at her sister's back. Elizabeth always slept like a log, but Annie couldn't sleep when she was troubled. "I'm to be content in all things," she muttered, wishing it were easy to put those words into practice. "If only I knew what my future would bring. How can I be content buried out here on the frontier where there is no one my age and no prospects of marriage? Will I live with my father and all his new children all the days of my life?"

She sighed deeply as she rose from her bed. The face that greeted her in the looking glass made her scowl. Annie's cheeks were freckled from the sun because she often forgot to wear her bonnet. Her curly brown hair refused to be tamed; so Annie had taken to wearing it pulled back in a knot at her neck. She pinned on her white lace cap, tucking the stubborn curls underneath.

"Good morning," her stepmother said, looking up fondly as she came into the room. "You look fresh this morning."

"I don't feel fresh," Annie confessed grumpily. "I feel uglier than sin, and my mood matches."

"Is it because your father has gone?" Dolly asked.

"No . . . though I wish he were done with politics. Just like I wish the war were over."

"May I ask you a question?" Annie blurted, feeling shy all of a sudden.

"Of course. What is it?"

"Do you think . . . um . . . " Annie hesitated and then started again. "Is it possible . . . Do you think I'll ever get married?"

"You're not yet seventeen," Dolly answered. "You'll have time."

"But will I ever meet someone and fall in love?" she asked.

"Poor dear," Dolly answered, rising from her chair and putting her arms around Annie. "If God has called you to marriage, then He'll provide a godly man to be your husband. But my Annie has never found it easy to wait, have you?" Holding Annie at arm's length, she suggested, "Why don't you go up and visit Clara Lesker? It'll do you good to see a friend."

It was a lovely May day. As the horse ran, Annie found her dark thoughts being replaced by a sense of well-being. She breathed deeply of the rich smell of damp soil and fragrant wildflowers. She saw rhododendron thickets so dense that a man could not cross them. Bees and butterflies hovered near their showy flowers.

Judge Lesker and his wife, Clara, lived in a house on a nearby parcel of land close to Martinsville, about two miles away. Mrs. Lesker was a young woman who had taught school in Williamsburg before moving to the frontier with her husband, a young lawyer. After several years he had become a county judge, riding circuit over Henry County, hearing cases in even the most remote locations. Several times Annie had visited with Clara, and the two enjoyed remembering life in Williamsburg.

The Leskers lived in a large frame house made of lumber planed in the lumber mill at Danville. Annie knew the house had been costly because the lumber had to be brought all that way over rough, hilly roads. But that was one of the reasons the girl liked to visit. It reminded her of Scotchtown; it was roomy and filled with pretty things from back East. And Mrs. Lesker was so happy in her marriage. "If only I could have her good fortune," Annie said to herself as she dismounted.

Annie tied the horse up at the fence and walked to the front door. The house seemed strangely quiet. She hoped the Leskers hadn't gone away. After knocking softly and getting no response, she examined the windows. They weren't shuttered. She looked up and saw that there was no smoke coming from the chimney. That was strange. People never let their fires go out because it was difficult to start another.

The door was not locked, and it pushed open easily. Feeling just a little skittish, Annie peeked into the hall, calling out softly, "Mrs. Lesker?"

There was no answer. Annie looked around nervously. "Don't be foolish," she told herself. "You are acting jumpy like an old woman. Why, the Leskers probably went away overnight and just forgot to lock up."

Pushing the door open all the way, Annie forced herself to enter the quiet house. She called out again, wishing that her voice did not sound so shaky. When there was no response, she began to feel better. Surely they had just gone away. "I guess I'll lock the shutters for them," she said to herself. "That way no squatters will be coming into the house while they're gone."

The girl closed the shutters in the front parlor and the study, wishing there was at least a fire in the fireplace to brighten up the dark rooms. She crossed over the hallway to the front bedroom and pulled its shutters closed, hurrying out to the hallway, which was well lit by the still-opened door.

There was one more room before Annie could get back on her horse and head to Leatherwood. She pushed open the door of a gloomy bedroom, which was shaded by a large bush growing outside the window.

Annie sniffed. *What is that smell?* she wondered, putting a handkerchief over her nose. She hurried to the window and pulled the shutter closed, wanting only to get out of the house as quickly as she could. As she began locking the shutter, she heard a quick intake of breath coming from the bed.

Annie spun around. There, huddled in the corner of the bed, was Mrs. Lesker, rocking back and forth, clutching a pillow between her arms. Her wild black eyes stared from her pale, tear-streaked face.

Without thought of danger, Annie rushed forward and threw her arms around the frightened woman. Stroking the woman's tangled hair, Annie said, "What's wrong? What has happened?"

Mrs. Lesker moaned, and the tears streamed down her face.

"Let me get you a drink," Annie whispered. She let go of Mrs. Lesker, but as she did so, the woman began trembling. Annie was crossing the room to fetch the water from the washstand when Clara let out a shriek, nearly scaring the girl to death. "Whatever is the matter?" she demanded. But suddenly she stumbled over something. To her horror, she saw that it was Mr. Lesker, who lay in a crumpled heap upon the floor.

Annie forgot the water. She bent down, her face close

to his, listening for a breath. There was nothing. Gently, she rolled the lifeless man onto his back. A crimson stain spread across the front of his shirt near a ragged, powder-stained hole. Annie's mouth went dry, and her stomach heaved as though she were going to be sick. She backed away, trying to keep from screaming, but her foot slipped in something sticky.

She regained her feet and looked desperately around the room, which was empty except for a woman in shock, her dead husband, and Annie.

"Help me, Lord," the terrified girl sobbed as she sat back on her heels, well away from the body. She covered her face with her hands and cried, giving herself over to her fear. Finally there were no more tears. As she wiped her eyes on the back of her hand, she recalled the words of Psalm 23 and began to say them to herself. When she came to the line, "Yea, though I walk through the valley of the shadow of death, I will fear no evil, for thou art with me," her voice trembled. But she felt comforted.

Rising from the floor, she smoothed her hair away from her face and looked with pity at young Mrs. Lesker, now a widow. "Come," she whispered, "we need to go home. I can't carry you, but lean on my shoulder, and I'll help you out."

She pulled on Mrs. Lesker's arm until the woman budged from the bed. First coaxing, then pulling, and at times even dragging the judge's wife, Annie managed to get her out of the house.

By the time they reached the horse, her back ached, and she knew there was no way she could boost the older woman up onto the saddle. Mrs. Lesker seemed to grasp the situation. She held onto the saddle and pulled herself up. Then Annie climbed on in front.

Mrs. Lesker's body seemed so limp that Annie feared she would simply slip off the horse. "You must hold onto me—do you hear?" she asked sharply. The older woman responded by clasping her arms tightly around the girl's waist until Annie began to relax. It was going to be all right.

They walked slowly over the trail that had seemed so pleasant only an hour earlier, with Annie content to let the horse set its own pace. When at last they reached the barn, her eyes filled with tears. God had preserved them. She patted Mrs. Lesker's hand and said, "We're home. You're safe here."

The next several hours were forever blurred in Annie's memory. She knew that someone helped her from the horse, but she couldn't remember who. She remembered being stripped of her soiled dress, bathed with gentle hands, and given a glass of warm milk to make her sleep.

Later Edward told her what happened next because the rest of the family thought she had suffered enough. It all went back to the war, Edward said. The British in South Carolina had occupied many towns. But having redcoats in their villages and seeing neighbors befriend the British soldiers had been more than some patriots could bear. They organized raiding parties to attack the British and their Tory helpers. The redcoats fought back, hanging any American raiders they caught.

Soon the South was full of these small, vicious battles. Things grew worse for settlers, Edward said, as angry Tories, made bold by the presence of the redcoats, no longer felt they had to hide their beliefs. Throughout the South they raided and pillaged. A Tory who had known Judge Lesker all his life had lurked in the bushes until it was safe to murder. The cruel man had done it while the judge's wife watched terrified from her bed.

The patriots returned swift justice, Edward announced proudly. They hanged the guilty man in the town square as a warning to other traitors. But the thought of justice did not cheer Annie, who wondered about a war that turned neighbor against neighbor.

Mrs. Lesker slowly regained her strength, but Annie wondered if her friend would ever rejoice again. Only by faith could she believe that God was in charge, even of this awful war.

7

On to Richmond

"If you eat any more of those berries, Edward Henry, you are going to be sick," Elizabeth said, speaking through purple lips and wiping her own blue-stained fingers on the apron of her dress.

Edward, deep in a blueberry thicket, only laughed. "I haven't tasted anything so good since . . ." The boy's memory obviously failed him as he continued popping the round, juicy berries into his mouth faster than he put them in the bucket.

"The mosquitoes are bothering me," Elizabeth fretted, slapping a large one on her arm. "At least they aren't as bad as they were in Williamsburg. Do you remember the mosquitoes there?"

It was late summer, 1780, and the Henrys had been at Leatherwood for a year already. For Edward, memories of Williamsburg and Scotchtown were fading. "I wouldn't trade Leatherwood for all the Williamsburgs in the world," he proclaimed.

"I would," said Annie, who had been quietly picking berries nearby.

"Oh, Annie. You don't mean that," her brother protested. "You hated all that Williamsburg la di da. You told me so yourself. You said you were never so happy as when you came back to Scotchtown. Didn't you say that?"

"Well, maybe I did. But Scotchtown wasn't Leatherwood," Annie snapped back.

Casting a surprised glance at her sister, Elizabeth said, "Don't you remember when I complained about Leatherwood, you told me to be content?"

With a great sigh, Annie straightened up and walked out of the thicket. "I'm not saying I'm not content at Leatherwood. I just said that I wouldn't mind being back in Williamsburg."

"Back in Williamsburg, you'd be right in the middle of a war," Elizabeth reminded her sister.

"Here at Leatherwood, we aren't that far from war," Annie retorted.

The war had gone on five years already, with most of the fighting in the north. Even though there had been no fighting in Virginia since the war's earliest days, the colony shared in the cost of war. Many of the soldiers were Virginians, like Annie's two older brothers, William and John. Andrew Thacker, a neighbor from Scotchtown, also fought with General Washington.

Virginians had sent more than soldiers. They had provided the army with food and money. Every family in Virginia felt the squeeze as prices rose and food became scarce. It was true that Leatherwood had forests full of game and wild berries. The Henrys had not gone hungry, but now the British army threatened to march through North Carolina and into Virginia. No one was safe from this long, expensive war.

"I bet you Annie has a beau there," Edward taunted, hoping that she would get angry and maybe chase him.

Elizabeth giggled, but Annie didn't find it funny. With an exasperated sigh, she turned and walked toward the house, her heavy bucket dragging at her side.

Behind her Edward and Elizabeth continued their teasing. "Who could it be? Let's see, Tom Jefferson is married. How about Mr. Madison? I bet Annie will fall in love with a graybeard like Mr. Lee. Why, he's as old as Father." That was enough to set the two youngsters laughing all over again.

Annie turned and glared at them, but they were having too much fun to notice. After leaving the berries at the kitchen, she stomped into the house.

"Annie, is that you?" Dolly asked from her bedroom.

"Yes, ma'am," Annie answered, fearing that she had aroused one of the sleeping children.

"We have a letter today from Sister Woods. Would you come here? I'd like you to read it."

Dolly leaned over a trunk, looking with displeasure at a soiled petticoat. When she heard her stepdaughter's footsteps, she turned, a smile replacing the frown. Tucking stray brown hair back under her cap, she motioned Annie to one of the chairs, pulling a letter from her apron pocket.

Annie bent over her aunt's spidery scrawl, trying to make out the words. When she had finished, she looked up at Dolly, who brushed at an invisible spot of dirt on a lace collar. "Poor woman," Annie said finally. "Two little ones to raise alone. I didn't know her husband was so ill."

"Nor did we. Mr. Woods was such a quiet man. He never complained over his ailments."

Dolly continued sorting out clothing from her trunk,

clearly not pleased with what she was finding. "Just look at this," she said, holding up an apron with a hole in the middle of it. "Chewed by mice, I imagine. I don't know if anything that I left packed away will be wearable."

"Are you looking for something in particular?" Annie asked, as she joined Dolly near the trunk.

Without looking up from her work, her stepmother said in a soft voice, "Your father and I thought you might go to Sister Woods and help out for a time. I thought I might find some wearable clothes for you."

For a minute Annie thought she had misunderstood. Could God really be answering her prayer to leave Leatherwood? "You mean I would go to Richmond?" she asked, trying not to appear too eager.

"Would you mind it terribly?" Dolly asked, looking up for the first time.

Trying not to seem too excited, Annie smiled. "If you think I could be helpful, I wouldn't mind going."

Dolly's eyes danced, but she hid her smile behind a handkerchief. Frowning deliberately, she said, "Of course I could send Elizabeth. . . . She's young, but she is so calming to be around. Don't you agree?"

"Much too young," Annie said more forcefully than she intended. "Besides, I can be every bit as calm as Elizabeth if that's what the situation requires."

"Would it be a great sacrifice for you?" Dolly asked solemnly.

But Annie caught the laughter in her eyes. She threw down the stockings that she held in her hand and said, "You know that I want to go, don't you? Please say yes."

"My only concern for you is safety. But your father says that the British are just as likely to attack near Leatherwood as they are to reach Richmond. It makes me sad to say that we can't protect you here. So the answer is yes, you may go," Dolly said. "In fact, you may leave with your father when he goes to the assembly."

Annie turned somber. "I didn't know Father was going again so soon. He hasn't been home more than a month. I don't want to abandon you."

"You aren't abandoning me," Dolly said. "I'll have plenty of help. In fact, Elizabeth is devoted to me and the children."

Annie fidgeted nervously, twisting her fingers on her lap and gnawing at her lip. She felt ashamed that she was so eager to leave her family. Dolly reached out a comforting hand. "There's no shame in wanting to start your own life, Annie," she said. "Every bird knows when it's time to leave the nest."

"You know I love you all," Annie said.

"Of course we do. And your father and I agree that it will be good for you to help your aunt."

After a week of preparation, Annie and her father finally set off for Richmond, now the capital of Virginia. They reached the city late on the evening of September 27, 1780. A boy in a tricorner hat rang a bell and called out, "Traitor's plot discovered. Arnold gets away."

Patrick Henry stopped the wagon in the midst of the busy street and beckoned for the newsboy. He scanned the newspaper eagerly, shaking his head when he had finished the story.

"What is it?" Annie asked, dismayed at the change in her father's expression.

"Benedict Arnold, one of General Washington's favorite and most trusted aides, has turned traitor and joined the British. A sad thing," he said. "He tried to betray his command at West Point but was discovered before the plot could hatch."

"Why would he leave now, Father? Does he think we have no chance of winning?"

"I don't know what he's thinking. He married a British girl, and he lost sight of honor. But if he thinks we will abandon the fight against tyranny at this late date, he's mistaken."

Around them the traffic surged forward as the once-sleepy town bustled with crowds who had business before the assembly. Men and women promenaded down the main street, dressed in their city best. Looking down at her own dusty dress and comparing it to the ones she saw made Annie blush. Turning to her father, who also carried plenty of road dust, she said, "I know it isn't important," Annie said, "but we don't look as though we belong in the city."

Her father chuckled. "We'll take you to your aunt's, and I'll grab a room at the inn. We'll both be able to bathe and put on our city clothes. You wait, Annie. In a matter of days, you'll feel right at home here. Besides, if Richmond ever becomes so much like London that a simple yeoman farmer and his family don't feel fancy enough, then we have already lost the war."

When Annie met her aunt, she was struck by how much the woman looked like Patrick Henry. But their appearance was all the brother and sister had in common. She was a dreamy, impractical woman who let her children run around like wild animals throughout her wood-frame house. To Annie it didn't seem as though her aunt was really there. Her mind always seemed somewhere else. And the poor cousins, Samuel and Amos, were the most unruly children that Annie had ever met. So starved were they for attention that they constantly misbehaved in order to get it.

At night, when Annie was in the quiet of her own room, she thought with wry amusement about the way God works. At Leatherwood, the young woman had felt crowded by all the people who shared such a small house. She had wanted time alone. In Richmond, she had a room alone. But her waking hours were spent shepherding two rowdy, needy children. Annie found herself missing Elizabeth and Edward and the little children. Mostly, though, she missed Dolly, whose steady calm had made a crowded house peaceful.

"I will have to learn to be the calm one," Annie told herself. "Right now this house has no loving center, but maybe it can develop one."

She buckled down to the job she had set before her. Each day, the two boys and Annie did an hour of school work. She took them outside for long walks along the river, where they talked to the boat captains. Other times they meandered along the creeks. She showed them how to make fishing poles, something her brothers had been born knowing how to do. She urged her aunt to resume their family Bible readings, and when the widow was too tired, Annie did it herself.

One cold winter day the boys were begging to go outside.

"It's too cold," she said. "Why don't you make something?"

"Teach us to whittle," pleaded Samuel.

"Me too," seven-year-old Amos added.

Annie threw up her hands. "I don't know how to whittle. Didn't your father teach you to do these things?

My brother Edward can do it. And he's not much bigger than you. I don't know how he learned. He just watched and did it."

"But who can we watch?" the boys whined.

Annie could teach them to sew, but they wanted nothing to do with "women's work." Finally, not knowing what else to do, she promised that on the first nice day they might walk up to the tavern and see if there would be some men whittling on the porch. Annie rather doubted it since it was cold.

There came a day in January, 1781, that was so balmy it seemed like spring. "Today is the day, boys," she announced to them after she had gone outside to test the weather.

They hurriedly pulled on their overcoats and boots. Soon they were ready to go.

The streets were peaceful. The newspapers warned that British troops were building strength at Yorktown, but that was more than a hundred miles away. No one thought much about it. The tavern was only three blocks away, but the boys were so full of energy after being cooped up that Annie let them run and holler for a while. Finally, each one armed with a pocket knife, they set off for the tavern. The boys pushed at each other until Annie feared they might do danger to themselves or someone else with the little knives they carried.

"Be careful with those knives," she scolded. "No more pushing or shoving."

With relief, she saw that several men were seated on the wooden bench in front of the tavern. Smoke curled from the pipes they held in their teeth, and their bellies strained against the buttons of their vests. The boys scooted over eagerly and positioned themselves where they could watch and listen to the conversation.

"You behave," she warned them before crossing the street to the milliner's, where she hoped to get new ribbons for her bonnet.

The nice weather brought everyone out, and Annie spent a pleasant hour in the store visiting with people she hadn't seen all winter. She occasionally peeked out the window to check up on the boys, who were contentedly carving on their pieces of wood.

A gnawing in her stomach reminded Annie that it was time for dinner. She opened the door of the shop and was astonished to see a horde of redcoats coming down the street. The color drained from her face as she watched the black-booted army march down Richmond's main street. Behind her, women gasped, and some burst into tears. All up and down the street, shutters slammed shut as the townsfolk hid behind the security of their walls.

All Annie could think about were the young boys across the street. Gathering up her skirts, she ran and grabbed them by the hands. They resisted her. "We want to watch," Samuel protested. Annie turned an angry face toward the boys. They were so impressed by the scarlet jackets, brass buttons, and white breeches that they couldn't pull their eyes away.

"Hurry. Hurry," she scolded, pulling on their arms. But they wriggled free of her grasp and began running down the street toward the oncoming soldiers. Annie stood motionless, frozen by fear of what the soldiers might do.

Several grinned and pointed at the boys who were marching alongside the procession. One even put his hat on Samuel's head. Annie trembled with anger at her cousins. What should she do?

Just then a young man walked up beside her. He was dressed in a gray vest and black breeches and wore his brownish hair pulled back in a simple ponytail at the neck. He bowed slightly and smiled. "Would you like me to capture the little scamps for you?"

Annie looked at him gratefully. "Would you?" she asked. In an instant, he had swept up beside the marching cousins, pulled one up under each arm, and tossed the redcoat's hat into a mud puddle.

He ignored the protests coming from the boys and the soldier. With a few graceful strides, he returned to Annie's side, holding the squawking boys by the ears. "You rascals have something to say to the young lady?"

Ducking their chins, they scowled at the pavement until the young man gave their ears a little pinch. "Ouch," they howled, wriggling to get free, but that just made their ears hurt more. Grudgingly, Amos apologized, and the young man let him go. Samuel wiggled a bit longer, but when he saw the determination in the young man's eyes, he apologized.

"Will that do?" the young man asked Annie before loosening his grip. She nodded shyly, wondering why he looked so familiar to her.

"The nerve of the redcoats marching into the capital in all their glory," he muttered as he stared glumly at the passing column of soldiers.

"I'll take these boys home," Annie whispered. "Their mother will be worried with all the commotion." Annie also was worried. How could the redcoats have taken Richmond without even a shot being fired? "I don't know how I can ever thank you for your help."

The young man bowed slightly. "It was my pleasure. Let me introduce myself. Spencer Roane, at your service."

Annie giggled. That's why he looked so familiar. She had met him in Williamsburg three years before. "I believe we've met," she managed to say after an awkward silence. "My name is Annie Henry."

Now it was Spencer's turn to be surprised. "But you were just a little thing then. I would not have recognized you," he said. "You've grown up."

"I'm seventeen," Annie said a bit smugly. "And how is your cousin Grace?"

"As much of a pill as ever. Her father has threatened to send her to the Caribbean until she learns to behave," he said shrugging his shoulders.

Just then a high-stepping white horse carrying a scarlet-clad soldier in a plumed hat pranced by. "The traitor Benedict Arnold," Spencer said, his face stony with disapproval. "I mustn't stay here any longer. I may do something I will regret." Impulsively, he grabbed Annie's hand and landed a kiss on it before turning and striding away.

Blushing furiously, she watched his retreating figure until he was out of sight. Next to her the cousins were nursing their sore ears and bruised egos, casting gloomy looks at her.

"You'll not tell Mother?" Amos pleaded.

"She wouldn't care," Samuel said with a note of belligerence.

"But she'd care if Annie got angry and went away," Amos retorted.

"I'm not going anywhere," Annie said sternly. "I made a promise to your mother and my parents that I would come help. But you boys must learn to obey."

"Why must we?" Samuel asked saucily.

"Because your life will be full of trouble if you don't. God won't put up with a rebellious spirit."

Taking aim, the boy kicked a rock with the toe of his well-scuffed boot. When they reached the little house where they lived, Amos scampered up the stairs, but Samuel refused to go in. Annie left him staring moodily at the soldiers who now filled the streets.

8

Redcoats

Throughout the night, gunshots shattered the silence. An explosion sent flames soaring into the heavens. Smaller fires burned here and there, and their acrid smoke filled the air. Annie paced nervously in her room, wishing she were back in Leatherwood. Where was General Washington's army?

Bonfires burned in the streets, and drunken soldiers danced on the sidewalks. Tory sympathizers, who had hidden their admiration for the king out of fear, now celebrated with the red-coated conquerors.

Sitting in her dark room, lit only by a candle, Annie dashed off a letter to her parents. Tomorrow she would take it to the post office. It was impossible to sleep with all the noise and confusion. At any moment, soldiers could be pounding at her aunt's door.

Morning came and found Annie slumped down in a chair, her head drooping awkwardly on her chest. She woke with a groan. After stretching her stiff muscles, she glanced at the desk.

Her letter was there as a reminder that she would have to go out to the post office.

She opened the shuttered window. Outside on her aunt's sidewalk lay two soldiers wrapped in blankets. All up and down the street, the soldiers littered the ground like so many red statues. "They aren't even in a camp," Annie muttered with disgust. "It's as though Benedict Arnold wants to soil the entire town with his British friends."

Annie feared that the presence of the British meant that General Washington was losing the war. She hurriedly washed and pulled on her dress, eager to go down on the street and hear some news.

Her aunt was drinking tea in the parlor. Her face was pale, and Annie could see that she had not slept well either. "What's the matter, Aunty?" Annie asked.

"I looked in on the boys. Amos is sleeping like a darling, but Samuel's bed is empty. I've searched the house, and he isn't to be found." Then looking down with a shamefaced expression, she added, "I'm afraid to go outside. Those soldiers are so frightening."

Annie looked at her aunt with pity. "I'll go," she said brusquely.

Her aunt watched as Annie pulled on a long woolen cape and tied her calash under her chin. "You aren't afraid of anything, are you?" she asked.

Annie stared at her aunt in astonishment. "I'm frightened of all sorts of things," she said. "It's only by the grace of God that I have courage, if that's what it is."

"With Samuel, it isn't courage. It's recklessness. I fear that he may do something foolish because he doesn't think. And he's very angry."

Again Annie was surprised. She hadn't thought her aunt paid any attention to the boys. The girl hesitated at the door, wanting to say something to comfort the anxious woman. "I think I understand Samuel," she said. "I felt awfully angry when my mother died. I did some foolish things, just like Samuel. It wasn't until I learned the Gospel—that Christ, the Son of God, died for me—that I put away the anger."

But from her aunt's wooden expression, it was hard to know if she understood.

The cold air put color in Annie's cheeks as she hurried through the streets, keeping her face turned to the ground. Here and there she saw from the corner of her eye other residents rushing along the sidewalks, being careful not to come too close to any of the soldiers. It was as if all the people in Richmond believed that if they stared at the ground, they would be invisible. Smoke continued rising from a building at the far end of town. With anger she saw that several other storefronts had been burned.

Outside the post office was a red-coated officer. Whenever anyone went in to mail a letter, he examined the address. Annie hesitated. It would not be wise to let that British soldier see that she was writing to Patrick Henry at Leatherwood.

Across the street, a small band of men had gathered. They ignored the pointed looks cast in their direction by the post office guard. Annie slipped over so that she could hear what they were saying. "The legislature has moved to Charlottesville," she heard one man say.

"The British would like nothing better than to catch the legislature—maybe Governor Jefferson as well."

"Those men would never let themselves fall into British hands," another man answered. "They're too wily for that."

Annie wanted to ask about her father, but looking around the group and seeing all the strange faces, she suddenly grew suspicious. How did she know they weren't spies? The Tories in Richmond would be rejoicing at the presence of the redcoats. And why weren't the soldiers breaking up this group?

Before she could decide, she felt a tap on her shoulder. Turning, she saw Spencer Roane, who looked at her quizzically.

"Are you sure it's safe to be out this morning?" he asked while guiding her beyond the hearing of the crowd.

"I thought I would hasten out to find the news," she said. "But my cousin Samuel, the stubborn one, is missing. He left sometime during the night, and my aunt is crazy with worry over him. I'm trying to find him." She looked into Spencer Roane's sympathetic face and felt a lifting of the burden. "If you were a young boy of eight, where would you hide?" she asked.

"I would have been in a barn with the horses," he said with a laugh. "I always liked a good horse."

"Well, Samuel has no horses," Annie responded, chewing her lip. "He seemed to like the soldiers, and that's what has me worried. Would he be with the British? Is there a camp?"

At the mention of the soldiers, Spencer's face darkened. His eyes looked moodily off into the distance. "Their camp is down the road," he said, pointing off behind her. "But they didn't bother sleeping there last night."

"Do you think Samuel would go there?" Annie asked with a growing sense of excitement mixed with dread.

"I guess it might be a likely place," he admitted. "But it isn't a safe place." Then he nodded at the cluster of men behind her. "The streets are not safe either. If one of these soldiers were to discover your identity, they would likely take you prisoner. Don't trust anyone, unless you know for certain that they are loyal to the cause."

Annie looked back at the soldier at the post office, glad

that she had had the good sense not to mail her letter. But her hopes for her young cousin withered. "What shall I do?" she asked, feeling dangerously close to tears.

"Don't you worry," the young man said gently. "I'll go to the camp myself. If I see the scamp, I'll bring him directly to your aunt's home."

A broad smile lit Annie's face. "You're so kind to me," she said gratefully. "I'll wait for you there."

It was three hours later that Spencer Roane returned with an angry Samuel in tow. After reuniting the boy with his worried mother, Annie sat in the parlor with the young man while he told his story.

Spencer sipped from his steaming mug of cider and stretched his long legs out on the hooked rug. "Just as you thought, the boy was in the camp. He was dressed like a redcoat from head to toe and was dancing to the fife. The men were having great fun at his expense, but he didn't mind. The more they joshed him, the more he danced."

"How awful," Annie said, closing her eyes and covering her face with her hands. "Just think what they would have done if they had known who he was."

Spencer Roane grew serious, though he couldn't completely extinguish the amusement in his eyes. "I'm afraid they did know. He told everyone his name, and when that didn't get any attention, he told them he was Patrick Henry's nephew. That brought even Benedict Arnold out of his tent."

Annie blushed a deep crimson. "That little . . . I'd like to strangle him."

"I'm afraid I beat you to it. He heard quite a lecture on loving family and country while I brought him home. I even told him how Doc Withers had his eyes gouged out for consorting with the enemy. I think it made an impression."

Annie nodded. "I appreciate that," she said. "His mother is too soft on him, and I don't really have any authority."

Spencer emptied his mug and rose reluctantly from his chair. "I would like to stay and visit," he admitted. "Perhaps when the present trouble is gone from our doorsteps, you would allow me to call."

Blushing furiously, Annie nodded. As she watched the dark-haired fellow stroll down the street, she threw up her hands in disgust. *Why can't I be more like Elizabeth?*

Later that week Annie walked to the apothecary to get some medicine for her aunt. She was waiting at the counter when suddenly from the street outside the shop came the sound of wild snorting, loud laughter, and screams. Looking out the door, she saw a herd of pigs running crazily from gutter to gutter, as if they didn't know which way to go. Other pigs spun in circles like tops as they chased their own curly tails. Behind them a mob of redcoats waved their hats, which only drove the pigs into a greater state of confusion.

Annie stepped back as a huge swine crashed into the door before dizzily stumbling back into the street. A few children chased the tiny ones while their mothers tried to get out of the way as the crazy animals plowed through the town.

Across the street, the tavern door opened and a whisky cask came rolling into the street. From its side flowed a trail of liquor. As the barrel wobbled down the street, the pigs chased it, greedily slurping up the liquid. Like dogs madly chasing a bone, the meaty beasts lunged after the barrel, snorting nastily at any other pig that got in the way.

The first cask was followed by another, and another, as the redcoats went through the tavern's supply of ale and whisky, ripping open the sides of each cask before sending it spinning out into the street where the pigs awaited. The smell of the sour liquid filled the air, and Annie looked with disgust at the pigs, who now wobbled on unsteady legs after the casks.

She felt her temper rise. Without thinking, she pushed the door open, ready to march across the street to find an officer to discipline his troops. Three steps out the door, she turned and stumbled over a pig that had fallen down drunk in the middle of the street. She caught her balance, but then proceeded to plop her foot right in the middle of a whisky puddle, splashing the sour liquid onto her dress.

Across the street, soldiers laughed, but none came to her assistance. With disgust mixed with embarrassment, she tossed her head as she turned back toward the apothecary. A voice behind her said, "Excuse my men. They have been fighting a long time and have lost their manners."

Annie turned to see a proud-looking man with mocking eyes staring at her, his lip curled in amusement at her distress. With a flourish, he doffed his plumed hat and made an exaggerated bow. "General Benedict Arnold," he said hautily.

Annie fixed her angry eyes on him. "I've always wondered what a traitor looked like. Now I know." She turned away, but the general grabbed her arm angrily.

"You are talking to a general in His Majesty's Army. You must show respect."

Annie raised her chin defiantly. "I will show respect to my God, to my parents, and to the rightful leaders of my country. You are none of those things. And a king who would allow himself to be represented by soldiers who carry on like this is not worthy of respect."

Pulling her arm away, Annie stalked away from the general, leaving him standing in angry astonishment. Before he could recover, she was in the apothecary, surrounded by her patriot neighbors. He glared at her through the glass before turning and marching across the street with a look that silenced the high spirits of his troops. In a sharp voice, he gave orders for them to assemble. Then as suddenly as they had marched into town, they marched back toward their camp, leaving behind the smoldering remains of burnt buildings, charred bonfires, broken casks, and drunken pigs.

9

Spencer Roane

In April, Benedict Arnold again sent his raiders into Richmond. They found little of value, especially since the legislature no longer met there. One day the boys went with their mother on a visit to some friends in the country. For Annie, it marked nearly a year since she had moved from Leatherwood to Richmond. Seeing that the day was warm and the sky clear, she packed a picnic lunch and carried it down to the river bank to eat.

The water lapped peacefully at the shore. As she gazed at the river, Annie watched gulls swooping low over the water, sometimes plunging their beaks beneath its glittery surface and coming up with a fish.

Lying back on the grassy slope, she watched the powdery clouds float by and remembered a picnic at the creek at Scotchtown when she had first met Andrew Thacker. Even now she could hear his fife playing in her imagination. Andrew, like her brothers John and William, had gone to be a soldier. She wondered wistfully if he had found it as exciting as he thought it would be. Had he been injured, maybe even killed? She hadn't heard a thing.

Annie found herself sinking into a melancholy mood as she considered her past and the sweet hopes she had for freedom in a new country. Judge Lesker's death at Leatherwood and Benedict Arnold's army had destroyed those hopes. Now she prayed only that her brothers would come home safely. What a waste if they should die and Virginia still be in bondage to the king. Annie shut her eyes against the dismal thought and prayed.

As she lay there praying, she heard a rustling next to her. Opening her eyes, she found Spencer Roane gazing at her so intensely that it made her blush and hurry to sit up. Embarrassed at being caught staring, he turned his eyes and looked out over the water.

"The housekeeper told me that I might find you here," he said. "I hope I'm not intruding."

"Not at all," she answered as she busied her nervous fingers with a fold in her skirt.

Silence followed this brief exchange as both were suddenly tongue-tied. Finally Spencer recalled why he had come. He pulled an envelope out of his pocket and handed it to Annie. "I brought this from your father," he said. "I thought you would want to read it right away."

Annie examined the letter. "Have you recently seen Father?" she asked curiously, turning the envelope over in her hand as though looking for a clue. Several curly locks sprang out from under her white cap and fell over her eyes, but the girl seemed not to notice.

Spencer reached out and brushed the curls gently back. His gesture startled Annie, who pulled away. "Excuse me, I don't know what I was doing," he stammered. "Those curls were just so distracting."

Annie's heart beat rapidly. She felt hot and wished she had chosen a shadier place for her picnic lunch.

"Go ahead. Open the letter. I won't find it rude," the young man said, seeing her discomfort and knowing he had contributed to it.

She slipped her finger under the flap and pulled open the seal. "Shall I read it out loud to you?" she asked shyly.

"I would love to hear it," he answered.

Dear Annie,

I trust Sister Woods is well and believe that you are proving to be a help to her. I write to let you know that the folks at Leatherwood are fine, although the British Army came close and threatened to enter Virginia through North Carolina. Had they done so, we might have been close to the fighting.

As you know, the assembly has been meeting without incident in Charlottesville, where we expected to be well out of the way of any trouble. Several nights ago, however, a young captain, Jack Jouett, overheard General Cornwallis ordering 250 cavalrymen to Charlottesville in order to overtake us. Had the plot been successful, I, along with my fellow legislators, Governor Jefferson, and other state officials would have all been captured. What a blow to the cause it would have been!

Jouett rode all night and warned the assembly. We immediately rose from our beds and made haste for Staunton in the Blue Ridge. I traveled with John Tyler, Speaker Harrison, and your uncle William Christian. We didn't dare stop, not knowing how far behind us the British cavalry were. (We later learned that they had stopped for breakfast, but we didn't know it at the time.)

On we scrambled through the dark night and into the next morning, until we could go no further. Tired and hungry, we decided to stop at a little cabin hidden in a mountain gorge. It was visible to us only by a tiny wisp of smoke that rose above the rocky summit.

An old woman answered the door and peered out suspiciously. "Who are you? Where have you come from?" she asked. I stood near the back, not wanting to draw attention to myself. Old Tyler said we were members of the legislature fleeing from the British cavalry.

"Ride on then, you cowardly knaves," she cackled, waving a broom at us as though we were chaff which she personally was going to sweep away.

I pushed forward and tried to reason with her, vainly I might add. Tyler interrupted me as I spoke. "What would you say if I told you that Patrick Henry fled with the rest of us?" he asked her.

She glared at him with a look I wouldn't want to see again. It made me tremble in my boots. (How glad I am that your mother, Dolly, is a gentle soul. You must follow her example when you marry. A husband is more likely to be won with kindness.)

When Annie read those words, she blushed because of the young man next to her. Taking a deep breath, she began to read again.

"Patrick Henry?" she asked in amazement. "I would tell you there wasn't a word of truth in it." She harumphed and shook her broom until all four of us almost turned and ran. "Why, Patrick Henry would never do such a cowardly thing."

I almost died laughing when I heard those words. Here she had me trembling with fear, and yet she was holding me up as a paragon of bravery. That's when the fun began. Tyler pointed at me and said, "But this is Mr. Henry."

The old woman demanded that I go inside and stand by the fire so that she could get a better look at me. Seeing something in my face that she liked, she finally relented, saying, "Well then, if that is Patrick Henry, it must be all right."

Next thing I knew we were sitting in her warm parlor, toasting comfortably in front of the fire, sipping warm cider and eating cornbread. Afterwards we all had a good laugh over the story.

We are now in Staunton, far from trouble. I know about Benedict Arnold in Richmond. Don't let it worry you. And don't let yourself be discouraged by concentrating only on the things you see around you. It is a much bigger world than you imagine, and much goes on that you don't know. Trust God.

I am giving this letter into the hand of Spencer Roane, who assisted some of our legislators in their flight to Staunton. Some of us aren't young and can't hazard the journey on horseback. Mr. Roane secured carriages and drove some of the men. Thank him for me.

Your faithful and loving father,
Patrick Henry

Annie looked up from the letter and caught a glimpse of humor in Spencer's eyes. With a smile she said, "Father must have enjoyed the scolding by the old woman. I wouldn't be surprised if he didn't invite her for dinner someday."

"Your father is a marvelous man," Spencer remarked.

"I think he is. He is not afraid to do what's right. And he is well loved by his family and his neighbors. That's important, don't you think?"

"Most men expect to be loved by their families," the young man mused. "It seems almost like part of the package. But to be loved, as your father is, by all the yeoman farmers of the state—that is a marvelous thing."

Annie beamed. Carefully tucking the letter into her pocket, she turned toward the picnic basket. "Would you eat with me?" she asked him, wanting very much for him to stay.

He hesitated just long enough for her to feel uneasy, as though perhaps he had someplace else to be. Forcing herself to smile, she said, "Go if you must. I didn't mean to keep you so long, for I know how busy you must be. I only wanted to carry out my father's wishes that I thank you for your kindness to his friends and colleagues."

"Is that really all, Annie?" he asked her, looking at her with such tenderness that she forgot the question. His eyes caught hers. For several minutes they sat that way, neither one able or willing to break away.

Finally the young man stood up. "I must go, Annie," he said in a gruff voice. "I would feel less than a gentleman if I were to speak my feelings for you before I had asked your father's permission. Please forgive me for being forward."

With a slight bow, he excused himself and walked away, leaving Annie sitting breathless on the grassy slope and not sure what she was feeling.

"I think it must be love," she whispered to herself after a moment.

10

A Reunion

Throughout the spring of 1781, Benedict Arnold and his men pillaged the Virginia countryside, setting fires to the storehouses filled with grain and tobacco.

General Washington was eager to capture the famous traitor; so he sent out the French General Lafayette with 1,200 men. When Lafayette and his men reached Virginia, however, the British recalled Arnold to New York. The raiding continued, now under the orders of the British General Cornwallis.

Annie learned not to despair. Though the news from Virginia was bad, there had been reports of American victories at Kings Meadow and Cowpens in North Carolina. Didn't her father tell her not to judge things based only on what she could see?

One day in October, 1781, Annie's quiet world erupted. She received a letter from her brother William telling her that John was very sick. During a hurried march with General Washington's army from New York to Yorktown, east of Williamsburg on the peninsula, John had taken sick with the flu. High fever and chills had made him unfit for fighting, and the army had abandoned him in Williamsburg. William pleaded for Annie to go to him.

If the situation hadn't been so grave, Annie would have found it amusing. Once again she was being sent off as nurse and comforter to the sick. It wasn't a role that she would have predicted for herself even a year earlier. But people asked for her, and she was glad to go. So many times in the past someone else had comforted her. Now it was her turn.

Her aunt sent her off tearfully. "You've been a balm to my family," she said. "We would not have survived the past year without your gentle love and patience."

The words startled Annie. How she had longed to have Dolly's grace, and now her aunt seemed to suggest that she had a touch of it. Had God done that?

Annie took the basket of food and medicine her aunt offered before turning to say good-bye to her young cousins. It grieved her to part with Amos and Samuel. The younger one clung to her and begged her to stay. But Samuel was too old for tears and begging. Unnoticed by his mother and brother, he slipped an ink-blotched note into Annie's hand as she climbed into the coach that would carry her to Williamsburg.

She watched them grow tiny through teary eyes as the carriage lumbered along the dusty track toward the coast. When they were no longer in sight, she opened the grubby piece of paper.

"I love you," it read in Samuel's childish handwriting. "And God loves me."

Annie smiled as she folded the little letter and put it back in her pocket. Many nights she had spent reading the family Bible to the willful child, despairing that its healing words would ever touch his stubborn heart. Maybe he had heard more than she thought.

She dozed away the hours and didn't wake until they reached the town. She watched out the window as they rolled into the familiar city where she had spent so much time in the Governor's Palace. The town was virtually empty now. Many people had moved with the capital to Richmond. Those who had stayed behind had been hard hit by the war. Many shops were closed, and the streets seemed nearly deserted.

The coach dropped Annie at the Wythes' house where her friend Kate Marsh still lived. The Wythes, like so many others, had abandoned Williamsburg to be farther away from danger, but they had left servants there to protect their house and property.

Annie stood hesitantly on the stoop, letting the memories flood back. Before she could knock, the door opened. Kate clapped her hands and tugged Annie inside. "Don't stand outside gathering moss," she laughed.

Annie smiled at the friend she hadn't seen for three years. Kate had blossomed. She no longer had the frail skittish look that had so provoked Grace to tease her. Now she radiated an inner calm that made her plain features seem beautiful.

"I know you feel dusty and dirty. Those coaches are awful, aren't they? I hope you didn't travel with any unpleasant people." A worried expression crossed Kate's brow.

"It wasn't so awfully bad," Annie said. "But it seemed long, since I was worrying about John. Do you know how he is?"

"That is one of the surprises that I have for you," Kate said with a smile. "He's upstairs in one of the bedrooms. I went to the infirmary and claimed him. We've been taking good care of him, but he seems dreadfully lonely for his family."

Annie threw her arms around her friend. "You are good!" she exclaimed. "May I go to see him now?"

"Even before you bathe?" Kate asked.

"I couldn't wait a minute now that I know he's here," Annie confessed. "I'll have a good wash after I've seen him."

She found her brother sleeping fitfully in a tall four-poster bed. He had kicked off his sheets, so she remade the bed, pulling the sheets up over him. While she worked, she studied his face. Her brother no longer bore a look of innocent mischief. His cheekbones jutted out of a gaunt, colorless face.

John looked so different that it almost broke Annie's heart. She turned away from the bed, her eyes full of tears as she realized how hard the war had been for General Washington's soldiers.

Kate met her on the stairs. After taking one look at Annie's sad face, she wrapped her arms around her. "He looks bad, I know. But the fever is getting better. You'll see, once he's back on the farm, he'll be a new man."

Sighing deeply, Annie said, "He looks so much like my father. It's troubling, for he isn't yet twenty, and he looks like an old man. Has everyone who has gone to be a soldier come back like that?"

"Not at all. Some are wounded in their bodies. But others, like John, seem to be more wounded in their minds. He is sick, but he also is so dreadfully sad. I think it will take awhile for him to get over the things he has seen."

By now the two young ladies were seated in the parlor where Kate had brought a warming cup of herb tea to

Annie. Despite the sad conversation, Kate seemed so bubbling with happiness that Annie couldn't keep from noticing. "What makes you so happy during this sad time?" she asked, setting her cup down.

"I wanted to tell you before," Kate said with a modest smile. "I'm married. Have been since last month. My name is not Kate Marsh, but Kate Wigglesworth, if you can imagine."

"Married!" Annie looked at her friend with new eyes. There were so many questions she wanted to ask, but they all became tangled up before she could ask them.

Kate's smile froze. "Aren't you happy for me?" she asked in a small voice that reminded Annie of the timid girl her friend had once been.

"Happy? Of course I'm happy. Only there's so much to ask, and I just don't know where to begin."

"His name is William, though I call him Bill," Kate said. "He's a glassblower, and he's trying to earn enough money to buy land out West. Maybe in Kentucky."

Annie listened, thinking about marriage and plans. She thought of Spencer Roane's words and smiled.

To Annie's joy, John did get better. Although he sometimes sank into a melancholy mood, for the most part he was cheerful, waiting quietly on the porch for the women to bring him food or drink or medicine. Annie didn't think she had ever seen her brother be so patient, and it worried her a bit. She longed to see a little of his old spark, but it wasn't to be found.

At night John and Bill smoked their pipes on the porch and talked of the war. Annie and Kate often joined them and listened as John described what he had seen. Winters in the North had been brutal, particularly for the south-ern soldiers who didn't even own the warm coats that their northern comrades had. Food was scarce. One hardtack biscuit sometimes had to last for days before a new supply of grain and meat would reach the troops.

This last march, though, had been more than John's body could take. For weeks General Washington had moved the troops here and there near New York, trying to convince the British that he was going to attack Manhattan Island. Having confused the British thoroughly, Washington ordered his troops to begin the long march south, leaving behind only enough soldiers to fool the British, who thought Washington's entire army was still in New York.

Throughout the sweltering August days the army marched despite the heat and lack of food. It was an orderly march, John said. Most of the soldiers were veterans of many battles. They were joined by a large army of French soldiers who had promised to fight with the patriots.

By September, the early columns had reached the mouth of the Chesapeake Bay. They loaded onto boats and began the trip to Williamsburg. That's when John had taken sick. Now it was October, and in Yorktown, just a little east of Williamsburg, a major battle was developing.

"Go see William's shop," Kate said one brisk October day when Annie seemed restless. She agreed and walked down to his little glass factory. It was a brick building, open on one side, where a blazing hot fire burned within an enormous furnace. Unlike most open fireplaces, this furnace had a door that closed. Inside was a vat of glowing orange liquid glass.

William stood in front of the furnace, his rotund belly

straining against his vest buttons. Though it was cool outside, he wore only a vest and muslin shirt. Sweat streaked down his face. Annie entered the shop just as he donned large leather gloves and scooped up a ball of molten glass on the end of a long iron rod that he held in his hand.

He sat down and rolled the iron bar on his bench. Under his skillful hands, the glass was changed from a rough glob to a smooth ball. When he was satisfied, he blew into the end of the tube, and the glass ball expanded, becoming hollow inside. He rolled it and swung it, and the glass ball changed into a vase before her eyes.

Annie was so fascinated that she didn't hear a man run up behind her. Only when he spoke, did she turn to see who it was. "William, could you spare some time?" he gasped. "Thomas was to take food to the troops outside Yorktown, but he is sick and unable to go. There aren't many young men available, but I thought you might be willing."

William wiped his brow on the sleeve of his muslin shirt. He removed the large gloves and set them on his table. Glancing quickly at Annie, he said gruffly, "I'll go. There isn't any work here that won't wait until tomorrow."

"The wagon is loaded at the cooper's. Should I tell them you're coming?"

"Tell them I'll come after I've said good-bye to Kate. You can spare me that time."

Bill and Annie walked back to the Wythes' together. "Will it be dangerous?" Annie asked.

"Not at all," William answered. "I hear the British are trapped in Yorktown. Our army stands between us and them. So I won't even cross enemy lines. There has been traffic back and forth all month."

Annie chewed her lip. "Do you think I could come?" she blurted. "Maybe I'll catch sight of William. I'd like to give him news about John."

Bill scowled, but behind the gruff expression, Annie thought she saw sympathy in his eyes. With a shrug, he said, "I'll ask Kate. If she says it's proper, then I wouldn't mind the company."

Kate didn't like the idea, Annie could tell. Turning to her husband with a sigh of exasperation, she said, "Bill, take good care of her. Don't let her out of your sight."

He promised, and Annie promised to be good. With those assurances, Kate sent them off with a basket of food for the journey.

Throughout the ride, they heard the unceasing sound of distant cannon. "Must be 100 guns," Bill muttered. "Hope they belong to us."

When they passed a wagon going the other way, he stopped the driver for news. "How goes the battle?" he asked.

"The patriots are shelling the British. They'll not be able to hang on much longer," the man answered.

Annie allowed herself to smile. Now if only William were out of harm's way. When they reached Yorktown, dense smoke hung over the field. Its smell greeted them long before they could see the cannons that produced it. William drove the wagon to the high ridge where the patriots had set up camp and unloaded the wagon while Annie waited. From their vantage point they could see over the whole field. Arrayed before them were the blue jackets of the colonials, and across the field, the scarlet of the British.

William had been right. There were nearly 100 cannon keeping up a constant barrage against the British lines. The gunners paused only to let the smoke clear so they could better see their targets.

During one such pause, as the smoke drifted away, there was movement on the British side. A small figure walked to a high perch and stood at attention. With all eyes focused his way, he began drumming. At first the beats came slow and soft. Then faster and louder. "What does it mean?" Annie asked the big man who stood next to her.

"I think it means parley," he answered. "The British are asking for a meeting."

"Then it's good news," Annie said, her face brightening with hope.

As they waited for the official word, a fifer began to play, and thousands of voices joined to sing "Yankee Doodle."

"Let's go closer," Annie begged. Together they ran toward the assembled army. They found themselves surrounded by jubilant soldiers who sent thousands of hats into the air as the buoyant sound of "Yankee Doodle" played.

Annie grinned as she heard whispers and then shouts of "Huzzah, they've surrendered."

"Did you hear that, Bill?" she screamed, trying to be heard over the soldiers who crowded around. Though Annie tried to keep her friend in sight, the pushing and jostling of the crowd soon separated them, and she found herself concentrating on not falling. Just then someone shoved her, and she fell backward into a soldier.

"Are you all right?" the young man asked as he helped her regain her balance.

Embarrassed by her clumsiness, Annie stared at the ground and began apologizing. "Excuse me," she said before a voice interrupted her.

"Annie? Is that you?"

When she looked up, she recognized her friend from Hanover. "Andrew!" she exclaimed.

Before she could hug him, he backed away stammering, "Wait here . . . I can't believe my eyes. . . . Don't you move, you hear. . . ." He rushed off, looking over his shoulder as if to make sure she wouldn't disappear. Within minutes he was back, dragging a dirty soldier behind him.

"William?" Annie asked hesitantly, scarcely recognizing the powder-smeared soldier as her brother.

"Annie Henry! What a sight you are," he whooped, swallowing her up in a big bear hug. Over his shoulder, Annie saw Andrew Thacker looking wistfully on. Giggling, she pulled away from her brother long enough to plant a kiss on Andrew's cheek. From the British across the field came the first notes of a mournful tune.

"What are they playing?" Annie asked softly.

"It's a lament," her brother answered. "It's called 'The World Turned Upside Down.' Listen to the words." As the singing from the patriot side subsided, the forlorn words sung by the British hung in the air: "If buttercups buzzed after the bees. If boats were on land, churches on seas . . . the world turned upside down."

"Is the war over?" she asked Kate's husband.

"If the British surrender here, then the war will surely be over," Bill promised.

"And the boys can come home?" she asked.

With huge smiles on their gaunt faces they agreed. "Yes! We'll come home."

Annie felt she might burst with happiness. At long last the war seemed to be coming to an end. Freedom was won. Love beckoned. Surely God is good!

Historical Note

Although these stories are fiction, Patrick Henry did have a daughter named Annie. She married Spencer Roane on September 7, 1786. Together they had six children. She died in 1799, the same year as her father.

Patrick Henry was elected governor again in 1784. He and his second wife, Dolly, had ten children. He spent the last years of his life happily retired on a farm called Red Hill where he read the Bible and played with his young family.

Many of the incidents in this book are true. The famous traitor Benedict Arnold did invade Richmond, burn the city, and tear open the liquor casks so that drunken pigs ran wild in the streets. Judge Lesker was murdered in his house while his wife watched from a nearby bed. Patrick Henry did barely escape ahead of the British cavalry led by Colonel Tarleton, a British soldier famed for his cruelty.

Following is a letter that Patrick Henry wrote to Annie on the occasion of her wedding:

My Dear Daughter:

You have just entered into that state which is replete with happiness or misery.

You are allied to a man of honor, of talents, and of an open, generous disposition. You have, therefore, in your power all the essential ingredients of that system of conduct which you ought invariably to pursue—if you will now see clearly the path from which you will resolve never to deviate.

The first maxim which you should impress upon your mind is never to attempt to control your husband, by opposition, by displeasure, or any other work of anger. . . . Little things that in reality are mere trifles in themselves, often produce bickerings and even quarrels. Never permit them to be a subject of dispute; yield them with pleasure, with a smile of affection. . . .

Cultivate your mind by the perusal of those books which instruct while they amuse. Do not devote much of your time to novels. . . . History, geography, poetry, moral essays, biography, travels, sermons, and other well-written religious productions will not fail to enlarge your understanding, to render you a more agreeable companion, and to exalt your virtue.

Mutual politeness between the most intimate friends is essential to that harmony which should never be broken or interrupted. How important, then, it is between man and wife! . . . I will add that matrimonial happiness does not depend on wealth; no, it is not to be found in wealth, but in minds properly tempered and united to our respective situations.

In the management of your domestic concerns let prudence and wise economy prevail. Unite liberality with a just frugality; always reserve something for the hand of charity; and never let your door be closed to the voice of suffering humanity.